"W
of
bl

"

"

"
as

bo

Books by Kylie Chan

Dark Heavens

WHITE TIGER
RED PHOENIX
BLUE DRAGON

Journey to Wudang

EARTH TO HELL
HELL TO HEAVEN
HEAVEN TO WUDANG

Celestial Battle

DARK SERPENT
DEMON CHILD

KYLIE CHAN

DEMON CHILD

CELESTIAL BATTLE
BOOK TWO

HARPER Voyager
An Imprint of HarperCollinsPublishers

First published in Australia in 2014 by HarperCollins*Publishers* Australia Pty Limited.

HARPER Voyager
An Imprint of HarperCollins*Publishers*
195 Broadway
New York, New York 10007

Copyright © 2014 by Kylie Chan
Cover design by Darren Holt, HarperCollins Design Studio, adapted by Alicia Freile, Tango Media
Cover images by shutterstock.com
ISBN 978-0-06-232908-0
www.harpervoyagerbooks.com

First Harper Voyager mass market printing: March 2015

Harper Voyager and) is a trademark of HCP LLC.

Printed in the U.S.A.

10 9 8 7 6 5 4 3 2 1

Gentle Reader, this is the eighth book in this story. Although you can choose to start here, you may find it more rewarding to read the story from the beginning with the first novel, *White Tiger*.

In response to readers' requests I've added a list of characters at the end.

Note for parents/teachers

My books are sometimes shelved as 'Young Adult'. This novel contains adult themes that a less mature reader may find disturbing. Parental discretion is advised.

For my grandfather, Clyde Alfred Lee,
who kept his half-Chinese heritage a shame-filled secret
from even his closest family.
My half-Chinese children cannot comprehend why he was
ashamed and I hope they never do.

The Serpent drifts between torture and nightmare
Unconsciousness its only escape
It seeks the Turtle's cool respite
Its cries receive no answer

The Turtle blocks the Serpent's pain
The future looms with blood and death
Children scream with grief and rage
Their murdered parents do not respond.

1

Zhenwu

John nodded in time to the music as he scanned through the spreadsheets. There was no way to avoid it: twenty-three of the newest Disciples had to go. No amount of training, even by the Shen Masters, would bring them up to a level where they could handle demons without mortal risk. He emailed the order through to Leo with a copy to the other Masters and Emma.

With a large group of the first-year students gone, the Mountain's entire defensive force was reduced to less than two hundred. John put his chin on his hand and studied the list. One hundred of them were trained and equipped well enough to handle demons, but the eighty-nine more junior ones were underequipped, undertrained, young and mortal. They'd been brought in by Leo after the last huge losses when demon copies had devastated the Mountain army.

John rubbed his eyes and leaned back. The coming conflict could very well wipe out his beloved Mountain; not the physical

Mountain, but the Disciples — the real heart of Wudang. He took a deep breath and went through the spreadsheets again. The Heavens must be defended; if necessary every single Disciple, Master, Celestial and himself would be thrown into the pyre to ensure that the Heavens did not fall.

He thought of Emma and Simone: young, human, mortal and deadly. The pyre would burn brightly with their brilliance in its flames.

Madam Emma and the Emperor of the West are here, my Lord, Zara said from John's office anteroom.

Turn that fucking awful noise off, the Tiger said.

John muted his computer's sound system and opened the office door for them without moving from his desk. Emma and the Tiger entered his office and sat across from him.

What the fuck have you been doing to her? the Tiger said, indicating Emma with his head. *She looks fucking awful.*

Emma did look older than her forty-two years: her brown hair was shot with grey and her eyes mirrored the suffering she'd endured at the hands of the demons. More than that, she'd experienced more stress and violence since meeting him than any normal human could possibly handle and she was still fighting. Everybody had tried to talk her into taking time off to recover, but with typical stubborn resilience she'd ignored them all and thrown herself into helping him prepare for the inevitable approaching conflict.

She just needs time to heal from losing our child as well as all her reproductive organs, John said, *and she won't rest until the Heavens are secure.*

You two are a matched set.

'Both of you are amazingly bad-mannered sometimes,' Emma said, and the Tiger and John shared an amused glance. 'I'll bet you're even talking about me.'

'He's worried about you,' John said.

She glared at the Tiger, her sharp blue eyes intense. 'Don't be. I'm fine. We have too much to do. Now show us what you have there — and it'd better not be another cat video — so I can go back to work.'

The Tiger put a tablet computer on top of the mess on John's desk and flipped it up onto its stand. A photograph of a European man in a hound's-tooth jacket was on the screen, and Emma jolted with alarm.

'What?' John said.

She pointed at the screen. 'That's the Western King of the demons.'

John turned his attention back to the screen. So that was him. He was dark and powerfully built, with bright intelligent blue eyes that were hard with cruelty.

'He's using the name Ineke Prochazka,' the Tiger said. He swiped the screen and a new picture appeared. It showed a man-sized black marble monolith etched with what was obviously a transferred photograph of the Western Demon King — or someone who looked very much like him — in a double-breasted suit and standing in front of an expensive sports car.

'Same man?' John said.

'This is the gravestone of a dead Russian gangster,' the Tiger said. 'Their Demon King appropriated his identity to take over his network.'

John leaned on his desk to study the photo. 'Well done. How did you find him?'

'Huge fuss, even as far as the west of my dominion, about how this Prochazka came back from the dead. Anyone who asks too many questions,' he shrugged, 'disappears.'

'Can we move on him?' Emma said.

'As soon as this business with our Demon King is sorted I'm sending a squad in,' the Tiger said. 'Your people are more than welcome to come along, Ah Wu.'

'We're allowed?' she said.

The Tiger emitted a growl that was more feline than human. 'Eastern Russia is in my territory. Fucking straight we can move on him, and it would be very much my pleasure.'

'Any sign of our Demon King over there?' John said.

'Both of them are all over the place. Bio labs everywhere. The operation's so massive I have three good people tracking it all down.'

He swiped the screen again and it changed to a bad photograph of Kitty Kwok and the Western Demon King in front of a café, both of them trying to avoid the camera.

'Where is that?' John said.

'Amsterdam,' the Tiger said. 'They have a lab there.'

'UK, Russia, Amsterdam ... Damn, that's huge,' Emma said.

'When was it?' John said.

'Six weeks ago. Second.' The Tiger flipped to a graphic image of a body opened wide for autopsy, revealing its internal organs. He glanced at Emma. 'You okay with this?'

She nodded silently.

John studied her: she really was completely unfazed. Fifteen years ago she'd fainted at the sight of gore and now she was unaffected. Something inside him died a little at her growing immunity to the violent life they led.

'This is a Western demon,' the Tiger said.

'No way,' Emma said.

'How much demon essence was in it? What level? How did it die?' John raised his hand. 'I know. One at a time.'

4

'Demon essence: as far as we could tell, none. Level: no idea. How it died: my Number Three stuck an extremely nice rapier through its head and it died like a living thing.'

'If it had no demon essence then it *was* a living thing,' Emma said.

'It sounds like a natural human,' John said.

'Yeah, she thought she'd made a mistake, but look.' He swept his hand across the screen and the same autopsy table appeared, covered in black sticky goo. 'Same corpse twenty-four hours later. The humans think it's some sort of flesh-eating superbug, but we know better. Fucking demon, all right.'

'Was it a Number One?' Emma said. 'Only a Number One has bones and internal organs.'

The Tiger leaned his elbow on the desk and his chin in his hand. 'That's what I wanted to ask you, Ah Wu. You were talking about having two Number Ones. Could these demons have that as well? Because this is the second one we've encountered. My Number Three was on her way home to show me photos of the first which was identical when she ran into this one.'

John stared at the image, considering the implications. In the East, only the Demon King's Number One had blood, bones and internal organs, but in the West things could be completely different. A whole range of possibilities opened up if there was more than one Western demon that was equivalent in power to a Number One …

The Tiger turned to Emma. 'You were there. Did you see the Western King's Number One?'

'No. He had a few extremely high-level demons in his closest circle — they were insanely powerful — but I never saw a Duke or a Mother. In fact, I never saw anything analogous to our demon hierarchy.'

5

'Possible,' John said, leaning back but still studying the disturbing picture. 'There's no reason their hierarchy should mirror ours.'

'Two Number Ones?' the Tiger said.

'I'd say several Number One equivalents, but no single Number One,' John said. 'More of a Western-style flat structure than our heavily hierarchical bureaucracy.'

'Would that be more efficient in a war setting?' the Tiger said, intrigued.

John thought about it, then shook his head. 'No. In a war situation, you need a structured hierarchy where orders are followed immediately and without question. Your personnel are divided into small manageable groups all reporting to a higher-up. A flat structure would allow for too much questioning and feedback. Communication would be slower and more cumbersome. It would be weaker.'

'They'd have to know that and compensate,' Emma said.

'Of course,' John said. 'But this information is invaluable. I'm glad you ran into two of them. We now know that taking out a senior demon with human characteristics isn't removing their Number One.'

'If there was no demon essence, then what prompted your Number Three to kill it?' Emma asked the Tiger. 'She'd see it as human and wouldn't attack.'

'Number Three was in Siberia tracking down Prochazka,' the Tiger said. 'She found the location of one of his villas, and went in.' He picked up the tablet, swiped the pictures away and pulled up a video. 'She's wearing a headcam.'

The view swung from side to side as Number Three walked through the crunching snow towards a grey stone house surrounded by dark leafless trees.

'Middle of nowhere,' the Tiger said.

6

The Tiger's Number Three spoke softly and her hands appeared in the camera's view as she ordered her squad into position. 'Two left. Three right. You two to the back door, and you to cover our backs.'

'You did me a huge favour when you talked me into promoting her,' the Tiger said.

'I shouldn't have needed to,' Emma said.

John hushed them without looking away from the screen. Number Three had hesitated at the front door, her hand poised over the door knocker. Then she obviously changed her mind and kicked the door in.

'Police!' she shouted as she stormed into the entry. She checked the side doors and up the stairs in front of her. 'There have been reports of a disturbance. Please cooperate peacefully.'

The house was completely silent. She lowered her gun and it disappeared from the camera's view.

'Checking silently. Back door clear,' she said for the benefit of those watching.

'She's good,' the Tiger said with admiration.

She turned left and checked the living room. It was sparsely furnished, the sofas covered in bright pink towelling bedspreads that were threadbare and stained. One of Number Three's people met her at the door to the kitchen and they went together into the dining room on the other side.

'Clear,' someone said from the front of the house.

'Three and four upstairs.' Number Three moved around the chipped dining table. 'I can't sense anything up there but make sure.' The camera view swung around. 'There's something alive below me and I can sense demons …'

A man appeared in the doorway between the dining room and entrance hall and she raised her weapon at him.

'Put your hands on your head and turn around,' she said.

Two more men appeared behind the first, all of them Europeans. They were tall and well-muscled and similar in appearance to the Western demons that had attacked John and Emma in the UK.

The man in front raised his hands and smiled. 'What's going on? Why did you break my door?'

'Stand still and keep your hands where I can see them,' Number Three said.

There were now five men. The front one pulled a pistol out of a holster under his jacket, still grinning. He raised it and emptied the clip at her, and the microphone on her headset went silent from the overload of noise.

'She has metal. Did nothing,' the Tiger said.

Number Three raised her gun and shot the man. He didn't stop moving towards her, his grin still frozen on his face. The gun clicked in his hand. The four men behind him pulled guns out as well and emptied them at her, with similar grins on their faces. More men appeared behind them, all copies of each other. There were only three different faces within the group.

Number Three switched her rifle to full auto and strafed them, again deafening the camera's microphone. The bullets went straight through without harming them. Demons.

'Fuck,' she said, and there was the sound of fabric against the microphone and the rasp of a sword being drawn.

Her squad drew their swords as well.

The Tiger grabbed the tablet and hit the fast-forward button. 'They took them all out. She was quite sure they were hypnotised humans right up until her bullets went through them without doing anything.'

'I would like to see that skirmish later,' John said.

The Tiger growled softly. 'The last thing she needs is you picking her technique to pieces. They took the demons down and achieved their objective. Leave her alone.'

'What he said,' Emma said to John.

John smiled slightly. 'Very well.'

The Tiger stopped the fast forward. Number Three was standing in the entry hall. She glanced back to show the rest of her squad, men and women, moving the pieces of the dead demons into the dining room.

'Once again: bones, blood and internal organs,' the Tiger said. 'If she hadn't seen the bullets go straight through them she would probably be beating herself up for killing humans.'

Number Three turned back to the entry hall. 'There's something underneath here ... I can sense it. There are humans below me.' She looked back at the rest of her squad. 'Everybody into the kitchen. I'm going to yang it.'

'She has yang?' John said.

'I'm thinking of doing the same thing as you and promoting her to joint Number One,' the Tiger said as the screen went completely white. 'She has two hundred years' experience on young Michael and would be excellent backup for him.'

'No,' Emma said, as the screen cleared to show a hole in the middle of the entry floor. 'Michael would be an excellent backup for *her*.'

'Didn't think of it that way,' the Tiger said. 'Maybe you're right; it isn't deliberate discrimination at all.'

'I think in your case it is,' Emma said.

John raised his hand and hushed them again, and Emma reached across the desk to tap his arm. He ignored her scolding. The Tiger grinned.

Number Three jumped down the hole and moved quickly in as her people followed her.

'Oh dear Lord,' Emma said when she saw the cages.

'Holy shit,' Number Three said at the same time.

Cages lined both sides of the basement walls, five on each side, filled with naked terrified humans who wailed with terror when they saw Number Three's squad.

She stopped in front of one of the cages. It held a huddled group of pale emaciated people, all white damp skin, jutting bones and huge hollow frightened eyes.

'I see them as human,' Number Three said. 'But I saw the ones up top as human as well.'

'They're probably demons. Shoot one and see if it does no damage?' one of the women in her squad said. 'If it doesn't do anything, then we can leave them here.'

'No,' Number Three said. 'Open the cage door, and if they don't attack they're human.'

She drew her sword and moved to the door of the cage. The people inside scrambled over each other to get away, knocking their waste bucket over and sliding through its contents in their haste.

'Leave them alone!' a woman shouted from the other side of the room.

Number Three glanced in that direction. The woman was standing next to the bars of her cage, shaking with either cold or fear, but probably both.

'We're the police. We're here to free you, but we have to make sure you're human,' Number Three said.

'Human as opposed to what?' the woman said. She pressed against the bars, her eyes wide with hope, then jerked away from the cold metal.

Number Three checked the humans in the first cage. They hadn't moved. She went to the trembling woman. 'Hold your hand out.'

The woman retreated from the bars, obviously frightened.

'I need to know that you're not the same thing as the creatures holding you so we can take you out safely,' Number Three said.

'Whatever you have to do. Just get us out of here. Please.' The woman visibly rallied, stepped back up to the bars again and stuck her left hand between them.

'Courage,' John said.

'Raw,' the Tiger said. 'I'm in love already.'

Number Three took the woman's hand and concentrated. 'I'm nearly completely sure that these are human.'

She released the woman's hand, and the woman drew it back through the bars and stared at it, then at Three. 'What are you?'

'A leopard,' Number Three said.

She moved to the door of the cage and held her hand over the lock to break it. She opened the door and watched the humans inside. The woman remained near the bars, waiting, but the rest of the captives scrambled to the back of the cage. Number Three beckoned the woman closer, and she approached to stand in front of Three.

'You said you're the police and you'd let us out,' the woman said.

'She's not attacking.' Number Three raised her voice. 'Take these humans out, find something warm to wrap them in, and call for transport.'

'Be careful,' the woman said. She pointed towards the rear of the basement. 'There's another room through there, with … things inside.' She shuddered. 'Horrible things.'

Number Three glanced at the door at the end of the room. 'I don't think anything could possibly be more horrible than this.'

11

She stepped away from the cage door and the woman ran out of her cell to another cell door, where she stood fidgeting, touching the bars and then flinching away from the cold. The minute one of Number Three's squad had the door open, the woman raced inside and threw herself into another woman's arms. They held each other, weeping with joy.

'Two and Five with me,' Number Three said. 'Watch my back.' She went to the door at the far end of the basement. It was made of solid steel. 'What needs a door like this to hold it in?'

She held her hands out over the steel and it melted. There were three large Western demons behind it, standing motionless against the back wall of a simple brick room. They were in True Form, three metres tall and all completely covered in black shiny skin.

'Shit,' John and Emma said together.

Number Three hesitated in the doorway and the demons came to life. They were so big that all three couldn't come at her at once, but she didn't wait for them. She closed with the nearest and swung her sword at its neck. The sword glanced off. The camera spun then lurched as the demon swiped her sideways into the wall, and she grunted with pain.

She pulled herself together and looked around. One of the other demons had grabbed a member of her squad and broken his screaming body in half, then thrown the sobbing remains onto the floor. Three raised her hands, full of shen energy, and launched it at the demon approaching her; but it did nothing. One of her squad tried to take the demon's head off from behind but again the blow was ineffectual. The demon turned and casually swiped the soldier sideways. The soldier's head hit the wall with a crack and she slid down, unconscious or dead.

12

'Dear god,' Number Three said as screams rose from the room outside. One of the demons had attacked the caged humans.

'Fall back! I'm yanging the bastards!' she shouted, and the screen blanked to white.

When the picture returned, Three was in the cage room and a black demon held one of the captive humans — the brave woman — dangling limply from its right claw.

There was the sound of gunshots and the pinging of ricochets.

'Hold your fire, you idiot!' Number Three shouted.

'I saw what you did to my brothers,' the demon said. 'Release me and I won't harm the humans.'

Number Three hesitated. 'If I yang it, the human will die too,' she whispered. She raised her voice. 'Release the human and go, and we won't follow you.'

'Your word, woman,' the demon said.

'You have my word,' she said with defeat.

The demon dropped the woman and she crumpled onto the concrete floor. It turned, its massive black shoulders and back shining under the harsh electric bulbs of the cellar, walked past Number Three's white-faced companions and jumped up through the hole into the house above.

'Hold,' Number Three said, and her squad stood alert and silently waiting among the gently sobbing captives.

'I don't know what else I could have done,' Number Three said. She raised her voice. 'Clear. Let's take these people out.'

She went to the woman who was unconscious on the floor and put her hand on the side of her throat. 'She's alive.' Her hands moved over the woman's pale waxy skin and she shifted her into a recovery position.

'The bus is here, ma'am,' one of the soldiers said.

'Shit!' Number Three ran to the hole, jumped through it and raced out of the front door of the villa into the snow-covered open area that passed for a yard. An ancient European bus stood there, its engine throbbing. Number Three leapt high into the air and the camera swept over the area. She landed, rolled and righted herself, then quickly checked the driver, inside the bus and the luggage compartment. She stood completely still for a long moment.

When she spoke, her voice was full of relief. 'It's really gone. The yang must have seriously spooked it.'

The video flickered and restarted from the beginning. The Tiger hit the pause button and the three of them sat silently.

'What did you do with the humans?' Emma said.

'They were too damaged to take to the Celestial Plane. I have them in one of my places in Mongolia. It's not luxurious, but for them it's like heaven to be warm and fed and safe.' He rubbed his chin. 'Never seen a bunch of humans so fucking broken in my entire life. They'd only been there for six months, but they're worse than any of the refugees you'll see coming out of the war zones. Most of them will never recover.'

'What about that brave woman?'

'Major internal injuries. We made it to medical help just in time. It will take her a very long time to recover from this, and I am marrying that woman as soon as she's well enough.'

'Don't you dare,' Emma said, stabbing her index finger at him. 'She deserves way better than being one of a hundred.'

'But I can give her a life on the Celestial Plane better than anything —'

She cut him off. 'She deserves a man who will give himself to her a hundred per cent. Not servants, not staff, but *him*.'

He hesitated for a moment, then smiled slightly.

'And besides, that may have been her partner she was hugging,' Emma said.

'Sister,' the Tiger said. When Emma opened her mouth to yell at him again he raised his hands. 'No, you're right, paws off. I'll just make sure that she's damn well cared for.'

'Good.'

'Are the humans providing you with any useful information?' John said, glancing back at the screen.

'They don't know anything,' the Tiger said. 'They have no idea what those black demons were. I'd love to know where they came from. I've never seen anything like them before.'

'Dammit, Bai Hu!' Emma said, exasperated. 'I wish you'd read the reports I send you.'

'Why? You've seen this before?'

She gestured towards the screen. 'That's what happened to me when they injected me with demon essence and it hit the AIDS in my blood. Shiny black skin that was as hard as glass and impenetrable as steel. The only thing that destroyed it was John's blood.'

The Tiger glanced at John. John shrugged; he didn't know what he could cure with his blood until it happened.

'The Demon Kings were holding a small group of AIDS patients in the Glass Citadel in the Western Heavens,' Emma said. 'They obviously used them to make armoured demons. We were hoping the process wouldn't work.'

'How many of these impervious demons do you think they made?' the Tiger said. 'Only a very few of us have access to yang, and if there's more than a dozen of them we'll be in trouble.'

'Only three of us in the North have access to yin. The Dragon won't let his people touch it so he's the only one in the East,' John said. 'I haven't talked to the Phoenix about it

15

lately, but last I heard she had three people, including herself, that could yang.'

'So that's … around ten altogether with access to the basic forces,' Emma said. 'Damn.'

'Did your people track down the Western King?' John asked the Tiger.

'As I said, I have three good people working on it. The network is huge, and they move quickly and silently. Every time I hit a location it drives them further underground. Should I stop harassing them and wait for them to move instead?'

'No,' John said. 'Continue to annoy them; it will keep them weak and preoccupied. You might find their centre of operations if you persevere.'

'I agree with your wise advice.' The Tiger folded up the tablet. 'That's all I have right now.'

'Try to capture one of those armoured demons so we can see what their weaknesses are,' Emma said. 'If they have an army of them, we're in serious trouble.'

'I doubt we can,' the Tiger said. 'They're completely indestructible, and if they hold humans hostage we can't even yang them.'

'We need to know if anyone else's blood destroys the armour,' John said.

'I'll do my best,' the Tiger said. 'Oh.' He raised his hand and a red envelope appeared in it. 'For you guys.' He handed it to John.

John opened it, and passed it to Emma. They were invited to Michael and Clarissa's wedding, to be held in one month's time at a Christian church in Hong Kong Mid-Levels.

'Her family don't know,' the Tiger said. 'Number One has asked me to keep them in the dark, and pretend that he and Clarissa are setting up house on the Earthly. They don't want to worry her family.'

'How is she?' Emma said.

The Tiger frowned. 'She spends most of her time in a wheelchair, but she's having therapy. No chance of kids for a long time, if ever; her system is still heavily damaged.' He ran his hand over his face and his voice filled with pain. 'I would very much like to sink my claws into the Demon King and make him pay for what he's done to this sweet and good-hearted young woman. My son is incredibly lucky to have her and I would love to see many grandchildren from them.'

'Getting soft in your old age, Ah Bai?' John said.

'I dunno,' the Tiger said, leaning his elbow on the desk. 'After seeing that ...' He gestured towards the screen.

'Never hurts to see some soft among the hard, yang and yin in balance,' Emma said.

John and the Tiger both looked at Emma for a long moment, then nodded agreement. The wisdom of serpents was often as unexpected as it was welcome.

The Tiger picked up the tablet and rose. 'I'll keep you posted.'

'Ah Bai,' John said.

'See you at the wedding,' Emma said, and stood to show him out. 'Are Leo and Martin invited?'

'Leo's best man,' the Tiger said. 'I'm looking forward to it. It will be a shaft of light and hope in the darkness that's gathering around our dominions.'

'Don't worry,' Emma said and gestured back towards John. 'The darkness is on our side.'

'That I am,' John said, and closed the office door behind them.

17

2

Emma

I rapped on the door of Persimmon Tree Pavilion, then opened it to poke my head around. 'Leo, I need to ask you about these students —'

I stopped. Leo and Martin weren't aware that I'd opened the door. They weren't even aware that I was there. They were on the couch in the living room, where they'd obviously been studying together; there were scrolls and brushes in a disarray on the floor. Martin was on top. Fortunately they hadn't gone too far; they still had their pants on, but only just.

They were kissing with a passion that I'd thought only John and I could generate. Martin had his arms thrown around Leo's neck. Leo was running his hands up and down Martin's back and along his smooth curves. Leo's hands went lower to slip inside Martin's pants and pull Martin hard into him. Martin responded by groaning and thrusting into Leo.

I pulled my head out and shut the door.

There were a few thumps inside and the door was thrown open. It was Leo. Martin appeared behind him, his face expressionless. The three of us stood there without speaking for a long moment.

Then Leo said, 'If it isn't life or death, Emma, get lost,' and slammed the door in my face.

'Next time damn well lock your door!' I shouted.

'Immortals know not to barge in!' he shouted back.

'Well, I'm not Immortal,' I grumbled as I stomped away.

I dropped the pretence of being irritated with them as I walked back to my office; it felt too good to have all the family finally together and in Heaven. I stopped and took a deep breath; the breeze was tinged with the warmth of spring, and the snow on the gardens was beginning to melt. The air of the Heavens was always clean and sweet, and as I walked along the path between the budding flowers I experienced a moment of true joy. We were all in Heaven together; we'd made it. Nothing would ever tear us apart.

I arrived at the barracks building, where some demons on ladders were hanging a brass calligraphy sign above the door. A delighted laughing group of students stood around watching them. John was under the sign at the front of the group, with his hands on his hips and a look of smug satisfaction. I took a short detour to see what the sign said, full of dread, and realised with dismay that I was right. It read *Turtle's Folly* in John's elegant flowing hand. Stone turtles stood on either side of the door to reinforce the point.

One of the students pointed at the sign. 'Have you seen this, Lady Emma? How cool is this?'

'That's what the barracks down in Hong Kong were called,' one of the seniors said.

19

John crossed his arms over his chest. 'It is a fitting description for all of you.'

One of the Chinese students raised both his arms in triumph. 'We are the Turtle's Folly!'

'Yes, we are!' another student yelled, and they all cheered and clapped, whistling at the demons who were finishing the placement of the sign.

'You are all completely insane,' I said, and couldn't hide my grin as I headed towards my office.

'It was your idea to call it the Folly!' John called after me, and the cheers and whistles increased.

* * *

I set the spreadsheet to print, and went out to Yi Hao's desk to collect it from the printer in the office anteroom.

'Needs more toner,' I said.

'Already?' Yi Hao said. 'I filled it up not long ago.'

'Did Yi Hao just scold you?' John said as he came in with Ronnie Wong.

'I would never scold Miss Emma,' Yi Hao said, indignant.

John and I shared a quick smile. Yi Hao didn't know it, but John and I had a bet that if I could make her full-on scold me John would have to buy me dinner. It was unheard of for a demon to approach free will so quickly — in only twelve years. Both Yi Hao and Er Hao agreed it was because they'd been tamed by me; and I wasn't just a bewildering Westerner, I was completely impossible to work for as well.

'Hi, Ronnie,' I said.

Ronnie placed his battered briefcase of fung shui equipment on the floor and saluted me. 'Lady Emma. The

Dark Lord is attempting to help me recover what I have lost, and is showing me how to set seals.'

'It would be wonderful if you could regain that skill,' I said. 'The Heavens need your ability at setting seals. The Dark Lord can't be going around scribbling on paper all day.'

'The seals on the Mountain are completely down and I can't spare a whole day to put them back up again,' John said.

Yi Hao squeaked softly behind me. Obviously she hadn't known.

'John, security,' I said with exasperation.

He flashed me a grin. 'I remember a young woman who hated it when secrets were kept from her.'

'Not secrets this important. The last thing we need is the Demon King knowing that our seals have faded.'

'Hopefully Ronnie will be able to reset them for us very soon.'

John crouched next to the briefcase and gestured for Ronnie to join him. Ronnie knelt on the floor, opened the case and stared at its contents.

I leaned on the desk to watch them.

John sat cross-legged on the floor and pointed at the items in the case. 'There's your compass. Remember we talked about it?'

Ronnie put his hand over the fung shui compass with its complicated series of characters around the edge that indicated the directions. He jerked his hand back, obviously intimidated.

'Take it,' John said.

Ronnie carefully slipped the compass out of its elastic tie-downs. He appeared confused as he moved the compass around in front of John.

'Why does the needle always point away from you?' he said.

'Because I'm North,' John said. 'It will be useless anywhere near me. For now, let's just set some seals on the door.'

'I need papers for that,' Ronnie said.

'Very good,' John said, pleased. 'Do you know which ones?'

Ronnie took some slips of paper, twenty centimetres high and three wide, out of the case. 'I think these are the right ones. But some have writing on them already.' His face screwed up with concentration. 'Is it important that they have writing on them?'

'Well done, those are the right papers. The writing is important; the writing creates the seal,' John said.

'Who wrote on these?'

'We did,' John said. 'We created them before we came in here.'

Ronnie glanced up at him. 'We made them just before we came here?'

'Yes,' John said.

Ronnie studied the seals. 'I don't remember doing it.'

'That's nothing to be concerned about,' John said. 'The more we do it, the more likely it is that you will remember.'

'I want to remember,' Ronnie said. 'I want to be useful.'

'You will be. Take one of the papers out. Let's start with one we've already done,' John said.

Ronnie carefully released the elastic band holding the papers together, and removed a seal as if it was very fragile.

'Good,' John said. He stood and turned to the door, and motioned for Ronnie to join him. He held his hand out towards the frame, as if he was holding the seal, and held his

22

other hand out to Ronnie. Ronnie took his hand and they stood silently for a moment.

'All right?' John said, nodding at Ronnie.

Ronnie nodded back, then he held the seal out towards the door and concentrated.

'Let it happen,' John said gently.

Ronnie's face crumpled and he closed his eyes, then sagged.

'Try again. Don't give up,' John said, still gentle.

I couldn't watch any more and gestured for Yi Hao to follow me into my office.

'Dear Lord, was I like that?' I asked her when we were inside.

'No, ma'am,' Yi Hao said. 'You were fifty times worse.' She raised her head. 'They've given up. The Dark Lord says they will try again later.' She shook her head and went back to her office.

About an hour later, Leo's personal assistant came into my office. He hesitated, then fell to one knee and rose again.

'What is it, Otis?' I said.

'Ma'am.' He took a deep breath. 'There are twenty students outside Lord Leo's office; he asked me to have them come see him. He's planning to expel them from the school. But,' he gestured helplessly, 'they're all outside his office, and he's not there.'

'Where is he?'

'I don't know, ma'am. He's not answering his phone or when I call him directly.' His voice gained a desperate edge. 'I don't know where he is! I hope he's all right.'

I picked up the receiver on my desk phone and called Leo's mobile. It rang through to voicemail and beeped for me to leave a message.

'Fine job chickening out on expelling these students,' I said. 'Do you really expect me to do it? Maybe instead of throwing them out for you, I should tell them to come back and see you later.' I hung up. 'Stone.'

'Ma'am?' the stone said.

'You're never asleep when there's something juicy happening.'

'I have no idea what you're talking about.'

'Where's Lord Xuan?'

Otis cringed at the mention of John's name. 'I really don't want to waste the Dark Lord's time on this, ma'am.'

'Lord Xuan is in the Northern Heavens,' the stone said.

'Where exactly in the Northern Heavens? Holding court or in the Residence?'

'Hall of Serene Meditation.'

That meant I shouldn't disturb him. I rose and walked around the desk. 'Come on, Otis, let's do this most unpleasant job ourselves.'

He followed me out of my office and across the courtyard in the centre of the administration buildings. I passed John's office and waved to Zara through the open door, then walked along a covered breezeway with a carved stone handrail that ran along the edge of the cliff. There was a bottomless drop on the left, disappearing into the clouds below.

Leo's office was in the student residential section: a small stand-alone house next to the long barracks buildings. The students to be expelled had overflowed out of his waiting room and into the wide paved walkway leading to the barracks. The air was full of the savoury aroma of the evening meal cooking in the mess, tainted by the sour smell of the students' anxiety. They had a good idea why they were there, and my heart went out to them. They'd be expelled and their memories wiped, and they'd never remember the joy they'd experienced here.

'Do you have the student lists inside?' I asked Otis as we approached.

'Yes, ma'am,' he said.

I sighed with relief when we entered the reception area and saw Meredith standing in front of Otis's desk. She would handle it better than I could.

'Otis, when I tell you, send them into the office in alphabetical order,' Meredith said. She gestured for me to follow her into Leo's office and closed the door behind me. 'He's not answering direct calls. Neither is Ming Gui.'

'You're *kidding*,' I said. 'They're off together *again*?'

'I'm here! I'm here!' Leo shouted outside, his deep voice resonating. He charged into the office and raised his hands. 'Sorry, sorry, I was caught up. Leave this to me, I have it.'

'Where were you?' I said.

He grinned broadly. 'Oh, just busy.'

Meredith and I shared a look, then both turned to glare at him.

Before I could open my mouth, he fell into the chair behind his desk, making it creak, and opened one of the student record folders. 'I know, I know, my fault, won't happen again.' He waved us away. 'Just go and leave me to it.' He looked up at me. 'Go and rest, Emma, you look terrible.' His grin turned mischievous. 'Don't you have an energy class to teach, Meredith?'

I crossed my arms in front of my chest. 'We will discuss this later.'

'Of course we will, and I'll be all guilty and stuff, but right now I have twenty students I need to counsel and you're holding me up.'

'Come on, Emma, let's leave him to it,' Meredith said. 'Doing this job is probably punishment enough.' She crossed her arms as well. 'But next time, don't make the poor kids wait like this. They've been standing here working themselves into a frenzy of anxiety, and you're about to make their worst fears come true.'

'I know,' he said, sobering. He brightened again. 'See you at dinner after this?'

'I think I may be at the Northern Heavens in Serene Meditation,' I said with quiet dignity, and followed Meredith out.

Meredith stopped me once we were out of the students' earshot. 'This is the second time this month he's done this. I would suggest that you talk to him, but you don't have the clout; he sees you as a friend. And Cheng Rong and I are colleagues, not commanders.'

'Dark Lord it is,' I said.

'Don't let that stop you from having one of your famous Emma shouts at him though. Leo and Martin are getting as bad as the Tiger for putting their dicks before their duty.'

'This is completely unlike Leo, you know that?' I said.

'Any idea what's changed?'

'I wish. I may have a talk rather than a shout.'

She nodded. 'I think I may as well.'

* * *

The late winter sun broke through the clouds and the snow-covered plum blossoms bobbed in the breeze outside the training pavilion's window. John was watching me as I performed a yang-style tai chi set, his long hair tied in a topknot and his hands behind his back. Both of us wore the

Mountain uniform of a plain black jacket and pants, with the cloth shoes and leg bindings of traditional practitioners.

I moved slowly through the set on the smooth polished timbers. When I came to the high kicks I couldn't tap my hands with my toes as I used to; I'd lost a great deal of flexibility while I'd been held by the demons.

'Stop. Again,' he said.

I took two steps back and performed the high kicks again. He moved closer and put an index finger under my knees as my legs went up, and my tendons loosened so that I could tap my toes.

'Back. Again,' he said.

I took three steps back and repeated the move, again unable to tap my toes. I tried to force it and he raised one hand to stop me.

'Again. Stop at the top,' he said when I'd completed the move.

I took the steps back and performed the high kicks. Again he helped me by loosening the tendons, allowing me to reach full extension easily.

'Continue,' he said, moving out of the way.

He watched, expressionless, as I completed the set and put my chi back.

He moved forward and held one hand out for me to take. He placed my hand, palm up, on top of his.

'Chi, about twenty centimetres across,' he said.

I generated the energy and his face lit up from its glow.

'Can you make it white?'

'I can try,' I said, and took a deep breath. I reached down inside me, twisted the energy, and it turned white.

'Good. Now black.'

I hesitated. He'd never asked for black before.

'Take your hand off me before I do,' I said.

He removed his hand from mine. I reached inside myself again, concentrated on the darkness within me, and turned the energy black.

'Can you hold it?' he said.

'No problem at all. Still feels like ordinary chi.'

'And your Western serpent knew many ways to use it?'

'Yes. There must have been nearly twenty things I could do with it, and I don't remember a single one.'

'Interesting.'

He held his hand over the energy, and before I could do anything it effortlessly slid up into his hand, turning his skin black as it moved inside him. The loss of the energy weakened me and my knees buckled. He caught me before I fell, hoisted me in his arms and carried me to sit on the mats piled on one side of the room.

'If this was ten years ago, you would be dead,' he said. He put his hand on my forehead and I shivered at his cool touch. 'Hold your hands out again.'

I held them out and he stood in front of me. He concentrated with his hand palm down over mine and a ball of black energy appeared under it.

'I can do it too,' he said with interest. 'I suppress my dark nature too much, I've never even considered creating such a thing.'

The energy drifted down towards my hands, which flashed black as it entered me. I shivered again, suddenly cold all over, and for a moment I was completely merged with him, seeing through his eyes and feeling his dark cool emotions. Both of us took a deep breath in unison and his eyes widened. He took a step back, alarmed, and the same feeling of alarm rocked through me. Both of us worked to control it and together we

28

stifled the panic. The experience diminished with time, and we stared into each other's eyes as the link between us faded.

John's final thought before the link disappeared was to move as far from me as he could. I clumsily rose to stop him and toppled again. He caught me.

'Don't run from it,' I said.

'I'm not running. I'm concerned about the proximity.'

'Same thing.'

He fell to sit next to me, making the air whoosh out of the mats, and put his head in his hands. 'Your nature is too similar.'

'You say that like it's a bad thing.'

He turned to me, unamused. 'I thought we'd fixed that desire to be one with me.'

I threw myself back to lean on the wall. 'Absolutely. No damn way am I letting you do that to me. I value my individuality, thank you very much.'

'Good.' He put his elbows on his knees, clasping his hands. 'How long is it now?'

'Ten weeks. No, twelve. Three months.'

He shook his head, his long hair shimmering around him. 'Even with our help, you're not a fraction of what you were.'

He stiffened and we shared a look. Both of us had been summoned by the Jade Emperor.

'And this is the reason,' he said. 'If he keeps summoning us like this, you'll never be strong enough to be Raised.'

'My report's finished. This has to be the last time,' I said.

He took my hand and helped me to stand. 'It'd damn well better be. And stop visiting the orphanages.'

'I'm the only one besides you and Jade who can sign the bank documents, John. Our accountant's flat out doing something much more important.'

'Give Chang access. He's trustworthy.'

'I'm in the process of doing it. You know how banks are with bureaucracy.'

'Hurry, love, we need you strong before this storm hits.'

I leaned into him, holding his hand. 'You know I want to be.'

* * *

Both John and I wore full Mountain uniforms, robes and armour, to answer the Jade Emperor's summons. He met us in the small audience chamber without a throne; just three long rosewood couches with tea tables between them, and a screen behind him depicting longevity cranes flying over mountains composed of semi-precious stones.

As senior Retainers, we both fell to one knee, heads bowed, then joined him on the couches. He waved for one of the palace fairies to serve us tea.

'I won't waste your time,' he said. 'I know how busy you are.'

'Anything you can tell us about the demons' plans?' I said.

'No,' he said, and left it at that. 'First, I want to talk to you about the appointment of your daughter as your Number One.'

'This is not negotiable,' John said. 'It is my choice to have two of them, and they are joint and equal.'

'What I was going to ask you, Ah Wu,' the Emperor said, glaring at John from under his white brows, 'was if you'd like to use one of the audience halls here for her investiture.'

John and I both sat straighter. Holding the investiture at the Celestial Palace would give Yue Gui's appointment an obvious and public endorsement by the Jade Emperor himself.

'You really don't have any problem with him having two?' I said.

'Of course not,' the Jade Emperor said. 'It's appropriate. With him being two creatures himself, the combined essence of yang and yin, two Number Ones, one of each gender, is harmonious.'

John saluted the Emperor. 'I am honoured by your most generous offer and humbly accept.'

'Good,' the Emperor said. He spoke to the fairy standing behind him. 'Liaise with the Dark Lord on the allocation of the Northern Xuan Wu Hall for Princess Yue's investiture.' The fairy nodded, and the Emperor turned back to us. 'Second. I hear rumours that you two are planning a quiet private wedding without the Celestial rigmarole.'

John and I shared a look.

'Thought so. Well, forget it. We need the ceremony, we need the celebration, and it will be a huge morale boost for everybody to see you two finally wed. Ah Wu, you vowed to Raise her first, and you will not risk Celestial Harmony by marrying before this has happened. Am I completely understood?'

We both saluted him with resignation.

'Emma, after you are Raised, you will have one of the grandest and most lavish weddings the Celestial has ever seen, and your opinion on the matter is irrelevant.'

Both of us sagged slightly. We'd hoped to have an extremely small, private wedding during the Chinese New Year break, and hadn't even told our families. We'd planned to spring it on them, have a quick ceremony, take a few days off while everything stopped for New Year, and get it out of the way. So much for that little escapade.

31

'Third,' the Emperor said, 'I understand that the House of the North is funding a number of orphanages on the Earthly Plane for young humans?'

John made an almost undetectable nod towards me.

'Yes,' I said. 'The House is funding them in conjunction with the staff of the Twelve Villages.'

'Evacuate the villages,' the Emperor said. He lifted one hand over his shoulder and spoke to the fairy without turning towards her. 'Accommodate them here.'

She nodded.

'When?' John said.

'Now.'

'What about the orphanages?' I said. 'A motherless child can't enter the Celestial Plane.'

'Station guards. I expect to see the villagers residing here within the next two weeks.'

'Two weeks?' I said, horrified.

'Two weeks. Last item.' The Jade Emperor shifted slightly. 'This is vital.'

John and I shared a surreptitious look.

The Emperor hesitated for a moment, then said intensely, 'You are completely forbidden from adopting a child from one of the orphanages as your own.' He glanced from me to John. 'Both of you are forbidden. Your duties are clear; you will not need the distraction of caring for a child. After what happened with Simone, I'm sure you agree with me. Maybe when this matter is settled I may release this prohibition; but for now it stays.'

John and I stared at him, speechless; then I said, 'I wasn't even considering it.'

'Good. Don't.'

32

'Why this limitation? What will happen to her?' John said, his voice raw.

'That entirely depends upon the choices you make; and one of these choices absolutely must be *not to adopt a child*. Is this understood?'

'Celestial Majesty,' we said mechanically in unison.

He raised his teacup. 'Dismissed.'

We saluted him and went out, unable to even begin discussing the implications of such an order.

3

'Mummy.'

I slithered through the tunnels, listening for the baby's call. A light ahead made me lift my serpent snout.

'Muu … my.'

I went through an archway into a Nest chamber. A huge demon egg, four metres across, sat in the middle of the nest hollow, glowing gently. The child inside had the bright, hard eyes of a tiny foetus, and undeveloped hands waved in front of its huge, misshapen head. Its fish-like gills opened and closed, and its heart was visible beating in its ridged chest.

'Mummy.'

'You don't exist,' I said. 'The biggest you could have been was three months, and that's not big enough to survive.' I dropped my serpent head. 'You didn't make it.'

'I made it!' the child said. 'I'm in an egg and growing.' Its voice changed to pain. 'Why did you leave me?'

'Because you died. You're not alive, and this is a dream. I have this dream all the time because I want you to be alive.'

'I want to be with you, Mummy,' the child said, its eyes unblinking. It put its hands against the inside of the shell, pushing it towards me. The egg rolled and the baby shifted inside so that it stayed upright.

I turned to move away and heard it behind me. I looked back and it was descending on me. It would crush me.

'You're not real!' I shouted at it, slithering for the door as fast as my body would take me. The egg wouldn't fit through the doorway, it was too massive. If I could make it through, it couldn't follow me. 'You died!'

I felt its cold touch on my tail and jerked upright with a huge gasp.

I was sitting in our bed on the Mountain, the fire in the fireplace burned down to softly glowing coals. John was next to me, his face peaceful in sleep.

I fell back onto the pillow. Even though I was aware of the dream when I was in it, it was still terrifying. I'd checked and double-checked with the medical staff as well as the demon masters. Everybody was sure that it was impossible for a three-month-old foetus to live, but there was always that tiny niggling doubt, and as long as it existed the dream would trouble me.

I pulled the silk quilt back over me. John and I had fallen asleep naked, skin to skin, after a warm evening of gentle lovemaking. I snuggled next to him, glad he hadn't woken, and stretched my feet under the quilt.

I felt something cold and slippery with my feet and stopped, filled with dread. Carefully, so I didn't wake John, I pulled the quilt off my feet; they were covered in blood. Trying to control the nausea, I lifted the quilt from John's legs.

They'd cut the ends of his feet off. Blood covered everything and the sight sent me over the edge.

I rushed to the end of the bed, leaned over it and threw up on the floor. Horrified at myself and even more horrified at John's feet, I tapped the stone.

'What?' it said, its voice sluggish.

I retched a few times as I held the stone over John's feet. I wiped my mouth on a clean corner of the quilt.

'By all the Buddhas,' the stone said, its voice soft with dismay. 'Give me a moment.'

I went back up the bed to John's face and put my hand on his forehead. He was unconscious, breathing gently, but his eyes were moving rapidly under his eyelids. They'd knocked him out but he was obviously feeling it.

'Edwin's on his way. Put something on,' the stone said.

My side of the bed was against the wall, so I was forced to climb over John to get out. I clambered carefully over him, unwilling to do any energetic moves that might disturb him, found his black silk robe and pulled it around me, the fresh scent of the ocean rising from it. I attempted to roll up the sleeves but they wouldn't go so I gave up. The bottom of the robe brushed the floor.

Edwin tapped on the door and came in, then stopped when he saw John. 'Can you carry him?'

'I'm strong enough to lift him but he's too big for me to carry,' I said. 'He drags on the floor. Bring a stretcher.'

Edwin moved to go out again but the stone stopped him.

'I have it,' the stone said. 'A couple of demons are coming to carry him to the infirmary.'

John made a soft sound in his throat and his face twisted.

'He's coming around, tell them to hurry,' I said.

'They're downstairs,' the stone said.

John's eyes snapped open and he bellowed with pain, arching his back. He clawed at the sheets then covered the entire bed with ice. The demons entered, and hesitated when they saw he was naked.

'John,' I said, moving closer. 'John, it's me, Emma. Edwin's here. Let us take you to the infirmary.'

The ice exploded outwards. I threw my arms in front of my face and some of the shards sliced my forearms with shallow cuts. John yelled again, then lay rigid, panting with effort.

'I'm … here,' John said.

'You okay, Edwin?' I said.

'Not hit. You?'

'Nothing major.' I pulled the bloodied quilt over John to cover his nakedness. 'Bring the stretcher.'

The demons crept closer as John flopped back.

'Holy shit, this hurts!' he said. 'What the hell did they do to me?'

I lifted him to slide him onto the stretcher. 'They cut half your feet off, love.'

His eyes widened as I settled him onto the stretcher. 'I won't be able to balance to fight.'

'That's the least of your problems,' Edwin said. He nodded to the demons. 'Bring him.'

I adjusted the robe around me and followed them.

* * *

'Can he take True Form and fix this?' Edwin said as we placed John onto the hospital bed. The quilt slipped off and I threw it to one side and replaced it with a clean sheet.

'No, he might rejoin.' I put my hand on his forehead. 'Do you need pain relief?'

37

'That would be good,' John said, his expression strained. I put my hands on either side of his head and he grabbed my wrists. 'Not you.'

I looked up at one of the demons. 'Tell Master Meredith what's happened.'

Edwin put on a surgical mask and gloves, then filled a syringe. 'This will help.' He injected it into the bottom of John's feet and pulled a trolley closer. He mopped at the blood. 'They cut right through the middle of your feet; all your toes are gone.'

'They cut the end of my tail off,' John said. 'It will take months to grow it back if I can't take True Form.'

Edwin glanced up from his cleaning effort. 'I didn't know you could grow back body parts.'

'Normally I'm in Court Ten before the process begins,' John said. He took a deep breath. 'That's working. Maybe don't wake Meredith up.'

'Too late,' Meredith said as she and her husband, Liu, came into the infirmary, both wearing old-fashioned flannel pyjamas with tartan dressing gowns over the top. She stopped when she saw his feet. 'Bloody hell.'

'How the hell are you supposed to practise the Arts like this?' Liu said, studying his feet. 'Your balance will be completely ruined. You may even need sticks to walk, like a woman with bound feet.'

'I know,' John said, sounding desperate. 'I need to see how bad it is.'

'The Demon King used to be a human girl. She had her feet bound,' I said.

'They've done the same thing to him,' Meredith said, understanding.

'No, they cut the end of my tail off,' John said. 'Hurry up,

38

Edwin, just roughly clean it up. I want to see if my Celestial Form is injured as well.'

'No. This will take at least an hour. I want to make sure it's a tidy amputation and there's no infection,' Edwin said.

'There won't be any infection. I'm a god and we're on the fucking Celestial Plane,' John growled. 'Just slap some hot tar on them and leave it. I need to see if my Celestial Form is damaged!'

Pain and shock making him irritable, Meredith said, and I nodded.

John raised himself on one elbow and glared up at her. 'Nobody speaks silently in my presence.'

'Shut up, I'm working on tying off the blood vessels,' Edwin said, unfazed. 'Give me any grief and I'll put you under.'

'Try me,' John said, then flopped back and closed his eyes.

'Send someone to wake my assistant, I need him to run suction,' Edwin said.

'I'll get him,' Liu said, and went out.

A shout went up outside. Every Disciple on the Mountain had gathered at the Great Court in front of True Way to perform the morning energy-work set.

John's eyebrows bunched together over his closed eyes. 'I need to be out there.'

'Audrey has it,' Meredith said.

'They need to see me. They need reassuring.'

'They will. Tomorrow,' Edwin said. 'Keep still, dammit!'

An hour later, the Lius had left for the morning meeting and Edwin tied off the last suture.

He leaned back. 'How's the pain?'

'Nonexistent,' John said.

Edwin glanced at me and I shrugged. We were both accustomed to him lying about things like this.

'All right, up you get,' Edwin said. 'Expect some dizziness from the blood loss. And take it slowly.'

John sat up and levered himself over the edge of the bed to stand leaning on it. I handed him some clothes. He pulled the black cotton pants on without underwear, then stopped when the waistband was at his hips. He'd have to stand free of the bed to pull the pants on all the way.

He spoke to Edwin over his shoulder. 'Leave me.'

'No,' Edwin said. 'I want to see how much physical therapy you'll need.'

John sighed gently and rubbed one hand over his face. I held my forearm out to support him, and he stared at it for a full minute before relenting and taking it with one hand. He leaned on me while he stood, his expression intense as he worked out how affected his balance was. He released my arm and pulled his pants all the way up, tying the waist string.

He nodded to me and I moved back. He dropped his head and concentrated, and his form shimmered. His expression grew more intense, his eyes closed, and his edges blurred then solidified. He stood straighter; his feet were okay. I breathed a sigh of relief.

'Excellent ... What?' Edwin said.

John shimmered again and went solid; his feet had reverted. He gave up and sagged. The damage was to his True Form and, like the other injuries the Demon King had inflicted on his Serpent, was too significant for him to heal in his human form for more than a couple of minutes.

John swayed from side to side, then forward to back. He took a hesitant step, and his face filled with triumph as he took a couple more. He was obviously having difficulty with his balance but he could move. He gingerly performed the first few moves of a hand-to-hand set, then stopped and nodded.

He glanced at Edwin. 'Nice job.'

'Take Celestial Form,' Edwin said. 'Do it without shoes so we'll be able to tell immediately.'

'Back, Emma,' John said, and I gave him room.

He took full dark ugly Celestial Form, still in just a plain pair of black pants. His hair came out and writhed around his head, and he had to stoop to fit under the ceiling of the infirmary.

'Shit,' he said softly. The ends of his feet were still gone.

'Go down to the Grotto for a couple of hours and take True Form,' I said.

'The Serpent is in too much pain. I wouldn't be able to resist its call,' he said, shifting back to his usual human form.

Edwin came around to check that the stitches were still in his feet, then moved back, satisfied. 'Back on the table and I'll wrap them up,' he said.

John levered himself back up to sit while Edwin bandaged his feet.

'Can you fly everywhere instead of walking?' Edwin said.

'No,' John said, and didn't elaborate.

'Don't walk too much, you'll open up the stitches,' Edwin said. 'I'd like to put them in plaster casts but I know you won't let me. Just understand this.' He looked John in the eye. 'It will take a few weeks for them to heal to the stage where the stitches won't be blown open by vigorous activity; and if you open them up too many times, I'll have to trim your feet back even further to have a clean seal.'

I sighed softly. It would be nearly impossible to stop John from practising.

'Most of what I'm doing right now is administration and planning,' John said, his voice low. 'Not a problem.'

Edwin and I shared a shocked look, and I shrugged again.

Edwin pinned the last of the bandages to John's feet. 'Put some slippers over them so the bandages don't wear. Leo's should be big enough.' He leaned back and studied his work. 'You can walk gently back to the Residence, but try to stay off them otherwise.'

John levered himself off the table and pulled on the Mountain uniform shirt. 'Come on, Emma, you're still covered in blood. Let's clean you up and find something to eat.'

He shuffled towards the door, putting a hand on Edwin's shoulder as he passed him. 'Thank you.'

'My Lord,' Edwin said, rolling up bandages.

John and I both stopped once we'd cleared the infirmary door.

'Tell me where you want me,' I said.

He linked his arm in mine. 'Does this look normal?'

'Depends whether the students know or not,' I said.

He was silent for a moment, checking, then sagged slightly. 'The household staff had to clean up the mess in our bedroom. They asked the demons who carried me down what happened.'

'So everybody knows?'

'Hn.' He shifted his weight, leaning on my shoulder with one hand instead. 'I'm not too heavy?'

'You're fine. Let's go to the Residence and you can eat something, then practise getting your balance back.'

'Not too fast,' he said, his weight heavy on me as I guided him back to our house.

* * *

While John, still weak from blood loss, had a nap, I went to my office. I was looking at the armoury stocks when Yi Hao spoke silently to me. *A son of the White Tiger is here to see you, ma'am.*

'Michael?' I called.

Marcus, husband of our ex-housekeeper, Monica, came in with Yi Hao behind him. 'No, it's me, ma'am.'

'Oh! Come on in, Marcus, I haven't seen you in ages.' I nodded to Yi Hao. 'Make sure I'm not disturbed while we're talking, and bring us a pot of Western tea or something, will you?'

'Ma'am,' Yi Hao said, and went out.

'Sit, Marcus, sit,' I said. 'Why didn't Monica come as well? We haven't seen her in a while either.' I raised the telephone handset. 'Did you bring her? I can round up Simone and Leo and we can have a family get-together. I'm sorry, we're always so busy we never seem to have time to talk to you, and we all really miss you both.'

He raised one hand. 'No need, ma'am, it's just me, and don't worry, we understand.' He sighed gently. 'Monica's very sick, ma'am.'

My heart fell. 'Too sick to come up here?'

'My brother brought me up to talk to you, but he says that the trip would kill her.'

'What is it, Marcus?'

'Cancer. She didn't tell anyone for a long time; she said she was on a diet and she was happy to be so thin. By the time we made her see a doctor it was too late. It's so far through her that the doctors don't even know where it started. She didn't want me to tell you. She said you were too busy to worry about her.'

I wiped my hand over my eyes. 'Simone will be devastated. We must go down and see her.'

'She doesn't want you to. She doesn't want you to see her like this.' His face was full of misery. 'She's very bad.'

'How long does she have?'

His voice thickened. 'We hope she will have Easter with us.'

'Oh dear Lord. That's only a couple of months away.'

'She doesn't want any of the family to know, ma'am. She has her sisters and her brothers and all their children around her, and she has me. We know you and the Dark Lord are fighting to protect all of us, and she doesn't want you to waste your time on her when you could be saving many.'

'Don't be ridiculous, she's family, we have to see her,' I said. 'Is she in hospital or at home?'

'She knew you'd say that.' He pulled a note out of his pocket and handed it to me.

Ma'am,

I know you will want to rush down and see me but you don't need to. I have my family all around me and seeing you would only make me very sad. I beg you, please don't tell them I'm sick. That way I can leave this world happy that you will all remember me the way I was when you were just the nanny and Simone was just a little tiny girl. Tell Mr Chen that I am happy that he found someone new after we lost Miss Michelle, and that someone is as smart and brave as you are. Tell Mister Leo that he is a special man and I hope he is happy; and tell Simone that I love her like my own little girl and I am so proud that she has become something so grand!

Please, ma'am, don't tell anyone. I really don't want them to know. I am content. I hope you respect my wishes.

Monica xxx

'I'll respect her wishes but it'll break my heart,' I said.

'She will be pleased.'

Yi Hao brought a tea tray in and went out again. I stared at the teapot without moving.

'Is there anything we can do?' I said.

'Just respecting her wishes is enough.'

'How about financial help to pay the medical expenses?'

'You already support us like royalty, ma'am. We have everything covered by your generosity, and my mother's legacy passed on from my father. We're well established and need for nothing.'

'Keep me up to date on her situation, Marcus.' I poured tea for us, more to keep busy than anything else. 'I just wish she'd seen a doctor before it was so bad. It wouldn't have progressed if she was up here, and she would have lived much longer.'

'She wouldn't come up here anyway, she loves her nieces and nephews too much.' He smiled slightly. 'They are all like our own children. We are terribly blessed.'

'We've been blessed to know her. Can I speak to her on the phone?'

'I think she would love that. And if she could talk to Simone without Simone knowing what's wrong with her, it would make her very happy. I'll let you know when's a good time to call after I've returned.' He rose without touching his tea. 'If you don't mind, I'll head back down. My brother's waiting for me.'

I nodded to him and he went out. I picked up the note from my desk and ran my hand over Monica's handwriting. I took a sip of the tea but didn't really taste it.

4

I sat at the table next to Lily, the court administrator, my mind wandering as I scribbled notes on the pad in front of me. John was holding court in the Hall of Dark Justice in the Northern Heavens, and his dark Celestial Form was grim and forbidding as he sat behind his desk on the dais above us. Minor functionaries from various departments of the bureaucracy that ran the Northern Heavens were complaining about the war preparations and their impact on the budgets.

My head nodded with fatigue as I tried to concentrate on my notes; I had so many things on my to-do list. John was directing the mobilisation of troops in defence of the entire Celestial Plane; Er Lang was travelling the Heavens to ensure the troops were stationed correctly; the Wudang Masters were drilling the armies; and I was helping by handling the operations side.

The student Disciples weren't usually called into battle, but general agreement was that the seniors could be needed as reinforcements for the Thirty-Six if things became as bad as predicted. That meant I needed to obtain steel for new weapons to be made, and many of the senior Disciples didn't have armour so that had to be made as well. The forge was working flat out, but a priority schedule would ensure that they produced items according to need rather than in the order they were requisitioned. The steel we had stored behind the forge would run out within a couple of weeks. Supplies of food and water needed to be stockpiled in case the Earthly fell and there was a siege of the Heavens, and when refugees arrived in the Northern Heavens from the evacuation of Hell and the Earthly they would have to be catered for as well …

John's deep voice stopped. The ensuing silence snapped me out of my reverie.

Emma, please go rest. You are not helping and it's obvious that you're fading.

I glanced up at him; his face was grim but his eyes were full of concern. I sighed, nodded, pushed my chair back and rose. I bowed and saluted him, he nodded formally in reply, and I went out.

I wandered through the Grand Court of the Northern Celestial Palace, winding my way between the soldiers as they stacked sleeping bags and tent canvas. Nobody had been evacuated into the Northern Heavens yet, but we had to be ready for them. A few soldiers saluted me, grinning, and I returned the courtesy; I'd taught them as juniors.

Someone fell into step beside me and I stopped to see what she wanted. It was one of the demon servants, in black pants and white shirt. She was shorter than me, round and plump with the full rosy cheeks of the mountain people of the West. She appeared in her early twenties, but her demon nature said she was about twelve years old.

47

'The Dark Lord sent me to escort you,' she said, bowing slightly and smiling with pleasure. 'I am honoured.'

'What's your number?' I said, touched by her enthusiasm.

'I have taken a name, if it pleases Your Majesty. I am Smally.'

'I'm not a Majesty, you can call me Emma,' I said. I turned back towards the gatehouse between the administrative and residential parts of the palace. 'Where's Jade?'

She was silent as she walked next to me, her expression stiff with mortification. She didn't know which Jade I was talking about.

'The Jade Girl,' I said, clarifying for her. 'Princess Jade, Eighty-Second daughter of the Dragon King.'

'I'm sorry, ma'am,' Smally said. 'I'm far too small to be speaking to someone as exalted as her. Someone as exalted as you, as well.'

'I'm just an ordinary human. Do you know where the Golden Boy is?'

'No, ma'am,' she said. She dipped her head as she walked. 'Perhaps the Dark Lord should have sent someone more senior to escort you. I am useless.'

'You're not useless, you can help me,' I said.

We went through the gatehouse into the residential part of the palace, and the black walls gave way to shades of ochre and khaki, blending into the gardens. The demons had shovelled away the snow and the warm sun reflected off the walls. I sighed as I felt myself relax; the grass and trees were very soothing after the stark black majesty of the administrative section.

'The Dark Lord suggested that I bring you tea and cookies, and has ordered me to ensure that you rest in the Ancient Dragon Tree Garden,' the demon said. 'He says that it is very important for you to eat … carbohydrates, I think it is called? Is that acceptable?'

'I'm not an invalid,' I said, mildly annoyed at his attitude. Then I took a deep breath; yes, I was.

'I apologise, my Lady,' Smally said, ducking her head with misery.

'I'm not annoyed at you, little one,' I said, patting her on the arm. 'The Dark Lord is wrapping me in cotton wool and it chafes.'

'How can cotton wool chafe? It is soft,' she said, confused.

I chuckled as we turned right to walk through a moon gate flanked by sculpted pine trees. 'What are your normal duties?'

'I boil linen in the laundry.'

'Could you be spared?'

'I would have to ask my mistress.'

We arrived at the courtyard between the Emperor's private residence and the Crown Prince's residence. Martin and Leo were off somewhere together again, supervising the evacuation of one of the villages and the defence of the orphanage. Simone was in Tokyo, organising her entry into Tokyo University. The quiet settled through the trees and I relaxed further. I hadn't realised I was so tense.

I sat on the stone bench beneath the famous Dragon Tree. It was believed this ancient tree had been present before the palace was built, and imaginative poets had seen the shape of a dragon in its convoluted trunk. The demons had set up a charcoal brazier next to the tree and its warmth spread through the courtyard. Smally knelt on the pavers next to the bench, head down and obviously deeply uncomfortable to be in the Emperor's own residential area.

'The demons in the Residence can give you tea and these magical biscuits that the Dark Lord wants to feed me,'

I said. I gestured towards the wood-framed door with its teak shutters carved with a Buddhist swastika motif. 'Go in there, around the central courtyard, then left and into the kitchen. The head demon there is Thirty-Eight; she'll look after you.'

Smally rose and bobbed her head. 'I will return directly, ma'am.' She took a deep breath, straightened, and strode through the door into the house.

Rest, love, John said. *Please. For me. Don't work, read a book or something. Relax. Whatever you need to do can wait a couple of hours and you need a break. We have to go to Hell later this afternoon.*

I sighed and leaned back against the bench, wincing as my insides twinged with the movement. I should have healed by now. Another trip to Hell was all I needed.

Thirty-Eight came into the courtyard with Smally trailing behind her. Smally had brought cushions and fussed over me as she positioned them around me. She put a blanket on my lap, and Thirty-Eight placed a rosewood table in front of me with a steaming pot of tea and some tiny southeastern provincial biscuits, oval and one centimetre across with a star-shaped dollop of pastel-coloured icing on the top.

Thirty-Eight stood back and studied me, her hands in her sleeves. 'Anything you need, ma'am, you send the little one.'

'I need less fussing,' I said.

Thirty-Eight ignored me and went back into the house.

Smally poured a cup of tea, then tucked the blanket around me. She stood back and nodded, then a swift expression of pain crossed her face. 'I should go, I am probably needed back in the laundry.'

'Would you rather stay?'

50

She brightened. 'I would be honoured if you would permit me to stay and serve you. I promise to be quiet, ma'am, and I will pour the tea for you and make sure you are warm.'

'I'd like that very much,' I said. 'The rest of the family are all over the place doing stuff and I'm stuck tagging along with His Royal Grumpiness until I'm a hundred per cent.'

Her eyes went wide and her mouth fell open, then she giggled behind her hand. 'You really call him that?'

'Among other things,' I said, and crunched into a biscuit. 'Can you read, Smally?'

'Yes, ma'am,' she said, her expression full of pride.

'Find my ereader on my bedside table?' I said, pointing at the doorway. 'In there, first on the right.'

'In your bedroom?' she said, breathless. 'The Emperor's own bedroom? Am I allowed?'

'You are if I say you are. The ereader has a black slipcover with my name in silver on it and a ridiculous number of silly blue stars that Simone drew all over it with a puff pen,' I said. 'You can't miss it.'

Smally nodded. 'Yes, ma'am.' She took a deep breath and marched into the house again.

I relaxed onto the cushions, enjoying the quiet. I smiled when Smally squealed. She'd found the mess. She was subdued when she returned, probably with disbelief. She handed me the ereader, poured me some more tea, checked my blanket, then knelt on the stones, head bowed.

I opened to the book I'd been reading, then changed my mind. I couldn't sit and read with her quiet and unmoving on the ground like that. I changed to a different book that I hadn't read yet, set it at the start, and held it out to Smally.

'Can you find yourself a chair and read it to me?' I said.

She nodded, and took the ereader from me. She looked at the screen, turning it in her hands.

'Do this to go forward one page. This to go back,' I said, showing her.

'This is in English?'

'Yes. Can you read it anyway? You should be able to, we're on the Celestial Plane.'

'I can.' She shook her head. 'I can't believe it. I'm reading in English to the Dark Lady.'

I picked up my teacup and threw a couple of biscuits into my mouth, then waved towards the house. 'Go find yourself something to sit on; the stones are cold.'

She went back into the house and returned with a low stool, only about fifteen centimetres high. I opened my mouth to tell her to find something more comfortable, then gave up; I didn't have the energy for that particular argument. She sat on the stool next to my feet, ready to read.

'Skip the parts in italics, read from the beginning there,' I said.

'Yes, ma'am. *God a was he said and Mahasamatman him called followers his …*' She stopped, confused.

'English is read left to right,' I said.

'Oh, sorry, ma'am,' she said, and proceeded to read it the right way around.

I settled back to listen, well aware that John had finally won the battle to appoint a personal demon maid for me. At least now he'd stop making terrible jokes about the state of the closet.

* * *

Two hours later, John hobbled through the moon gate into the garden. He was in human form and leaning on a walking stick. He stopped when he saw Smally reading to me, and smiled slightly. I nodded; he'd won. He inclined his head in acknowledgement. I looked down at the walking stick then up at him, and he looked me up and down as well. His hair was greying and his face was lined, making him appear sixty years old. We both smiled slightly; he appeared as old as I felt.

Smally was still reading, unaware of the silent communication that had passed between us. John edged further into the courtyard, his feet obviously bothering him, and Smally stopped and glanced up. Her eyes widened with horror and she shot to her feet, then fell to her knees and touched her forehead to the grass.

'Wen sui, wen sui, wen wen sui,' she said, her voice quivering. She was shaking.

'Rise,' John said. 'What is your designation, little one?'

She lifted her torso but remained on her knees, hunched over with terror. 'I am Two Hundred and Ninety-Seven, Celestial Highness.'

'Her name's Smally, John, and she's perfect. Thank you for finding her. She's wasted in the laundry.'

Smally shot a quick, delighted glance at me, then audibly gulped and turned back to carefully study the grass.

'We have to be in Hell in half an hour,' John said. 'Something's not right, Emma. I think you should suit up.'

Smally tittered, then choked.

'You understand the reference?' John asked her.

She fell over her knees again, desperate. 'I apologise for laughing, Highness, it will not happen again.'

'Don't be afraid. He thinks you're cute,' I said.

'Smally, Emma needs to put her armour on. Help her to do it up,' John said. 'I will sit here and wait. Have Thirty-Eight bring me fresh tea and some fruit.'

'Come on, Smally,' I said, pulling myself up from the bench. 'The old man's right, I could use your help with the buckles and the robe always goes wrong.'

Smally climbed to her feet and kept her head down as she escorted me to the doorway. She snuck a glance back as John lowered himself to sit on the bench, leaning heavily on the walking stick. He shooed her away with one hand and she flitted to join me.

In the bedroom, I pulled my jeans off and threw them on the bed. Smally turned away, embarrassed.

'You have to help me, and you can't help if you're not looking,' I said, sorting through my wardrobe to find my robe and black pants.

She turned back and I handed her the robe, then pulled the pants on.

'Ma'am, your staff here are lax and should be reprimanded,' Smally said as she helped me into the robe. 'This untidiness is completely unacceptable for someone as senior as you.'

'They're not allowed to touch it,' I said.

'But your beautiful clothes ...' She stopped as she realised that I didn't own anything that could be remotely considered beautiful. 'Your clothes are crushed here.'

'While I'm in Hell you can sort them out for me,' I said. 'But on one condition.'

'Anything. I would love to be of assistance,' she said.

'You will have to know exactly where everything is the minute I need it. I like being able to grab stuff quickly. I don't have time to waste messing around with my wardrobe.'

'That will not be a problem, ma'am,' she said, quietly delighted. 'This will be sorted when you return from Hell and you will have no trouble finding anything.' She glanced around. 'Where is your armour?'

I gestured towards the wall next to the wardrobe doors. 'Walk through there.'

She hesitated, unsure, and I took her by the hand and led her through the wall. John's battledress and my black enamel armour sat on wooden dummies in the small room behind.

Smally turned back to where we'd come through the wall. 'I would never have known that was there.'

'That's the idea,' I said, lifting the armour off its stand. 'Help me get this damn thing done up, will you? He won't want to be late.'

'He looks unwell, ma'am, is he all right? We rely on him,' she said as she helped me into the armour.

'Nobody is to know that he requires the walking stick,' I said. 'If you tell anyone he will be extremely upset. *Nobody must know.*'

'I understand, ma'am, you can trust me.'

We would see. John was obviously testing her ability to stay quiet, but it would be a major concern if word went out about his feet.

'Did you order him the tea and fruit?' I said, and her eyes widened. I patted her on the arm. 'Just tell Thirty-Eight and she'll do it. Ask her to bring him some pain-killing medicine as well.'

She nodded, obviously communicating, then snapped back and studied my armour, her voice thick. 'I've only been working for you for an hour and I've already ruined my chances of staying.'

'No, you haven't. You've been very useful already, and I'll keep you around at least for the next week or so. Talk to Thirty-Eight about having quarters allocated here in the Residence.'

She lit up, her smile wide with joy that made me feel good as well.

'I thought your armour appeared out of nowhere,' she said, glancing back at John's battledress.

'I can't do that. He can, but right now it's easier for him to have some physical armour standing by so he can pull it to him.'

'I never knew he could become weak like this,' she said, her voice soft. 'It's very scary.'

'I know.'

'He thinks I'm cute?' she said as she helped me with the buckles. She stopped for a moment. 'If I was to work here, would part of my duties ... I mean, it's an honour, ma'am, I understand that it's often part of the duties ...' She flushed and busied herself with the buckles. 'I don't mind, really, it's an honour.'

It was a valid question to ask any traditional Empress; it was the Empress's job to provide the Emperor with as many sexual partners as he required. Expressing any anger at what she'd suffered in Hell would probably make her shut down in self-defence so I deliberately kept my voice very even when I answered.

'I understand what you're asking, Smally, and no, that won't happen here. Has it happened to you before?'

She shuddered, making herself busy to cover it. 'I was a small demon in Hell, and I was noticed by one of the Princes.' She nodded to herself, choosing her words carefully. 'He singled me out for special attention and told me that I was honoured. I did feel honoured; I never thought I'd be pretty enough to gain anyone's attention. But what he did ...' She took a deep breath. 'I took a chance and escaped with my nest mates to join the Dark Lord. I never thought I'd make it, and here I am.'

'Was this about ten or twelve years ago?'

'Yes, ma'am.'

'I remember that.' I smiled as she tightened the buckles. 'A whole bunch of you turned up on our doorstep. We didn't know what to do with you all.'

'We worked hard to rebuild the beautiful Mountain,' she said with pride. 'The Dark Lord treated us with care, and we did our best to repay his kindness. When the rebuilding was complete, they even asked where we would like to be assigned! It was so different ...' Her voice trailed off.

'Nothing that happened in Hell will ever happen here, Smally. We will protect all of you and treat you with respect.'

She visibly relaxed and let out a tiny sigh of relief. 'Sometimes, ma'am, I stop and think: today, nobody will hurt me, nobody will do anything bad to me. I don't have to be afraid.' She wiped her eyes. 'Sometimes I just stop and ... relish the feeling of being happy. It's something I thought I would never have.'

'Since the Dark Lord came back, I feel the same way.'

'You've been hurt too, ma'am?' she said, wide-eyed.

'Nothing compared to what you've suffered, but it's wonderful to have the Dark Lord back after so many years alone.' I raised my arms and swung them, and the armour didn't pinch anywhere. 'Good job. Can you put my hair up in the ebony spike for me?'

'I can do your make-up, ma'am,' she said, pleased, 'and put ornaments in your hair.'

'No make-up, no ornaments, just the spike.'

'What, like a man?' she said. 'You should have a prettier hairstyle than that. Something more decorative. I would be delighted to put your hair into a feminine style, I have practised.' She studied my hair. 'Some gold ornaments and a comb would be much more suitable for someone of your rank.'

I tapped the breastplate. 'I'm a warrior.'

'But with no make-up, you'll look like a man. They let you dress as a man?' she said. 'I didn't realise — I mean, I know you wear armour and you're a warrior, but dressed like this you look like a man.'

'I'm not dressed as a man,' I said. 'I'm dressed as me. I'm not here to be decorative, I'm here to do a job. Come on.' I walked back through the wall and sat at the dressing table. 'Put it up and put the spike through it.'

'Yes, ma'am,' she said. She shook her head as she pulled my hair up. 'You are turning everything upside down. You make the world look so different. I feel like I don't know anything any more.'

'Then you're probably ready to begin learning,' I said.

I pulled my Doc Martens on, and Smally laced one while I laced the other. When we were done we went back out to the courtyard, where John was waiting for us with a sliced nashi pear and some grapes in front of him. We shared a nod and I went to him.

He stood with effort, leaning on the stick, and glanced over my shoulder at Smally. 'Return to your duties.'

Smally's voice was soft with disappointment. 'At the laundry?'

'No,' John said.

I turned to her. 'Smally, you were planning to clean out my closet. We'll be a while so take your time.'

Smally lit up and bowed low with a huge grin. 'My Lady.' She spun and nearly skipped back into the house.

I turned back to John. 'All set?'

'Just arranging a private place to land.' I waited for a moment, and then he nodded. 'Fixed.'

He held his hand out to me and I took it. We stood, hands clasped, gazing into each other's eyes, then the world spun and I blacked out.

* * *

I came around on a simple coconut-fibre mattress laid on the floor in a bare room. John was sitting cross-legged next to me, and nobody else was present. I sat up, then lowered my head as a moment of dizziness took me. I breathed deeply, aware of his concerned attention, then sat back up and shook out my shoulders.

'How long was I out?'

'Half an hour.' He took his hair out, leaned forward, tied it into a topknot then tossed it back. 'I was out for fifteen minutes.'

'Are you okay?'

He nodded, his dark eyes full of restrained emotion. 'You aren't.'

'I'll get there.'

I leaned on the wall to pull myself upright, my insides protesting, then bent as another wave of dizziness made the room spin. I carefully levered myself to vertical, then waited for John. He did exactly the same thing, also stopping before he could be completely upright. He concentrated and grew to his mid-forties form wearing his black robe and armour, same as me.

Yanluo Wang, Lord of the Underworld, opened the door and poked his head around. 'My Lord.'

'We're ready,' John said.

Wang looked from John to me, his expression carefully controlled, then opened the door wider. 'This way.'

When we arrived in his office, Wang leaned on the back of his big leather executive chair and put one hand out towards John. 'Surely you can take True Form or come through the Courts? This must be driving you crazy.'

'The damage is to the Serpent, and it's infected,' John said, grimacing with pain as he sat. 'Even if the Turtle goes through the Courts the damage will still be there. We have to make a hard decision: give me antibiotics in the hope that they'll transfer to the Serpent, or let me suffer and hope that I die of it.' He corrected himself. 'The Serpent dies of it.'

'I understand your nature. What are the demons doing about it? Are they treating it?'

John leaned on the table and rubbed his eyes. 'They hadn't been in the holding pen in months. I was totally unprepared when they came in and chopped my tail off, and I haven't seen them since. I sincerely wish my Serpent was a small enough Shen to die of starvation.'

Wang quickly went to the door of his office and poked his head out to talk to someone, then sat behind the desk. 'Can you use donor energy to rebuild yourself?'

'I would drain any donor,' John said. 'They would be gone.'

'I used to wonder why the Ancients talked about the Jade Emperor's multiple souls,' I said.

'The Celestial hasn't done it in a very long time,' Wang said. 'It is very much a last resort, because it takes him a century of solitude and meditation to extricate the life force

60

and release it again.' He tapped the table. 'Find a willing donor. Pay the price later.'

'I don't know how to extricate them,' John said. 'If I take them, they're gone.'

'This just gets better and better,' Wang said grimly. 'How many souls have you consumed in the past, Ah Wu? Surely the Jade Emperor taught you the technique when you did it?'

'I have never done it,' John said with fierce dignity.

'Never? What about before you turned to the Celestial? I've heard the stories.'

John's face was rigid with restraint. 'That was not me. Here and now I am the Celestial Xuan Wu, and I have never drained anyone's life force.'

'But a couple of years ago you absorbed the Heavenly Star ...' Wang said, glancing at me.

'The Star gave me his energy and reverted to a mindless nature spirit. I did not absorb him completely,' John said.

'I see.' Wang rubbed his chin. 'The reason I've called you in here is a very high-security matter, but I'm sure you won't be too surprised when you hear what it is.'

One of his assistants, wearing a Qing-style robe in black with a red border, brought a massive book into the office and put it in front of Wang. Another assistant placed a jug of water and some glasses on the table. Both of them bowed to us and went out.

'Holy shit, is that the book?' I said.

It was thirty centimetres to a side and twenty thick, with a heavy dark brown leather cover and pages stained by age to a similar colour.

'You're not supposed to see it,' Wang said with amusement.

John poured himself a glass of water and drank it quickly. 'Show her where Sun Wu Kong defaced it.'

I stared at John. 'He really did that?'

'Damn monkey,' Wang growled. He opened the book on the table, then held his hand over it and the pages flipped backwards and forwards by themselves. They settled onto a page with a red ink-brush stain and splotches across it. 'He was Immortal already, he'd learned to dance the stars and ride the wind, and he came down here and defaced the book anyway. Asshole.'

'So he crossed his name out?' I said.

'In vermilion ink, insulting the Jade Emperor at the same time,' Wang said.

'Stupid bastard crossed out the wrong name too,' John said. 'That's not him.'

'Yeah, this is a kid born on Hainan Island who had the same name,' Wang said. 'Gained Immortality through a clerical error.'

'So what's the problem now?' John said, raising his glass of water at Wang. 'I assume the demons haven't tried the defences yet. What's going on?'

Wang held his hand over the book and the pages flipped again. It stopped and he read down the characters. 'It's very reassuring to have some of the Thirty-Six here, but I'm beginning to wonder if their first assault will be Celestial Hell after all.'

'It will be. If they can control all of Hell, every one of us who dies will be trapped here. It has to be their first strategic target.'

'There don't seem to be any of them left on the demonic side at all,' Wang said. 'They've stopped releasing people from the Pits.'

'What?' John said, his voice flat.

Wang tapped the book. 'Here's one. Went in mid-Qing Dynasty. Sentenced by every single court; he was a nasty piece of work. Bribed and murdered his way to provincial governor: he killed people and took over their positions, then raped and murdered their wives and children. Raped three babies to death. Embezzled fifteen million yuan from his citizens. Allowed health care and infrastructure to fall into ruin while he lived a lavish lifestyle of cruelty and excess. I watched with a great deal of satisfaction as he was released from each level only to be sentenced by the Courts to suffer in the next.' He looked up at John. 'Was due to be released last week after two hundred and fifty years of torture. Never came out. Nobody's been released from the demonic side in two months.'

'How many haven't been released?' John said.

'Four.'

'How many are still in there?'

'One thousand, three hundred and ...' Wang checked the book. 'Seventeen.' He looked up at John. 'We need to get them out. Their sentences are complete. You could go undercover and find your Serpent at the same time.'

'The JE won't let him,' I said. 'If both of him are trapped, we'll lose for sure.'

'So what do we do?' Wang said.

'Try a diplomatic solution first; we're the good guys here,' I said. 'Give the King a chance to do the right thing. Call him or a senior lieutenant for a meeting on neutral ground halfway across the first causeway, and try to talk them into releasing the people who are due.'

'My Lord?'

'Emma speaks for me; she always knows what I'm thinking and right now she has twice the brains I do. If I

63

am silent I agree with her and you do not need to confirm with me.'

Wang looked from John to me. 'You share your thoughts?'

'No,' John and I said at the same time, and both of us winced.

'Maybe the Serpent —' Wang began.

'No!' John and I snapped in unison and shifted uncomfortably, then went still when we realised what we were doing.

Wang was smart enough to leave it there, but it was obvious what he was thinking.

'She knows everything that's going on and she's not putting up with these goddamn painful feet,' John said. 'I'm relying on her right now.'

'Opium could ease —'

'No,' John said.

They matched glares for a moment and Wang backed down. He raised his hands. 'I will ask them for a meeting.'

'Arrange a time with his assistant, Zara,' I said. 'I'm free when he's free.'

'Done,' Wang said. 'And when the diplomatic talks fail?'

'We'll cross that causeway when we come to it,' John said. 'If you or one of your Generals can think of a way to get these people out without starting a war, I would appreciate it. It burns to have people who have completed their sentences still being tortured there.'

'They may just be sitting under a tree doing nothing if all the demons have left,' I said.

'They haven't,' John said. 'I can smell them. They're trying to goad me into going in.'

'Don't,' Wang said. 'Emma's right. I thought it would be a good idea for you to go in, but with you in this state ... it's not.'

'I know,' John said, wiping one hand over his forehead. He took another sip of the water; he was feeling the Serpent's dehydration and starvation. 'I'll ask around quietly and see if we can find someone to investigate down here. Until then, we'll go with the diplomatic solution first.'

'I agree with your wise advice,' Wang said. He pushed the book away. 'Let me show you out.'

'Both of us need an hour to rest in the same room to rebuild our strength before we return,' John said.

'A whole hour?' Wang said, looking from John to me.

Neither of us replied.

'I'll make sure you're not disturbed.'

'Good,' John said.

5

'Tiger.'

'About time you answered,' I said. 'I've been trying to talk to you forever!'

'This had better be fucking good, I'm busy.'

'Do you have time for a simple question?'

'How simple?'

'Can you synthesise two metric tons of weapons-grade steel in the next eight weeks?'

'Two thousand kilos?'

'Yep.'

'Damn. Let me think. Um ... no. Number One could ... No. Sorry, Emma, can't be done. I can't free anybody up for that amount of time, and with a couple of my biggest guys working on it ...' He thought for a moment. 'No. I can't spare them, not unless you can't find another way.'

'Okay. I thought that would be the case, but it was worth a try. I'll give my connections on the Earthly a call.

Do you know anyone who sells this stuff?'

'Of course not, we make our own. We're the last people you should ask.'

'Could you provide me with a smaller quantity of Celestial-weapons-grade steel with energy spun through it to make it more effective against demons?'

'How much of that would you need?'

'Probably a hundred kilos to start off with.'

'I can put my Number Three and Number Five on that — should take about three days ... No, wait, Number Three's still in Russia, so about a week. You can have it faster if you provide the raw steel for Five to work with after you've bought your big lot. Satisfactory?'

'Thanks,' I said, noting it down. 'That's all I need for now.'

'Do you know —'

'Yes, I know I sound like him,' I said. 'Bye, Tiger.'

'Wait,' he said. 'Why are you asking for this now? We sent you a bunch of steel ...' I heard papers shuffling. 'Not long ago.'

'Wait ... are you actually at your desk?'

He sounded sheepish. 'Maybe. So the steel. What happened to it all?'

'I've had the forge working nonstop, and some of the steel was wasted on the materials-fusion experiments with the Phoenix's people.'

'How did that work out? Ceramic would make an excellent edge. Much sharper, and would hold the edge for significantly longer.'

'It didn't. The ceramic was too brittle — one good hit and it was gone; and when the steel flexed it shattered.'

'Carbon fibre?'

67

'Major fail on that one: much too soft, completely destroyed the edge.'

'Well, damn. Okay then, send the steel over to me when you've bought it and I'll put a couple of my boys onto the energy enhancement.' He shuffled papers again. 'Yep, should be possible, but send it fast because we're heavily occupied with war preparations.'

'I know. All of you Winds are flat out — hell, even *you're* being productive. Just hold a minute. There.'

'What?'

'Marked it in my diary: *Tiger at his desk*. Is that an unofficial holiday in the West?'

'No, it's a day of mourning because I'm not in the harem. Fuck it, it's more fun in there anyway. Bye, Emma,' he said, and hung up.

* * *

'Wei?'

'Simone, where are you? You're supposed to be here for this call to Monica.'

My mobile phone dinged with a text message and I picked it up to see: Leo.

'I can't come right now,' Simone said. 'I'm stuck outside the student accommodation office, they're running late for my interview. If I leave now I won't have a place in the residences. Can't it wait?'

'No, I've made arrangements with her family so that she'd be in to speak to us. We haven't talked to her in ages.'

'I know, Emma, but I really can't leave! Look, as soon as I have it all settled here I'll pop over to the Philippines and see her, that'd be much better anyway. Oh, my number's up,

I have to go. Say hello to her for me, will you? Tell her I love her. Bye.'

She hung up. I read Leo's text.

Sry can't come up rght now stuck @ Singpre with orphans, gov't being trble w ID docs. Will talk to M next time, k?

Not even John was able to come; he was in a meeting with the Generals about the defence of Hell that had already gone an hour over time and looked like taking most of the afternoon.

I dialled Monica's number.

'Hello?'

'Hello, is Monica there?' I said.

'Who is asking?'

'It's Emma Donahoe.'

'Oh! Oh! Yes, ma'am, sorry, ma'am.'

I sighed with exasperation. 'I'm not ma'am. Just call me Emma. Monica's part of the family!'

'Yes, ma'am. Just a second, I'll get Monica.'

I heard a torrent of Tagalog, many excited voices on the other end of the line, then Monica came on.

'Ma'am.' Her voice was thin and weak.

'Oh, Monica,' I said. 'I'm so sorry this happened.'

'It's God's will, ma'am.'

'Will everybody stop with the ma'am business! Just Emma. Please.'

'You're a queen, ma'am.' Her voice became breathless. 'I knew that Mr Chen was a special man, but when Marcus told me ... I never knew. Marcus explained that even though Mr Chen doesn't say much, and most of the time doesn't seem much, ...he's a king — or more like an angel, a Chinese angel. I am very privileged to have been a part

69

of such a noble family. I never would have met Marcus if it hadn't been for Mr Chen and his friend Mr Tiger. I have Marcus, I have my family, I am so happy. Oh! My sister's daughter is pregnant, she'll be having the baby soon, so much excitement.' She sounded genuinely delighted. 'How are Miss Simone and Mister Leo? Are they well?'

I winced. 'They were supposed to come and talk to you, but Simone's held up organising her university accommodation in Tokyo —'

'University! That's wonderful! I have nieces and nephews that are going to university, the first time in our family. And it's because of your generosity, ma'am, that we can afford for them to go. They will do great things, just like Miss Simone. One of them is even studying to be a *doctor*! We are so proud. What will Simone study?'

'Marine biology. She'll be learning to save the oceans.'

'Of course, since Mr Chen is ...' She hissed with restrained laughter. 'What he is. Please tell her I said hello.'

'I'm sorry she couldn't speak to you.'

'No! She's doing important things. It's fine, it's fine.'

'Leo's running some orphanages all over Asia. He's stuck in Singapore arranging for some children to be looked after and couldn't get away, but he sends his best wishes.'

'I always knew he would do great things. You know, the first time I saw him, he scared me to death. And the first time I found out ... about him ... I thought he was ...' She hesitated. 'Sinful? I don't know the English word. But then to see him care for Simone and protect all of us ... I think that God has a special place in his heart for a noble man like Leo.'

'I agree completely.'

'How is Mr Chen?'

'He couldn't come and talk to you, he's off doing ... king stuff,' I said. 'He's defending all of us.'

'I know, I understand, I understand, he's always been so important.' Her voice filled with amusement. 'You'd never know it from his clothes. I hope you and Leo are making him wear something nice.'

'Hey, this is Mr Chen we're talking about,' I said with similar amusement. 'Anything he wears is immediately scruffy no matter how new it is.'

'I know!' She giggled. 'And you, ma'am? Are you happy?' Her voice became mischievous. 'Are you two married yet? I expect many children from both of you, you know. They would be like my own grandchildren.' She sighed with bliss. 'I only wish I could last a little longer and have the chance to see you be a mother and Mr Chen be a father again. That, I think, was the happiest time of his life, when he had Miss Michelle and little Simone ... Oh!' She sounded horrified. 'But you make him happy too, I didn't mean —'

'I know what you mean, and he's said that it was a happy time for him as well, and you helped him and Michelle to make it happy. He says he's been more blessed in the time you've been with him than any other time in his very long life.'

She dropped her voice. 'You say too much, ma'am.'

'I'm a better person for having known you, Monica. All of us are.'

'Thank you. Um ...' She choked on the words. 'I think I need to go now. I'll put Marcus on.' Her voice thickened even more. 'Thank you so much for calling me, ma'am, it means so much to me ...'

She obviously broke down, and the receiver filled with the sound of Tagalog again. Then Marcus spoke. 'Thank you, ma'am. She's crying, but smiling, and she needs to rest.'

'I'll try to have Simone and Leo talk to her soon, okay?'

'That would be wonderful, ma'am. Thank you for calling.'

There was more Tagalog, and the phone disconnected.

I leaned back in my office chair, pulled out a couple of tissues, wiped my eyes, and turned back to the weapons inventory spreadsheets.

* * *

The meeting between the demons and the Celestial was held the next day. The Demon King sent his Number One so John was obliged to send Er Lang, a Celestial of matching rank. Number One had demanded that they meet one on one with no Retainers, so Er Lang took Zara with him, as jewellery, to relay, and we watched the meeting from Yanluo Wang's office in Hell.

After the bows and formalities had taken place, Er Lang and Number One sat at a table on the middle of the causeway. They spoke for a tedious five minutes about families and happenings on both Planes, then settled into silence as each waited for the other to broach the subject.

Er Lang finally relented and pulled a scroll from the side of the table. 'I have been directed by the Celestial to request that the four humans who have completed their sentences be returned.'

Number One's expression remained carefully blank. 'There are no humans who have completed their sentences.'

'There are four,' Er Lang said, pushing the scroll at Number One.

Number One didn't look at it. 'We do not have any humans to return to you.'

'You must return them. That is the agreement that you have with the Celestial.'

Number One rose and pushed his chair back. 'Come and get them.'

'We do not wish to go to war with you,' Er Lang said without rising. 'You were soundly defeated last time. Do not repeat your mistake.'

Number One grinned menacingly. 'Guns don't hurt us.'

'We don't use guns.'

'No,' Number One said. 'But we do.'

John's fingers twitched on the table next to me and I put my hand on top of his to still them. He inclined his head slightly in thanks without looking away from the transmission.

Er Lang pushed his chair back and rose, then summoned his halberd and held it upright next to him. 'You will defer to the authority of the Celestial, demon, or face the consequences.'

'What the hell are you doing, Number Two?' John said.

Number One summoned a similar weapon. 'We do not defer to turtle eggs,' he said with relish.

Er Lang's halberd was a blur as he swung it straight at Number One's head. Number One blocked it and pushed it down, then spun his own weapon and drove the pointed butt into Er Lang's throat.

John jumped to his feet and leaned on the table to stare at the transmission with astonishment. 'What the fuck?'

Number One ripped the point of halberd out and blood gushed from Er Lang's throat. Er Lang tottered for a minute, eyes wide and breath gurgling through the throat wound, then fell sideways. The transmission blinked out and Er Lang appeared on the floor of Yanluo Wang's office. We knelt next to him and John summoned a pad to put over the wound.

73

'You'd better have a very good reason for this, Number Two,' John said to him.

Er Lang's breath bubbled through the blood in his throat. He attempted to speak, and made more horrible gurgling sounds. He changed to silent speech.

There was a small memory device attached to the point. They are ready to go to war and will attack soon. This memory device has intelligence on their plans and an outline of their strength. You need to keep me alive until you can remove it. If I die, it's gone.

John checked the wound. 'This isn't fatal. He's missed your carotid and pierced your trachea.'

He held one hand over Er Lang's throat and the blood lifted free. Er Lang gasped with relief, the breath whistling through the wound in his throat. He panted until blood started to well from the wound and blocked it again.

'We need a tracheotomy tube to clear your breathing.' John looked around for Yanluo Wang, who had already gone. 'We're finding one. He told you to attack him?'

He said to make it look good.

'You didn't. He defeated you easily in front of everybody.'

I wasn't expecting him to be quite as good as he is. He's faster than me. He did defeat me easily. His breath sucked through the blood. *Help, Ah Wu, I'm drowning!*

John lifted the blood free again and Er Lang panted with relief. He turned his head to see me. *What did you teach them?*

'Nothing,' I said. Er Lang's dog appeared and pushed me aside. 'The Jade Emperor restricted me from teaching.'

'This is all my fault!' Zara wailed from her ring on Er Lang's right hand. 'Never ask me to be jewellery again. I am bad luck!'

Just take the device out of me so I can go! Er Lang said, his breath still bubbling.

John studied the wound. 'I can't see it. I'll have to open you up further to find it.'

Er Lang's dog whined.

Zara rose from her setting in a ring on Er Lang's finger. 'Let me do it,' she said, her voice hoarse with emotion.

She shrank as she swept through the air towards the wound, then disappeared into Er Lang's throat. His face went rigid with pain and he gritted his teeth, arching his back.

'I have it,' Zara said, re-emerging covered in Er Lang's blood. 'My Lord Er Lang, I am so very sorry. I vow I will never be a piece of jewellery again.'

'It's not your fault, Zara,' I said.

'I am cursed!'

Yanluo Wang entered holding a tracheotomy tube in a sterile bag. 'Sorry. Took a while to find one.'

Don't bother, Er Lang panted through the blood, his face a fierce grimace of pain. *Do me a favour, Ah Wu? You are the quickest and cleanest way.*

John hesitated, then glanced up at me. He didn't want me to know he could do it.

'Do it, John, I know you can,' I said.

John dropped his head to speak intensely to Er Lang. 'You ask a great deal; you know how difficult this is.'

I know. Please, Ah Wu, let me go, Er Lang said.

'Only for you, old friend,' John said.

He put two fingers on the side of Er Lang's throat and concentrated as if taking his pulse. Er Lang's breathing stopped and he went limp. He disappeared, and his dog fell over his front paws then disappeared as well.

'Hold your hand out,' Zara said to John.

He opened his palm and she dropped a tiny, blood-covered micro-SD memory card less than a centimetre to a side into his hand.

'Will it still work after being soaked like this?' I said.

'It's an expensive waterproof one,' Zara said. 'Uh, my Lord, did you just kill him with your touch?'

John didn't reply.

'It's part of what he is,' I said.

'You are as cursed as I am, Dark Lord,' Zara breathed. 'I am glad it is difficult for you.'

'It isn't. The difficulty lies in not killing everything else around me.' He glared up at her, his voice icy. 'Do not tell anyone.'

'My Lord,' Zara said. 'Forgive me, I think I'm going to be sick.' She disappeared.

'I'll head over to Court Ten and talk to Judge Pao,' Yanluo Wang said. 'We need Er Lang back as quickly as possible now we know they're about to attack.'

'Don't,' John said, summoning a bubble of water to wash the blood off the SD card. 'He'll blame us for the fact we're at war and delay Er Lang's release.'

'He's not really that uncooperative, is he?' I said, then raised my hands. 'Never mind. I know the answer to that.'

John released the bubble and the SD card fell out of the air into his hand. 'Let's go back to the Mountain. I think in the very near future I will be needed in three places at once.'

'You can do that?' Yanluo Wang said.

'Best I can manage is two, and right now one of them is slightly stationary,' John said with grim humour. He leaned on the desk to pull himself to his feet. 'Pass the message on to the Celestial that I'm on my way. I'll be there as soon as I can.'

He reached and helped me to stand, holding me upright when another wave of dizziness made me hesitate. 'I'll take us straight back to the Mountain, Emma, and put us on the bed. We'll probably be unconscious for a while.' He raised his head and concentrated. 'The staff are ready for us.' He gazed into my eyes. 'Ready?'

I lost myself in his eyes. 'Always.'

6

The next morning we sat side by side meditating together in Serene Meditation, the pavilion I'd had built to replace Serpent Concubine in the Northern Heavens. We had half an hour before the first hearings in the Hall of Dark Justice, and were using the respite to rebuild our energy. We didn't know exactly when the demons would attack; the memory card only carried basic information on the demons' plans and didn't have any details on the Western army or a projected timeline. Zara was analysing further, but there was a renewed sense of urgency around us as people prepared.

The chi thrummed between us, a satisfying feeling of togetherness that nevertheless distressed John and made him slightly lose his concentration. We shouldn't have been able to do that.

Yue Gui approached across the stepping stones in the pond in front of the pavilion, and gracefully fell to one knee on the open timber veranda. John opened one eye but didn't address her, and she knelt waiting.

'What, Ah Yue?' I eventually said.

'My Lord. My Lady. You have been immediately ordered to the Azure Dragon's Palace Under the Sea.'

John snapped open his eyes and I sat straighter.

'Both of us?' John said.

Yue rose and nodded. 'Yes.'

'What, now?' I said.

'Right now.'

'Is this a joke?' John said. 'Hell is about to attack and he sends us to have a tea ceremony with the Dragon?'

'I know,' she moaned. 'But it's from the Jade Emperor himself. He won't leave you two alone.'

John and I shared a look. He'd suspected for a while that the Jade Emperor was dragging me all over creation to ensure I'd never be strong enough to take the Elixir of Immortality, and I was starting to believe it.

John pulled himself to his feet and summoned his walking stick. 'Notify Emma's maid that she'll need to dress up.'

'No need, Father,' Yue Gui said. 'The Dragon himself contacted me and said that this does not require any regalia. It is a private matter and your usual,' she smiled slightly, 'scruffiness will suffice.'

'Did the Dragon say why we're being dragged over there?' I said.

She shook her head.

'Can you do it?' I asked John.

'I can.' His face went rigid with concentration as he warned the Dragon of the state we were in. His expression softened. 'He's ready for us.'

He nodded to Yue Gui. 'Reschedule the hearings, Mei Mei. We will recommence as soon as we return.'

Yue Gui glowed with pleasure at the affectionate familiarity of her father calling her 'little sister', and headed back to her office in the administrative section of the palace.

John held his hand out to me. 'I think I will have a talk to the Jade Emperor about this.'

I took his hand and gazed into his eyes. 'Make sure you take me with you. I want to speak to him as well.'

His eyes crinkled up as the world changed around us. 'Don't scare him too much.'

* * *

I came around on a brilliant peacock-blue couch in a room of shining crystal walls. A chandelier hung from the ceiling, looking like something grown rather than crafted, the light gleaming from within its transparent tentacle-like arms. John was sitting cross-legged across from me on another sofa, his eyes closed in meditation.

I sat up and rubbed my eyes. 'How long this time?'

He took a deep breath in and out. 'Forty minutes.'

'Shit.'

'Language, Emma. You insult our host.'

'He's not even here.'

The Dragon surged through the crystal wall in huge blue True Form. The walls weren't crystal; they were the interface between air and water. 'Yes, I am.'

'Hey, Qing Long,' I said. 'Take human form so I can give you a hug.'

He folded up into his tall slim human form and held his arms out. 'Deal.'

I went to him and embraced him around his waist — the highest I could reach — and he kissed the top of my head. He turned to John with me still in his arms. 'You guys ready?' His voice changed to patient exasperation. 'Oh, Ah Wu, look at your feet.'

I sighed with similar exasperation. The stitches had come open again and blood stained the bandages.

'This had better be good, Ah Qing, we have a war to prepare for,' John growled. He picked up his walking stick and gingerly stepped off the couch to stand next to us.

Qing Long released me and I went to John and put my arm around his waist. He rubbed my back affectionately.

The Dragon bowed slightly and put his hands in his turquoise and silver embossed sleeves. 'It's not good. It's very bad. But I think, in the circumstance, it is the right thing to do.'

John's expression darkened. 'What is?'

'I can't say. You'll see when you see. Just come with me and all will be made clear.'

'This is all very mysterious and disturbing,' I said as I walked between them down the corridor. It appeared as a normal breezeway with columns and a roof, but instead of open walls the sides were the water–air interface. Our reflections followed us as we walked, and flashes of brilliance lit the other side, blurred by the water.

At the end of the breezeway, the Dragon held one hand out. The water interface in front of us shimmered and he walked through. 'This way.'

We followed him down a wide series of steps and he opened a pair of gates at the end. We entered what appeared to be a cell complex, with barred doors and long corridors. I stopped.

'Don't worry, Emma, these aren't cells,' John said, reading my mind.

'This is my storeroom,' the Dragon said, leading us to the end of the corridor.

As we passed the cells I saw inside: it was a treasure house. Each cell had shelves around the walls; some held pieces of Celestial and mundane jade, carved into delicate sculptures that enhanced their value; others held ancient gold Buddhist icons and priceless Imperial porcelain.

Another pair of doors, this time wood and red, opened before us and we went down a narrower set of steps.

Qing Long stopped at the bottom and turned to eye me. 'I would appreciate it if you would not tell anyone that this is here, and what's in it.'

'You have my word,' I said.

The Dragon nodded, his turquoise hair shining in the reflected light of the crystals illuminating the tunnel. 'Thank you.'

He led us through another barred gate and generated a ball of light so I could see. This tunnel was dark and featureless, with large solid wood doors at regular intervals on either side. The light didn't penetrate to the corners, putting us in a pool of brightness with the darkness around us.

Qing Long stopped at the end of the tunnel and put his hand on a door that was embossed with the circular motif of the Blue Dragon. The door split vertically into two pieces, which slid smoothly sideways. We went into a brightly lit room that was four metres to a side and contained only a carved wooden box, forty centimetres wide, standing on a metre-tall pillar.

'The Jade Emperor says to give this to you,' the Dragon said. 'In your current state, it's probably a good idea.'

82

He opened the lid of the casket and John and I both took a step back. The casket contained a cage of what appeared to be Celestial Jade, the same size as the interior of the casket and sitting flush with its walls.

'Oh, dear Lord, is that what I think it is?' I said.

'What are you doing with one of these?' John said, his voice a horrified rasp.

The Dragon put the lid back on the casket. 'This is the safest place it could be.'

'You should destroy it,' John said.

'I was as distressed as you are when the Celestial gave it to me four hundred years ago, and I wanted to destroy it. The Celestial told me not to; he said there would be a time when such a thing is needed.' He lifted the casket in both hands. 'And now is the time. Take True Form in this and you can heal without risk.'

'You should have told me about this when my feet were first injured. The demons are preparing to attack now,' John said.

The Dragon dropped his head slightly. 'The Jade Emperor suggested I give it to you three days ago and I ignored him.' He put one hand on top of the casket as he held it with the other. 'I didn't want to see you trapped inside this awful thing.'

'And now the Jade Emperor's changed it to an order,' John said.

'I know, I know,' the Dragon said with resignation. 'Obey the Celestial, he knows what he's doing.'

'No,' I said softly.

John took a step forward and accepted the casket from the Dragon, his face grim.

'No!' I said. 'We can't risk this.'

'Enter it and rest here,' the Dragon said. 'You will be safe under the sea.'

'I will go to the Grotto,' John said. 'I will reap the most benefit in the heart of my Mountain.'

The Dragon nodded. 'Good idea.' He ducked slightly to gaze into John's eyes; he was a good head taller. 'Let me come to ensure you aren't imprisoned by a demon seeking advancement.' He put his hand on John's shoulder. 'I'll watch you, Ah Wu.'

'Emma can watch me. You have more important things to do.'

'And I don't,' I said. 'I can sit with him for as long as it takes.'

The Dragon glanced at me, seeing the lie, then obviously relented and nodded.

He stood more upright and turned to me. 'He won't be able to do anything while he's in it. He can't call or travel or carry.' He held his hand out and one of his AI phones appeared in it, slim and blue–silver. 'Go down with him and watch him, and the minute you think anything is wrong, contact me immediately. I'll be right there.'

'Thanks, Dragon,' I said, my voice small. 'God, this is such a bad idea.'

'And it's not one of yours for a change,' the Dragon said with grim humour. He turned to John. 'Let me know when you enter, and also when you leave. I'll be on alert while you're in it.'

'Thank you, Ah Qing,' John said, and gave the Dragon a clumsy one-handed embrace while he held the casket with the other. 'I'll be very glad to have my feet back.'

'My pleasure,' the Dragon said. 'Please don't tell anyone it exists. Its presence imperils us all.'

'Hopefully very soon it will be destroyed,' John said.

'Hopefully you are right,' the Dragon said.

7

John was sitting in an armchair next to the fire in our bedroom when I came around after the journey back. His long hair was damp from the shower and he was wearing his black silk bathrobe, loosely tied and open to his waist. He was studying some of the reports, the papers held casually on his crossed knee as he read. I lay for a moment watching him, wishing I could take a photo of him like this, relaxed and elegant — until I saw the blood on his bandaged feet.

He smiled slightly without looking away from the papers.

'When do you want to do it?' I said without rising.

'Immediately.' He didn't look up. 'After we've decided whether to go into lockdown or continue normally while I'm in it.'

'What did the Masters say?'

'Continue normally.' He glanced up at me. 'Do you agree?'

'What do *you* think?'

He sighed and placed the reports on the floor next to him, then rubbed his eyes. 'Lockdown. We'll be vulnerable while I'm bound and we need to take every precaution.'

I sat up. 'I agree with you. We should go into lockdown for the duration.'

He nodded and unfocused, giving the order. He snapped back as the bells started to ring in the slow rhythm of lockdown.

'Let me use the bathroom and we can go down,' I said.

He concentrated and changed out of the robe into a Mountain uniform, then bent and picked up the jade cage, which had been sitting in its casket beside his chair, and put it in his lap while he waited for me.

Students were wandering back to their barracks, sharing their confusion about the reason for the lockdown, as I helped John from the Residence to the wall that held the entrance to the Grotto. We paused at the entrance and waited for the bells to stop, indicating that all the students had been accounted for. I studied my feet as we leaned side by side on the rock wall. John shifted slightly.

The bells stopped ringing, and John nodded acknowledgement as the Masters told him the lockdown was complete.

We levered ourselves off the wall and turned, and John put one hand out to open it. I put my hand on his arm to stop him before we went in.

'Talk about it inside where it's secure,' he said.

I nodded and followed him down the stairs, conjuring a ball of chi to see by when the wall closed behind us.

'You can manage the light yourself?' he asked softly.

'Yes.'

When we reached the bottom, he placed the casket on the floor of the ledge next to the lake, opened it and took out the jade cage.

'John ...' I said.

He straightened to see me.

I ran my hands through my hair. 'Are you absolutely sure the Western Demon King can't flash into my eyes and see what we're doing?'

He sagged slightly. 'I was wondering when you'd work it out.' He straightened again. 'Why didn't you tell me when you knew?'

'Because I'm no longer controlled by them and they can't do it any more.' I shook my head. 'At least, I hope I'm not. Are you sure they can't do it any more? I don't feel any different. I just feel like me.'

'They can't do it any more.'

'How many others know it was me?' I said.

'About four of the Celestial Masters. The Lius pulled me in for a meeting about it after you came back from the West. They'd worked out the Western King was doing it, and wanted to be sure that it wouldn't happen any more.' He saw my face. 'The Western King could only flash into your head for less than a second each time, Emma. It wasn't a major security breach.'

'Are you absolutely sure it won't happen again?'

'You broke their hold. You stopped obeying them so you became ...' He searched for the words. 'Completely human. You are no longer under their control.'

I looked into his eyes and saw the lie. 'The Western King said there was enough demon there for him to control. There was enough demon there to fill me with Eastern demon essence.'

'You regained your free will. You are now human.'

'You know that's not possible. When a demon becomes human they Ascend, and I know that hasn't happened to me.'

'I can't talk about that and you know it.'

'I know how powerful the Jade Emperor's orders are. I also know I can't have Ascended. That hasn't happened to me, so I'm still a demon.'

'You are not a demon and you never were, Emma. You're a human with a very small amount of demon in you that's been overcome. There's no distinct line between human and demon; with interbreeding, the grey areas are huge. You were very far on the human side of the border. You are so human it doesn't matter.'

I sat on the bench and leaned my elbows on my knees. 'You need to stop living in denial, John; you've been doing it for more than ten years. Face the fact that I'm a demon and I'm a security risk.'

'You're human.' He shrugged. 'I'm not in denial.'

'You need to check me and make sure.'

'I have seen all I need to see inside your head.'

'That was before I went to the West and the Western King controlled me.' I studied him, seeing his conflict. 'Who knows what they did to me while they'd taken my will?'

'I won't do it, Emma.' He paced in a circle, then crouched to open the jade cage. 'You broke their hold, that's all that matters.'

'Face the fact that I may be a security risk and check me again.'

He didn't reply, studying the cage.

'If I am a security risk, we do *not* want the Western Demon King to know you're in that,' I said, pointing at the cage. 'You need to double-check, John.'

'No.'

'Please.' I went to him and crouched next to him. I put my hand on his face. 'I want to be sure. Do it for me. If you're right, then it makes no difference.'

'I am right. I don't like looking inside your head.'

'It would ease my mind and it won't hurt me. Just do it, John.'

'All right. If I must. Let's get this over with so we can stop arguing like the old married couple we are and I can have my nap.'

He stood and waved for me to rise as well.

'Why didn't you see my demon nature when you looked inside me before?' I said as I moved closer. 'Never mind; you've been in denial for years.'

'Your Western demon nature was not visible to me, and it was dormant until you encountered the Western King,' he said, putting his hands on either side of my face. 'Your mixed Western nature was something we haven't encountered in the past, and it is so small that there's hardly any of it.'

'I remember. The Western King said that one more generation and he wouldn't be able to control me.'

'That's right. The grey area is huge, and your demon nature is minuscule. There is also something about you that is very hard to spot — the same as our Demon King when he is disguised as human, as Kitty Kwok.'

'Kitty was originally human.'

'So are you, you see?'

He raised his face and closed his eyes, and his dark cool essence flowed through my nerves, up and down my spine.

'It feels like there's ice water running through me,' I said.

'I'm not hurting you?'

'No. It feels ...' I hesitated. 'Really good, actually.'

'Oh, Emma,' he said, his voice soft with awe. 'No wonder we are so in tune. You're right, you haven't Ascended at all. You have done the same thing as I have: you've turned. You broke their hold and disobeyed their orders, and turned to the Celestial by choice. Every other demon has required taming with the Fire Essence Pill to control their nature. You have done it by yourself.'

'I'm still a demon?'

'Am I?'

I paused at that.

'Exactly,' he said. 'You have overcome it and it is no longer part of your nature, same as me.'

'How many demons have done this? Overcome their natures and turned without being tamed?'

'There are very rare cases of it happening. Very few of us have done it. I hoped Ronnie Wong would do it, but he remained obedient to Number One and had to be tamed. A couple of the Generals are the only ones I know of apart from me — and now you as well.'

'I don't feel that special,' I said, unconvinced.

'You have done this by force of will, and through the love you hold for your family. By the Heavens, Emma, you are a very strange creature.'

'Oh, that's a true compliment coming from you, Xuan Wu.'

'I know.' He removed his essence from me and I shivered. 'I wonder if your Western heritage and growing up in the South had something to do with it? Bred in the West, grew up in the South, trained in the East. Maybe there are other cross-nation spirits that are as complex as you are. When all this is resolved, we must go and speak to the Grandmother. In the meantime, you are no more a danger to the security of the Celestial than I am.' He put his hands on my shoulders. 'Now that you have transcended your demon nature and the training I have given you is approaching its full potential, you have grown into something astonishing. When we have that Elixir inside you, it will be a sight to see.'

'So there's no chance that the Western Demon King can see through my eyes?' I said. 'I'm sorry for doubting you. You were right.'

'No, you were right,' he said. 'I was absolutely positive you weren't a demon, but I think to some degree I have been in denial. I didn't want you to be something I have vowed to destroy, however slim that possibility is.'

'Maybe we should have kept it casual and not gone into lockdown then,' I said.

'Even so,' he said, turning back to the jade cage. 'Even without a single untamed demon on the Mountain, you can never be sure that nobody will try us. And since we have no seals I'd prefer to be safe.'

He handed the lid to me and I readied myself. I would have to be fast to shut the Turtle in the cage before it took off to merge with the Serpent.

John attempted to stand inside the cage to make it easier for me, but even with his mutilated feet he didn't fit. He put one foot in and turned to face me.

I crouched with the cover in both hands, ready to imprison him, then stopped and shook my head. 'I can't put you in and close the lid at the same time. We need another person here to make sure you go into the cage.'

'Leo's on the Earthly with Ming. Yue is at the Northern Heavens. None of them can come in now that we've locked down.' He was silent for a moment. 'Simone is here.'

'She's perfect. You should have asked her first.'

'I don't want her to see me imprisoned.'

'I don't want to see it either, John,' I said, my voice hoarse.

The Grotto lit up as Simone opened the doorway far above, then darkened as she came down the stairs to us.

'I'll put him in, you slam the lid on,' she said, her voice thick with tears.

'Simone.' John put one hand on her shoulder. 'It's okay. It'll be like a rest for me. Nothing will happen.'

'I just have a really bad feeling about this.' She raised her head to see him. 'How will we know to let you out?'

'I'll just ask,' he said. 'When I'm in control enough to speak to you, take the lid off.'

'Okay,' she said. 'Ready, Emma?'

'I have it.'

'I'm going to mess this up,' she whispered.

'No, you aren't,' John said. 'Are you ready?'

'How big will you make yourself?' Simone said.

'As small as I can. It will be about the same size as the cage. If I'm too big …' He hesitated. 'Never mind.'

Simone glanced at me and her expression matched my own dread. If he was too big, we wouldn't be able to put him in the cage and he would be gone.

John pushed one leg out towards her. 'Hold behind my knee. When I change, you will have one of my back legs. Use it to put me in.'

Simone silently shook her head. She threw her arms around him and embraced him, and he rested his face on top of her head and kissed her hair.

'I'll be fine,' he said.

She nodded, knelt, and did as he suggested.

'Ready?' he said.

'I love you,' I said.

'I love you too, Daddy,' Simone said, her voice still thick with tears.

'Both of you are my life,' he said. 'I will count to three and change. One, two … three.'

He collapsed into his small tortoise form and Simone swept both hands around it. She nearly threw it into the cage and I slammed the lid on, hoping that I didn't catch any fingers or feet. I held the lid on against the tortoise's struggles.

'We did it,' Simone said with disbelief as I closed the latches on the lid to hold it in place.

'You don't have to hang around now. I'll sit with him,' I said.

'I'll stay a while too, just to make sure nothing bad happens,' Simone said. 'He's fighting it.'

She was right: the tortoise was banging its beak against the bars of the cage. It was nearly as big as the cage itself so couldn't turn around, but it raised its feet and stamped at the bars.

'He's really distressed,' Simone said.

The tortoise raised its head, beak wide, and made a pathetic hissing sound, then banged its beak on the cage. It slammed the top of its head against the lid. It opened its mouth and hissed again, then tried to prise its beak between the bars of the cage. When it didn't succeed, it squatted with frustration and systematically banged its beak on the inside of the cage.

'I can't watch this,' Simone said, and turned away.

'Go out. I can mind him,' I said.

She stood and went up the stairs and out of the Grotto. I picked up the cage, which was surprisingly heavy with him in it, put it on the stone bench and settled next to it to supervise as the tortoise struggled and hissed.

Half an hour later, the tortoise was still banging its beak on the interior of the cage and was bleeding from its nose. This process was causing more damage instead of healing him. I pulled out my mundane phone and called Simone but she didn't answer. I called the Dragon on his AI phone instead.

'I'm on my way,' he said, and hung up before I could say anything.

I immediately called him back.

'How bad is it?' he said. 'Be quick, I'm taking True Form.'

'You don't need to come. He's fighting it and hurting himself. I need you to call Simone for me and tell her to come back down and try to calm him. She's not answering her phone.'

'Oh.' The Dragon was silent for a moment. 'All right. You don't need me? Nothing happened?'

'Apart from him stressing out and hurting himself, no. All's secure.'

'I should come anyway.'

'Hold off, Ah Qing. If Simone can't calm him, I'll have you bring a reptile-type sedative and we'll knock him out so he'll be forced to heal.'

'Good idea. I'll stand by. Let me see what I have around here.'

'Thanks, Ah Qing. Bye.'

'Do you know you sound an awful lot like him sometimes?' he said, and hung up.

'Yes,' I said as Simone opened the doorway and the light flooded in again.

When she reached the bench, she knelt so that her face was next to the cage. The tortoise ignored her, continuing to hiss and bang its beak on the bars.

'Daddy,' she said, and pushed her finger between the bars to stroke its leg. It moved faster than was visible, its beak snapped and she ripped her hand back and shook it.

'Ouch! He bit me.'

I knelt on the damp stone next to her and checked her hand. The sharp beak had cut her deeply, but the wound disappeared as I watched.

I pulled out the phone and called the Dragon. 'I think we need you.'

'He's still doing it?'

'Yes. Do you have something that will work on a reptile?'

'Yes. How much would you say he weighs?'

'Three or four kilos?'

'On my way.' He hung up.

Five minutes later the Grotto lit up again as the door above us opened. The Blue Dragon came down the stairs in human form.

'You were right,' he said, 'this whole thing was a terrible idea.' He held a Tupperware container with two syringes in it. 'This should do it. My own vet says it's the correct dose; and there's a second syringe to increase the dose if it doesn't affect him like a normal turtle.'

He took a syringe out and crouched in front of the cage.

'What is it?' Simone said.

'Diazepam. Valium. Should work on reptiles. I've used it myself in dragon form for panic attacks, and it doesn't matter whether it goes into a muscle or a vein, it'll work either way.'

'Panic attacks? You?' Simone said.

'Sometimes.' He studied the tortoise. 'You said he was distressed.'

I crouched next to him to look. The tortoise had stopped fighting and was squatting with its eyes half-closed.

'A minute ago he was frantic,' Simone said. 'Maybe biting me let some of the anger out.'

'He bit you?' the Dragon said, glancing up at her.

She shrugged. 'He's all animal.'

The Dragon put his elbows on his knees and levered himself upright. 'Well, he's settled now and he should heal.' He put his hand on my shoulder. 'Do you want me to stay, Emma?'

I hesitated.

'It's no bother, really,' he said, gently rubbing my arm. 'I'm just hanging around at home worried sick about him anyway.'

Simone stared at the Dragon.

'Let's sit and see if he becomes distressed again,' I said. 'If he does, we'll use what you brought.'

Qing Long nodded, then took full huge True Form and settled himself on the rock, resting his head on his crossed forelegs. 'I hope he heals up; those feet were torturing him. It was most painful to see.'

I sat on the other side of the cage from Simone. 'His feet have already stopped bleeding. How's his beak?'

'No change so far,' Simone said.

'We'll just wait and see.'

'I hope this works. It's been heartbreaking to see him like that, it really has,' the Dragon said. 'I'm just glad I could help.' He raised his head slightly. 'Is Jade here today?'

'No, she's on the Earthly arranging the orphanage accounts at the bank,' I said.

'Well, damn,' he said. 'Can't have everything, I suppose.' He sighed and his dragon nostrils flared. 'She's my whole world and she won't have anything to do with me. She has three times the integrity I ever will. She makes me feel small and worthless.'

'Drop the act and she's yours, Ah Qing,' I said.

'I doubt she'd have me even if I dropped the act.'

'What act?' Simone said.

'Me,' he said. 'All of me. Everything.' He let his back end fall sideways and stretched his hind legs like a cat. 'I thought it was about time you saw the real Qing Long.'

She was silent for a long time.

'Ask,' he said gently, his huge turquoise eyes glowing in the dark.

She started to say something, then changed her mind. She thought for another long moment, then said, 'Why?'

'It is in my nature to be … graceful, delicate, soft, kind? There's no real word for it.'

'Effeminate,' Simone said. 'You? Really?'

'So there is a word for it,' he said. 'There was a time when people did not respect a soft and gentle man, so I became the opposite — an extremely macho arrogant dick. Looking back, it was a stupid idea. Now I'm stuck with it. I can't admit I've been living a lie for these thousands of years.'

'So you're like, more feminine than the Phoenix?'

'I am the Lesser Yin. She is the Greater Yang. Of course I am.'

'Are you gay too?'

He chuckled and his scales rippled along his body. 'No. You know about me and Jade.'

'She won't marry you because it's all an act?'

'That's right.'

'I don't blame her,' Simone said fiercely.

He dropped his head on his forelegs again, and when he spoke his voice was full of grief. 'Neither do I.'

8

I was wrenched out of my meditation by my phone ringing.
The Dragon's phone rang as well, and he snorted and raised
his head. Simone floated out of the water; her phone was
ringing too. All three of us answered them at the same time.

It was Marshal Ma on my phone. 'Emma, we can't
contact Ah Wu. Where is he?'

'In retreat. Resting. What's the problem, Ma? Did
something happen?'

'Hell is under attack. We need him.'

I rose and paced. 'Who is defending? What's the status?
Wait.' I bent to peer at the tortoise in the cage; his eyes were
still half-closed. I tapped the bars and he didn't respond.
I returned the phone to my ear. 'He's ... unavailable.
Defending? Status?'

'Three battalions are defending. Looks like a good four
thousand demons.'

'Dear Lord. Level?'

He was answering already without waiting for me to ask. 'Not too big, about level forty. Each about the same strength as one of ours, with a similar level of training.'

'Which battalions?'

'Ninth, Sixteenth and Thirty-First.'

'How about we add the Third and Twenty-Second?'

'Most of the Third was lost when we tried to win back the Serpent. I already mobilised the Seventeenth and Twenty-Second.'

'Sorry, I forgot; that's John's area of expertise. But five battalions should be enough if we can bring a couple of Winds down as well. Anything bigger that we can't handle?'

'According to the intel their Number One gave us, this attack was planned with elementals too.'

I let my breath out in a long gasp. The Dragon took human form, his face rigid with restrained fury.

'Metal or wood?' I said.

'How did you ...? Never mind. Both types. I believe the Dragon knows about it already, but I don't have the authority to summon the Phoenix or the Tiger. It has to be Ah Wu.'

'Can it be me? Never mind, I know it can't.' I checked John again; he was insensible. 'Tell Er Lang. He can let the Winds know.'

'Actually, Emma, yes, it can be you,' Ma said. 'You're a better option than Er Lang to talk to the Winds. They don't acknowledge his seniority, and they all have a soft spot for you. Go ahead and talk to them.'

'Anything else you need me to pass on?'

'Tell them to mobilise their defences. This may be a diversion while they try for the rest of Heaven.'

'Understood. Keep me up to date. Bye, Ma.'

I hung up and quickly called the Tiger. He didn't answer. The Phoenix did when I called her.

'I know. I'm on my way,' she said.

'Is the Tiger aware of what's going on?' I said.

'He isn't responding. His Number One is dragging him out of his harem.'

'Geez, poor Michael,' I said under my breath.

'The Dragon told me what you're doing with the cage,' the Phoenix said. 'How is Ah Wu?'

'Completely out of it.' I rubbed my free hand over my forehead and paced in a circle. 'He was beating his brains out on the cage, then suddenly stopped. I thought he'd settled, but they obviously hit him with something before they attacked. I should have seen it for what it was.'

'Either way, he would still be in that cage so we have to manage without him. Let me call up some elementals and take some Red Warriors and we will deal with this.'

'Mobilise your Red Warriors in the Southern Heavens as well. This may be a distraction,' I said.

'Already.' She hung up without another word.

The Dragon lowered his phone. 'I need to go as well.'

'Go,' I said.

'Wait for me,' Simone said. 'I'll take some water elementals with me.' She smiled with grim delight. 'My new weapons need blooding too.'

The Dragon turned to me and opened his mouth.

'We'll be fine. I have my phone. The Mountain is in lockdown.' I waved them away. 'We can't afford to lose Hell. Go!'

'The phone I gave you will be useful. Place it on the floor and tell it to show you what's happening,' the Dragon said.

The Dragon and Simone ran up the stairs together, and light flared above as they went out. The sound of the bells ringing for battle stations echoed through the Grotto, then they closed the door and I was left in the darkness with the dozing tortoise. I placed the phone on the floor as the Dragon had said and hesitated, wondering what to do with it. I pressed the button on the front and it spoke with a young girl's voice.

'Please ask me a question.'

'Show me what's happening in Hell.'

'I have no sources to show you what is happening in Hell.'

I rose again and walked in a circle, then remembered that the Jade Building Block had dealt with these AI things before.

I tapped the stone in my ring. 'Stone.' It didn't reply. 'Stone! Jade Building Block.' I hit it harder. 'Stone!'

'Huh?'

'Are you hungover or something? Hell's been attacked. John's in a cage of jade here, knocked out. Help me get this phone thing to work, will you?'

'Why is the Turtle in a cage and knocked out?'

'The cage will force his feet to heal up, but the demons knocked him out before they attacked. Help me out. I'm sitting here in the dark and Hell could fall.'

'Damn, I hate these things,' the stone said. 'Phone.'

'Please ask me a question,' the phone said.

'Perverted unnatural piece of shit,' the stone said under its breath. It raised its voice. 'Project a screen above yourself showing us what's happening in Hell.'

'I tried that,' I said. 'It didn't do anything.'

'I have no source of information from Hell,' the phone said.

'What information sources do you have?' the stone said.

'The Lord Qing Long is carrying a camera.'

'Then show us that,' I said, exasperated.

'Why didn't you show us that?' the stone said at the same time.

'He is not in Hell,' the phone said, and a moving 3D image, forty centimetres across, appeared floating above the phone. It was the view from Qing Long's eyes.

'How did he do that?' the stone said.

'Headcam,' I said. 'I'd like to know how he fits it to his True Form.'

'Confirmed,' Qing Long said. 'Emma, I'm wearing a headset, but stay off the channel, please. Haruna, I need you to keep an eye on the situation and liaise with the Celestial. Keep me informed on the status in Heaven as well.'

'Understood, my Lord,' a young woman said, then her voice filled with awe. 'Emma? The Dark Lady's on the channel?'

'No, she's off the channel and watching. Mind your console, Haruna,' the Dragon said. 'Is the comms room fully staffed?'

'Yes, my Lord,' Haruna said.

'Does the Tiger finally have his dick put away and his damn pants on?'

Haruna sounded amused. 'He's on his way.'

'I'm moving to Hell now,' the Dragon said, and the signal dropped out to snowy static.

I checked the tortoise; he was still semi-conscious.

'Greetings, Dark Lady,' Haruna said.

'Hi, Haruna. Better keep quiet or your dad will have both of us for breakfast.'

'I know,' she said, breathless with excitement. 'Where is the Dark Lord? I think they will need him.'

'I'm hoping he'll be back soon.'

'But where …?' The signal popped back on above the phone. 'Never mind.'

The Dragon was prowling at the back of a waiting army of the Phoenix's Red Warriors and his own dragon soldiers, all standing tensely at the end of one of the causeways that linked the sides of Hell. A massed troop of demons stood on the causeway a hundred metres away, but not moving to attack.

'White Horsemen are in position on causeway nine,' a young man said. 'Seventeenth are in place. Twenty-Second are on their way. The main force is on causeways seven through nine.'

'Someone give me another headset for Ma,' the Dragon said.

The transmission filled with the sound of a microphone being rubbed against fabric, then Ma spoke. 'Testing.'

'Confirmed,' Haruna said.

'Are you *sure* this is better than silent speech?' Ma said.

'Haruna's in Heaven and she can relay for us. The battle is won on information, and she can coordinate from above. I have three dragons carrying cameras above us — she can see everything. Haruna?'

'The cameras are up and visibility is good,' Haruna said. 'I can't see who's heading the demons; there doesn't appear to be a leader. No senior officers to hit; they're all grunts.'

'Their leader is running it by remote control,' the Dragon said. 'Look for flyers carrying cameras the same way we are. I can't see any elementals. Haruna?'

'I have no visual on any elementals,' Haruna said. 'Maybe they didn't bring them along?'

'Good,' Ma said. 'Damn, perhaps you're right about these headset things. Marshal Deng of the Seventeenth.'

'My Lord,' Deng said, his voice rasping.

'Marshal Xiao of the Twenty-Second,' Ma said.

'Moving into position across causeways three to five now,' Xiao said in his usual old-man voice. 'We have your back.'

'Why aren't they attacking?' I asked the stone softly.

'That's what we'd all like to know,' Ma said.

'Wait, did you hear that?' the Dragon said. 'My lizard ears heard a vibration. There it is again. Can anyone else hear that?'

There was silence.

'No,' Ma said.

'Haruna?'

'Uh …' Haruna's voice was uncertain. 'There's some vibration across causeway eight … I have a visual.'

'I hear it now,' Ma said. 'It sounds like a huge machine …'

The screen flicked. I fell to sit on the bench next to John when I saw the tank.

'There's a modern army tank on causeway eight,' Haruna said.

'How the fucking fuck did they get a fucking tank into Hell?' the Tiger shouted.

'Haruna, quickly. Strategies,' the Dragon said.

'Accessing,' Haruna said, her voice strained with urgency. 'This is an ex-Russian army tank, bought surplus and restored. Weaknesses. Hold.'

The tank moved its turret gun and fired into the Tiger's White Horsemen on the eighth causeway. The shockwave knocked the Dragon backwards, and the sound was so loud that it deafened the microphone for a second. At the end of the causeway, men, women and horses flew through the air in a cloud of gravel and dust, and some fell into the lake.

'Holy shit,' the Tiger said. 'Back! Retreat! What's the range on this bitch, someone? No, we can't fight that. They have guns?'

There was a blast of automatic gunfire for twenty seconds and more of the Horsemen fell.

'All sides,' Haruna said. 'We're being mowed down on all three causeways.'

The Tiger roared with fury. 'Retreat, everyone! Back *up*. We can't fight these!' He roared again. 'Three! Five! Nine! Where the *fuck* is One! One!' His voice became deeper and louder. '*One!*'

'I'm working on it!' Michael shouted. 'I am trying to *concentrate* here! We're on causeway eight, regrouping. The tank's too far away to use metal abilities on it.'

'Well, stop talking and build a goddamn shield to block these blasts —'

The Tiger was interrupted by the tank firing again. It blew a huge crater in the grass at the end of the causeway and flattened all the White Horsemen and their mounts in a ten-metre radius.

'I said I'm fucking working on it,' Michael said through his teeth. 'Having trouble pulling together enough metal from the ground —'

'Grab the metal from the bullets and stop them, you fucking idiot!' the Tiger shouted. 'Someone stop that damn tank!'

A White Horsewoman charged on her horse through the carnage towards the tank — it was Number Three. When she was fifty metres away she stopped and concentrated, and the tank's treads and the muzzle of its turret gun visibly softened.

A machine gun below the tank's turret gun fired a short barrage and both she and her horse fell, shredded by the bullets. Another Horseman charged in to finish the job, and was also shredded before he was fifty metres from the tank.

'We can't stop all the bullets, there's too many of them,' Michael said. 'We're building a wall, but we can't grab enough —'

'To hell with this,' the Dragon said, and the camera switched to his viewpoint.

He leapt to fly and the camera slid dizzyingly up and down as he writhed through the air. The tank followed his progress with its turret gun and fired at him as he approached, but its aim was ruined. He dived onto the tank through the bullets from the other demons' guns, picked it up with his forefeet, flew over the water and dropped it into the lake with a massive splash that caused waves to cascade over the causeways.

He lifted into the air. 'I'm hit. Never mind, just a couple of bullets. I'm fine.'

'We need archers,' Ma said. 'Dragons to rake the gunmen from above. Where the hell did they get so many automatic weapons?'

'Obvious place,' I said under my breath as I watched.

'Range on these is two hundred metres,' Haruna said. 'Dad, we're severely outgunned. It's like the twenty-first century meets the fifteenth.'

'They're not carrying extra ammo,' the Tiger said. 'At full automatic their weapons will go for thirty seconds max. Obviously nobody's taught them to conserve their ammunition.'

The Dragon's viewpoint remained floating above the three causeways. The demons were close to the ends of the causeways and beginning to overrun the defending armies. As the demons ran out of ammunition they dropped their weapons and charged to fight hand to hand. The Heavenly army held them at the end of the causeways and the demons weren't able to invade the island, but it wouldn't be long. The defending armies were outnumbered and the demons seemed to go on forever.

'Hold the line!' Ma shouted.

'Air support incoming,' the Phoenix said. 'I need ground reinforcements where my people were standing.'

'Twenty-Seventh are in position,' Yang Piao said. 'Just let us know where to go.'

'Yang, bring your battalion in to reinforce where the birds were,' Ma said.

'Squads one to five, reinforce causeway eight. Six to ten on nine. Pull them back, I'm going to lift the earth,' Yang said. 'In five.'

'Everybody back! Yang's going to lift the earth!' the Dragon shouted.

'Back! Back!' the Tiger yelled.

The armies retreated to the island at the end of the causeways, and the demons surged to follow them. The ground fell out from under the demons' feet and the last ten metres of the causeways became deep holes, which the demons toppled into. The demons still on the causeways tried to stop their rush towards the Celestial army, but were pushed into the holes by the demons behind them. The holes filled with water and the demons thrashed and screamed, eventually disappearing beneath the water. The ends of the causeways peeled upwards like ribbons, sending the demons on them sliding down towards the demonic side of Hell. Demons tumbled as the causeways became almost vertical, some demons hitting the water and others landing on their companions and crushing them.

'Birds, go,' the Phoenix said.

Glittering red phoenixes, each with a wingspan of four metres, fell into view from the sky above the Dragon and blasted the demons with fire from their beaks.

'I have a visual on camera three. Elementals just appeared on the other side of the Celestial island,' the young man said over the comms. 'Wood and metal. Thirty of them.'

'I've stopped time around them, but I can't hold them forever!' Xiao shouted. 'I could do with a hand here!'

'Elementals at causeways three and four,' Haruna said. 'Wood and metal.'

'I have two fire elementals on camera six,' the young man said.

'Where the *fuck* is Ah Wu?' the Tiger shouted.

'Never mind him. Squad five, are you still with the Dark Princess?' Ma shouted.

'My Lord,' a demon soldier said.

'Escort her to the causeways where the elementals are and guard her with your lives, you hear me?' Ma's voice dropped. 'Anything happens to her, we're all quite majestically fucked.'

'I'm already there,' Simone said. 'Shut up and let me work.'

'Haruna, can you relay a visual of Simone for me?' I said.

'Hold on and I'll send a dragon around,' she said.

The screen still showed the phoenixes mopping up the ends of the causeways. The demons on the causeways had fled back towards the demonic side of Hell, and there wasn't much left moving on the battlefield except for the injured soldiers from our side being examined by field medics and the occasional lost and bewildered demon being torched.

'Phoenix, tell your people to stop destroying the stragglers and try to tame them instead,' I said.

My ordinary phone rang in my pocket and I answered it.

'Emma, it's Yue Gui. The Northern Heavens are under attack and we need Father. Where is he? He's not answering.'

'This is ridiculous!' I said. 'He's unavailable. He's healing. He can't help. Where's Martin?'

She was silent for a moment. 'He's not replying either. Is he with Father?'

'No. What about Leo? Is he with Martin?'

'No answer from him either.'

'This is insane. Where are they?' I said. 'Do you need reinforcements?'

A man's voice came on the phone: Martin's second-in-command and general of the defensive legion of the North. 'It's these damn insects. We've locked down and everybody's inside the screens, but the seals are gone and the wasps are so big that they're actually beginning to tunnel through the mesh. How did the Horsemen take them down? The minute my soldiers try to fight them, they sting us and we're dead.'

'Tiger!' I shouted at the Dragon's phone on the floor, which still displayed the deserted ends of the causeways on the screen. 'How did you destroy the wasp demons?'

'We tried everything and the best thing to hit them with is fucking tennis racquets,' the Tiger growled. 'You smack them out of the air and squash them. What, we have them? Where?'

'Northern Heavens.'

'Well, fuck. I'll have people take a bunch of racquets over to the North for you and hand them out. Your people are trained by Ah Wu; once they have something to hit the little bastards with, it won't take long.'

'You should have told us this before,' I said to the Tiger.

'These are too big — I can't stop them!' Simone shouted from the phone on the floor. 'It doesn't do anything. Help!'

'Fall back!' Ma shouted. 'Fall back! And pray to the Buddhas, because we need their help.'

'My elementals did *nothing*,' Simone said, distraught.

'Neither did mine, little one,' the Phoenix said. 'We're out of options. We have to retreat.'

'Emma?' Yue Gui said into my ear, drawing me back to the situation in the Northern Heavens.

'Tennis racquets take them out; the Tiger's sending you a bunch of them,' I said.

'Well, that's a new one,' she said with amusement.

I turned on the spot, trying to keep the anguish from my voice. 'Hell's falling, Ah Yue.'

'No,' she whispered. 'No!' She yelled, 'Smash it! Don't let it near you!' The line went dead.

'Where the *fuck* is Ah Wu?' the Tiger shouted. 'Hold them off as long as you can! Simone, encase them in ice.'

'I am!' Simone shouted, then screamed so loudly that the screen above the phone flickered.

'Come on, little one,' the Tiger grunted. 'We're not letting you go now, you're not Immortal yet. You still have a lot to do.'

'Michael?'

'Hold on to me, Simone.'

'Oh, Michael,' she said. 'You came for me.'

'Not Michael, I'm Uncle Tiger,' the Tiger said with gentle affection.

'Oh. I thought you were Michael.' She coughed. 'We're leaving? We can't leave Hell, we need it.'

'How is she?' I said.

'She'll live,' the Tiger said.

'We have a camera over the … carnage,' Haruna said.

The screen flicked to a view over the central island. Four-metre-tall metal and wood elementals were striding through the demonic and Celestial soldiers on the island and indiscriminately tearing them to pieces. The Generals and Winds had retreated onto the roof of Yanluo Wang's office building, and the Horsemen and Celestial demon soldiers were defending them against a couple of wood elementals and a fire elemental that were attempting to make their way up the stairs. Simone was leaning against the Tiger; her face and arms were blackened with burns and soot and she seemed semi-conscious.

The Dragon became visible as he dropped over one of the wood elementals, picked it up in his claws and flew it over the water. Long branches whipped out of the tree-like elemental and stabbed him in the eyes, killing him. He dropped it and fell into the water.

'All evacuate at the same time!' Ma shouted from the middle of the rooftop garden. 'On my mark!'

'Wait,' someone said, more a rumble through the earth than a sound.

The people on the roof looked around, bewildered. A fire elemental, a human shape of flame, hesitated halfway up the stairs to the roof.

'Haruna?' I said.

'Do you know what that was?' Haruna said at the same time.

'What was that?' Ma said.

A swirling cloud of dust materialised above the roof. 'Everybody stay put,' it said, sounding like the wind.

'It's stones! Do as they say!' Ma shouted, and everybody on the rooftop stopped moving.

The cloud of tiny stones swirled so that parts of it became thicker and then thinned again. The cloud split into several, and parts of it blew over the fire elemental, surrounding it. The cloud shrank and changed from dust to a single huge boulder that continued to shrink. When it was the size of a basketball, it fell onto the ground.

Another cloud of stones encased a wood elemental that was making a try for the stairs and contracted that down to a similar size.

The stones encasing the fire elemental lifted from the ground and flew up to hover in front of Simone.

'Princess, we need your help,' they said.

The Tiger assisted Simone to stand upright.

'I'll do my best,' she said, then bent to cough, wincing at the pain.

'The wood we can kill without difficulty, but we need your help with the fire ones,' the stones said, sounding like hundreds of people speaking in unison. 'We will make a hole in ourselves. Can you push ice into it?'

'Yes,' Simone said, her voice a hoarse whisper. She straightened with difficulty and raised her hand towards the stone ball.

'Not water ice,' the stones said. 'Frozen oxygen.'

'That's a very bad idea,' she said. 'It'll explode.'

'We'll hold the blast. Can you do it?'

'Yes.'

'Be quick. The elemental will try to escape through the hole.'

'I'm ready.'

'On three.'

The stones counted, and Simone slapped her hand on the side of the ball. It expanded then contracted quickly. It fell open in two halves and dust came out.

'Thank you. Can you do the other one for us?' the stones said, returning to their cloud form.

Simone leaned on the Tiger again and he held her. 'Yes,' she said. 'Just bring it here and I'll do it.'

'Dragon's daughter on the comms,' Ma said. 'What's your name?'

'Haruna,' she said.

'Do you have a visual on the other demons on the causeways? Are they returning?'

'Yes. No,' Haruna said. 'I can see them and they're not returning. I've sent one of my brothers to fly over them and they're headed back to the demonic side.'

'Give me a visual,' Ma said.

The view over the phone switched to one of the causeways. The demons were running, checking behind them and obviously terrified. It appeared that whoever was controlling them had let go and they were fleeing the battle in panic.

'They won't be permitted back into the demonic side if they run,' Ma said. 'Twenty-First, follow them and mop up. Maybe recruit a few.' He dropped his voice. 'Heavens know we will need them.'

The camera zoomed in on the air above the fleeing demons. A pair of flyers with riders were hovering, their wings flapping too fast to see. The camera zoomed in closer but the resolution was too poor to show any detail of the riders.

'Who is that?' Ma said.

'Could be the Demon King, hard to tell,' the male dragon said. 'And a really small demon on the other one. They saw me — they're taking off.'

The two flyers spun in the air and headed back towards the demonic side of Hell, faster than the running demons below them.

'The day is ours,' Ma said. 'Haruna, we need transport and care for the wounded and collection for the dead. Can you arrange that?'

'I can coordinate from here,' Haruna said, her voice thick with relief and grief at the same time.

'And we need that goddamn Turtle back as soon as possible so he can reassign defensive units back here and we can build some barriers,' Ma said. 'How much longer will he be washing his hair, Emma?'

'I'm not sure,' I said. 'I'll keep you informed.'

'War room on the Mountain in two hours to debrief, I suppose,' Ma said. 'I'm sending Simone home with the Tiger, and stationing the remaining legions here to make sure the demons don't try to come back.'

'Thanks, Ma. Simone, are you okay?'

'Burnt,' the Tiger said. 'I'm taking her to the Mountain infirmary. Be there soon.'

I sat on the bench and rested my head in my hands. The turtle didn't move.

9

'Emma,' John said, waking me.

I sat up; I'd fallen asleep with my head on the cage. The tortoise was sitting inside with a wise, ancient grin on his face.

'Let me out, love,' John said.

'You're completely yourself?' I said.

He nodded. 'Open up, let me out. I must do this more often, it's a huge relief to have my feet back. You have lines on your face from the cage ...' He saw my expression. 'Something happened.'

'We nearly lost Hell.'

I opened the latches, lifted the lid, and the tortoise floated out of the cage. He changed to his human form and landed lightly on the rock in front of me.

'How nearly?'

'We won, but it was a close thing. How are you feeling? You're not dizzy or weak or anything?'

'No. Why do you ask?'

'They did something to you. You were completely out of it when they attacked Hell.'

He unfocused for a moment, remembering, then his face went rigid with shock for a second before he composed himself.

I sagged on the bench. 'They can see through my eyes. They waited until you were in the cage and then they attacked.'

'No,' John said. 'They knocked the Serpent unconscious to have me out of the way. I heard what they said: they were hoping my Turtle would be somewhere dangerous and killed and I would rejoin. They didn't know the Turtle was in the cage. They can't see through your eyes, Emma, you don't need to worry.' He crouched in front of me. 'Tell me what happened in Hell.'

I pointed at my forehead. 'Too much to tell. Just take it out directly.'

He shook his head and sat on the bench on the other side of the cage. 'No need. No rush. Just tell me.'

'The Generals are waiting for us in the war room for a debrief.' I took his hand and placed it on my forehead. 'Go ahead, you know I don't mind.'

'I mind. I hate invading your privacy like this, and twice in one day is too much.' He moved his hand so his index finger was directly over my third eye. 'Go.'

I quickly ran through everything that had happened and he absorbed the information.

He took his hand away and leaned on his knees. 'Just a minute.'

He communicated silently for a while as I put the lid back on the jade cage and returned it to its casket.

'Are you all right?' he said, studying me. 'You look ...' He searched for the word.

'Wrecked,' I said. 'I watched it all happen.' I raised one hand and dropped it, feeling helpless. 'I feel the same way that I did when the Mountain was attacked by those copies and I had to bring you back. We won, but it feels like we lost.'

'That's because we did.' He took the casket from me and helped me to rise with his other hand. 'The minute we take up arms, we lose.'

'We don't have a choice when it's demons; they can't give up. No room for compromise.' I leaned into him and we started back up the stairs. 'You need to put that casket somewhere safe before we go to the war room.'

'I'll put it in the armoury on the way.'

'Did you ask about Simone? The Tiger says she's all right.'

'He is with her. He says her lungs were burnt and all her breathing passages are damaged. Nothing terribly serious; she'll just have to rest for a few days. He's helping out with some energy healing.' He squeezed me around the shoulders as we walked. 'Are you okay to join the meeting? As you said, you look wrecked.'

I hesitated; I really was exhausted. I sighed deeply. 'I need to be there.'

'I know. Duty calls,' he said, and opened the door for us.

It was late afternoon. The sky was grey and cold, stinging rain was falling. Smally was waiting outside the Grotto, holding an umbrella and a warm padded silk jacket for me.

* * *

The five Generals from the battle were waiting for us, seated at the table already. The Phoenix was there too, talking softly and intensely to Yue Gui. They all stood and saluted John and me as we took our places at the head of the table.

'Did it work?' Ma said.

'It did,' John said.

'Good. We've just been discussing reassignments. Five more battalions were nearly destroyed today.'

'Zara, post the losses,' John said.

A list of the five battalions and their losses appeared, floating above the table.

The Tiger came in, saluted John and joined us. 'Simone will be fine.'

'Thank you.' John scanned the list of casualties. 'Field promotions are confirmed. Xiao is relieved. Twenty-Two and Thirty-One are to merge under Wang's command.'

'I'm not objecting to losing my command, but why?' Xiao said. 'My demons will be sorely upset.'

'I'm freeing you to concentrate solely on manipulating time in battle if necessary,' John said.

Xiao nodded. 'Makes sense. I'll talk to my soldiers.'

The list items shuffled to show four battalions.

'The other three to stay as they are.' John wiped one hand over his face. 'I'm ordering Zhao to find a way to recruit more demon soldiers. We're down to twenty-eight battalions and losing soldiers faster than we can replace them. Did we lose any civilians in the palace, Ah Yue?'

'Zara,' Yue Gui said, and Zara replaced the floating list with a new one showing the losses in the Northern Heavens: at least twenty names.

'That many?' I said with dismay.

'The Tiger's warriors were able to electrify their bats, which killed the insects on touch,' Yue Gui said. 'We couldn't do that. If they survived the first blow, they became angry and even more deadly.'

'Liaise with the Dragon to find a technological way around this,' John said. 'A larger version of the electrified fly swatters they use on the Earthly.'

'My Lord,' Yue Gui said.

'Did you find Leo and Ming Gui?' John said.

Yue Gui shook her head. 'I am deeply concerned. Neither of them is answering their phones or direct calls.'

John's face went grim as he concentrated, calling them. Obviously he'd spoken to one of them because he became even grimmer.

'They were at a movie and turned their damn phones off,' he said. 'Completely unacceptable. When they return to the Heavens, they are to attend me in my office.'

'My Lord,' Yue Gui said, carefully keeping her expression composed. She shot a glance at me, and from her face we were both thinking the same thing: why the hell were they ignoring direct calls if they were only at a movie?

'Zara,' John said, 'reviewing the data that Number One gave us: what is their plan if their attack on Hell should fail?'

'They didn't plan for failure,' Zara said. 'They assumed they would succeed.'

'No alternative strategy if they failed to take Hell?' John said.

'No, my Lord,' Zara said. 'Our information is already out of date.'

'What were they planning to do after they'd secured Hell?' I said.

'Take an army through the Gates to the Western Heavens and conquer that, then proceed to the South.'

'Take the South?' the Phoenix said. 'Not possible.'

'How?' John said.

'Stones,' Zara said, her voice weak with dismay. 'They have artificial stones, and they will use them to take the South.'

'Completely impossible,' the Phoenix said. 'Any artificial stone they create would melt in the heat of my nest. Our sweet lava is the essence of molten stone.'

'We don't melt, Highness,' Zara said. 'We natural stones enjoy a lava bath. These … things may have similar properties.'

The Phoenix went silent, her long face thoughtful.

'Anything else?' John said.

'It's started on the Earthly,' the Tiger said. 'I have reports coming in from the far west of my domain. Two in Europe, one in the Middle East, beyond our jurisdiction.' He rubbed both hands over his long sideburns. 'Same scenario each time: there'll be a peaceful protest about the economy or political incompetence. It'll be noisy — shouting, drums — but peaceful. The police will be relaxed, almost on side, it's a bit of a carnival. Then suddenly a large group of young men will show up out of nowhere, armed with clubs, sticks, some with machetes or even guns. They'll charge straight into the police and attack them. The protesters shout at them to stop but it's too late and the police are forced to defend themselves, and in their panic they counterattack hard. Carnage. Lives lost. The protests turn into riots and the protesters are arrested and vilified in the press for being violent anarchists.' He shrugged. 'It's a perfect environment for recruiting an army intent on toppling the cruel government.'

'Is there nothing we can do to stop this?' the Phoenix said. 'We have to help the humans.'

'I have people investigating. We'll move as soon as things are settled in our region,' the Tiger said.

'We should send some of our armies in to protect the humans in these situations,' the Phoenix said. 'My Red Warriors —'

'We can't, much as I would love to,' John said. 'We're already stretched too thin. We need to concentrate on protecting the East. The West has already fallen; we have to stop it from happening here.'

'Won't be long before it does,' the Tiger said, looking pointedly at the Phoenix. 'Some parts of the southeast are ready for political turmoil and ripe for exploitation.'

'Your domain in the West is just as bad. If the human governments did their jobs properly this would not be an issue,' the Phoenix said, tapping the table with her index finger. 'Anywhere there is corruption and deceit from the government, the populace will be ready to listen to those who would change things, uncaring as to what sort of change it is.'

'Anything more to report?' John said.

Everybody either remained silent or shook their head.

He placed his hands palms down on the table. 'Ma, with me. Let's head down to Hell and shore up the defences. Everybody else, dismissed.'

'Me?' I said as they rose and gathered their notes.

'You're not needed. Go and rest,' Ma said.

'He's right, Emma,' John said. 'Go.'

I nodded and went out. Smally was waiting for me in the courtyard. She passed me the silk jacket again, and held the umbrella over me. I shrugged the jacket on and headed towards the infirmary. Edwin was at his desk.

'How is she?' I said.

'A couple of hours' rest and she'll be fine,' Edwin said. 'She's absolutely remarkable. I never saw her father when he was whole, but I think she must have close on his healing

121

power. She can recover in a day from something that would take a normal human a week.'

'Can I sit with her?'

'Of course.' He opened the door of her room. 'She's asleep, but you can stay as long as you like.'

I turned back to tell Smally to wait for me, but she had already settled herself in one of the chairs and obviously switched off: she sat stiff, unmoving and completely blank, with my jacket in her lap.

I went into Simone's room and had a moment of panic: she wasn't in the bed. Then I heard the water running. She was in the shower. I sat beside the bed and waited for her to come out. She stepped out of the bathroom naked.

'I'm here,' I said.

'Whoops,' she said, and scooted back in again.

'I've seen it all before, I know what it looks like,' I said, smiling as I leaned one arm on the chair.

She opened the door slightly and poked her head out. 'If you tell me that you used to give me baths when I was little, I will blow you up with the biggest ball of shen ...'

'Just get dressed,' I said, waving one hand at her.

She grinned and pulled her head in. A few minutes later she came out wearing a hoodie over her underwear. She towelled her hair, which fell to her waist in a thick dark gold tangle, and dropped the towel on the bed. She took some jeans from the end of the bed and pulled them on.

'That feels better,' she said.

'How are the burns?'

She held her arms out in front of her. 'Nothing to see. All healed.'

I rose to check. 'Edwin's right. That's remarkable.'

'Uncle Bai helped. I'd still be healing if it wasn't for him.'

122

She concentrated and her eyes unfocused. 'I should go down to Hell and help Dad.'

'He doesn't need you. Go back to Todai.'

'Uh …' She turned away and dropped her head.

'What?'

She started making the bed, angrily tugging at the sheets. 'All Celestial students have been pulled off the Earthly, by Edict. We've all been drawn back to Heaven. That includes me.' She dropped the blanket and turned to me. 'I haven't even started and I can't go!'

'It's only temporary.'

She hopped up to sit on the bed. 'How long do you think this whole thing will take? Please don't say years. I don't want to wait until I'm much older than the other students. I want to go now.'

I sat next to her and took her hand. 'I don't know. A lot depends on the outcome of our next skirmish with Hell. If we win, they'll probably call it quits.'

'And if they win?'

'That isn't an option.'

'Oh well.' She shrugged. 'I suppose I should be up here anyway. I have to help fight them.'

'Only if you're sure you want to. Today was tough.'

'I'm my father's daughter,' she said with an edge of cold menace. 'Go rest. I'm heading to the training room in the Residence to work with my elementals and my new blades.' She patted my hand. 'When you're feeling better, come and spar with me. I want to see what my swords say to your sword.'

'Deal.'

* * *

At the Imperial Residence, Simone went into the training room and I collapsed on our bed. I woke an hour later and stared at the ceiling for a while, then pulled myself up.

I checked on Simone in the training room, but she wasn't there. She'd obviously given up waiting for me. I headed to my office to go over the requisitions and outfitting of the Disciples.

Leo walked in fifteen minutes later. 'John's not back yet, and they said to come see you.'

I leaned over the desk to shout at him. 'Where the hell were you?' Yi Hao squeaked at her desk so I controlled my voice. 'The Northern Heavens were attacked, we nearly lost Hell, and both of you were offline.'

'Can't a couple of guys have a minute of privacy?' he said with false bravado as he sat at the other side of the desk.

'It was more than two hours,' I said. 'You didn't even check your phone messages. What. The. Hell, Leo?'

'We were busy.'

'That's obvious,' I said, leaning back and glaring at him. 'But for two hours? Where *were* you?'

'We were in the Peak apartment, checking it over and making sure the seals were still secure.'

'You were busy in John's and my bed?' I said with horror.

'No, of course not,' he said, indignant. He grew sheepish. 'My old bed.'

'Even so,' I said, waving one hand over the desk. 'Two hours? Really?'

'We really did check the seals and the fittings. We left our phones in the bedroom and didn't hear them.'

'Why? We hardly use the Peak apartment any more. Was this nostalgia or something?'

'We want to move in there.'

That stunned me to silence.

He saw my reaction and explained. 'I'm spending most of my time with Chang and the orphanages — I might as well move full-time to the Earthly. Martin can keep an eye on the Earthly situation there as well. As soon as John returns, we'll ask his permission.'

'He won't give it,' I said. 'Martin's needed in the Northern Heavens. He's John's goddamn Number One, Leo. We need him here when we're attacked.'

'Yue Gui's just as good and she's his Number One too.'

'Don't be ridiculous! She's a genius, but a peacetime administrator. Martin's a fighter and strategist close to John in ability. We're at war, and when it comes to defending the Northern Heavens Martin is second only to John himself. This is a stupid made-up reason if ever I heard one. Why do you really want to live on the Earthly? What's happened?'

'Really, to help out down there with the orphanages. It'll just save us a lot of time moving around.'

'John won't give permission, so you may as well not ask him.'

'We'll move down there temporarily then.'

'You'll do it anyway?'

'We're needed on the Earthly. We'll free up Persimmon Tree Pavilion, and your family can use it when they're visiting.'

'Leo,' I bent to speak intensely to him over the surface of the desk, 'tell me what's really going on. You can trust me. Is one of you in trouble? Has something happened? Maybe we can help you fix it.'

'Nothing to fix. We'd just like to live down there. That's all.'

'We can't let you do this.'

He leaned back in his chair. 'Do you have any idea how much you sound like him? Doesn't it bother you?'

I slapped the desk. 'No.'

He rose. 'As soon as he's back, I'll ask him. I hope you'll help me out here, Emma. A good word from you could make all the difference.'

I glowered at him. 'You won't be getting it. Both of you are needed here.'

'A lot like him,' he said, an edge of concern in his voice.

Simone appeared in the doorway. 'Emma, there's something —' She saw Leo. 'Oh, hi, Leo. Sorry.' She turned to go out again.

'No, it's fine, I'm leaving anyway,' Leo said. He gestured towards me. 'Come in and ask Emma whatever it was.'

'You are in so much trouble, Leo. Daddy's going to cut your head off,' she said, coming in.

He grinned. 'Wouldn't be the first time.' He waved to me. 'A good word, Emma, that's all I ask.' He went out.

'A good word for what?' Simone said.

'He wants to go down to the Earthly and live on the Peak with Martin,' I said.

'What on earth for?'

'He's given me a list of stupid reasons that make no sense. If you could find out what's really going on, I'd appreciate it.'

'I'll talk to them,' she said. She leaned her hip on the desk, crossed her arms and tilted her head. 'Um.'

'What?'

'Uh …' She furrowed her brow. 'Today, in Hell … um.' She straightened and flipped her hair over her shoulder. 'Actually, never mind. I'll go talk to Leo and find out what's happening. It's nothing.'

She shrugged and went out without another word.

'It's not nothing!' I shouted after her. 'Come back and tell me what the problem is.'

'It's really nothing,' she said from outside my office. 'Just a stupid small silly thing. You have more important stuff to worry about.'

My outer office door closed.

'Secrets, secrets everywhere,' the stone said.

'Was Leo lying about wanting to live on the Earthly?' I said.

'No,' the stone said. 'But you were right: he was lying about his reasons for doing it.'

'Why won't he trust me? He's always trusted me.'

'This must be extremely big.'

'I hope Simone can find out for us.'

'You should ask him to find out what's going on with her as well,' the stone said.

'Good idea. Is the Dark Lord back?'

'No, he's still in Hell organising the defensive legions. I think he'll be a while.'

'Thanks,' I said, and returned to the spreadsheets.

* * *

John came into my office a couple of hours later. He sat on the other side of my desk looking old and haggard, but at least his feet were whole.

'All that good work to make you rest in the cage is gone already,' I said.

He rubbed one hand over his face. 'We're outnumbered and outgunned. They'll try for Hell again and we're thinning our defences elsewhere protecting it. If they attempt the Celestial at the same time they try for Hell, we will be sorely tested.'

'We can do this,' I said fiercely. 'We have to.'

'We will.' He leaned back and composed himself, turning back from mid-sixties to his usual late-forties self with visible effort. 'Did Leo and Ming come in here after I spoke to them?'

'No. I'd already shouted at Leo before he spoke to you. Do either of them have some trouble on the Celestial Plane that they're trying to avoid?'

'I have Zara checking.'

'Ming can't live on the Earthly, John. He's your Number One and we need him in the Northern Heavens.'

'That's exactly what I said. He insisted. He said that Yue can handle it since I made her Number One as well.'

'That's a stupid reason, but from what Leo said we don't have much choice.'

'I know. If I deny them permission, they'll move down there anyway and say it's only temporary. I might as well allow them. It'll free up Persimmon Tree Pavilion and we can give it to your family when they come visit.'

'What about BJ? She lives in Persimmon Tree too.'

'We will need to speak to her as well.'

'I'd still like to know their real reason for moving down there. Do you want me to talk to Leo? Maybe I can get more out of him if I speak to him as a friend instead of as Lord.'

'Stop it.'

'Stop what?' I realised what he meant. 'We're just in tune. That's all. It's nothing.'

'You just said *exactly* what I was thinking. Even to being his Lord.'

I waved it away. 'Form of words. Don't worry about it.'

He concentrated, checking that his Serpent was still imprisoned, and his edges grew fuzzy. I could see the chair through him; he was going transparent.

I shot to my feet. 'Stay with us, John. Stay here!' I ran around the desk and crouched to put my arms around him to hold him with me. 'Don't leave me. Don't leave us. We need you!'

He took a deep breath in my embrace, grabbed me and buried his face in my shoulder. 'Sorry. Sorry. I had to check. You sounded so much like me ...'

'Next time, don't check. Don't touch it. Don't look for it. We will find it and we will release it and you will be whole, but not just yet.'

'Hurts,' he said into my shoulder, so softly I could barely hear it.

'I know,' I said, my voice hoarse. 'I can see.'

He patted my back to show he was okay. I pulled away, then moved back in and kissed him hard. He put his hand around the back of my head and returned the kiss just as hard until I released him and wiped my eyes.

'That was so close. And all you did was check on it.'

'I'm in so much pain,' he said. 'All it wants to do is die and it's denied that release. I should sleep in the jade cage. I hear its cries in my dreams and I may go to it.'

I leaned on the desk behind me and dropped my head with misery. Now that he'd returned, sleeping beside him was one of life's greatest pleasures. Sleeping alone again would be very hard.

'Do you want me to arrange a roster of senior people to mind you at night while you sleep in the cage?' I said.

'Not yet.'

'Don't risk it, okay?'

His eyes were dark with sorrow. 'I know.'

10

I jerked upright, banging my head on the ceiling. I was in the cage again. I looked around; nobody was nearby. I felt the needle in my back and tried to reach around to remove it, but it was too close to the back of my head. I dropped my head and flicked my tongue, tasting the decay of Hell and the traces of demons that had come and gone. None had been near in a very long time. The IV bag on the outside of the cage was empty. I tried moving as far from the stand as possible, hoping to pull out the needle, but the intravenous line was long enough to reach from one end of the cage to the other.

I gave up and flopped on the floor. I was roasting hot and it wasn't pleasant heat. My scales felt raw and painful, and I was dizzy with thirst. My tail throbbed with pain in time with my heartbeat, making me wish for the release of unconsciousness again. I didn't have enough energy left to control the suffering, and the IV had cured the infection so that it wasn't killing me any more.

I had to find a way to die. Everything I'd tried had failed. Banging my head repeatedly on the inside of the cage was ineffectual. I was immune to my own venom. As long as I stayed in the cage, there was a chance that the Turtle would merge with me and be trapped as well, which would be a disaster for everybody. I rested my head on the floor of the cage, dreaming of being whole again, and showing Emma what I was really capable of.

I shot upright with a huge gasp and cast around, confused. I was in our bed in the Residence and John was lying next to me, watching me. I'd woken him.

'Bad dream?' he said.

I dropped back to cuddle into him. 'Yes.'

He nuzzled my hair. 'Do you want to talk about it?'

'No. It's just the stress from all we're doing. I worry about our family.'

He kissed the top of my head and pulled me closer. 'I do too.'

I closed my eyes, hoping that I wouldn't see the interior of the cage again, and again vowed not to worry him about it. He was stressed enough already.

The dream wasn't real anyway; the Serpent didn't have any IVs stuck in it. It was just my imagination.

* * *

To: David Hawkes
From: Emma Donahoe
Hi David,
I know this is a strange request but I need your help.
I need 2000 kg of either iron or mild steel in a form
that can be forged (like ingots or pellets), delivered to a

warehouse (White Tiger Godown) in Belcher's Street in
Western District. As you deal with car manufacturers,
is there any way we could swing a small amount like
this? I'll pay exceptionally well for it.
Regards,
Emma

Smally stood in the doorway of my office, hesitant.

'It's fine, come in,' I said, still looking at the screen.

She sidled in, holding a large Ninja Turtle figurine in front of her.

I leapt to my feet. 'Oh my *god*, you found it! Where was it?'

She was frozen for a moment, then said, 'It was on the top shelf of your closet here on the Mountain, right at the very back.'

'You are totally wonderful,' I said, and she lit up. I went around the desk and gestured for her to follow me. 'Come with me, this will be priceless.'

I stopped in front of Yi Hao. 'Tell Zara to be ready to take a photo of the Dark Lord's face when we show him this?'

Yi Hao unfocused and came back. 'Done, ma'am. What is it?' Smally raised the Ninja Turtle so she could see it and her eyes widened. 'The little demon found it!' Her expression grew sly. 'Are you taking it to him now? Can I see his face as well?'

I nodded.

Yi Hao dropped her pen and came around her desk. She patted Smally on the back. 'You have done us all a great favour, Smally. This will be very good.'

We went across the courtyard and into John's anteroom. His office door was closed; he had his music on and the heavy bass thrummed through the floor. Zara was waiting for us, and pulled her earphones out of her ears when we entered.

She saw the figure. 'That's it?'

'I don't understand all the fuss,' Smally said, bewildered.

I tapped on John's office door. Nothing happened; he hadn't heard me. I looked at Zara. She concentrated, and the music stopped. I opened the door and ushered everybody in.

John stared at us. 'This looks serious.'

'Oh, it is,' I said. I gestured to Smally, who was cowering behind Zara. 'Put it on his desk.'

She crept around Zara, inched to the desk and placed the Ninja Turtle in front of him.

He leapt to his feet with joy. 'Yes! You found it! Where was it?' He looked around at us. 'I have been looking for this *everywhere*! Who found it? I want to thank them.'

I indicated Smally, who was again trying to hide behind an uncooperative Zara. 'It was right at the back of my closet and she found it when she was cleaning it out.'

He pointed at her and she cringed. 'Bringing you in to be Emma's personal maid is the best decision I have made in my entire life,' he said sternly. 'I hereby promote you to Chief Turtle Finder. Your uniform is to have green and blue cuffs added to honour you.'

Smally stood straighter. 'Really?'

I patted her back. 'The least you deserve.'

'Considering what you have to put up with,' Zara said with good humour. 'Her closet is worse than his desk.'

I opened my mouth to protest, but John and Yi Hao were both nodding agreement.

John grabbed a pile of papers and dropped them on the floor behind him. Zara made a small sound of pain and he ignored her. He shuffled the rest of the papers on his desk to make some space, picked up the Ninja Turtle and placed it carefully next to the monitor.

'Now,' he said with satisfaction, 'I have officially returned.' He sat at the desk and pulled his chair in. 'Me and Leonardo here have things to do. You lot disappear.'

He turned the music back on and the thump of the intensely loud German industrial metal made the Ninja Turtle quiver on his desk. Smally cowered and put her hands over her ears. I put my arms around Yi Hao's and Smally's waists and guided them out, and Zara closed the door behind us. I couldn't wait until Simone discovered that the turtle had been found.

There was a message on my voicemail when I returned to my desk: David. I called him back.

'David, it's Emma.'

'Emma. What. The. Hell? Two thousand kilos of steel? Why?'

'You don't want to know. Believe me.'

'Police Superintendent Cheung wants to talk to you. Says it's urgent.'

'It's always urgent.'

'This is more urgent than usual. He's called me twice already today asking to be put in touch with you. He says the Brigadier has disappeared and there's nobody he can contact. Please talk to him, Emma. I can't get anything done while he's harassing me like this and it sounds important.'

'Okay.'

'Promise?'

'Yeah, I will. So … iron, steel. Can you do it?'

He sighed with exasperation. 'Of course I can't. Melt down a car.'

'Too much aluminium.'

'Really?'

'And plastic. Our forge can't handle the impurities. We're stuck in the Tang Dynasty.'

'Your forge? Wait — you're making two thousand kilos of *weapons*?'

'Like I said, you don't want to know.'

'Tell me.'

I thought about it for a moment. 'No.'

'Then you'll have to look elsewhere for your steel, and you promised to talk to Cheung. I'll hold you to that: I know how you people are about keeping your word. Bye, Emma.'

You people? I brushed it aside. As his voice faded, I said, 'If I told you why I needed it would you be able to swing it for me?'

His voice returned. 'Maybe.'

'You won't thank me, David.'

'I need to know everything if I'm to make valid decisions. Don't withhold information from me.'

'This is more than just information. Trust me, you really do not want to know. It will change everything you see in the world around you and make your life ten times more stressful.'

'It can't be that bad! Tell me.'

I took a deep breath, heavy with dread. 'The Celestial and the forces of Hell are at war.'

'What? But ...' He was silent for a long moment. 'Okay, I believe you. Why hasn't it affected us? It's still business as usual on the Earthly.'

'You said Cheung wanted to speak to me urgently?'

He hesitated, then, 'I see.'

'We won the first battle. We lost a few legions, but we won. This isn't settled, though, and we need to prepare for the next conflict.'

'Can I protect my family from this?'

'Things are about to become very bad around here. Move them to anywhere but Europe or Asia. America or Australia would be a good idea. The gods in Europe are all gone, and Africa's too close to Europe. I recommend Australia; there's a powerful spirit there who's on our side. The spirits of the other regions have gone completely silent. We think the ones in Africa and America are waiting to see how this turns out.'

'The European Shen are gone? Our whole extended family's back in the UK!'

'Move everybody you can to Australia.'

'What about here in Hong Kong?'

I dropped my forehead into one hand, still holding the phone with the other. 'I'm not surprised Cheung wants to speak to me. Our part of the world is about to have some very nasty things happen. It won't be anything obviously supernatural, but it will happen.'

'What sort of "not obviously supernatural"?'

'Riots. Insurrection. Coups d'état. Crime. Kidnappings. Violence.'

'Emma, that sounds like business as usual in much of Asia.'

'Yes. It's been brewing for a while.'

'And it'll get worse?'

'Count on it.'

'How much steel did you need again? Wait, I can see your email. Two thousand kilos. That's an awfully small lot; it's a tiny fraction of a forty-tonne cradle. Let me see what

I can do.' I heard him typing. 'I can't get you guns, so don't even ask.'

'Guns don't work on them.'

'Well, that's just completely wonderful. I'm glad they don't have any to use on you.'

'They do. They threw a *tank* at us during the last skirmish.'

'Holy shit. This is getting better and better. Australia, you say?' He typed again. 'Emma, what if ... what if you lose? What if the demons take over?'

'There was a time at the dawn of recorded history when any attempt by mankind to build a civilisation was promptly and ruthlessly crushed by an invading barbarian horde. Humans were kept weak and their technological advances were destroyed. It made them ideal fodder for enslavement and exploitation in a feudal system where demon lords ruled them with absolute control.' I wiped my hand over my forehead and turned away from the monitor to study the scroll with the character *si* — thought and remembrance — behind my desk. 'We would prefer not to see that situation arise again.'

I realised I had said 'we' and 'them'. Okay, maybe he had a point with the 'you people' comment.

He was still typing. 'This is strange. Why has the price of raw iron skyrocketed in the last six months? That's completely against the trend for a primary resource.' He inhaled sharply as he understood. 'Oh shit. They're ahead of you and buying it up. Damn, how many of them are there?'

I hesitated, then said, 'Move your family to Australia.'

'Sounds like a good idea. I'll get back to you on the steel, but understand,' he brushed his hand over the telephone receiver, probably wiping his eyes, 'I may not be able to swing such a small amount of raw materials. It's completely outside our usual realm of operations. I might have to ask my business contacts.'

'I appreciate your help.'

'I really wish you hadn't told me this,' he said, his voice weak. 'You were right.'

'I know. Keep safe.'

'Call Cheung, okay? Even if you can't help him, you can reassure him.'

'I will. Bye, David.'

He hung up without another word. I really hadn't done him a favour.

'Cheung.'

'Superintendent.' I deliberately made my voice upbeat. 'I hope all's well with you.'

'Miss Donahoe.' He sounded desperate. 'You have to stop doing this to me. It's making me look extremely bad.'

'Doing what?'

'You know what. I'm in serious trouble, you have to stop.'

'Whatever this is, it isn't me,' I said. 'We're in the middle of a big offshore operation, really top-level stuff, and we don't have the time or resources to mess with you. What's happening?'

'It's not you?' he said, sounding genuinely shocked.

'Tell me what's happening, Wyland.'

'All my triad arrests disappear from the cell block. Nobody knows how it's happening. The ICAC is investigating me for corruption. You have to talk to them! They think I'm releasing Little Brothers because I'm being paid off.'

'Oh,' I said, my voice small. Cheung thought I was Chinese Secret Service, and I had to give him a reason for the disappearance of the demon gangsters that was within the realms of possibility. 'I have no idea what's going on. Let me investigate and get back to you.'

'If it's not you, then who is it?'

'Demons, has to be,' I said with forced cheerfulness. 'Appear in the cell block, steal the prisoner, disappear again.'

'I'm more than half-way inclined to believe you,' he said, playing along with the joke. 'These cells are secure and they seem to be walking out through the walls.'

'Let me talk to some Shen I know and we'll see what we can do about destroying the demons,' I said.

'I knew I could count on you to provide the ideal solution. Get Guan Gong, we have an altar to him in the office, and he'd be perfect,' he said with grim humour. 'Please call me when you know something. At least give me your direct number so I don't have to bother the Gweilo.'

'I'm a Gweilo,' I said.

'The other one.'

'Racist. I'll have my secretary text you her number but I'm not in the office much at the moment with the operation we're doing so you may not be able to contact me anyway.'

'Is it something to do with the Diaoyu Islands?'

'No.'

'Oh no, it's not North Korea, is it?' he said with dismay.

'No. The entire region. Something seriously big is going down, and I think your little disappearing gangsters are a symptom of the problem. Leave it with us, Cheung, the Brigadier knows what he's doing.'

'Can you get the ICAC off my back?'

'Like I said, I'll see what I can do. What I need,' I tapped on my computer keyboard to sound official, 'is the names of the relevant ICAC officers who are chasing you about this, and the location the prisoners are disappearing from.'

I gave him my generic non-Wudang email address, inwardly cringing. Nobody had time to help him with his problem. Then I had an inspiration: Simone had nothing better to do since being called back from university, and this small task would be perfect for her.

'I will email them to you.' He sounded relieved. 'Thanks, Emma. Keep in touch, okay?'

'I will.'

Five minutes later, just as Simone and Martin came into my office, the phone rang again. It was David. Simone and Martin stopped at the door and I waved them in while I answered.

'David. That was quick.'

'You know how I said that was less than a cradle?' he said.

'Yes?'

'Would twenty-two hundred kilos do?'

'That's slightly more than I need ... would it be easier?'

'Yes, because that's how much an empty shipping container weighs.'

'They're solid steel?'

'Yes.'

'Oh my *god*, you are a lifesaver. This is brilliant. Thank you. How much do I owe you?'

'Nothing. It's just sitting in the yard. It's past its use-by date so it's being used for on-site storage. How will you transport it up there?'

'I have a dragon who's big enough to carry it.'

'Are you serious?'

'Yep. Give me the details and I'll send her over to pick it up.'

'Damn, I cannot wait to see that.'

'Isn't there some way I could pay you?'

'Would my family be safer up there with you? In your Mountain fortress place?'

'Yes, they would. But I can't give them a big house of their own. They may have to share with someone.'

'That's the payment.'

'Okay. I'll have Simone manage the move up...' I raised my eyebrows at her and she stared at me, shocked. 'I'm flat out doing other things. She'll be in touch shortly. It might be best to hold off moving them until we know we're going into battle.'

'Can she manage it?' he said, sounding unsure.

'Absolutely. She's extremely capable and has had extensive managerial training in her role as Celestial Princess. Leave it with us; she'll call you soon.'

He sounded relieved. 'I really appreciate this.'

'I appreciate it too. That steel will be a lifesaver.'

I put the phone down and turned to face Martin and Simone.

'You're giving me jobs to do?' Simone said, stunned.

'I need your help.' I turned to Martin. 'Is this private?'

'Not so private Simone can't hear.'

'Okay. Simone, if you can help out, I really do need you. Not just arranging the evacuation of David's family, but to take over my job liaising with the Hong Kong police. Cheung's in serious trouble; his arrested gangsters are disappearing from the lockup.'

Simone's eyes went wide. 'You want me to do your spy act thing?'

'Only until this business in Hell is sorted. Just keep him off my back until this is over.'

'I can't get away with it, I'm too young!'

'Make yourself older.'

She paused for a moment, then said, 'Okay. Give me the info and I'll take it over from you. Is there anything else you need me to manage?'

'At the moment, no, but I appreciate your help. Go ask Yi Hao for the details, and call David.'

She smiled slightly. 'Okay, I'll call him.'

She rose and I stopped her. 'Wait, you didn't tell me what you wanted.'

'It's nothing. Talk to Ge Ge. I'll go ring David.' She went out.

'What's the big disaster this time?' I asked Martin.

He shook his hands in front of his face. 'Both the Lion and I sincerely apologise for our recent negligent behaviour. We would like to show you the reason for our distraction.'

'It had better be a good one. I hope it isn't what I think it is.'

'What do you think it is? Never mind, it's the very best. We need you to come down to Dragon Village in Sha Tin and see for yourself.'

'Just tell me.'

'I cannot. We promised each other we wouldn't divulge the information to anyone. I have to show you.'

I sighed and pushed my chair back. 'I'm supposed to minimise my travelling. I'll never be a hundred per cent if I don't stop plane-shifting like this.'

He smiled slightly. 'We'd show my father but we're ... not really sure how he'll react.'

'If it's what I think it is, my reaction may be similar.'

11

'Is this security new? It doesn't look it,' I said as Leo drove us through the main gate of Dragon Village and past the gatehouse staffed with two uniformed security guards.

The small estate high on the hill above Sha Tin was a circle of brown houses jammed next to each other around a central open area. It had a spiked perimeter fence four metres high, topped with razor wire and motion detectors.

'This is standard for this part of the New Territories,' Martin said in the back seat next to me. 'It's identical to every other estate on top of the hill here.'

'Shame you can't see Sha Tin from here,' I said, studying the tree-covered hillsides around us. 'The view from the top must be really good.'

'The dragons used to go up to the top to launch themselves to fly, but strategically it's too exposed up there,' Leo said. He made a soft sound of amusement. 'Gross, too. All the taxi and minibus drivers stop at the lookout and toss their urine bottles out. The ground is covered with them.'

'Lovely,' I said. 'Is that an English school on the other side of the road outside the estate?'

'Yeah, the dragon kids go there; they all speak excellent English,' Leo said. 'One of the reasons why kids from Dragon Village are so damn up themselves.'

'Apart from being dragons,' Martin said.

Leo wound around the narrow four-storey brown-tiled houses and down a ramp into an underground car park that was deserted except for one other car.

'I've never been to Dragon Village before,' I said. 'Very classy. How are they finding it up at the Celestial Palace? There isn't nearly as much room there.'

'They didn't want to go,' Martin said. 'The Jade Emperor had the Dragon King himself send one of his emissaries to move them along. They argued for a long time.'

'I'm not surprised.'

Leo parked the car and we went up the stairs to the central plaza of the estate. A communal clubhouse and pool sat in the centre with a small dragon fountain. The tall narrow houses had only one room on each floor, covering the full three-metre width; and a couple of three-storey apartment blocks stood at the end. The silence was eerie. All of the houses were obviously empty, even though furniture was visible through some of the windows. The entire estate seemed deserted.

'They'll be up in the playground,' Martin said, and patted Leo on the shoulder as he walked around him towards the far end of the estate.

'The orphans live in the apartment block,' Leo said. 'Chang took the whole building, since the dragons lived in the larger houses. He considered moving them to the houses after the evacuation, but they seemed happy in the apartment dorms so he left them there. Some of the other orphanages were moved around after the villages were evacuated.'

We rounded the corner to where the gardens stood at the back of the estate and the playing children came into view.

A little girl of about four years ran to throw herself into Leo's arms. He hoisted her up and she kissed him on the cheek, then leaned away from him and reached to be held by Martin. Her intelligent dark brown eyes sparkled under her close-cropped dark frizz; she was obviously half-black and half-Chinese.

She hugged Martin around the neck. 'I missed you, Ba Ba! Where have you been?'

I sighed with dismay. 'Oh no. No way. Do not do this to us. We need you up there.'

Leo came to stand next to Martin and put his hand on Martin's shoulder. 'Too late. The adoption papers have nearly gone through.'

Chang came and saluted us all. 'Ma'am. My Lords. It's gone through. She's all yours, Master Leo.'

'Yay!' the little girl yelled, then burst into tears and hugged Martin fiercely around his neck. He spoke softly in her ear, reassuring her, and she nodded into his shoulder.

Leo spoke silently to me. *Her mother gave a false ID and walked out of the hospital without her when she was less than twenty-four hours old. We think her father was African but we really have no idea. She was bullied by the other kids at the old place she was at; they were only too happy to let us take her.*

Martin handed the child to Leo, and he held her tight and changed to speaking out loud. 'She already has Hong

Kong residency, and if she wants, she can have American citizenship from me. She can choose to live anywhere she pleases when she grows up.' He spoke into her hair. 'I'm your real Daddy now, it's all legal and everything. They can never take you away from us.'

'I want Ba Ba to be my real Daddy too,' she said into his chest.

'The names on the papers don't matter, Butterfly. He's as much your real Daddy as I am, and we'll always be here for you.' Leo shrugged as he spoke to me. 'The legals won't be important when we move up in ten years or so. It's a small price to pay to have ...' He tickled her, making her wriggle and giggle. 'This little bundle of terror all our own.'

'All ours,' Martin said with wonder, and Butterfly turned in Leo's arms and reached for Martin to take her again.

'She'll be his first daughter,' Leo said with a sad smile. 'Four thousand years and he's never fathered a child.'

'I thought I'd never have a child of my own,' Martin said. He spoke to Butterfly. 'We will have a home, and you will have your own bedroom, and we will be a family.'

She sniffled and ran the back of her hand across her nose, then threw her arms around Martin's neck again. 'I love you, Ba Ba.'

He closed his eyes and his face went fierce as he rested his cheek on the top of her head. 'I love you too, my Butterfly,' he said, his voice hoarse.

'So can we have the Peak apartment?' Leo said.

'John will be furious,' I said.

'Like I said, a good word from you would make all the difference,' Leo said.

'How long have you two been planning this?'

'It wasn't planned,' Martin said, holding Butterfly close. 'About three months ago, Leo helped Chang set up the orphanage here in Dragon Village. There was some extra space, so he scouted to see if we could take some children that needed a good home from other places.'

'And from there it just happened,' Leo said.

'It's more like she adopted us, actually,' Martin said. 'When she saw Leo for the first time she was hysterical. She'd never seen a black man before; she'd always thought she was some sort of deformed freak. When Leo explained that being black is perfectly ordinary and normal, she cried for a long time.'

'I'm normal!' Butterfly said with triumph, her head on Martin's chest.

'No, you're special,' I said. 'And smart and lovely and very lucky to have these two great men for your fathers.'

'I know,' Butterfly said, turning her head on Martin's chest to see Leo. 'So lucky.'

'Does she know?' I said.

'Of course she does,' Martin said.

'Do I know what?' Butterfly asked me without moving her head from Martin's chest.

'That Daddy and Ba Ba love each other and want to get married together.'

'Oh, I know *that*,' she said dismissively, waving one tiny hand through the air. She dropped her voice. 'They are so cute and mushy sometimes.'

'Does she know the full situation?'

'Yep!' Butterfly said.

'As much as we can explain to one so small,' Martin said. 'The real me may be an issue. But we'll deal with that later.'

147

'I don't think it'll be an issue. She's seen the real me and thinks I'm awesome,' Leo said with pride. He turned back to me. 'So … apartment? If you say no, we'll just buy or rent something. But the Peak apartment has the best seals anywhere and nobody's living there right now. Can you ask him?'

'I don't need to, I'm in charge of that.' I sighed with resignation. 'I suppose you might as well start moving in. But please try to spend as much time as you can helping out with the …' I skipped the word, 'effort. Martin, you particularly are needed in the Northern Heavens and they will make another try for … the place below.'

'We know this is very bad timing,' Martin said. 'And if we could take her up with us, we would. We also need to work out a strategy for defending the orphanages. Every single child is in the same situation as Butterfly — without their mother, they cannot travel to a safer place — so we must defend them here.'

'I'd appreciate Lord Leo's help,' Chang said as he passed us with a ball he'd retrieved from the roof of the apartment building. 'I can't be everywhere at once, and you know we're a target.'

'I'll be spending most of my time arranging the defence of the orphanages now recruitment's been halted,' Leo said. 'I might as well be living down here. It's easier to travel around the Earthly when I'm already on it.'

Chang went to join the children in an impromptu game of soccer.

A skinny fourteen-year-old boy raced up to us. 'Mr Alexander, the truck is here with the TV people.'

'What?' Leo checked his watch. 'They're early? Unheard of.'

'TV people?' I said with horror.

'Martin, explain. I'll show them where to park,' Leo said, and walked off with the boy.

'We've been liaising with UNICEF about caring for kids all over Asia.' Martin shrugged. 'Chang's foundation has become somewhat famous, and the UN wants to do a documentary on us as a fundraising vehicle.'

I dropped my head and ran my hands through my hair. 'Dear Lord, what a bad idea.' I looked up at him. 'Our entire operation and every location will be identified. The foundation will become a huge target. Why on earth did you agree to this?'

'We've taken precautions, don't worry. We won't identify specific locations, only the country; and adults won't be shown in enough detail to be identified.' He turned to watch the children playing. 'Only the happy kids will be shown, and our efforts to find them good homes if we can and remedial help if they need it. Besides, demons can't harm humans: it's in the agreement that my father made with them all that time ago. Not a single human has been harmed on the Earthly since Father returned.'

'If you were where you should have been during the most recent debriefing, you'd know that the demons have been harming humans all over the West,' I said grimly.

'No,' he said, pulling Butterfly closer.

'What, Ba Ba?' Butterfly said.

'We need to move you to the Peak as quickly as we can,' he said. He turned back to me. 'Do you have Monica's phone number? Leo was wondering if she'd be willing to return and help us.'

'Monica's nearly sixty years old,' I said. 'And ... um ...' I tried to word it so that it wouldn't scare Butterfly. 'Carcinoma.'

149

'Oh, that's terrible. Does Leo know?'

'No.'

'She should move up to the Heavenly Plane. The disease won't spread there.'

'She's too ill to travel. She let it go too far before seeing a doctor.'

'What did Simone say when she found out?'

I hesitated. 'I've known about it for a while, but you're the first one I've told. And I request that you respect Monica's wishes and don't tell anyone else. She doesn't want to be remembered as she is now, but as she was. She's not alone, she's surrounded by loving family, and it's her choice.'

'Simone will be heartbroken.'

'Simone's heart has been broken so many times that there aren't many pieces left to break. All of us have left her at one point or another, Martin.'

'I will never leave you,' he said to Butterfly, and kissed the top of her head. 'I have something to show you,' he said to me. 'Will you come with me upstairs? I think you will like it.'

'If it's a particular baby in the orphanage then don't bother.'

His eyes widened. 'How did you know?'

I dropped my head and kicked at the ground. 'The Jade Emperor has strictly forbidden us from adopting a child.'

'He knew?'

I looked up at him and tried to keep my voice even. 'It seems so, and he's right. We're at war, Martin. We don't need this sort of distraction.'

'A child would bring you both so much joy, and there's this little half-European girl who could be a little sister for Simone ...'

I turned away and gazed up at the apartment building, not really seeing it. 'Stop there. I don't want to know. Look after them and guard them but don't let me see them.'

'I'm sorry,' he said softly behind me.

'Just keep them safe,' I said. 'I'll take a taxi back to the gateway. You take Butterfly upstairs and pack for her. I'm sure you're eager to set up house and be a family.'

'One of the staff can drive you down.' He stopped and concentrated. 'One of the dragons stayed on to help — he's bringing the spare car around. Meet him at the car park exit.' He spoke to Butterfly, still in his arms. 'We can move you to our new home now, then we need to go shopping for furniture for you.'

'Furniture?' she said, wide-eyed and breathless. 'Can I choose?'

'Of course you can. There's the car,' Martin said. He put his free arm around my shoulders and pulled me in to kiss the top of my head. 'Thanks, Mom.'

I squeezed him around the waist and let go. 'You're as bad as Leo.' I waved to them both as I headed down to the car. 'And I can't be your Mom, John is,' I called back as I opened the car door.

Shh, nobody's supposed to know!

* * *

I climbed into the car's front passenger seat.

'Where to, ma'am?' asked the slim young driver.

I turned and stared at him; I knew that voice. He saw me looking and grinned.

'Lok?'

His smile widened.

151

'Oh my *god*, Lok — where have you been? How come you're human? What happened to you? We searched everywhere!'

He put the car in gear and eased us down the narrow lane between the houses and the high brick perimeter wall. 'I'll tell you everything, but you have to let me know where I'm dropping you.'

'Celestial gateway in Wan Chai. Now where the hell have you been?' I gasped. 'Not Hell?'

'No, not Hell.' He sighed and patted the steering wheel as we waited for the guards to open the electric gate for us. 'I miss everybody at the Academy. I must come up and say hello.'

'Lucy Chen would love to have you back. She's run off her feet trying to manage the armoury, and I'm having a good few hundred new weapons made. So what happened to you? You broke the curse?'

'The bitch that cursed me died. I was suddenly a dragon again and I was free.' He winced. 'I took off — I'm sorry, ma'am, but I was free and I could fly and swim and ...' He smiled slightly. 'Well. I'd been a dog for a long time and it was a truly wonderful feeling.'

We headed down the steep road that led from the hilltop estates to the industrial area of Fo Tan, which was packed with multistorey factory buildings. Sha Tin Racecourse complex, more than a kilometre from one end to the other, spread out next to the artificially constrained concrete banks of the Shing Mun River. It was a long time since I'd lived in Sha Tin New Town, in a tiny flat with Louise, and I felt a pang of grief at her loss. Then I pushed it aside. I missed her terribly, but there were many people relying on me and I had to stay strong and focused.

At the bottom of the hill, Lok merged into a multi-lane road that would join the expressway to take us into the

Tate's Cairn Tunnel, which cut through the steep mountains surrounding Kowloon on the other side.

'Why didn't you come back to us?' I asked him.

'I heard that the Dark Lord had returned, and I knew I'd be in serious trouble for deserting my post.'

'Don't worry, I'll handle him,' I said. 'We could use your skills, either in the barracks or the armoury. Particularly in the barracks now that Leo's moving down here.'

'That's why I've been hiding here, waiting for you to come down so I could talk to you,' Lok said. 'I never worked for the Dark Lord, only for you, and I don't know how much trouble I'll be in now he's back. I hear he's executed deserters in the past. I hope you can put in a good word for me.'

'No need. The Dark Lord has much more important things to worry about than a single rogue dragon,' I said. 'And any help is most welcome, Lok. You know the students and the armoury, and your skills have been sorely missed.'

After five kilometres inside the tunnel, we shot out the other side into the grey congested high rises of Kowloon. The eastern part of Hong Kong Island was visible through a haze of pollution across the harbour, but before we could go back to the Central area we had to head even further east to take the Eastern Harbour Crossing. The high rises towered around us as Lok smoothly slid the car onto the raised expressway that carried cars straight from one tunnel to the next over the streets of East Kowloon. The distance was much further than going directly through the Cross-Harbour Tunnel straight into Wan Chai, but the lack of traffic on this less direct route made it a faster option most of the time. The narrower roads at ground level below us were choked with traffic and busy with pedestrians.

'Can you do me a favour, ma'am?'

'I'll call him now and make sure you're not in trouble.'

'Thank you.'

I pulled out my phone.

'Wei?' John said.

'John. I was right.'

'Damn,' he said, his voice soft. 'Boy or girl?'

'A very sweet half-black girl. She's delightful.'

'Give them the Peak,' he said with resignation.

'I already did. Do you remember Lok, the dog who used to look after the armoury and the Folly?'

'Dog?' He was silent for a moment. 'Oh yes. You told me about him. You said he disappeared?'

'I found him. The curse was broken, he's a dragon again, and he'd like to come back.'

'Sure.'

'He deserted his post.'

John's voice was full of amusement. 'He's a reptile, Emma.'

'We have to stop giving reptiles special treatment. We'll be accused of favouritism.'

'You have a point,' both Lok and John said at the same time.

We shot into the Eastern Harbour Tunnel and travelled a kilometre under the water, exiting at the far eastern end of Hong Kong Island.

'Punish him with something minor and bring him back,' John said. 'Lucy would love the relief. Can you handle the rest? I'm flat out with the disposition of the army.'

'Sure. I found the steel, by the way. I need a big dragon to go down to the Earthly and collect it.'

'There's your punishment.'

I turned to Lok. 'Can you fly carrying twenty-two hundred kilos of steel? A shipping container?'

Lok guided us onto another raised expressway that would take us back towards the centre of Hong Kong Island. Dusk was falling and the buildings on the other side of the harbour in Kowloon lit up in a splendid array of colours, although blurred by the smog.

'Not in one go,' he said, 'but I can take it apart with my claws and bring it up in pieces.'

I put the phone back to my ear. 'Thanks, John. See you at dinner?'

'Before then, I hope,' he said, his voice soft with desire.

His tone resonated within me and I dropped my voice as well. 'Me too.'

'Celestial Highness?' someone said in his background. 'This is quite urgent.'

'Dammit. Sorry, Emma, bye,' he said, and hung up.

12

'Emma,' the stone said.

I stopped working on the spreadsheets and raised my head. 'What?'

'Silica requests that she and Ronnie be permitted to come to your office and try to set seals again.'

'Without John?'

'The Dark Lord doesn't have time. Ronnie has advanced to the stage where he knows what to do; he just needs to manipulate his energy successfully. Silica would like to bring him to your office for an attempt.'

'Tell them sure.'

'Thank you.'

Five minutes later Ronnie's and Silica's voices echoed outside my office. I went out to see how they were going.

Yi Hao glared at my stone. 'You tell me when you arrange things with the Dark Lady!'

'Sorry, Yi Hao,' the stone said.

'Not good enough,' she grumbled, sitting behind her desk. 'Next time tell me.'

'I'll make sure it tells you,' I said.

Ronnie seemed much more confident and in control as he placed his suitcase on the floor, smiled and saluted me. 'Dark Lady.'

His wife, Silica, bowed slightly. 'Lady Emma.' She appeared as a slim woman in her early fifties with steel-grey hair and wearing a grey robe.

'You're looking way better, Ronnie.'

'I'm feeling it. The Dark Lord's assistance has been the main reason I've come so far, I think.'

'Are you ready to try?' Silica said.

'I am.' He knelt and opened the case, then pulled out a bunch of seal papers. He took the ink stone and ink block out of the case and placed them on Yi Hao's desk, then poured some water from a small bottle he kept in his case onto the stone.

'This was much easier with the Dark Lord around. He just summoned water for me,' he said as he ran the ink block over the stone until the ink was satisfactory. 'Here goes.'

He inked his brush and with quick precise strokes created the seal symbols on the paper. One of them was recognisably the seven stars of the Big Dipper, the symbol of John's power. Ronnie placed the brush carefully on the stone, waved the paper around a few times to dry it, then held it out towards the office door.

Everybody held their breath as he stood silent and concentrating.

Nothing happened and he dropped his head. 'I can't do it.'

'You can.' Silica brushed her hand over his shoulder. 'Try again, Ronnie. I know you're close. I can feel it. Don't give up.'

He nodded once sharply, held the seal out towards the door and his face went from strained to beatific. A gentle smile spread across his features. The seal went blindingly white and snapped from his hand to hit the door frame with an audible smack. It glowed too brightly to look at, then disappeared.

Silica and Yi Hao both applauded, with Silica making little squeaks of delight.

Ronnie stared at the door frame with his mouth open. 'I did it.' He turned, grabbed Silica and spun her. 'I did it!'

'You'll have your free will back in no time, Ronnie,' I said. 'I have a very long list of places that need new seals. Can you travel to Hell?'

'I've never tried,' he said, his voice thick with emotion. 'I haven't been there since I escaped. We'll have to see if I can travel to the Celestial side of Hell.'

'Either way, every single Heavenly dominion has places that need new seals, and not enough people to do them,' I said. I went into my office, set the list to print in Yi Hao's office and came back out again. 'But I think you two should go and have a small celebration first.'

'I don't want to,' Ronnie said, and Silica's expression fell. 'No! I mean, I just learned how to do this again. I want to do it a few more times to make sure that I really have it back.' He touched her hand. 'Then you and I are having the celebration of a lifetime.'

She smiled broadly, threw her arms around his neck and they held each other for a moment. When they broke apart, I handed Ronnie the list of buildings that needed refreshed seals.

'You're a slave driver,' he said with disbelief as he scanned the list.

'Hell is the most important right now, then here on the Mountain and the Northern Heavens. The other realms have their own masters, but they're so overworked you'll be welcome there as well. But we have nobody apart from the Dark Lord himself, so we're relying on you,' I said. 'I am so very glad you have this back, Ronnie, we really need you.'

He saluted me with the list in his hand. 'You have no idea how glad I am to be back.' He turned to put his equipment away. 'Let's see if I can go to the Celestial side of Hell.'

'I'm not sure that's a good idea,' Silica said.

He gazed into her eyes. 'I'll be fine as long as you're with me.'

She smiled and dropped her head.

He finished packing up his equipment, closed and picked up his case, then saluted me Western-style, hand to forehead. 'I'll be back later to do the Mountain.'

'Thank you,' I said. 'And Ronnie?'

'Hmm?'

'Congratulations again.'

'Thank the Dark Lord for me when you see him. I would never have come so far so quickly without his help,' he said.

He nodded to me and Yi Hao, then he and Silica left.

'Free will so quickly,' Yi Hao said with longing, staring at the door.

'He's half-human, not pure demon, and that's not free will quite yet,' I said. I patted her shoulder over the desk. 'You will get there.'

'I'm happy right here looking after all of you,' she said with a smile of bliss. Her expression went stern. 'Despite your meddling stone.'

'I said I was sorry!' the stone said.

Yi Hao just grinned and shooed me back into my office.

An hour later, Simone stormed into my office, her face a mask of fury, and threw herself to sit across the desk from me. I turned towards her and waited.

'Why didn't you *tell* me?' she said.

'Tell you what?'

'I went to the Philippines to see Monica after I talked to Cheung.'

I leaned back. 'Oh.'

'She asked you not to tell me?'

'She did. I respected her wishes.'

Simone turned away and crossed her arms. 'I hate both of you.'

'She's dying.'

Simone glared at me. 'Thanks for pointing that out. Anything else you want to be particularly insensitive about?'

'Is she unhappy?'

Simone's frown disappeared. 'Actually, no. She's very happy. She's weak and thin and really frail, but she doesn't stop smiling.'

'She'd be unhappy up here, away from her family.'

'But we're her ... No, we're not.' She rose. 'You don't need to say any more. It's my own stupid fault for not speaking to her on the phone.' She leaned on my desk. 'She says she's looked after. Are they? They're okay for money and things?'

'Yes, they are. Remember that her mother-in-law was one of the Tiger's wives. They're supporting a massive extended family and giving them opportunities they wouldn't have otherwise. They treat her like royalty. The family has members going to university for the first time.'

She tapped the desk. 'Okay then. I can't wait to do that too when this is over, and go from being an old woman Chinese spy to a uni student my real age again.'

'You forgot half-Shen and weird-ass snake thing.'

'That too.' She smiled. 'Thanks for not telling Dad.'

'I still think you should.'

'I will. One day. Hey.'

'Hmm?'

'Get some rest, Emma, you look terrible. Maybe I could handle some more of your stuff? Yi Hao can help me.'

Lok came into the office and stopped. 'Sorry, I didn't realise the Princess was in here.' He saluted us both. 'Dark Lady. Princess.'

'Wait!' Simone studied him. 'I know your chi. Um ...' Her brows creased, then her eyes went wide with recognition. 'Lok?'

He grinned and bowed slightly to her. 'Ma'am. You've grown into an impressive young woman, Princess, and the Mountain is a sight to see.'

'Thanks. Nice human form yourself,' Simone said. 'Present yourself to Master Chen at the armoury immediately for —'

'No, wait,' I said. 'Leo's moved to the Earthly and he was in charge of counselling the students and managing the residential barracks. You can take that over; it's exactly the same as running the Folly ...' My voice trailed off.

'Because Daddy put a sign up over the entrance to the barracks that says *Turtle's Folly*,' Simone said with humour. 'Back to work at the Folly, Lok. There's a demon there called Otis; he has the student files and can help you catch up.'

Lok smiled broadly. 'It would absolutely be my pleasure. I can't wait to see everybody again.'

'Bring that steel container up first. I've been waiting for it,' I said, and passed him a document. 'Here's the address and your contact on the Earthly. Make sure your claws are in terrible shape afterwards and you complain most mightily about how difficult it was.'

Lok's smile didn't shift. 'Ma'am. Anything else?'

'Yes,' Simone said. 'What were you going to ask when you came in?'

'If you had anything you needed me to do, and where this container is,' Lok said. 'Looks like the question's answered.' He bowed to us again. 'Lady. Princess.' He went out.

'That solves that,' Simone said. She straightened. 'Daddy's home. Oh.' She slumped again. 'He went straight to your room.'

'Oh dear.'

'What?'

'He's been working nonstop for more than twenty-four hours, and Smally's in there tidying up. He probably walked right past her, stripped off and fell on the bed ...'

'You'd better get in there now and rescue her,' Simone said, but I was already out the door.

* * *

The Northern Xuan Wu Hall stood on a raised platform at the northern end of the Celestial Palace complex, its black polished walls and roof gleaming in the late afternoon sunshine. A black marble ramp led up to the front door, sculpted with the Xuan Wu's True Form floating through heavenly clouds. Stairs on either side of the ramp led up to the twin doors guarded by the Door Gods themselves. The hall was one of the smaller ones, being only fifty metres to

162

a side, and invitations had been restricted. Everyone in the Heavens had wanted to attend even though the ceremony itself was a short formality.

We stopped when we saw that a crowd had gathered in the square outside the hall. Imperial Elites in their red and gold palace armour formed an honour guard on either side of a cleared aisle, keeping the people back so we could pass through. One of the Elite guards approached us. As she neared us, people in the crowd saw us and cheered. They were soon joined by others until everyone was applauding.

'It's a simple five-minute ceremony, Cloud,' John said to the Elite, exasperated. 'Why are they wasting their time out here when they won't even see it?' He swiped one hand through the air. 'And why are Elites on crowd control? This is highly inappropriate!'

She saluted us all. 'It's not often the entire royal family of the Dark North appears together in full regalia, Highness.' She turned to look at the crowd, then back to us. 'Can you wait a couple of minutes while we set up a relay for them to watch?'

John spread his hands. 'It's a five-minute ceremony!'

The air shimmered above the entrance to the hall and a rectangular image of the black throne on the dais inside appeared. The crowd cheered again. Someone threw chi into the air and made it explode like firecrackers and people shrieked with delight.

'It's a huge morale boost,' Martin said with satisfaction.

'Please give us plenty of notice when you set a date, Highness,' Cloud said. 'We'll need to arrange reinforcements if this is what we can expect.'

'Elites on crowd control,' John growled. 'Unbelievable.'

'They honour you, Xuan Wu,' I said.

'So stop complaining and let's do this!' Yue said.

Cloud bowed around at us, grinning.

John grumbled something unintelligible and stretched to his most massive height, towering four and a half metres above me. His long hair was down to his waist and his square dark face had a thin black beard. He wore his formal dress armour: black enamel embossed with a silver Big Dipper on his breastplate, and twining silver snakes and turtles on nearly every surface. The armour sat over a black silk robe embroidered with more silver snakes and turtles.

The crowd went wild and more chi explosions rang out.

Simone took her largest Celestial Form as well. She was close to her father's height, and her blue–black robes glittered with stars within their depths. Her immensely long honey-gold hair floated around her on a celestial breeze that wasn't there, with particles of ice appearing and disappearing among the strands. Her huge eyes were completely black in the pale ferocity of her face. Her twin curved swords sat in matching deep blue and gold enamel scabbards on her back.

Yue Gui's warrior livery was completely black, like her father's, and her robes and armour were similarly embellished with the Big Dipper. Her black hair was held in a topknot with a simple ebony spike. The long strands would have touched the floor if they weren't floating around her in a breeze that wasn't there. Her robe was embroidered with silver dragon-headed turtles and her black armour was etched with a silver turtle-shell design. She had a sword strapped to her back, the black scabbard decorated with the markings of a turtle shell and ba gua symbols.

Martin rarely took Celestial Form. He was slim and elegant, the same size as Simone, and much leaner than John's massive bulk. His waist-length black hair, tied in a topknot and bound in a small gold crown, did the same thing as his sisters', floating around him. His robes and armour were black to honour the House, with green and gold trimmings that mirrored his sea turtle nature, and he had his sword, the Silver Serpent, hanging from his belt.

I was small and felt tatty in my well-worn robes and armour. A few of the wires holding my armour plates together had worn through and there was a large chip in the breastplate that Moaner, the forge's head demon, hadn't had time to repair. I wore the Murasame clipped to my back, and cringed every time one of the others took a step.

'Me middle, Ming right, Simone left, Emma behind Simone,' John said. He glanced down at me. 'Sorry, Emma, but —'

I raised one hand to stop him. 'I know the protocol, John. I've been putting up with it for more than ten years. And as a concubine, I shouldn't even *be* here.'

'Consort.'

'Concubine.'

'Consort, Emma.'

'I'm a concubine.'

He glared down at me from his massive height. 'I am the Dark Emperor of the Northern Heavens and I have decreed that you are my consort and not a concubine and the matter is settled.'

'Whatever. I shouldn't be here.'

John dropped his voice. 'You're not getting out of this that easily. If we all have to put up with this formal bullshit then you do too.'

'Oh look, Father's breaking with tradition,' Martin said, his voice heavy with sarcasm.

'And I'm way too small. I'm sure one of you monsters will tread on me,' I grumbled under my breath.

'Don't worry, we'll be careful.' John turned to speak to Yue Gui. 'I'll give you the signal when we're settled and you can come in.' He looked around at everyone. 'Let's make this quick; we all have much more important things to do. Ready?'

'I hope someone has a video camera inside, I want to see what you all look like as you enter the hall. It'll be magnificent,' I said.

'We're recording it, ma'am,' Cloud said. She gestured towards the hall. 'Shall we?'

'Oh, and you won't need to touch me when the water comes,' John said, his voice full of amusement. 'I'll hyper-oxygenate it and you'll be able to breathe.' He nodded to Cloud.

'Wait, what? What water?' I said.

'Oh, that's mean, Daddy,' Simone said.

The Door Gods opened the doors and Cloud escorted us through the ecstatic crowd. John floated up the black marble ramp and Simone, Martin and I strode up the stairs at the sides and behind him. The interior of the hall was much quieter, the crowd inside silent as a show of respect. The carpet stretched in front of us, black with a silver twining snake along its length.

The four of us strode up the carpet and everybody in the hall fell to both knees. John swept up the stairs to the dais and stood in front of the black turtle throne, his dark face fierce. Martin stood behind him to the right, Simone to his left, and I stood behind and to the left of Simone and hoped that nobody could see me. Cloud took position below the dais to our right, her hands on her belt.

The crowd outside went completely silent.

'Wen sui, wen sui, wen wen sui,' everybody in the hall said in unison, and the people outside echoed the supplication.

John flicked his robe and sat with his legs spread wide and his hands on his knees. 'Rise.'

Everybody stood, and John waited for them to settle. When there was complete silence he spoke.

'The Northern Heavens decree that Princess Xuan Yue Gui, the Moon Turtle, is to present.'

Yue came in, her face fierce and her stride confident. When she was in front of the dais she fell to one knee as a senior Retainer and stiffly saluted John. 'This small Shen is present and honoured, Celestial Highness.'

'Rise, Princess.'

Yue Gui stood with her head bowed and her hands held in front of her face in the salute as a show of respect.

Both Simone and Martin shifted slightly. They knew their father. I remained completely still, but I knew him as well. The urge to break with protocol and do something chaotic would be almost irresistible for him.

Don't worry, the Jade Emperor just warned me off, he said, and all three of us relaxed.

Yue Gui saw our reactions and smiled slightly with her head bowed.

John stood and took two steps forward to stand with his hands resting on his wide belt and the hilt of Dark Heavens, which had grown to match his size.

He raised his voice to be heard throughout the hall. 'The Northern Heavens decree that within their realm, Princess Xuan Bei Yue Gui, the Moon Turtle, is second only to the Northern Heavens themselves in seniority. She is to be given equal distinction and merit to her brother, Xuan Bei Ming

167

Gui, the Bright Turtle. Each of these officers are of equal stature in the eyes of the Heavens and the Celestial.' He raised one hand towards Yue. 'Ascend, Princess Xuan Bei Yue Gui and take your place as the Dark Emperor's Number One.'

Yue Gui bowed to John, put her hands on her belt and strode up the stairs, taking her place next to Martin at John's right hand.

'This matter is concluded,' John said, his voice still carrying through the hall, then he sat on the throne again.

'Pay homage to your Sovereign,' Yue said at a similar volume.

Everybody in the hall fell to their knees again, heads bowed, and chanted the supplication, with the crowd outside repeating it.

John rose again. *Close up*, he said, and gestured with one hand for us to follow as he walked down the stairs. *Don't hold your breath.*

As we moved to follow him, a sphere of water appeared around us and we all lifted to float in it. The water glowed with John's shen energy, glittering with rays of light that shifted and spread to shine in dots on the walls and ceiling of the hall. The water floated above the carpet and we all hung suspended within it, our hair and robes flowing around us as it carried us back out the doors.

As soon as the doors closed behind us, John dropped the water and we landed lightly on the stone pavers of the raised platform around the building. The crowd outside the hall went wild, and we stopped for a moment to have our photos taken.

'Hurry, Father,' Yue said.

'Around the back,' John said, and walked quickly around the hall. 'Can they see us?'

'Clear,' Martin said.

John changed to human form, then fell face first, like a dead tree. Martin caught him.

'Get him out before anyone sees,' Yue said.

Martin nodded and disappeared.

Yue put her hand out to me. 'I'll take you back to the apartment.' She nodded to Simone. 'Are you okay to get there by yourself?'

'I'm good,' Simone said, and disappeared.

'Don't carry me, I'll walk back,' I said. 'The travelling's wearing me out.'

'Not an option, sorry, Emma,' she said, taking my hand. 'They can't see us leave without him.'

She dropped her head and the square disappeared.

* * *

Martin was placing John on the bed in the Celestial Palace apartment when we arrived. I took his hand and fell to one knee next to him, then ran my other hand over his forehead. He had severely drained himself with this ridiculous performance.

I dropped his hand and went to the end of the bed to pull his boots off as his children hovered, concerned. I was right: blood stained his socks. I pulled them off. His feet weren't gone, but they were skinless and bleeding raw.

'Oh god,' Simone said, and rushed out, gagging.

I looked up at Yue and Martin. 'You need to freeze this now to stop the bleeding.'

Martin froze the ends of John's feet. Ice formed around them.

'Yue, tell the Blue Dragon that John's feet are like this and we need his help,' I said. 'He's to tell you the nature of the item we're holding that can fix it.'

169

'The Dragon? Why?' she said, and her brow creased with concentration, then comprehension. 'Oh, I see.'

She concentrated on Martin and he understood as well.

'I'll carry Father. Ah Yue, take Emma to retrieve the ... thing,' Martin said.

I rose and turned to Yue Gui. She took my hand and the Celestial Palace disappeared.

* * *

Yue and I hurried down the stairs into the Grotto to find Martin next to an unconscious John, who was lying on the ledge near the water.

'Did you dismiss the fish?' I asked Martin.

'I did.' He inhaled sharply. 'That's it?'

I put the casket on the ground next to John and removed the cage from it.

'We need to wake him up and make him take True Form.' I looked up at them. 'Grab his turtle form before it takes off and slam it into the cage.'

Martin and Yue nodded, their expressions grim.

'We should anaesthetise his feet first,' Yue said.

'I already did,' Martin said.

'You try waking him, Emma,' Yue said. 'He's been with you the longest.'

'You're his children,' I said, and stopped. That didn't mean as much to a reptile. 'He's been with both of you for thousands of years.' I knelt next to his head anyway, and touched his cheek. 'John. John. Wake up.'

His eyes snapped open, unseeing, but not black. It was the Turtle, not the Serpent.

'John,' I said, brushing his cheek. 'You need to take True

Form. Your feet are damaged again. We have to put you into the cage.'

'I'm slipping into True Form,' he said, his eyes wide. 'Simone, Emma, are you there?'

'I'm here, John, just let the form take you.'

'Simone,' he said, his voice hoarse with emotion. 'Emma … Yue, Ming, Leo, I'm losing it.' He took a deep breath and closed his eyes, his brow creasing. 'I can't hold it. When I rejoin, don't try to pull me out, just leave me there. It's too dangerous. Emma?'

'I'm here, John,' I said, still stroking his cheek.

He grabbed my hand and held it so hard it was painful. He spoke with fierce urgency. 'Emma, this is only temporary. Even if the Heavens fall, I will be back for you. Simone, I am so damn proud of you. Ming, Yue, Leo, you are all magnificent. This is a direct order: nobody is to attempt a rescue. Stay away from me. It'll be a massive trap and they'll be waiting. You are needed on the Celestial. Huh? Mei Mei?'

Yue dropped her head, her eyes wide and concentrating.

'I'll try my best,' he said, and grunted with effort. 'You have no idea what you're asking here.'

'He may not be able to take a small enough form,' Yue said from a million miles away. 'Help me, Di Di.'

Both of them concentrated on him.

'Look after each other. I love you all,' John said.

He shimmered into True Form and Martin grabbed him. Yue helped him to put John in the cage and I slammed the lid on it. We all fell back to crouch on our heels and breathed a sigh of relief. He was too exhausted to fight being in the cage and sat with his eyes half-closed.

'He's worse than even he realises,' Martin said.

'I'll stay with him,' I said. 'You guys have stuff to do.'

'You're as exhausted as he is.'

'Simone will come down and relieve me later. I'll be fine.' I sat on the stone floor next to the cage. 'Both of you need to attend the investiture banquet and keep up appearances.'

Yue and Martin shared a look, then rose.

Martin patted me on the shoulder. 'Call us if you need anything.'

'I have everything I need right here,' I said, and settled myself to wait for him.

13

I was woken by his voice next to me. 'What happened? Emma?' He banged his head on the lid. 'I can't get out!'

'Relax, John, you're in the cage again,' I said.

I opened the lid and he floated out to land on the platform next to the lake.

'What happened?' He saw my blanket and inflatable mattress. 'How long have I been out?'

'You've been here for nearly six hours. It's 1 am.'

'Last thing I remember is leaving the hall ...' His face filled with comprehension. 'I overdid it.'

'Your feet lost all their skin.'

He winced. 'I remember.'

I put the cage back into the casket. 'Are your feet whole?'

He nodded. 'Being in the cage the first time helped me to grow my tail back, but it wasn't complete.' He shifted slightly, checking. 'I still need to completely regrow the scales, but this is much easier to hold. It's more like a mild burn than a complete loss. Has anything major happened?'

'No. All's quiet.'

'Good.' He took the casket from me and put his arm around my shoulder. 'Are you hungry?'

'No, just tired. Simone and I took turns watching you while we ate dinner. I just want to go to bed.'

He yawned widely. 'Me too. That's so strange; I just had a six-hour nap and I still feel exhausted.'

'So do I,' I said, leaning into him.

The stars blazed above us when we climbed out of the Grotto; the black banners had been furled and taken in. The chill wind made me shiver and he pulled me closer to him, sharing his warmth. Lights bobbed on the battlements as the Disciples on sentry duty walked along the top of the wall.

We dropped the cage in the armoury and walked through the spring-fresh gardens to our house. Before we entered the Residence, John stopped to check on everyone. He nodded silently and we went in.

Smally was waiting for me in the entry hall with a tray of tea and biscuits and a blanket over her arm. John concentrated on her. Her face filled with understanding, and she retreated to the servants' quarters at the back of the house.

We held hands as we headed up the stairs to our bedroom. As we approached, John moved closer and put his arm around my shoulders so that his body pressed into mine. I leaned into him as we went into our room and closed the doors together. We turned to face each other, and I threw my arms around his neck to pull him down.

Every time we had some private time to share our feelings, it was like the first time again. I lost myself in the fresh scent of the sea, the cool skin of his hands, the silken feeling as I ran my fingers down the side of his throat. I reached around to release his hair and he shook it out into a wild tangle. He pulled back, his expression intense, and led me past the warm glowing fire to the bed. I stopped and gently tugged at his hand.

He nodded understanding, made his clothes disappear, and hopped up to sit cross-legged on the bed to wait for me. I stood for a moment admiring him, and he spread his hands slightly and smiled.

Then he obviously remembered something. 'While you're in there, can you leave the stone for me? I'd like to ask it something.'

A million thoughts raced through my head. 'What do you want to ask it? Something personal about me?'

His smile turned wry. 'You can always see right through me.'

I sat on the bed next to him and ran my hand over his thigh. 'I like to think you trust me enough to ask me anything.'

'This I'm not so sure about.'

'Like when you told me about your run-in with the marine biologists?' I shifted my hand to the inside of his thigh and watched his reaction with delight as I lightly traced over him with my fingertips. I grinned up into his eyes. 'Mister porn star.'

He sat silently for a moment, then gently lifted my hand away. 'Similar. This is much more ... difficult. I know you are very accepting, even adventurous, and that's something I really love about you, but I know how offensive this could be, and I need to ask the stone.'

'Offensive?'

He shrugged silently.

'Your animal form,' I said, working it out. 'I know the Tiger does it ... You want to have sex with me as a *turtle*? John, that thing's massive!' My voice trailed off as I understood. 'My serpent?' I pulled away slightly. 'I don't think that's a very good idea.'

'No. Your human form. I don't want to try anything with your serpent form. Our natures are too similar and I could possess you while I'm broken like this.'

'But you'll take off and join with your Serpent ...' I understood. 'You won't if you're in the middle of being a Turtle. And you'll be in True Form, so it'll be really good for you ... and I don't just mean pleasurable.' He waited as I thought about it. 'Can you even do that with my human form?'

His face remained completely expressionless: yes, he could.

'Have you done it before?'

'No. You're the first human I've even considered asking.'

I shifted slightly more away. 'Let me think about it.' I looked up into his eyes. 'I want to be positive that it won't hurt me. Land tortoises have huge barbed penises with nasty spikes on them. Do sea turtles?'

'How do you know that?' he said, aghast.

'I'm marrying one. Well, do they?'

'It won't.'

'And I know damn well that it's half the length of your lower shell ... There's a scientific term for that ...'

'I have no idea.'

'So that thing is enormous, barbed or not. Are you *sure* you won't hurt me?'

He spread his hands slightly. 'I will be in control of my shape.'

176

'And I want to be sure that you won't take off in the middle of things.' I shook my head. 'I really don't think this is a terribly good idea.'

'I agree. Go and prepare for bed. I'll be here waiting for you in one hundred per cent human form.'

'Stone,' I said.

'I would prefer not to be involved in this particular discussion,' the stone said.

'If he had asked you, what would you have said?'

'I would have said that he's pushing you too far, that even you have limits to your acceptance of his strange nature, and to not even ask.'

'You're wording it as a challenge!' I said. 'You think it would be that good for him?'

'She can see through you as well,' John said with amusement.

'Exactly how good for him?' I said.

'It would bring him back to close to full strength. The benefit would flow on to the Serpent and heal it as well. It is part of his true nature and would be very, very good for him.'

I took his hand. 'Would you drain me?'

'In turtle form, absolutely not. Exactly the opposite: it would probably have health benefits for you as well.'

'Taoist turtle sex magic.'

He squeezed my hand. 'That's it.'

'And you're too damn faithful to find a female turtle Shen to help you out.'

'I know how you'd feel about that. You'd say you understand and it's for the best, and be totally betrayed.' He shrugged. 'And you're right. For me, only you.'

I dropped his hand and climbed off the bed. 'Let me think about it.'

I went to the bathroom without saying another word, and he slipped under the covers.

I came back out naked. His hair was a wild tangle on the pillow and his dark eyes watched me as I approached. He pulled back the silk quilt for me. I climbed over the top of him and he brushed his hands over me as I did. I settled next to him and cuddled into him. His hands roamed over my back, and I ran my own hands over his chest, tracing his abs, then slipped them around his behind to pull him hard against me.

'One question,' I said into the side of his neck.

'Only one?' he said, and his voice rumbled through his chest. He held me tighter. 'Good. Make it fast, because I have better things to do. It has been a while since I have adequately demonstrated to my Lady exactly how much I love her.'

I breathed in the scent of him, cool and fresh. 'It wouldn't be animal, would it? It would be you? You could talk me through it? Because it would be wrong if it was all animal.'

He pulled back to see me, his dark eyes intense. 'It would be me. The inside would be all me. The outside would be ... one of my many outsides. I can talk you through it. It will be me.'

'I'm still not sure.'

'I'm absolutely certain that it's a bad idea.'

I put my hand on the side of his face and looked into his eyes. 'I love you whatever form you take.'

'Leave it for now,' he said. 'We've had a hell of a day. A hell of a week. Rest.'

He kissed me and we wrapped around each other, losing ourselves in the sensation of sharing our bodies and minds so closely.

He pulled back to speak. 'The decision is: no. If you change your mind, I will still be here, and either way it makes no difference.' He buried his face in the side of my throat. 'I love you,' he breathed into my ear.

He stopped moving and remained completely motionless for more than a minute.

'Holy shit I do not believe this, and whoever this is will get a piece of my mind,' I said.

'A bomb just went off in Tiger Village,' he said. 'Multiple casualties, most of them civilians. Children.'

He threw the covers off, jumped out of bed and conjured his armour. He looked down at me and opened his mouth.

'Go,' I said. 'I'll stay here and cry for them, because they were our orphans and their carers.'

He disappeared and I turned over to bury my face in the pillow.

'Don't do it,' the stone said.

'The whole Celestial needs him strong. This is a tiny sacrifice for me to make.'

'If you do it when you don't want to, then the demons have won,' the stone said. 'The essence of the Celestial is respect and care for all life. If the two of you do this, then you will betray everything that the Celestial stands for.'

'If I'm not completely into it, he won't do it anyway.'

'And you should not even be considering it if you aren't.'

'But it would be very good for him, you said that yourself.'

'That would be nullified by your suffering.'

'What if I like it?'

The stone was silent a moment. 'Turtle Shen have something of a ... reputation. But you're human, and what he's suggesting is a very long way past normal experience for a human. It's possible that the strangeness of the experience would outweigh any pleasure he gives you.'

I sighed again. 'I'll never be able to sleep now. I'll worry about him while he's out there, and our children are dying.'

'No.'

'Come on, help me out here.'

'You need to stop using me as a sleeping aid; you'll become dependent.'

'Would you rather I took a sleeping pill?'

'Could you at least try cycling your energy?' the stone said.

'It's nearly two in the morning. I can't be lying here all night hoping I'll fall asleep; I need to be alert tomorrow. Just this once, okay?'

The stone's voice filled with resignation. 'You said that last time. Put me to your forehead.'

I did as it said and didn't remember anything else.

* * *

'Emma,' the stone said, waking me.

'Huh?'

'Emma, another bomb went off. We have more casualties and he's injured.'

I threw the covers off and turned on the light, blinding myself. When I could see, I rushed to find some clothes. I pulled on underwear and searched for my Mountain uniform, then gave up in frustration when I couldn't find it in the reorganised closet.

'How bad is it?' I said.

'Just a minute, reports are coming in. Serious injuries. Many of them are too serious to be taken to the Celestial;

they've been taken to hospital on the Earthly. The Dark Lord is among them ...'

The stone fell silent. I fidgeted, checking my phone, but there were no messages. He'd probably ordered them to leave me alone and let me sleep.

'Was it Tiger Village again?'

'Yes. The first bomb was to draw some Celestials there, and the second was to finish them off.'

I hissed under my breath. 'We should have seen that coming.'

'Shit-eating turtle eggs who fuck their own mothers' filthy stinking cunts —'

'Stone!'

'Two children and one staff dead. Sixteen children and three staff injured. The Dark Lord tried to shield them from the second blast ... Oh.'

'Stone?'

'Critical. Intensive care. This is very serious.' The stone dropped its voice. 'He's dying, Emma, and they can't take him up to the Celestial without killing him.'

'Find someone to take me down there!'

'Nobody will. You're safer where you are.'

I fell to sit on the bed. 'No.'

'He's just had six hours' rest. He may be able to hold it together and land in Court Ten. I'll let you know.'

I put my head in my hands.

Emma, I will try to hold it together, John said, and my head shot up. *I will do my best. Unh ...* It was a soft sound of pain. *Stay safe and I will be back. If I do rejoin, I ask you, my Lady, do not attempt to find me ...*

'Tell him I won't.'

Thank you. Now I'm saying goodbye to Simone and letting go. Remember: I will be back as soon as I can.

'Tell him I love him.'

I love you too.

Simone slammed the door open and raced into the room in her pyjamas. She grabbed me and pushed her tear-filled face into my shoulder, then collapsed to sit next to me. I wrapped my arms around her and held her as the tears ran down my back.

'I asked Kwan Yin to help and she didn't even reply,' she said.

'No Bodhisattva will ever assist any people who are at war. We'll be on our own until this is resolved,' I said.

'I *hate* this. Stone? What's happening?'

'He's gone. We have to wait and see whether he's rejoined, or he made it to Court Ten.'

The next five minutes of silence stretched for an eternity. We sat unmoving, holding each other. Simone occasionally shook with silent sobs.

'He's in Court Ten,' the stone said, and Simone let go into my shoulder.

After crying for a couple of minutes she released me and looked around, then went into the bathroom to find some tissues.

'If he hadn't spent that time in the cage he would be gone,' the stone said.

'Good. That means they really can't see what we're doing,' I said.

'Precisely,' the stone said. 'Now go back to sleep and there's an excellent chance that he'll be having breakfast with you tomorrow.'

Simone came to me with the box of tissues in her hand, sat next to me on the bed and hugged me again.

'Do you want to stay here?' I said.

'No. He might come back before we wake up, and we'll find him sleeping on the floor again.' She kissed me on the cheek and smiled into my eyes, her own red and swollen. 'Sometimes I'm very glad I have you, Emma.'

'I'm glad I'm here for you.'

I kissed her back, we shared another embrace, and she went out. I crawled under the quilt, still in my underwear, wrapped it around me and closed my eyes.

14

I was woken by someone tapping on the bedroom door. I looked beside me: John was gone. I had a moment of disorientation and remembered what had happened.

'Ma'am?' Smally said outside the room.

'Come in, Smally,' I said.

I checked the bedside clock and sighed: 10 am. I sat up with the quilt wrapped around me to spare Smally's modesty.

She sidled into the room and stood wringing her hands. 'Miss Simone's still asleep as well, ma'am. Should I wake her?'

'No, let her sleep. We had a very bad night. One of the orphanages was attacked, and we nearly lost the Dark Lord.' I wiped my hand over my face and through my tousled hair. My mouth tasted awful and I needed a shower. 'What's on for today? Do I have anything urgent right away? I need to check on the injured orphans and their carers from Tiger Village.'

'I just received a phone call from Lord Bai Hu. It's his Number One son's wedding today, ma'am,' Smally said, obviously anxious, 'and both you and Miss Simone are supposed to be there in less than an hour. He said people are handling Tiger Village and not to worry about it, but to —' She winced. 'He said things I can't say, ma'am.'

'No, we had the investiture Wednesday, and then the wedding's on Thursday … isn't that tomorrow?' I said, then, 'Holy *shit*, today's Thursday!'

I jumped out of bed. 'Simone! Simone!' I ran around the balcony in my underwear and rapped loudly on her door.

'Go away,' Simone said from inside.

'Michael and Clarissa's wedding is in less than an hour and we should be there already!'

'Oh *shit*!' Simone yelled. 'Oh god oh god oh god … Go!'

I ran back into my room and skidded to a halt in front of Smally. 'I need my dark blue skirt suit, the modern Western one. Oh geez.' I undid the rough ponytail in my hair. 'Just pull the suit and some undies out, put them on the bed, and go help Simone. She's the *bridesmaid*!'

I charged into the bathroom and shut the door in Smally's face, then opened it again. 'Tell Simone that if she's ready first to go without me.'

'Yes, ma'am,' Smally said, completely bewildered.

I was ready before Simone, and went in to find her in her dress and make-up with Smally doing her hair.

'How much time do we have?' she said.

'I called Michael. They're waiting for us, but the church will throw them out if they don't start within twenty minutes of their time slot.'

'So that gives me …?'

185

I sighed. 'Yeah. Now. Clarissa's waiting for you in the bride's prep room, so they can start as soon as you're there.'

'Close enough, Smally,' she said, and stood. She put her hand out to me and her eyes unfocused. 'Okay.' She nodded. 'Just finding you a spot to faint.'

'Oh, thank you very much.'

She took my hand and the world spun around me.

* * *

I fell onto my back and my head hit the wooden floor with a crack. I looked around. I was in a small wood-panelled room with a low ceiling and a demon had just dropped me. Two huge demons in human form were backing away from me towards the wall.

I lifted my head, still stunned from the impact, and saw Michael and Simone advancing on them, their expressions full of menace. They generated identical balls of shen energy and threw them at the demons to destroy them at the same time; obviously they were coordinating telepathically.

Simone knelt next to my head. 'Are you okay?'

'I'm fine. Has it started?'

'They're halfway through.' She glanced up at Michael. 'Go back. I'll be along when I've checked her.'

'You can't just leave the wedding halfway through!' I said. 'What did people say when you ran off like that?'

'All the humans are frozen, and we're the only Shen apart from Uncle Bai and Leo.' She put her hand on my forehead and concentrated. 'You're fine, but you'll have a lump the size of a grapefruit later.' Her healing energy moved through the back of my head, as cool and fresh as her father's. She

186

looked over her shoulder. 'I need to go. Uncle Bai can't hold them much longer without them realising that something happened.' She turned back to me. 'Come out when you're feeling better, okay?'

'I'm okay now.' I raised my hand and she helped me to stand. I had a moment of dizziness and then nodded. 'I'm good. Let's go.'

We walked out of what had obviously been the bridal preparation room. Everybody in the church was frozen. Simone went to the altar, took her bouquet from Leo and stood in position next to Clarissa. Clarissa had shed the wheelchair and was standing with the aid of crutches next to Michael. We'd had concerns that she wouldn't make it up the aisle on the crutches, but she'd been adamant. I felt a thrill of joy for her because she'd clearly succeeded.

'Everything good now?' she said.

'Sorry, Clarissa, all fixed. They tried to kidnap Emma,' Simone said.

Clarissa looked back at me and I raised one hand to indicate that I was okay.

Simone nodded to the Tiger, who was sitting in the front row next to Clarissa's parents. 'Let them go.'

Everybody let their breath out at once. The minister continued his speech as if nothing had happened. I crept up the side of the church and slipped into the back pew to sit. A couple of people nearby glanced at me without interest then turned back to the service.

Thank you, I said to the stone.

I love how they keep forgetting that I'm here, the stone said. *But in this case it wasn't me. Both Simone and Michael sensed the demons and dropped everything to help you. It's a*

187

good thing the Tiger was here, otherwise this wedding would be the talk of the newspapers.

I sat back to watch, the lump on the back of my head beginning to pound. I used a small amount of energy to block the pain.

It was a beautiful ceremony. The church was decked with white and pink flowers, matching Simone's bridesmaid's dress. Clarissa's dress was long and full, detailed with antique lace that highlighted her perfect fair skin and shining black hair. Michael wore a standard black Western-style tuxedo, but he'd left his hair blond and in a short ponytail. His expression was full of adoration as he spoke his vows, and his voice echoed through the church.

Leo stood next to Michael in a matching black tux, glowing with pride. Simone's smile was wide and her eyes glittered with unshed tears.

John appeared next to me in the pew wearing his black Western suit, shirt and tie. Nobody noticed his arrival. He took my hand in his and I leaned into him, and we silently watched the ceremony together until he dozed off on my shoulder. I had to wake him when the ceremony was finished and we all stood to watch the married couple leave.

We followed them outside, and Leo opened the limo door for Clarissa and Michael. When the couple were inside, Simone spoke to them through the door and they smiled and nodded in reply. Clarissa took Simone's hand and squeezed it, then Simone closed the car door.

The Tiger gestured for John and me to join him and Simone in the other car, and pulled himself in behind the wheel.

'Where's the reception?' John said, taking the front passenger seat.

'The hotel in Western. At least it'll have seals and reasonable protection,' the Tiger said. He growled with frustration. 'Clarissa's stupid family had to have the goddamn Christian fucking wedding with all the trimmings, and this church wouldn't let me come in and do a fung shui thing to set seals on it. Her parents even objected to me,' he hesitated, then said with emphasis, '*me* taking the second parking spot so we can follow the bridal car back to the reception and make sure they're all okay.'

'What, they treated you like an ordinary human instead of a Celestial Emperor?' John said with amusement.

'Totally unacceptable,' the Tiger said. He glanced into the back seat. 'You okay, Emma?'

'Yeah, they didn't have a chance to do anything.' I patted Simone on the hand. 'Thanks.'

'I'll only be able to stay long enough to pay my respects,' John said. 'Then I have to pull Leo out to plan the evacuation of the orphanages. I need to find somewhere safe on the Earthly to put them.'

'I heard about that. Didn't you have guards posted at Tiger Village?' the Tiger said.

'Guards are completely useless against a rocket-propelled grenade,' John said. 'They had a human stand outside the compound, shoot the grenade through one of the second-storey windows, then go to ground. We were lucky: most of the children had moved from that particular building after the village was evacuated, but we still lost two in the blast. After the grenade went off, we searched and didn't find any demons so we thought they'd gone. I summoned some rain to put the fire out, and I'll be damned if they didn't do exactly the same thing again and take most of us out.'

'Holy shit,' Simone said softly.

'You should have seen that coming, Ah Wu,' the Tiger said as he drove down the steep Garden Road towards the main five-lane highway that edged the harbour.

John ran his hand over his face. 'I know. The Snake would have seen it. The Turtle's a complete imbecile. Once again the Jade Emperor saved many lives with a single simple command. But the demons are using humans more and more to interfere with our ability to pick them, and I should have anticipated it.'

'We need to get that Snake out,' the Tiger said. 'I miss your brains, and I'm glad we have Emma.'

John sighed with feeling. 'Pao wanted to keep me for seventy-two hours. The Jade Emperor had to intervene to let me out.'

'That long? Why?' Simone said.

'Because children died in my care.'

'He doesn't give a damn about the kids — he just wants to cause trouble.' The Tiger left the five-lane road and entered an overpass that would take us to Western District. 'Every time one of us lands in Court Ten he does his damnedest to get in our way. One day I am going to punch that asshole square in the face. Let me see if one of my hotels or something in Europe can take them.'

'The demons are in Europe too. Do you own a hotel in Australia or America?' I said.

'I have a family-style resort in North Queensland in Australia, would that do?'

'Perfect,' I said.

'It'll cost you putting up a bunch of kids there. They'll bring it down from five stars to four,' the Tiger said. 'Ah Wu.' He looked sideways at John. 'Ah Wu! Wake up.'

John jerked awake. He and the Tiger went quiet and the car filled with the background buzz of telepathic communication.

'Hey!' I said.

They ignored me.

'God, they're rude,' Simone said.

'No! And that's final!' John said.

Let him do it, the Tiger said to me. *It wouldn't hurt you and it would do a fucking lot of good for him.*

'Do what?' I said.

'Tell me,' Simone said.

'No,' John said.

Stick that massive turtle dick up you. You should see that thing — it makes me look under-endowed. Every chick who's ever been fucked by a turtle has said it's a transcendental experience, even better than me. I've never done a female turtle — they refuse to have anything to do with me — but I've heard stories, and I can guarantee it won't hurt you and it would be incredibly fucking good for him.

'Leave it!' John said.

'What?' Simone said, becoming frustrated.

The Tiger shrugged. *Just think about it.* He switched to out loud. 'I'll email you the contact details of the hotel manager in Queensland.'

'Thanks,' I said, and attempted to change the subject. 'Thank god for the internet; I don't know what I'd do without it.'

'Thank Gold for the internet. He did something of a miracle connecting the Planes,' John said with amusement.

'That little asshole only did it to make sure he never ran into any of the *many* people who wanted to drop him in a vat of acid,' the Tiger said.

191

'Why would anyone want to do that?' Simone said. 'He's never been anything but perfectly honourable ...'

The Tiger made a loud sound of derision and John choked with laughter.

'Wow, suddenly I'm in a car full of frat boys,' Simone said.

'Damn straight, honey,' the Tiger said. 'Here we are.' He pulled into the hotel's driveway. 'And think about it, Emma. It would be,' he dropped his voice to a throaty rumble, 'unbelievably good for both of you.'

'What are you talking about?' Simone said.

'I said leave it!' John snapped.

The Tiger opened the car door and got out, then ducked to speak to John who was still sitting inside. 'Don't rush this orphan business. Let Emma do it. Go home and get some sleep.' *And let your Turtle show your missus what it's really all about.*

John roughly pulled himself out of the car, slammed the door shut and glared over the roof at the Tiger. 'Do I have to order you to shut the *fuck* up about this?'

The Tiger glared back. 'Try me. I can take you.'

John slapped the roof of the car so hard he dented it, then turned away to storm into the hotel. Simone and I shared a look.

'What's all this about, Emma?' she said as we got out of the car. 'He *never* loses it like that.'

'Trust me, you don't want to know. Suffice to say it's something to do with the Tiger's specialty.'

'Metal?' Her eyes went wide. 'Stop. Stop! No!' She stared at the Tiger. 'I cannot believe you just said that!'

The Tiger waved her down. 'I've had wives younger than you. Grow up.' He turned to follow John.

Simone dropped her head and shook it. She looked up at me with disbelief. 'Really?'

'What your father said. No,' I said, and headed into the hotel.

'Stupid Shen. Animals, all of them,' she said as she followed me.

* * *

We used the Wan Chai gateway and a cloud to return to the Mountain; the slower route was less stressful on both of us. When we arrived in the middle of the afternoon, John went straight into our bedroom. He pulled the suit jacket off and threw it on the floor, loosened his tie and collapsed face down on the bed.

I stood over him with my hands on my hips. 'Take the clothes off.'

'Too hard. Close the shutters for me, love?'

I rolled him onto his back and slipped his tie off, then unbuttoned his black shirt. 'Don't pass out yet. Let me get your clothes off.'

He grunted. 'Too hard.'

I lifted him to take the shirt off, tossed it aside, and began to work at his belt.

He raised his head slightly. 'That's more like it.'

'You'll be too uncomfortable sleeping in these pants.' I unzipped him. 'Lift your butt up. Good.' I pulled his pants off, taking the socks with them and leaving him in his black silk boxers. 'There. Isn't that better?'

He spread his hands, still lying on his back. 'I can think of a few things that would be better.'

'I thought you were exhausted,' I said, eyeing him.

His eyes fell closed and his head flopped sideways — he'd passed out. I saw his feet: the skin had disappeared again.

'Oh, for heaven's sake. Stone. Stone?' I tapped it.

'Yes? Oh, look at the Turtle, isn't he cute?'

'See his feet?'

'Dammit. At least they're not completely gone but he's losing blood there. What do you want to do?'

'Ask Edwin if he can come and cover them up without moving him.'

'Just a moment, I need someone to relay ... Edwin's on his way.'

I sighed and sat on the bed next to John. I ran my hand over the smooth skin of his chest, feeling the muscles beneath my fingertips. He was completely out of it.

'You heard the Tiger in the car?' I said to the stone. 'Now *he's* at me about it.'

'He's been pushing me to bring it up with you as well. He knows how good it would be for the Dark Lord.'

'I knew it had to be serious for John to even consider asking me — but really that good?'

The stone hesitated for a moment, then said, 'Yes. The exhaustion and these feet would not be a problem if ... Never mind. I don't want to freak you out even more than you already are.'

I raised my head; someone was crying. I went to the door to listen: Simone. I checked John again — he didn't move. I went out and around the balcony to Simone's door and tapped on it.

'Simone? Are you okay?'

She sniffled and I heard tissues being yanked out of the box. 'I'm fine.'

'Is there a problem?'

'No problem!' she said, her voice strained. 'Just leave me alone, okay? I'm fine!'

'What's the matter, Simone?'

'Nothing! Go away.' She collapsed into loud sobs, then the door of her bathroom closed. 'Go away!' she said, even more muffled.

Any idea, Emma? the stone said.

Michael.

Do you want me to call someone to talk to her?

No, best to leave her to it. She knows the situation. Tomorrow she'll be smiling and talking about what a great wedding it was.

Poor kid, the stone said.

I turned to see Edwin coming up the stairs with his doctor's bag, and guided him to the bedroom, where John was still lying unconscious and bleeding all over the sheets.

* * *

I woke slowly and with the profound feeling of bliss of lying next to John. My head was on his chest and his arms were around me; I'd cuddled up to him in my sleep. The morning sun shone through cracks in the shutters and the fire had gone out, filling the room with the comforting scent of the fragrant embers. Birds called across the Mountain and others replied, echoing through the gorges. There was a shout below: the morning energy session had started. I wrapped myself tighter around him.

'Morning,' he said, his voice resonating through his chest.

'This feels like the first time in forever I've woken up and you've been here,' I said, running my hands over him. 'You'd usually be called away by now.'

'I know,' he said. 'I was just enjoying the feeling as well.'
He lifted his head slightly. 'Did I lose my feet again? They're
bandaged. They're sore but not as painful as they were.'

'No, but they're raw and the top layer of skin is gone,'
I said.

'My tail has mostly grown back. It doesn't hurt nearly as
much.'

I looked up into his face and he rubbed his chin on my
forehead, his stubble scratchy on my skin.

'Do you want to go back into the cage for a while and
completely heal?' I said.

'No, I can manage. I can't spend all my time in that
damn thing.'

I dropped my head on his chest again and heard his heart
beating, strong and slow. 'I just want to stay here forever.'

'I remember you saying that at the Western Palace, and I
said we had to go back.' He pulled me closer. 'And now we
don't. We can spend every night like this.' He lowered his
voice. 'The best part is they all think I'm still sleeping and
nobody's called me yet.'

'I was thinking about what the Tiger said. We should do it.'

He squeezed me. 'Is it what you want?'

I hesitated.

'Tell me the truth, Emma. Not what you think is for the
best, not what you think I want to hear. The truth.'

'The truth is … no. It's too freaky.'

'Then the decision is made.'

'But the safety of the whole Celestial is at stake.'

'We could kill a tree to open the gateway. We could be
up in the European Heavens tomorrow to spring a surprise
attack on the demon army.'

'I know that,' I said.

'Should we? The safety of the whole Celestial is at stake there too.'

'Okay,' I said, and he stiffened beneath me. 'No! I don't mean we should kill a tree. I mean: if the need is dire, if the Earthly and Celestial could both fall, then we should reconsider. I think if one of the trees is willing to make the sacrifice, then we should consider it to save all the Planes from much greater suffering. And we should also consider letting your Turtle have me if the alternative is the Heavens falling.'

He made a soft sound of pleasure.

'What?' I said.

'Letting my Turtle have you. You have a way with words sometimes.'

'I love your Turtle,' I said, and he made another soft sound in his throat.

'Your Turtle is the sexiest thing on the planet,' I said, and slipped my hand inside his silk boxers.

He reached down and gently pulled my hand out. 'Please stop talking about it — you'll bring it out yourself.'

'Then I'll just stop talking altogether,' I said, and put my hand back inside.

He reached around me to pull my camisole off. 'Don't do that. Tell me what you think about the rest of me.' He spoke softly into my ear. 'Just don't mention turtles.'

'Last time we were at this stage you were called away,' I said.

'I'm switched to answering machine,' he said. 'I've been aching to finish the matter.'

He leaned into me and kissed me, and we shared the feeling for a long time. Our fingertips traced each other's curves, enjoying the touch of smooth skin and the warmth of our shared connection.

He pulled away to whisper in my ear. 'Did you know you are massively oversexed? You want it way more than any human woman I've ever been with.'

I pulled back to see him. 'Wait, hold on … You've only ever loved one human woman apart from me, you're famous for it.'

He smiled slightly.

'I'm not really human anyway,' I said. 'I'm a snake. And part demon.'

'Oh yeah,' he said. He watched me, his dark eyes intense, as I pushed him onto his back and climbed on top. 'That explains it.'

'Can you take female form right now?' I said. 'It's not too hard on you?'

'No, it's easy.' He raised his eyebrows. 'You want that?'

'No,' I said, putting my chin on his chest. 'I want that for you.'

He changed beneath me, becoming female. I didn't move and my chin was between her breasts. Her dark eyes crinkled up. 'You are completely wonderful.'

I moved my mouth slightly so that I was on top of a nipple, and sucked and teased it with my tongue. I gently tweaked the other one with my fingertips, and she arched her back with a soft sound of delight.

I raised my head. 'I wonder what happens if your eyes go black and you lose control in female form?'

'Don't push me too hard. I might change.'

'Tell me if I am,' I said, running my mouth down over her tight abdomen. I gently tugged the boxers off her, then moved back up to hover above her.

She moaned softly. 'Don't be surprised if I suddenly go male.'

'Let's see how close we can get then,' I said. I lightly touched her with my tongue, then pushed harder into her and enjoyed her quivering reaction.

I stopped, raised my head, and looked up into her eyes as she panted beneath me. 'When I take the Elixir ...'

'Yes?' she said, her voice husky with need.

'Will I be able to change gender too?'

She snapped into male form and his eyes went black.

15

To: Emma Donahoe
From: Brendan Donahoe
*Your mother and I have decided to stay here for now,
you don't need all of us up there at the same time! I
know you think we'd be safer, but honestly, nothing's
happened. Greg's here and we're fine. Don't worry
about us.*
Dad

* * *

To: Emma Donahoe
From: Jade Girl
*Brother Chang is very smart and trustworthy and
should be able to handle the bank accounts easily. His
new assistant Alvin is very capable as well, although
being in a wheelchair will be a difficulty for him on
the Earthly. I have made arrangements for us to do
the transfer of the bank account documents Tuesday*

of next week at 3 pm. Unfortunately these must be witnessed by the bank, so you have to go down to the Earthly to sign them. I already have a few ideas for your Raising ceremony and we can discuss that as well.

Another request, if it pleases my Lady. If his Celestial Highness the Emperor of the Eastern Heavens comes looking for me and asks you where I am again, could you please tell him — on my behalf — to go shove something long, hard and sharp up his blue scaly ass, screw it in tight and set fire to it. Thank you.
I am your humble servant,
Jade

To: Emma Donahoe
From: Wyland Cheung
Re: Re: Re: New Liaison
Many thanks for assigning the agent. All fixed. No more disappearances and they're off my back.

Do you know if she's single? She wouldn't say and seemed shy, which is strange for someone so capable. V. impressive. I really like her. So ... is she? Maybe you could put a word in for me ... are you her superior?
Anyway thanks again
Wyland

I forwarded Cheung's email to Simone with a note suggesting that in future she make it clear that she was married when dealing with Earthly liaisons. Unless, of course, she was interested, but in this case I knew Cheung was way too old.

* * *

'Is Emma in?' a male voice said outside my office.

'She's awfully busy, can you make an appoint—' Yi Hao began, but the young man came in anyway, accompanied by a middle-aged intelligent-looking European woman with shoulder-length brown hair, wearing a pair of slacks and a navy cashmere sweater.

I tried to place the man. He was Chinese, obviously a human Immortal, and was in his mid-thirties, tall, slim and extremely good-looking in a nerdy way, wearing a tailored black silk robe that flattered his slender shape, and fashionable rectangular metal-rimmed spectacles. His chi aura was vaguely familiar. I knew I'd met him before, but had no idea where or when.

I rose and saluted them both and tried to work out who they were as I sat.

The woman studied me appraisingly without returning the salute, and he shook his hands in front of his face before flopping into one of the visitors' chairs.

'Sit, Margie, don't mind about the saluting business,' he said, and she took the other chair. 'Hi, Emma.'

Any idea who this is? I asked the stone, but it didn't reply.

'Forgive me, sir,' I nodded to her, 'ma'am, have we met before?'

He rested his chin in his hand and studied me, full of amusement. 'You don't know who I am?'

I spread my hands. 'Most of you Immortals change your appearance so much I lose track. I have no idea who you are.'

He widened his eyes in mock offence. 'You Immortals?'

The European woman's expression went severe. 'Are you being an ass again, Archie?' she said with a soft Welsh accent.

202

He turned to smile at her and reached to touch her hand. 'Can't help it.'

'Archie. Archie.' I shook my head. 'Nope. No idea.'

'He's the Archivist,' she said with exasperation. 'Apparently everybody's used to seeing him as a pompous twelve-year-old boy and now he's a pompous thirty-year-old,' she glared at him and said the last word with emphasis, '*ass*.'

'Margie?' I said, studying her. 'Oh my god. Margaret Anathain.' I went around the desk and held my hand out for her to shake. 'I owe you so much. Thank you. Thank you!'

She stood as well, took my hand and turned it into a hug. 'I wanted to thank you, actually. And John.' She pulled back, smiling broadly. 'He introduced me to Archie.'

I looked from her to the Archivist. He grinned.

'Don't you have an actual *name*, Archivist?' I said.

He shrugged. 'I don't remember, it was so long ago. I've just been the Archivist for nearly a thousand years, so that's me.'

'Love the look, much more appropriate,' I said as I returned to my seat.

He promptly changed back to his twelve-year-old boy form.

Margaret put her forehead in her hand. 'I really wish you wouldn't do that. What are you saying about me?'

'That you're a disgusting old pedo,' he said with glee.

Her face went rigid and she walked to the door.

'Wait! Wait!' He leapt to his feet, changed his form back and took three huge strides to her. 'I'm sorry.' He took her hand. 'I apologise. Please, come and talk to Emma. I'm sure you and she have a lot in common.' He raised her hand to his face and kissed it. 'Please?'

She turned him around and pushed him back towards the desk, and winked at me behind his back. I was hard-pressed to control my amusement.

'We both wanted to thank you,' he said, flopping into the chair again. 'You and the Dark Lord brought us together.' He glanced at her and some of the adoration leaked through his expression. 'You changed our lives.'

She nodded, her face controlled but her eyes full of joy.

'So where's the Dark Lord?' he said.

'That's really what he's called?' she said with disbelief. 'His name isn't —'

'Nah, he's not nearly cool enough to be called Voldemort,' I said, and we laughed together.

'See? Told you you'd have a lot in common,' the Archivist said.

'Yi Hao!' I yelled at the door. 'Where's the Dark Lord?'

She was silent for a moment, then when she spoke it was full of urgency. 'Oh, ma'am! He's in the infirmary, Edwin has already —'

The outside door burst open. 'We need Lady Emma in the infirmary right now,' a male voice said in Yi Hao's office. 'It's happened again.'

I ran out to Yi Hao's office. 'How bad is he?'

'He's unconscious.'

'Battle stations, Yi Hao,' I said, and stormed back into my office. I picked up my phone and texted Gold.

'What's going on?' Margaret said.

'Emma?' the Archivist said.

'Give me a minute,' I said, pacing up and down in front of my desk. 'Why aren't those damn bells ringing? Yi Hao!' The bells started to ring outside. 'Never mind.'

Gold came in and stood in front of me. 'Ma'am?'

'He's unconscious. Send the message through the network. Confirm by text when you're sure that the Masters, Ma, Er Lang and the Winds are informed.'

Gold froze, his eyes wide, and stopped breathing.

'Good,' I said. I quickly bowed to both the Archivist and Margaret. 'My apologies. I have to go.'

I hefted my phone and rushed to the door.

'Wait, were we attacked?' the Archivist said. 'What's going on, Emma? He's unconscious?'

'I suggest you head back to the Archives and lock it down. We're about to be attacked,' I said on my way through the door.

'The Archives are safe. I need to know what's happening,' he said behind me, and chased me out the door with Margaret trailing him.

I stopped and turned to speak to him. 'Back off, Archivist. You're not cleared for this information —'

'I'm cleared for all information; information is what I do!' he shouted. 'I have top-level clearance and I might be able to help you.'

'You can't. I'll talk to you later.' I nodded to Margaret and headed for the infirmary.

'What's going on?' Margaret said behind me.

'You Europeans are all the same,' the Archivist said to my back as he followed me. 'Always so damn superior.'

'You're going to lose me if you don't drop this incredibly racist attitude all the bloody time,' Margaret growled. 'Fighting racism with more racism isn't the way to improve anything, and she *wasn't* being superior anyway.'

'You try putting up with it for a few hundred years ... but you're right,' he said, still following me. 'So why's the Dark Lord in the infirmary?'

I raised my hand. 'Keep it quiet, and if you must come don't say anything. Need-to-know.'

'Understood.'

The students scurried around us, pulling on armour and carrying weapons as they took their positions for battle stations. Margaret made sounds of astonishment as she followed us.

'It may be ugly,' I said, dropping my voice but still walking as fast as I could. 'His injuries could be severe.'

'Margie, you can stay outside ... Never mind,' the Archivist said.

'Now we're getting somewhere,' Margaret said with amusement.

We arrived at the infirmary. A couple of students who were standing guard outside let us through. I gave up trying to hold back to a walk and ran into the treatment room.

John was attended by Edwin alone. He was unconscious and his face was ashen.

'What did they do to him?' I asked Edwin. My phone dinged and I raised my hand. 'Wait.'

It was a text from Gold. *All informed.*

An order came through from the Jade Emperor to prepare for attack.

'Good, everybody's aware and ready,' I said, and sat next to John.

'Good Lord, I felt that,' Margaret said. 'Prepare for attack?'

'You're safe here,' the Archivist said. 'What happened to the Dark Lord?'

'I don't know,' Edwin said. 'Just when we have his feet back, this happens. He's unconscious, his blood pressure is dangerously low, his blood oxygen similar, his temperature has dropped to nearly freezing —'

'That's normal for him when he's stressed,' I said.

Edwin shrugged. 'I have no idea what they did to him. We can only hope that if he dies, the Serpent dies as well.'

'Do you mind if I have a look?' Margaret said. 'I'm a doctor too.'

I listened to them with half an ear as I watched my phone. I texted Gold: *Updte plz.*

No attack so far, he replied.

'Uh ... I appreciate your offer,' Edwin said, 'but he's not really human and this situation is unlike anything you'll have ever encountered before.'

'Explain for me then,' Margaret said, taking John's pulse, then dropping his wrist when she felt how cold it was. 'Damn.'

The Archivist concentrated on her and she nodded a few times, then stepped back. 'There's no way I could be of any use to you. This is completely out of my league.'

'Stone,' I said.

'Still no movement,' the stone said. 'The Tiger's most senior sons are manning the Hell barricades. The Earthly is quiet, and no incursion on the Celestial.'

'I haven't met you before. Are you a resident of the Celestial?' Edwin asked Margaret.

'Maybe, sometime in the future,' she said.

'Would you like to learn to deal with this sort of thing when you are?' Edwin said. 'I'm run off my feet and another trained physician would be a tremendous boon. I'm overworked and stressed to the point that I'm not providing the best of care.' He gestured towards me. 'She's watching to see if we're attacked. The last time we were, there were hundreds of casualties and we could really use any medical help we can find.'

207

'Absolutely!' Margaret said. 'If I could learn things like this, I'd move here right now.'

'Stone?' I said.

'I'll let you know if anything happens, I'm connected to the remaining network,' the stone said. 'So far, nothing. No movement whatsoever. The Generals are considering downgrading the alert.'

'They may be holding off and waiting for us to do that,' I said.

'That's why they haven't.'

'You'd move here?' the Archivist asked Margaret. 'I thought you were planning to return to Britain.'

She pushed him out of the way without looking at him and moved next to John's head. 'I just said that to scare you. This sort of variety, with strange and powerful people ...' She put her hand on John's forehead, then lifted it off again. 'This would be ... wonderful.' She smiled at the Archivist. 'Truly.' She looked back down at John. 'Dear John, I came all this way to thank you for changing my life and you may not make it through the night.'

That drew my attention back to them. 'He has to. He can't die now.' I turned to Edwin. 'How out of it is he? Can we wake him up and talk to him?'

'He seems to be in an induced coma,' Edwin said. 'I tried to rouse him but he's insensible. I'm waiting for a stone to come do a brain scan to see how much activity there is ...'

'Gold will be here as soon as he's done relaying,' the stone said. 'The Generals have decided to stay on high alert for another hour. They request that we keep them updated as to the Dark Lord's state. If he comes around we can assume they won't attack.'

'Why does everything depend on how awake he is?' Margaret said.

'I'll explain later,' the Archivist said.

'No, you won't,' I said. 'Need-to-know.' I rested my hand on the cold cloud above the blankets and spoke to Edwin. 'If he's brain dead will he rejoin?'

'No. The body has to die. Even if the brain's no longer functioning, while the body lives the spirit cannot be free.'

'Good,' I said, and he stared at me with shock. 'Keep him alive. Whatever it takes. Do not let him die.' I sat next to him and ran my fingers through his wild tangle of hair. 'All we can do now is wait.'

'Is there anything we can do?' Margaret said.

'I think I'll head back to the Archives just to make sure,' the Archivist said. 'You should stay here. It's safer.'

'No. I'm staying with you,' she said fiercely.

They had a quick, silent argument composed entirely of meaningful looks, and she won. They turned to me.

'Lovely to meet you, Margaret,' I said. 'Keep in touch, Archivist. Contact me if you need help protecting the Archives; the knowledge you have stored there is one of the Celestial's most valuable assets. The Jade Emperor will warn us again if they do attack, but the first target will be Hell.'

I didn't hear them leave. Five minutes later, Gold and his daughter, BJ, came in.

'No movement, ma'am,' Gold said, answering my question before I asked it, and I sagged with relief.

'We need to know if there's any —' I began.

'Brain activity. I know,' Gold said. He gestured with his head towards BJ. 'Do you mind if I show my child how to do this?'

'Go right ahead.'

'Okay, BJ, hook up and let's see what we can find,' Gold said.

He took his stone form and BJ followed shortly after. The two stones rested side by side on John's forehead. They extended long feelers and touched, and remained silent for a while.

'There's activity,' Gold said, and I breathed a sigh of relief. 'Would you like me to make an attempt to wake him?'

'If you could,' I said.

'It will hurt,' Gold said.

'Don't hurt yourself ...'

'Not us. Him.'

I wiped my eyes. 'The Celestial needs him. Do it.'

John's eyes snapped open and he made a sharp noise of pain. Both stones flew into the air above his head.

'That worked,' Gold said.

John cast around unseeing, his eyes completely black.

'It's okay, John — the Turtle's in the infirmary on the Mountain,' I said.

'Emma?'

'I'm here.' His hand was still too cold to touch.

He dropped his voice to a near-whisper. 'I have to get out of here.'

Edwin was checking the monitors. He turned and saw John's eyes. 'Serpent?' he said.

John turned his sightless black eyes towards Edwin. 'You are the physician, correct?'

'I am,' Edwin said. 'Do you know what they did to you?'

'They inserted an IV into me to cure the infection, but the bag's been empty for a while. Today they came in and put something into the line. I have no idea what it was. I tried to neutralise it, but it knocked me out too quickly.'

210

Fortunately no one saw my reaction when the Serpent mentioned the IV. It hadn't been my imagination.

'Can you reach the IV to pull it out?' Edwin said.

'I've been trying,' John said. 'It's too close to the back of my head. Emma?' He turned his head and obviously had difficulty focusing on me.

'I'm here, John,' I said. 'Do you know if they're readying to attack?'

'I don't think so,' the Serpent said. 'They knocked me out and put some sort of metal grid under me, like a barbecue grill. I think they're planning to turn up the heat.'

'Holy shit,' Edwin said softly.

'Gold, pass the message on,' I said, trying to control the emotion in my voice as the horrible images filled my head.

Gold nodded, and he and BJ went out together.

The Serpent turned its black eyes to Edwin. 'How much of me needs to be burnt and to what depth to guarantee I won't survive it?'

Edwin was silent for a moment. 'If you were human ...' He stopped. 'I don't believe I'm having this conversation. If you were human, then the skin would need to be burnt off to the muscle beneath for at least fifty per cent of you. Snake ... I have no idea, but I can ask a vet.'

'No need, I'll lose contact soon anyway. Emma.'

'John?'

'The Turtle is concerned that I'm absorbing you.'

'Leave us, Edwin,' I said.

'She sounds more and more like you every day, my Lord,' Edwin said. 'Are you absorbing her?'

John closed his eyes and his eyebrows creased. 'I just want to be out of here and complete, Turtle and Serpent together again ...'

'She's a snake, not a turtle. You shouldn't be absorbing her if you want to rejoin with your turtle,' Edwin said.

John's eyes snapped open and he glared at Edwin. 'You know nothing of my true nature.'

Edwin was obviously taken aback. He glanced at me.

'I asked you to go out, Edwin,' I said.

'Leave. Us,' John said with the force of an imperative.

Edwin, moving like an automaton, left the room.

'I'm not doing it deliberately,' John said.

'Of course you aren't.'

'Why did I have to love someone who's so damn similar to me?' he said. 'Down to our demonic origins. We should have known this would happen when we first laid eyes on you.'

'Too late now,' I said with forced cheerfulness.

'You need to stop spending so much time with the Turtle. I love you ...' His eyes changed back to normal. 'Emma? Are you still here?'

'I'm here.'

'Good,' he said, turned his head away and went limp.

'Edwin?' I called. 'Quickly!'

Edwin came in and checked the monitors. 'He seems to be in a normal sleep now. His blood pressure is back up.' He put his hand on John's forehead, then jerked it away again. 'Let him rest.' He leaned on the monitor. 'He is absorbing you?'

'No.'

He silently watched me for a long moment.

'Leave us,' I said.

'Enough of the "leave us" business. Don't ask me to leave you again — you can trust me. He has good colour, his blood pressure and oxygen are up, and it's a normal sleep.

212

You don't need to be here. Go home and rest. I'll let you know if his condition changes.'

He was right, but I needed to go back to my office just in case the demons still attacked.

'Call Zara, have her sit with him,' I said.

'Will do.' He took my elbow and helped me to stand. 'Go home or you'll end up in here as well, and if I'm any judge, the weaker you are the easier it is for him to take you over.' He looked from John to me. 'You two should split up; your whole existence is at stake here.'

'He vowed to Raise and marry me. It won't happen.'

'I sincerely hope you're right.'

I dropped my voice. 'Don't tell anyone he's absorbing me.'

'If I consult with some other physicians —'

'No. Don't tell anyone.' I shook his hand free from my arm. 'The Celestial comes first.'

He stood silently for a moment, then shook his hands in front of his face. 'Ma'am.'

'Thank you.' I headed back to my office.

16

Yi Hao came in and stood in front of the desk glaring at me, her arms crossed in front of her chest.

I ignored her.

She made some huffy noises and recrossed her arms.

I scooted behind the monitor so I couldn't see her.

She slowly and with deliberate care pushed the tray containing my lunch — some vegetarian won ton ho fan soup noodles — closer to me so that I couldn't ignore it.

'I can't eat while he's in a coma,' I said.

'That's exactly why you should eat.'

I sighed, scooted my chair back again, picked up the chopsticks and ceramic spoon and waved them at her. 'Happy?'

'I want to see that bowl empty when I come back,' she said, turning to go out.

'All right, all right,' I said, and dropped my voice. 'Mother.'

'To quote Master Leo, "I heard that",' she said loudly from the doorway.

An hour later she was back, hesitating at the doorway.

I looked up from the printouts. 'Yes?'

'He's asking for you, ma'am.'

I jumped up and ran to the infirmary. John was awake and sitting up, having an argument with Edwin.

'Emma, talk to him,' Edwin said with exasperation as I entered. 'He can't just leap out of bed and go fight a war like this. He needs to slow down.'

'Are you feeling okay?' I asked John.

'Tired, and I ache all over, and some painkillers for the headache would be most welcome. It feels like Gold stuck a glass blade through my brain, but I'm good.'

'Do you need a hand back to your office?'

'Hold Edwin down while I escape.'

We both turned to Edwin. He gestured angrily towards John. 'You need to rest!'

John levered himself off the bed and winced as his feet hit the floor. He bent to put his forehead in his hand. 'Just something for the headache, Edwin.'

Edwin made a loud sound of frustration and stormed out.

I held my hand out and John looked at it for a long moment. I shoved it at him to make the point. He slumped even further and took my hand so I could check him.

'Don't do anything, just check,' he said.

I looked inside. The pain in his feet and head were feeding off each other, running through his meridians and multiplying with the stress, but his energy levels weren't as bad as I thought they'd be.

And then I was sucked into a huge dark vortex and I was *inside* his meridians, riding the energy through him, experiencing the rawness of his feet and the pounding in his head, and my centre was a huge gaping abyss that I needed to keep carefully under control to protect my beloved family when it would be so very easy to release the darkness and destroy everything ...

My brain exploded with a blast so cold it was like a brain freeze, and I jumped back and took a long defensive position. I cast around for whoever had struck me, checking behind me as well. I dropped my hands when I saw John standing in front of me.

'Just call my name, dammit! There was no need to snap-freeze my brain.'

'I did call your name, multiple times. I tried everything. We've been merged for nearly a minute.' He leaned back on the bed, grim with defeat. 'The Serpent is right. We're absorbing you.'

I took a step closer to him and gazed up into his eyes, and he stretched back, still pinned against the bed, to avoid touching me. I wrapped my arms around him and he relented and hugged me back, resting his cheek on the top of my head.

'Can you swallow me slowly until I'm completely lost into you?' I said. 'Never mind. Of course you can. That's how we snakes devour our prey.'

He pulled me tight. 'Focus on being yourself, a separate entity from me.'

'Is that a yes, you can swallow me?' I said.

'I've never done it.'

'This is a unique situation.'

'That it is. But I like to think both of me love you too much to do this to you.' He dropped his voice. 'If we ended this relationship, separated and lived apart, then neither of us would ever have to worry about this again.'

I pulled back to see his miserable face. 'Do you want to end our relationship?'

'No. Of course not.'

'Then we'll stay together.'

'Emma …'

'But we may consider a temporary separation as a last resort.'

'Very well. Once I am whole I will be able to control it. But if we become too much in synch, I warn you now that I will ask you for a separation until this is no longer an issue.'

'And I'll reluctantly agree, but I won't be happy about it.'

'Good. That's a relief.'

I shrugged. 'We're both so busy we hardly see each other anyway.'

'That's true. I have a million things I need to do.'

We released each other.

'Uh … if you two merge and she becomes a part of you, part of the Immortal Dark Lord,' Edwin said from the doorway, '…does that count as you Raising her?'

We gazed into each other's eyes again. We both knew the answer to that, and replied together.

'No.'

* * *

'Go right in, sir,' Yi Hao said outside my office.

Leo walked in and sat across the desk from me. I shuffled the student files to one side.

'You wanted to see me?' he said.

'They drugged him through an IV in the Serpent's back,' I said. 'Whatever it was worked so quickly he didn't have

217

a chance to neutralise it. Edwin analysed his reactions and says they probably anaesthetised him.'

'At least they didn't attack while he was out.' He studied me intensely. 'And you need to get some rest, Emma. Both of you are pushing yourselves too hard.'

I gestured towards him. 'You haven't been using your wheelchair lately.'

His expression went emotionless.

We sat looking at each other in silence for a long moment. Eventually I caved and put my forehead in my hand. 'Martin's turtle?'

'This is really none of your business,' he said.

'Maybe I should talk to your husband.'

His voice sharpened. 'Maybe you should butt the hell out.'

'Leo, John's a turtle too.'

'And?' he said, still irate.

'He's asked me.'

'He's asked you what? Stop talking in riddles and come to the point.'

I struggled to explain it without being crass and direct, then gave up. 'He asked me to have sex with his turtle.'

His face went blank, then filled with sympathy. 'Are you okay?' He reached across the desk to hold my hand. 'I hope this hasn't put a rift between you two. Your relationship is like a solid rock that holds the Mountain together.'

'Same with you two and the Northern Heavens,' I said, squeezing his hand. 'I'm not upset with him, I understand why he's asked. It would heal him. He'd have his feet completely back. He wouldn't be in pain any more. He'd stop trying to merge with me —'

He interrupted me. 'What?'

I waved it away. 'He's desperate to rejoin, and I'm close and I'm a reptile too.'

'You should have told me, Emma. If you're at risk then you should separate.'

'That's one of the reasons I'm asking you about this turtle thing. If we were to do it, he'd stop trying to merge with me.'

'I see. But …?'

'But it's just so damn freaky!'

'Damn straight it is,' he said. 'It's something I thought I'd never do. Hell, I was freaked out more than you are when Ming brought the subject up.'

'And?'

He released my hand and leaned back. 'Exactly how much do you want me to share here? I know you women discuss just about every single damn detail of your sex lives, but I'm a guy and you're like my sister and this is starting to feel really awkward.'

'Would I regret saying yes?'

'To having sex with him as a turtle?'

'Yes.'

'What form would you be in? Human or snake?'

'What form are you in with Martin?'

He hesitated for a long moment, then said, 'Both.' He saw my confusion. 'Sometimes human, sometimes lion.'

'You've done it more than once?'

He smiled slightly. 'Hell, yeah. So human or snake?'

'Human. He doesn't want to have anything to do with my snake.'

'That's a shame,' Leo said, the smile not shifting. 'The truer your form, the better it is.'

'Are you saying I wouldn't regret it?'

He visibly relaxed. 'It would be one of the greatest experiences of your life. Absolutely euphoric. Completely transcendental.' His eyes turned inward and his smile widened. 'Like a really good shen energy meditation, but with all your brain's pleasure centres lighting up at the same time. I don't know how he does it, but *damn* it's good.'

'Those are some of the words the Tiger used.'

'Don't ask the Tiger about this. Martin says he has no experience in the matter — the female turtles won't have anything to do with him.'

'I know. I didn't ask the Tiger; he's been pushing me to do it so that it'll heal John.'

'It will. It'll heal you too,' Leo said. He spread his hands slightly. 'Look at me. Out of the chair for a week every time we do it.'

'Way too much information.'

He waved me down. 'I think we've shared more information in the last five minutes than we ever have.'

I smiled at him. 'I know, and it wasn't nearly as awkward as I thought it would be. Thanks for being frank. I am so glad I have you.'

'Anything else you need, ma'am?'

'Should I do it?'

'That's your choice. If the idea freaks you out too much you won't be able to fully appreciate the experience. But ...' He leaned over the desk to grin knowingly at me. 'If you're willing to let go of your inhibitions and relax into it, it is completely worth it. It would be incredibly good for both of you. It would be so good for him — and make him so strong — that I'd like to say go right ahead and do it, because having him back to full strength will give the Celestial an edge we really need.'

'You are the last person in the world I'd expect to say go have sex with an animal,' I said.

'Hey, we're all animals. I'm a lion, you're a snake and these two are turtles.' He shrugged. 'It's a goddamn zoo around here. Couldn't get much weirder if we tried.'

'How's Butterfly?'

His grin widened. 'Buffy. She's settled in, decorated her room completely in pink lace and sparkles, loves fairies and princesses, and is the most wonderful thing ever to happen to us.'

'You make sure you give her trucks and Meccano as well as fairies and princesses,' I said sternly, poking my index finger at him. 'Don't you dare limit that child's experiences just because of her gender.'

He nodded. 'Don't worry, she has cars. She just likes the girly stuff, you know? Maybe it's because she didn't have anything really *pretty* at the orphanage. I'm sure she'll grow out of it in no time and hate pink as much as Simone did.'

'Simone had a Hello Kitty T-shirt on the other day,' I said. 'She said she was wearing it ironically.'

'Damn,' he said. 'Our daughter the hipster.'

'So many children in our lives. We have to protect them and keep them close.'

'And having him strong will give us an edge,' he said. 'So seriously, think about it. It won't hurt you — in fact, the experience is thoroughly worth it — and it would be really good for him.'

'That's very similar to what the Tiger said. Have you been talking to him?'

'Absolutely not,' he growled. 'That damn cat stays well away from me. You can't have two big male cats anywhere near each other. One day I will take him on in True Form and we'll see whose claws are sharper.'

'I would like to see that.' I went around the desk to give him a quick hug around his huge shoulders. 'Thanks, Leo.'

'No problem, honey,' he said, and went out.

I sat behind the desk and opened the spreadsheets but didn't really see them. Having John strong could possibly mean the difference between victory and defeat.

A stone appeared above my desk with an audible pop.

'Can I help you?' I said.

'Help, General Danahuo,' she said. 'My Ronnie — there's something terribly wrong with him.'

I leapt to my feet. 'Where is he?'

'In the demon quarters here on the Mountain.'

I tapped the stone and didn't wait for it to reply. 'Stone. Ronnie Wong's in trouble. Call Edwin —' I changed my mind; he needed a demon master, not a human doctor. 'Call LK.'

'LK's with him,' the stone said. 'Silica, you know what this is.'

'Your demon master is wrong. He's just sick,' Silica said, floating next to me at eye level as I headed towards the demon barracks. 'He looks so old, and he hardly knows who I am.'

I stopped. 'Oh dear Lord. I am so sorry, Silica.'

She changed to human form. 'No, he's sick. He's unwell. He has to be.'

'He's Ascending, dear one,' the stone said with compassion.

Her face crumpled. 'He's just sick.'

'Go directly back to him. You don't have long to say goodbye,' the stone said.

Silica released a huge gasping sob, changed to stone form and disappeared.

222

'Does the Dark Lord know?' I said.

'He does. He abandoned a meeting to be present at Ronnie's Ascension. This is a momentous occasion.'

'Not for Silica.'

'It is highly unusual for a demon to Ascend and leave loved ones behind.'

'I know. Ah Yat cried for a long time because she didn't want to leave Simone when she went.' I dropped my voice. 'I wonder where she is now.'

'She is on a journey. She is searching for the Way. Now that she has gained free will and a higher consciousness, she will find it more easily. Be happy for her, Emma,' the stone said.

'I am.'

I arrived at the demon barracks to find a group of demons gathered around the door. I went inside and through the sparsely furnished main quarters to Ronnie's private rooms at the end.

'... and I refuse to go,' Ronnie was saying.

He was lying on his bunk with Silica, LK and John kneeling around him. Silica was next to his head and held his hand. Ronnie was hardly recognisable: he had aged twenty years, but at the same time seemed glowingly youthful.

'The fact that you deny Ascension is proof that you are ready for it,' John said, his voice calm and low. 'Be glad that you are Ascending. Your will is now your own.'

'But I won't remember who I am!' Ronnie said, trying to lift himself and failing. 'I won't leave Silica and forget what I had with her!'

'You will remember eventually,' John said.

'Do *you* remember all of your past?' Ronnie said.

'When you are Raised it becomes part of you again, but not a complete memory — even the mind of an Immortal

223

cannot handle the weight of all history,' John said. 'It is said that when you attain the highest level and become a Buddha, all of your past lives are laid before you and the full wisdom you have gained from many lifetimes is finally accessible.'

'Let yourself go,' Silica said, now much calmer, but with tears streaming down her face. 'You will have free will and the opportunity to be something much greater. I love you and I will miss you, but this is what you need to do. I will go on without you and I will be just fine.'

'I will find you again, Silica,' Ronnie said. 'I will always love you, you made my life so happy for this short time. Search for me, because I will always be searching for you ...'

He collapsed back onto the bed then exploded into a cloud of glowing black particles.

We held our breath as the black particles hung suspended in the air. They changed to gold, coalesced into a shining ball of light, and descended through the floor. We all let out our breath with relief.

I wiped my eyes. He'd made it, but it was hard to feel happy for him with Silica sitting next to the bed, her face blank with shock.

'It happened so fast,' she whispered.

'That is often the way when we lose the ones we love. It takes only a moment and they are gone,' John said, his voice mirroring her grief.

'I am glad I had a chance to tell him I loved him.' She looked up at John. 'Is that possible? For him to find me?'

'The long answer to your question is: if your bond is true and your hearts are destined to be together, then nothing can keep them apart.' John glanced at me, then turned back to Silica. 'The short answer is: yes.'

She nodded. 'Thank you, my Lord, you have eased my pain. He will find me.' She disappeared.

John took my hand to help me to stand, and we went out.

LK followed us. 'While I have you here, can I talk to you for a moment?'

'As soon as we've resolved the current Hell situation we'll find you a successor,' John said.

'I already had a successor lined up — but he just Ascended.'

'A demon can't be demon master,' I said.

'Just because it's never been done before doesn't mean it can't happen now,' LK said. 'There's no reason why a smart strong demon can't be demon master, and they won't have the problems that we do.'

I nodded. 'You have a point. Do you have anybody else who would be suitable?'

LK shook his head.

'Take your time and find a new master when everything has settled down,' John said.

'I can't. Look.' LK raised his hands. His fingernails and the tips of his fingers were black.

John studied them. 'You should have told us. Does it burn?'

'It's keeping me awake at night.'

'Then we need to find someone right now,' John said.

'Nigel's offered to take the job back until we can find someone new,' LK said. 'We just need to do the handover in your office.'

'Nigel can't do it,' John said.

'He has to; he's the only one available with the knowledge to handle it,' LK said.

'He'll deteriorate quicker than you,' I said. 'You have to find someone new.'

LK spread his hands. 'Everybody's busy with this war business. Nobody's free.'

'Did you ask the Tiger?'

'He can't spare anyone either.'

'You are stood down,' John said. 'You are to have no more contact with demons. Your full-time position is now finding a replacement for yourself. Search the Celestial from top to bottom — and I include Hell — to find someone, because you are off demon management immediately.'

'But —' LK began.

John glared at him. 'You are not to have any more contact with demons. That is an order. Am I completely understood?'

'We can't run the Mountain with nobody to manage the demons!' LK protested.

'Then. Find. Someone,' John said, very slowly and clearly. 'You are no longer demon master. I gave you an order. Don't make me back it up with an imperative.'

LK shook his hands in front of his face. 'My Lord.'

John stopped for a moment and concentrated, and the order went throughout the Mountain that we needed a new demon master immediately and all applications were welcome.

'A quick hug, then I'll go over to the Celestial Palace and announce it there so all the Heavens know,' John said to me, and put his arms out.

'No need, my Lord, I'll do it,' Franklin said as he scurried across the square towards us.

'Look at you,' I said, gesturing at him. He was panting from the mild effort and leaned his hands on his knees. He was completely emaciated, his sallow skin hanging in folds and his dark-rimmed eyes sunken and red. 'You need to go to the West right now.'

'I appreciate the offer, Franklin, but it would kill you,' LK said. 'Go to the West.'

'I'm glad I caught you,' Franklin said. He straightened to speak to John. 'How long do you think it will take me to recover there?'

'You need to be there permanently, Franklin. Here is much too far from your Centre,' John said.

'But I can do it!' Franklin said. 'I want to be useful. If someone can shuttle me back and forth I might be able to — but how long do I have to stay there before I can return?'

John thought about it for a moment, then waved Franklin closer. He held out his hand and Franklin took it.

John studied him, his dark eyes intense. 'You are very close, Franklin. Three weeks.'

'Back here?'

'How long has he been living here, Emma?'

'Three months.'

'Three months and you've deteriorated to a life-threatening level, but three weeks in the Western Heavens is worth double any stay in the Earthly West. It will be six months before you need to return there,' John said.

'Three weeks in the West, then six months here. I can do it, provided someone will take me there,' Franklin said. 'It can work!'

'What do you think, Emma?' John said.

I folded my arms over my chest. 'He certainly has the brains ...'

Franklin lit up.

'He has the attitude, he's a hard worker.' I shrugged. 'He'd be perfect if it weren't for this Centre business.'

'LK?'

227

'Delighted to see a demon doing the job. It's about time,' LK said. 'I know damn well nobody else will step forward. Until I found Ronnie no one showed any interest in the job.'

'Just tell me what I need to do,' Franklin said.

'Very well,' John said. 'You can take it on when you return.'

Franklin held his hand out for LK to shake and LK raised his own hands. 'Sorry, my friend, look at me.'

Franklin dropped his hand, concerned. 'You're in a worse state than me. You should show me the job remotely so I'm not too close to you.'

'Do it over webcam,' I said.

'That works,' LK said. He nodded to Franklin. 'Come to my office, we'll set it up.'

'No,' John said. 'No close contact. Have Gold arrange the link. Franklin, pack immediately and I will take you to the West right now; you won't last the day. You should have told me.'

'He's that bad?' I said.

'He's that bad. Franklin, go and put some stuff in a bag and meet me at the entrance to the Folly in five minutes.'

Franklin stood with his mouth open.

'Move!'

Franklin jumped and scurried a few steps to the demon quarters, then staggered and walked more slowly.

'Liaise with Gold to set up the webcam,' John said to LK. He turned his intense dark gaze on him. 'Under no circumstances are you to have any contact with demons in the next three weeks before Franklin returns. We will manage without a demon master until then.'

'My Lord,' LK said.

'Dismissed,' John said, and LK headed back towards the administration section.

John smiled down at me. 'Are you free for about thirty minutes or so when I'm back from taking Franklin to the West?'

'Oh, absolutely,' I said with enthusiasm. 'I can give you a whole hour.'

His smile widened. 'Good.'

17

The next morning, I was at my desk when the tower bells began to ring. I tapped the stone.

'Hm?'

'The bells are ringing for battle stations. Find out what's up.'

'Okay.'

I headed out of my office towards the centre of the administrative section. The weapons master, Miss Chen, was locking up the armoury and I went to her.

She spoke before I was close enough to say anything. 'Go to the Residence and stay there with the doors shut. Dark Lord's orders.'

'Where is he?'

'Don't bother looking for him.'

'Okay.' I moved to walk around her and continue to the administrative section.

She put one arm out to stop me. 'No, Emma, damn. Please go back into the Residence and lock up. This is big.'

I ignored her and went towards the southwest corner of the wall where it joined with the administrative section and John's office, and provided a good view over the mountains.

'Stone?'

'Actually, Emma, locking yourself in the Imperial Residence is a good idea. It's the King himself.'

I stopped halfway over a moon bridge that spanned one of the Mountain's immensely deep gorges. 'Here? He's attacking the Mountain?' I turned to go to the Residence where I'd be safe. John himself kept the seals on the Residence fresh.

'To parley.'

I turned around again. 'Ask John if he needs me.'

'He'd prefer you stayed in the Residence. Zara will relay to me and you can advise from inside where you're safe.'

I hesitated, undecided. 'He needs my moral support. He's hurting badly, stone.'

'New message. The King has guaranteed your safety. The Dark Lord and Princess Yue request your counsel in Stone Boulder House.' The stone's voice filled with caution. 'The King says he wants to say hello.'

'I'll say hello with the Murasame between his third and fourth ribs,' I growled, heading for the west gate.

'You are aware that would be completely ineffective because he doesn't have a heart?'

'That has become intensely obvious over the last fifteen years.'

I ran five metres up the wall at the west gate until I was on top of the battlements. I ran an eye over the defending Disciples stationed on top of the wall, then selected two of the finest warriors of their cohort to accompany me.

'Scotty, Julie, you'll be at my back while we talk to the Demon King,' I said.

'We're profoundly honoured, ma'am,' Julie said.

We jumped off the wall to land lightly on the rocks fifteen metres below. They followed me, alert, as I walked down the path to the village house that the Mountain personnel used to meet with demons who were unable to enter the Academy's seals. The seals that we were pretending still existed.

'The Demon King's in there talking to the Dark Lord,' I said softly as we approached the house. 'You're more of a formality than anything. I would lose face by going in alone and we need to put on a show. Station yourselves behind me, weapons sheathed, and be ready for trouble if the demons do something to the Dark Lord. Princess Yue Gui is there; follow her lead.'

'Ma'am,' they said.

I took a deep breath to calm myself and went into the house.

John was sitting on one of the couches with Yue standing behind him. She wasn't in her usual black and silver Tang robes and hair ornaments; she was wearing a plain Mountain uniform with her hair tied back in a simple bun. The Demon King sat across from John, with his Number One son standing behind his couch mirroring Yue. I nodded to my guards and they positioned themselves next to the wall.

'Ah, here she is,' the Demon King said, jovial. 'Now that the Dark Lord's brain is here, we can begin.'

'I needed my brains,' John said, unfazed.

'So how are you feeling, Emma?' the King said as I pulled a rosewood chair closer and sat in it. 'Sorry about leaving you out in the cold like that, but it was your choice. You look like you're recovering well.'

'I'll get there.'

He leaned one elbow on the arm of the couch. 'Offer's still open, honey. I hear you can come and teach now. We'd love to have you.'

I gestured towards John. 'Talk to my husband. I have nothing to say to you.'

'You'll both be in trouble referring to each other that way when the ceremony hasn't taken place yet. The Jade Emperor is very big on proper procedure,' the King said. He turned to John. 'I wish to parley under terms of truce.'

'Speak your mind,' John said.

The Demon King leaned back and studied John, his eyes full of amusement. 'Looking good, Ah Wu. I hope you're feeling better — we didn't know your poor snake's tail was infected. The antibiotics fixed it right up, it should be fine. Can you grow it back? We want to do that again, it was great fun.'

'I doubt it will grow back.'

'How far up did it go on you? Did you lose your feet entirely? Your ankles as well?' The Demon King grinned. 'I'm surprised you're not bleeding all over the place, to be honest. Tremendous force of will to keep your poor sore feet whole like that, must be exhausting.' He leaned forward to speak intensely, the grin growing vicious. 'You stood silently by and watched as this was done to women for a thousand years. You still stand and watch as they're mutilated today. We would cut your dick off as well if we could. How does it feel when it's happening to you?'

'Do you have a point, or are you just here to taunt me?' John said. 'I have places I need to be.'

'Oh, come on, Ah Wu,' the Demon King said, spreading his hands. 'It's not every day we can share a cup of tea like this.' He swept one hand over the coffee table and tiny cups of black liquid appeared. 'Or even better, something to banish the winter chills.' He raised one of the cups. 'Yum sing.' He downed it quickly.

Yue shot me a look. John sat unmoving. The black liquid in the cups was snake bile, harvested from the snake as it writhed in its death throes, and drunk, as the Demon King said, to banish winter chills.

John rose and bowed slightly to the King. 'I apologise. I am vegetarian. I cannot share your hospitality. If this is what you came for, I suggest we not waste each other's time.'

'Damn. Emma is so much more fun than you are,' the King said. 'Okay, okay, sit down, playtime's over. Let's put the deal on the table.' He gestured and the snake bile disappeared, to be replaced by a stack of ordinary A4 paper. 'You know damn well you nearly lost Hell the other day, and it's only a matter of time before we wear you down. Once we have Hell, the rest will be easy. But we can end this now. Nobody else needs to die. You can keep your half of Hell, and we stay on our side. Sign this now and the war is over. We can shake hands and go home, and your precious Celestial Plane is safe.'

'If I give you the Earthly, you will raise an army and try for the Celestial anyway.'

The Demon King put one hand on the stack of paper. 'You can't have seen this yet. How do you know it gives us the Earthly?'

'I know you. You've been trying to retake the Earthly ever since I drove you off. This treaty probably forces us to relinquish the Earthly Plane to you with no restrictions. In return, you give us guaranteed safety on our side of Hell and everything on the Celestial Plane. But there'll be a loophole in the treaty that allows you to raise an army on the Earthly and make a try for Heaven.'

The Demon King's eyes went wide with admiration. 'Damn, Ah Wu, you are seriously good.'

John flicked one hand over the stack of papers. 'How long would it keep you out of the Celestial before you tried us?'

The King hesitated, then said, 'Three years.'

'Plenty of time for you to raise an army on the Earthly. We're better off taking our chances now.'

The Demon King tapped the treaty with his index finger. 'Are there any changes we could make that would result in a signature?'

'No time limit. No loopholes. You give us the Celestial, we give you the Earthly in perpetuity,' John said. 'Hell we divide as it's always been.'

'You'd sign that? You'd let us out onto the Earthly with no restrictions on harming humans?'

'Only the Jade Emperor would have sufficient seniority to sign such a treaty, but we'd definitely give it serious consideration after what happened in Hell. Redraft it and halt your attacks for a week while we look at it.'

'Stalling? I don't think so. I'll give you forty-eight hours to look at it,' the Demon King said.

'I want a ceasefire while you draft it and while we look at it.'

'Done,' the King said. 'I'll send you a revised treaty in twenty-four hours. You have two days after that to make your decision.' He leaned forward to speak intensely to John. 'Understand, Ah Wu, we have the Western horde as well as our own. What you saw in Hell was *nothing*; it was just our weakest and most expendable.' He leaned back. 'And we nearly had you. If you lose Hell it's all over, my friend, so let's finish this now. Agree to the new treaty and we can be friends again. No one else need suffer. The Earthly is the world of ruin anyway, it's not worth your time to defend it. Stay up here where it's pure and bright, and leave the humans to their hatred, greed and corruption. It's their world anyway, and they're making such a mess of it that they deserve to have us among them.'

'I will give you my answer in three days,' John said. 'Until then we have a ceasefire.'

'Done,' the King said. He rose and put out his hand.

John eyed it without moving from the couch. 'Seriously?'

'Good faith Western-style,' the King said. 'I know you are a creature of your word.' He smiled slightly. 'You're not the only one dipping into the pleasures of the West and learning a whole new set of skills.'

John rose, shook the Demon King's hand, then sat again. The King and his Number One left.

'Number One, escort them from the Heavens,' John said without looking up.

'My Lord,' Yue said, and went out to join them.

Emma, you chose two Europeans as your honour guard, John said. *Think more carefully next time.*

'Oh damn,' I said softly. 'It never occurred to me. I just selected the most talented two that were there.'

'I can see that,' John said. He sighed, leaned forward to put his elbows on his knees and rubbed his hands over his face. 'If I give him the Earthly, the war will be over. Many lives will be saved.'

'That's not an option, is it?' Julie said from her post next to the wall. 'Really? Because my mom —'

'I know, Julie. We know,' I said.

'If it came to all-out war, could they beat us?' Scott said, his voice weak. 'He said they could win.'

John looked at them, his gaze fierce. 'It would be a close thing. But if it comes to war, win or lose, many lives are destroyed.'

'And if they take over the Earthly?' Julie said.

'It's hard to imagine which is a worse option,' I said.

'We have a very tough decision to make,' John said.

'I'm glad I don't have your job,' Scott said.

'It's not a job I'd wish on anyone,' I said.

John waved the Disciples closer. 'Come and I'll wipe your memories.'

'No need,' I said. 'They're senior Disciples. Neither of them will share anything they learned here today.'

'I know, because I'll make sure of it.' John stopped and concentrated for a moment. 'Yue says that the King really is leaving; he's keeping his word about the ceasefire. Let's use these three days to prepare.' He nodded to the Disciples and they approached him.

'Don't do this,' I said.

Julie and Scott fell to their knees in front of John. Julie turned on her knees to speak to me. 'It's okay, ma'am, it's definitely for the best. I shouldn't know about this.'

'She's right,' Scott said.

'They'll forget everything up until what Julie just said,' John said, putting his finger on Julie's forehead. 'They'll remember agreeing to have it done.'

I leaned on the wall and crossed my arms. 'It's wrong. You shouldn't mess with our own people's heads.'

'I don't need to do it often, because I'm aware of security,' John said, unfocused. He changed to Scott, and Julie rose to stand next to me. She patted my arm.

'It's part of our duties, ma'am. If the Dark Lord doesn't want us to know, then we shouldn't know.'

John finished Scott and helped him to his feet. 'Both of you wait outside.'

After they'd gone out I asked him, 'Have you ever made me forget anything I shouldn't have heard?'

He rose from the couch and went to the door without looking at me, his expression full of restraint.

'You have?' I said with horror.

I tried to push past him to go out, and he turned to stand in front of the door and leaned on it, blocking me.

'Emma, stop. No. I haven't. Never.' He pointed at his nose. 'Look at me. No. I never have.'

I looked up into his eyes and saw the honesty there. 'Never?'

'Never. Trust me.' He uncrossed his arms and sagged. 'You've given your permission every time we've been inside your head.' He made a helpless gesture. 'That's one of the reasons why I don't like doing it. You're correct: it's wrong.'

'You had no trouble doing it to them,' I said, pointing at the door.

'And next time you won't bring low-security humans along when we have a high-security meeting.'

My breath left me with a gasp as I realised. 'You had to do that because of my mistake in bringing them here. Even though they can be completely trusted, they could still be captured and their minds read by a powerful enough demon. I should have brought an Immortal or Shen, not ordinary humans.'

'Now she understands.'

I leaned my head on his chest and he wrapped his arms around me. 'I am totally unfit for this job.'

'So am I.' He levered himself off the door, still holding me. 'But we do our best, and make mistakes, and hope that not too many lives are lost when we mess up. In this case, it

238

was just a short-term memory for a couple of students and they'll be proud to have made the sacrifice.' He opened the door. 'Let's go up and find something to eat. Neither of us had breakfast and it's already lunchtime.'

'I don't feel like eating,' I said.

'Neither do I. But we will eat anyway because we need to be strong.' He raised his head and his eyes unfocused. 'The Jade Emperor has requested an immediate report on this meeting.' He turned to me. 'You weren't summoned too?'

'No, thank the Heavens,' I said. 'He's finally giving me a chance to recuperate.'

The summons hit me and he saw it. I sighed and he took my hand.

* * *

The trip to the Celestial Palace never knocked us out: the Jade Emperor was probably helping. But it didn't stop us from clutching each other, dizzy, as we landed. We nodded when we were both ready and strode into the minor audience hall. The Jade Emperor was sitting there as if he hadn't moved since we'd seen him last. We knelt before him and he waved for us to sit.

'What is your opinion of sacrificing the Earthly to retain control of Hell and Heaven?' he said as we sat.

John and I shared a look; this level of directness from him was unheard of.

'I think we can hold the Earthly without compromising control of our side of Hell,' John said.

'I agree. When he returns tomorrow with the new treaty, wait the full two days then tell him no. He will immediately attack Hell. Be ready, Ah Wu.'

'I will, Majesty,' John said, his voice cold and grim.

'Dismissed,' the Emperor said. 'Use these three days to prepare our defences.'

'Majesty,' we said in unison, rose, saluted him and went out.

* * *

Your eleven o'clock appointment is here, ma'am, Yi Hao said the next morning.

'Come on in, Kenny,' I shouted at the door.

Kenny was a sweet American senior who was a complete genius with energy. He'd arrived after the Mountain had moved back to Heaven and had never known Lok, so he'd asked to speak to me about a personal matter. Lok needed to rebuild his status as a trusted advisor for the students, but it wouldn't take long.

Kenny fell to one knee and saluted me, and I waved for him to sit on the other side of the desk. 'What can I do for you, Kenny?'

He looked down at his hands, obviously uncomfortable. 'I love being here. This is the greatest place I've ever been, I've learned so much ...' He looked up into my eyes, his own full of pain.

'There's no shame in leaving,' I said. 'It's completely your choice and we respect that.'

His eyes went wide. 'How do you know I want to leave?'

'You're the fifth student this morning.'

'Who else ... No, it doesn't matter.' He dropped his head again. 'Do you remember what I was like when I first arrived?'

I made a soft sound of amusement. 'You were a complete tool.'

He grinned. 'That's the word for it! Although Mui Linh uses the word "douche". I can't believe that stupid car was so important to me. And wearing other people's names across my chest ...' He shook his head. 'What was I thinking? I took martial arts purely to kick people's asses. To feel like a big man by beating people up, by physically ...' He searched for the word.

'Dominating them,' I said. 'It's the ultimate argument winner, the ultimate proof that you're better: by violently defeating someone. Back then, it was all around you and it was important. I'm glad you saw through it.'

'So am I. "Things" were important,' he said with regret. 'Competition to have things. I had that damn car, I had designer shit ...' He winced. 'Sorry, ma'am. Well, I had stuff. Things. And they didn't make me happy. Showing them off to other people was supposed to make me feel big and important, and maybe it did for like, five minutes, and then the other people walked away.' He smiled slightly. 'So I bought more stuff to feel more important. Shinier stuff, gold stuff, more expensive sunglasses ... damn.' He shook his head. 'I was such a tool.'

'I have to admit that I was completely astonished when you passed the DN4.'

He opened his mouth to say something, then stopped, confused. 'What's the DN4? I don't remember taking any test called that.'

'You'll know when I describe it. Back in the first week, you were called out of bed at 4 am and told to report to the mess. Remember?'

'Oh yeah. There was nobody there, so I waited a while and then realised it was probably Juan's idea of a bad joke and headed back to the barracks. But there was this girl outside ...' His expression filled with understanding. 'That was a test?'

'Anyone who would behave even slightly inappropriately towards a drunk naked woman they found outside the barracks at 4 am isn't worthy of the Mountain uniform.'

'I never even thought of that. I just wanted to help her.' He smiled, remembering. 'I gave her my T-shirt with the designer name on it.'

'That was the beginning of you finding out what really makes you important.'

He lit up again. 'You helped, ma'am. Remember how much I complained when you gave me two first-year students to mentor instead of one? I thought you were picking on me.'

I hissed with laughter. 'I was.'

'And then they both moved up and thanked me for helping them — and that was worth more than any name on my chest.'

'I'm glad.'

'Anyway, that's all behind me now. I just wanted to say thank you. But I don't want to be involved in a war. I don't want to fight in an army. That's not me any more; I'm not a soldier.'

'You have gained so much wisdom in three years, Kenny.' My voice thickened. 'I am so damn proud of you.'

He was silent for a long moment, then wiped his eyes. 'You're not disappointed?'

'Of course not. I'll arrange for someone to take you home, with our blessings, and I hope that you can return when this is all finished, because you are a fine practitioner and a magnificent human being.'

'I don't want to go home.' He saw my confusion. 'I mean, I do want to leave, but I don't want to go back there.' He wiped his eyes again. 'Is there a monastery somewhere that would take me? Or can I join one of the temples here? I want to continue to help people.'

'No,' I said. 'You're not ready to withdraw from life. You're far too young and have a lot of living to do. Maybe when you're older, but for now: no.'

'But it's what I want.'

'Good. You should go home and be with your family.'

'They're abusive fucks,' he said with venom, then winced again. 'Sorry. It's just ... they're not good people. I talked to Master Liu about it, and she agrees with me. If people are toxic then sometimes it's just best not to be near them.'

I had an inspiration. 'Okay, then, I have a job for you. The orphans are being moved to a tropical beachside resort in Australia, and we need guards and,' I smiled slightly, 'the kids will need "camp counsellors". I think you'd be perfect for the job.'

He grinned broadly. '*Seriously?*'

'Leo will be there too.'

He sat straighter, bouncing in his chair. 'You really mean it? This is true? Wow, ma'am ...' He was wide-eyed with delight. 'Helping kids? Orphans? On a *beach resort?*'

Tears started to stream down his face and I handed him the box of tissues.

He ripped a couple out and unselfconsciously wiped his eyes, then blew his nose. 'Count me in.'

'Stand up,' I said sternly.

He jumped to attention, serious but still tearful.

He watched me, nervous, as I rose, walked around the desk and gave him a hug. He was much taller than me and he jerked with surprise, then bent to hug me back.

'Thanks, Emma,' he said.

243

'Yi Hao,' I said loudly without letting him go. 'Contact Brother Chang. Tell him that this young man is to join the orphans in Australia, to help guard and care for them.' I released Kenny and patted him on the shoulder. 'You'll do great.'

Kenny fell to one knee, saluted me, then took some more tissues and went out.

He poked his head back in with a huge grin. 'You're the *best*, Emma.'

I waved him down and went back behind the desk. I thought with regret about what I was doing: war was the ultimate way of winning an argument by force.

I stiffened; John had summoned me exactly the same way the Jade Emperor did, demanding my presence in the war room. I rose and stomped out of my office.

At Yi Hao's desk I stopped and spoke to her. 'I've been called. I'll be back as soon as I can.'

I patted Kenny on the back and stormed towards the war room.

Sorry, my mistake, John said. *That was just a general summons to some senior Mountain and Heavens staff. We have a difficult decision to make.*

I shook my head as I headed towards the war room at a more leisurely pace.

18

The demons had already set up the war room for a meeting. A black and silver embroidered cloth depicting ancient warriors in battle on horseback and on foot covered the conference table. Some of the warriors on the cloth were recognisably John and the Thirty-Six.

John sat in the centre of the group and all of the senior staff were there: the Lius, Martin, Yue Gui, Ma, and even Guan Yu had come from guarding the Gates. I stopped when I saw them all sitting grimly at the table. John gestured for me to join them, sitting at his right hand. I nearly argued about the inappropriateness of him having a low-ranking human concubine at his right hand — a more senior position than both his Number Ones — then decided to leave it. This looked serious; they hadn't even saluted.

When I was sitting, John opened a scroll and read from it.

'Supreme Emperor of the Dark Northern Heavens, Celestial Master of the Nine Mysteries, et cetera et cetera, from

His Loathsome Majesty King of the Demons and so on.' He glanced up. 'I'll skip the formal bullshit. He wants to give us the treaty at noon today.' He dropped the scroll and raised his hand. 'Before you all shout at me for dragging you here when we knew it was noon today anyway: he wants to give us the treaty in person, in his own throne room in Hell, and he will only give it to Emma and myself. The two of us, and only the two of us, must go there to collect it, otherwise the deal is off.'

There was complete silence.

'Don't,' Meredith said.

'Are we ready for war now?' Yue said.

'Yes, but another two days would be significant,' Ma said.

'More significant than losing me?' John said.

Ma leaned back. 'Hard to say.'

John spread his hands. 'That's why you're here. Risk me, or go to war now. Choose.'

'Has he guaranteed our safety?' I said.

There was a chorus of derisive noises.

'Yes,' John said. He indicated around the table. 'And it's obvious what everybody thinks of that.'

'Make the choice, then check the future to see where it leads,' Liu said.

'I am,' John said. His eyes went wide. 'No.' He looked around at the gathered Shen. 'We can't do this! There has to be some other way.'

'We must,' Guan Yu said. 'We are sworn to protect the Celestial. All of us are. It must be done.'

'Well?' I said.

John didn't reply. He studied the Demon King's scroll. The other two Generals shifted uncomfortably.

'Tell me!' I said. 'I can't advise you if I don't know all the facts.' Then I realised David Hawkes had said nearly the same thing to me. I looked around the table, then back at John. 'Dear Lord, it's really that bad?'

'We smaller Shen need to know as well, my Lord,' Meredith said, her voice full of compassion.

John stared into her eyes.

'Not good enough,' I said. 'Out loud. You tell her, you tell me.'

Meredith's face filled with shock, then dismay. She rose and went out.

'So we lose,' I said. 'Either way, we lose. Which choice gives us a loss with fewer casualties?'

'No, we may still win,' John said. 'If both of us go down and collect the treaty, we could still win this. If we don't go down there, we will definitely lose. We will lose everything: Hell and the Earthly will be overrun, and Heaven will fall.'

'Then we go collect the treaty,' I said. 'Why the grim faces? We just go get it.' I understood with an electric shock down to my feet. 'We lose Lord Xuan.'

'We aren't sure of that.' John fingered the scroll, his face a mask of misery. 'I cannot be predicted. I am too primal and chaotic.' He gazed into my eyes. 'But your future is easy to see.'

'What?' I said, glancing around the table at their rigid faces. Nobody said anything. 'What?'

'Tell her,' Ma said, gesturing towards me. 'She needs to know, my Lord. This is just as much her decision as it is ours. More, even.'

'No,' John said.

'Tell me,' I said.

John was quiet for a long time, studying the scroll.

'Only one of you will return,' Guan Yu eventually said.

'Which one of us?'

'That is our choice. Him or you.'

'If you return with the treaty, he will remain in Hell, joined with the Serpent and imprisoned,' Ma said.

John put his forehead in his hand.

'If he is imprisoned, we will lose. That is definite,' Guan Yu said.

'So he has to come back with the treaty,' I said. 'But without me?'

'If he returns with the treaty, he will return alone,' Ma said.

'So what happens to me?' I said. 'They'll hold me hostage?'

'You will die,' Guan Yu said.

Everything blanked out for a minute as the shock of the knowledge hit me, then I pulled myself together. 'The only way we have a chance is if I die?'

'Yes,' Guan Yu said.

'I will definitely die?'

'Yes,' Ma said.

'So it's either me or the whole Celestial?'

'Good,' Guan Yu said. 'You understand what's at stake. Not just the whole Celestial. The Earthly and Hell as well. You, or … everything.'

I dropped my head for a moment, saddened that I didn't have time to say a proper goodbye to everybody.

Ma spoke, his voice soft and urgent. 'Please be willing to do this.'

'Of course I'm willing,' I said.

John slumped in his seat, still with his face in his hand.

'You'll Raise me,' I said to him. 'You promised.'

He didn't move or speak.

'That is not something we can predict. The Dark Lord is too primal and powerful to foresee; we can only see the future around him,' Guan Yu said. 'But if we are to have any chance of winning this war, then you both must go down and collect this treaty, he must return with it, and you will die.'

'Will you shut the fuck up and stop telling her she has to die!' John shouted. He spun in his chair and turned away.

'Is there another option?' I said.

'Of course not,' Ma said. 'If there is, hurry and think of one. You have less than an hour to be there. But I don't think even you are that clever.'

'What does the Jade Emperor say?'

They went silent.

'We must decide,' Ma said. 'He says the decision is obvious but we must make it ourselves.'

'Seeing into the future isn't an advantage sometimes, is it?' I said. 'We would all sacrifice ourselves in a second if it would keep the Heavens safe.'

'This is not sacrificing myself. This is sacrificing the one I love,' John said, still turned away.

'This is not your sacrifice to make. This is mine,' I said. 'You have no say in the matter.'

He spun to face me and glared into my eyes for a long moment without speaking.

'Thank you for not arguing with me.' I shrugged. 'You vowed to Raise me anyway. It will happen.' I rose. 'Let the Demon King know that we'll go down and collect the treaty. I'll be outside passing my final wishes on to Meredith. You know what needs to be done.'

I kissed the top of John's head, patted his shoulder, and went out to find Meredith. She was sitting on a bench in the courtyard outside the war room with her head in her hands.

I sat next to her and put my arm around her shoulders. 'You really shouldn't let the students see you like this.'

Her voice was hoarse with emotion. 'Bloody good for them to see that we're not invincible.'

'Don't be so upset at the prospect of losing me. I'm just a friend. You've lost thousands of friends over your long life.'

'You're more like a daughter, dear,' she said.

'He'll Raise me.'

'I hope so.' She wiped her eyes with the back of her hand. 'It's not just you. There's a very good chance that we could still lose this war, the Heavens will fall, and everyone we love will be enslaved. Our students and families will be singled out for particular torment.'

'Losing is not an option. There's a couple of things I want you to do for me.'

'Anything.'

'Call Simone in so I can say goodbye.'

'She's already on her way.' Meredith's expression filled with wonder. 'She understands.'

'Of course she does. Tell my family goodbye, and that I loved them, and that I'm sorry I put them through so much grief. Where's Leo?'

'On the Earthly with his daughter.'

'Tell him goodbye for me as well.'

'He's not replying.'

'I'm not surprised. If I don't return, destroy the Murasame. That damn blade should have been melted down a long time ago. I can barely control it, and I doubt anyone else short of John himself is capable of holding back its destructive nature.'

'Done.'

'Care for my demons. Smally isn't to return to the laundry, she's to be given something more rewarding.'

'Who's ... Never mind. I'll find her.'

'Thank you.' I shrugged. 'I'm sure I've missed a lot of things but that's all I can think of right now.'

'One thing before you go down there,' she said.

'Yes?'

'For god's sake, Emma,' she smiled slightly. 'In more ways than one. For all of our sakes — don't let him use Seven Stars. Don't even let him take it. Don't let him summon it. For god's sake, don't let him use Seven Stars on the Demon King.'

'I know, believe me. The knowledge of what it would do keeps me awake at night,' I said.

'He told you what it would do?'

'The King's essence will wipe out John's chakras in the sword and his sentience with them. He'll become a mindless nature spirit, and he may even lose his Celestial alignment.'

'Don't tell Simone, but his vow to Raise you will be destroyed as well. He must not use Seven Stars.'

I considered for a moment. 'Can you stop it from leaving the armoury?'

'No. It's part of him; that's why this is so damn dangerous. If he loses his temper and attacks the King with it ...'

'I'll talk to him before we go.'

'Thank you.'

She looked over my shoulder, and I turned to see behind me. It was John.

'Meredith, out,' he said.

Meredith nodded, rose and left. John sat next to me on the bench and held both my hands in his, then bent and touched them to his forehead.

'Let's just run away together,' he said. 'We can find somewhere safe and quiet on a mountain top on the Earthly and disappear. We can live out our lives as humans and share a happy existence, at one with the Tao and at peace.'

'And Simone?'

He was silent.

'And Leo? And Martin and Yue? And our students? All our friends, our family, our colleagues, our subjects?'

He still didn't reply.

I squeezed his hands, still on his forehead. 'You can do this.'

'It's so easy to sacrifice myself to keep the Heavens safe,' he said. 'It takes so much more courage to sacrifice you.'

'You will Raise me. I trust you.'

He bent with grief, still with my hands on his forehead. 'I wish I trusted myself as much.' He straightened, lowered my hands and looked into my eyes. 'Are you absolutely sure about doing this?'

'Yes, I'm sure.'

'Say it again,' he said.

'I'm sure. I trust you. You will Raise me.'

He hesitated. 'Are you really …?'

'I just said I'm sure twice. Now I'm saying it for a third time. Yes, I'm sure. You know I would do anything for our students, and most of all for our family, and I trust you. You will Raise me. Now if we're to do this on time we need to go.'

He rose without releasing my hands and I rose with him. 'Come inside then. We need to talk.'

* * *

Everybody was standing around the table in the war room, including Simone.

'We don't have long to say goodbye,' John said, putting his arm around my shoulders. 'If we're to be conscious at noon, we have to go in the next ten minutes.'

'I'll be at the Gates,' Guan Yu said, and disappeared.

Ma looked me in the eye. 'Make sure he Raises you, you owe me a hazelnut latte.' He disappeared as well.

Martin strode to me and embraced me. 'From both of us,' he said, kissed the top of my head and disappeared.

Yue embraced me, held me for a while, then pulled back. 'You rescued me from the cooking pot and freed me from a stone holding me captive. I thank you, my Lady. Return as a Raised Immortal and show us all what you are fully capable of.' She hugged me again and disappeared.

'What she said,' Liu said, and stormed out the door to find Meredith.

Simone sighed and put her hands by her sides. 'Here we go again.'

I hugged her and she embraced me back.

'He'll Raise me,' I said. 'He promised.'

'Make sure you do, Daddy.'

'Leave us now. I need to talk to Emma,' John said, gruff.

'I need more time!' she said.

'We don't have it. You need to leave,' he said. 'I'll be back soon, and I have promised to Raise her.'

'Look after her,' Simone said.

'I will,' he said, his voice low. 'Go.'

She went out without looking back.

'Tell me what to do when it happens,' I said. 'Can you?'

'I can. This is the first time the Jade Emperor's treated your death as a real possibility and allowed me to talk about it.' He waved for me to sit at the table next to him, and leaned on it to speak intensely to me. 'Our best hope is that you are a Celestial Worthy and land in Court Ten. If you do, I will be able to enter the Court with the Elixir, Raise you myself, and Pao won't be able to do a damn thing about it. If you aren't Worthy, you will be profoundly disoriented and you will land in Court One.'

'Who decides whether I'm Worthy? Who decides whether I go to One or Ten?'

'You do.'

'What, I can decide which Court I land in?' I leaned back, relieved. 'That's easy. I've been in Ten before, I can just go there.'

'No, you can't. It is not a choice you can consciously make, so don't even try. If you land in Court One, you will lose your memory and be unaware of who you are. Your personality may be strong enough to keep your awareness together so you can distinguish yourself from the rest of the ... inhabitants. If you do, I can find and Raise you anyway. I wish I had a piece of my shell to give to you. A piece of one of us — a Dragon's scale or a Phoenix's feather — will help you to stay together during the transition.' He rubbed one hand over his face. 'I don't have time to give you one. Concentrate if you feel it happening —'

'Wait,' I said. 'I have one of the Tiger's claws. Will that do?'

'When did he give you one of his claws?'

'A very long time ago.' I put my hand out and the claw appeared in it. It appeared to be made of platinum and was fifteen centimetres long. 'He told me not to give it back, it might prove useful.'

'Hold on to it. Put it in your pocket. If you feel it happening, or you see it happening, put your hand on the claw and concentrate on who you are.' He appeared relieved. 'It will help me to recognise you.'

I put the claw in my pocket, then took his hand and clutched it. 'You promised to Raise me. So you must not take Seven Stars.'

'I know,' he said, gazing into my eyes.

He bent closer, our mouths touched, and the world around us spun into nothingness.

19

After we'd come around in Yanluo Wang's office building, we rode a cloud across the lake and landed on the other side very close to noon. As we approached the main entrance to the demonic side of Hell, the doors smoothly opened towards us. They were fifteen metres high, black with massive metal studs on them, and an honour guard of horse- and bull-headed demons, all wearing brown trousers and naked from the waist up, stood inside waiting for us.

John took Celestial Form as we approached, with Seven Stars on his back; then obviously remembered and dismissed the sword. He raised one hand to indicate he realised his mistake and I nodded in reply.

We walked down the deep black tunnel with the demon Dukes flanking us. The tunnel was four metres wide and so high that the ceiling was invisible. The honour guard formed neat rows on either side of us and paced us as we went down the tunnel towards the King's throne room.

Is it very dark and misty for you too? John said.

'No, it's dim but not very dark, and there's no mist,' I said.

'Welcome home, Dark Lord,' the horse-head next to me said as it walked beside us. 'It has been an age since you left the Brotherhood. We had some good times.'

'Those times are behind me,' John said without emotion. 'And this was never my home.'

The horse-head raised its muzzle. 'There was a time when this place was not our home either. His Loathsome Majesty works with industry and diligence to provide us a new home in the sunlight, something we have not had in millennia.'

'And I will fight till my last breath to ensure that he does not succeed,' John said.

The horse-head eyed me. 'No comment, Lady Emma? You let your man do all the talking? I have heard that you are,' it pulled his lips back, revealing even horse teeth, '*equal*.'

'As equal as any Snake Mother,' I said. 'Why not go ask them about your attitude towards equality?'

The demon tossed its head and rolled its eyes.

Another pair of doors stood before us, this time black with red trimmings and embossed circular motifs of Snake Mothers in the middle.

Deep breath, Emma, John said. *This will be ugly.*

I had already used energy manipulation to calm myself. I knew what was on the other side of the doors and I wasn't looking forward to it. Some of the most distressing experiences of my life had happened in there. I was surprised as I realised: the certain knowledge that I was about to die was much less terrifying than the concern about how I would die. I sincerely hoped it wouldn't be too slow and painful — and really sincerely hoped it didn't involve any Snake Mothers. With luck, it would be quick, and after it was done, he would Raise me. He had promised. I wrapped my hand around the Tiger's claw in my pocket and gripped it.

The doors opened and we stepped into the Demon King's throne room.

Red pillars embossed with good-luck motifs held the majestically high roof above us, and the windowless wooden room was three hundred metres to a side. What appeared to be the entire horde of Hell occupied the room, not in orderly ranks on either side of a central aisle the way the Shen in Heaven did it, but packed in randomly, all the way to the edges of the room, and in some places piled on top of each other until they were nearly waist-deep in a writhing dark mass. The King's throne stood at the end of the room, three metres above the floor on a raised dais. He'd given me to Simon Wong on that dais.

As we approached, the demons parted before us, allowing us to walk to the dais.

The King was on the dais, and I took another deep breath. That *bastard* was in Kitty Kwok form. She appeared as a Chinese woman, ageless as the result of a serious amount of plastic surgery that had turned her face into a tight waxy mask and pulled her hairline up close to the top of her head. She stood next to the throne with her arms crossed over her chest and smiled with satisfaction as we neared.

All the Snake Mothers were gathered at the base of the dais in True Form, the terrified demons closest to them giving them as much space as possible in the crush.

John bent and grabbed my hand. He was so tall that I had to raise my arm to hold it but I gripped it tight, giving whatever comfort I could and feeling comforted myself.

The Serpent in its Celestial Jade cage came into view behind the throne as we drew closer. Its scales were dull and grey and its eyes were white: they'd blinded it. Its tail had regrown but it was red raw skin without scales. The IV on the outside of the cage fed into its back.

This is not fair, I said to the stone.

I completely agree. Don't let go of his hand. No, wait; move to his right and hold his right hand in your left. I'll touch both of you and can relay silently.

I pulled John towards me. 'Me on the right.'

He looked down at me, bewildered, and it took all of my courage to move to his right side and make the demon horde recede to give me room. I swapped hands on the Tiger's claw and took his right hand in my left, again having to reach high because of his Celestial Form's size.

I see, he said. *Good idea.*

Can he feel it? I asked the stone.

John dropped his head slightly. *I can feel everything. All of it. I'm half-blind already. Guide me, Emma, I can't see.* He raised his head, his expression determined. *Both of us must walk out of this alive. We will walk out of this alive. We must.*

You will Raise me.

I promise.

We arrived at the base of the dais, and the demon Dukes formed an honour guard in front of it, the floor of the dais level with their shoulders. A pair of Dukes remained as escorts on either side of us as we stood facing the throne. The Snake Mothers parted and moved away from us, obviously intimidated by John's Celestial Form. If it came to a battle, there was no way we could take all of them at once. Even if we destroyed the King, we were doomed. I had to ensure that even though I died, John made it out of there free and alive, because all that we loved was at stake.

'Hi guys,' Kitty said, and her voice was George's male voice. 'How's things?'

John released my hand and saluted her. 'Mo Wang.'

'No, no, don't stand on formality, we're all family here,' she said, waving him down. 'Have you met my son? I think you have.' She raised her voice to be heard to the end of the hall. 'Number One, you're demoted. Get your ass up here.'

One of the horse-head Dukes changed to male human form — the Demon King's Number One — and walked up the stairs onto the dais. He moved stiffly, his eyes wide and his face fierce with effort. The King was controlling him. He stopped at the throne and turned to face the gathered horde.

The Demon King sauntered up to him. 'Someone gave the forces of the Celestial about sixteen gigs of data with all our strengths and plans on it.'

The gathered demons hissed with venom.

'Do you have anything to say for yourself?' the King said.

Number One stood rigid and silent. He opened his mouth and closed it again.

'Go on, you may speak,' the King said.

'Seppuku,' Number One said. His voice gained a desperate edge. 'Death with honour, Loathsome Majesty. I beg you.'

'Oh, that's very good considering what you've done.' The King turned to speak to the gathered horde. 'He betrayed us all, and he will be punished.'

The King turned back to Number One, took his chin in her hand and moved his face from side to side. 'Such a shame, your human form is so very well constructed. Did you have help making it?' She pushed his face away. 'Never mind.'

She turned to John. 'You're not even strong enough to put him out of his misery?' She looked from Number One to John. 'I'm sure he's asking you for a quick release. He has a good idea what's next.'

John didn't reply, and the Demon King turned back to Number One. 'Are you wearing contacts, son?'

Number One shook his head.

'That's the natural colour of your eyes? Really? You went with blue, even without coloured contacts?'

Number One nodded.

'A wonderful addition to my collection, particularly since I'm starting a new one.' The Demon King studied Number One. 'This is going to hurt.' She changed to male human form and turned his blood-coloured eyes onto me. 'This is really going to hurt. I could let him go quickly and painlessly, Emma. What would it be worth to you?'

'The only things you want from me are things I cannot give you,' I said.

The King studied Number One. 'How about a Tiger's claw?'

'I won't give you a piece of my friend the Tiger. I'd be mad to,' I said.

'You know what?' the King said to One. 'Taking your eyes would be altogether too quick and easy. I'll end up with them anyway, and I'm starving.' He took a step closer and gazed almost lovingly into the young man's eyes. 'Go to my private quarters, strip, bathe and wait for me. I'll be along shortly.' He grinned without humour. 'I'm absolutely starving, but you, I think, I will take my time with.'

Number One disappeared and the gathered demons all sighed.

'Lucinda,' the King said, facing the horde.

261

A Snake Mother slithered to the front of the dais and stood in front of us as if we weren't there. 'Majesty?'

'Do you want the job?'

'With all due respect, Majesty, I love you with all my heart, but I would prefer to remain where I am. I would be honoured to advise and counsel you, but I do not wish to hold that sort of power.'

The King pointed at her. 'See? That's why you're the smartest one here.'

She bowed gracefully over her coils. 'Loathsome Majesty.'

'Okay, position vacant,' the Demon King said. 'Go for it, kiddies. As soon as we're done with the Dark Lord here, whoever who has the tits for it can take it.'

The demons rumbled with subvocal comments.

'And now be quiet, because I'm going to give the Dark Lord his treaty,' the King said. 'Come on up, Ah Wu.'

I took John's hand to speak to him through the stone. *I'll do it. Don't go near the cage.* I tried to release his hand but couldn't; he held me. *We can't win this, John. Let me go.*

No. Don't sacrifice yourself. The Heavens can fall, I don't care. Let's just go.

Simone is in the Heavens, John. Simone, Leo, Ming, Yue — my family on the Earthly — we must protect them all.

He hesitated, then said, *I love you. I will Raise you.*

You are my life, Xuan Wu, and I trust you with it. I shook his hand free. 'I'll do it.'

The Demon King linked his hands behind his back. 'Sure. Come on up.'

I walked up the stairs onto the dais, full of dread. I had to find the treaty and make sure that John left with it.

'Where's the treaty, George?'

He gestured to a large plain binder sitting on the dais next to the Serpent's cage. 'Just take it and go.'

'Emma?' the Serpent said in its warm female voice.

'Do not approach the cage door,' the King said.

'I'm not planning to. I'm just here to collect the treaty,' I said.

I went to where the binder was, and stopped when I saw the Serpent. They'd spray-painted over its lidless eyes.

'I'm here, John,' I said.

Take care, the Turtle part of John said. *I cannot see you to defend you, and there are a great many big demons between us.*

'Hello, Emma,' the Serpent said. 'You taste lovely.'

'Thank you,' I said. 'We will get you out. Stay strong.'

It moved towards my voice and blindly slammed its snout on the cage. I winced; I knew how much that hurt. The Serpent moved more slowly, and leaned its head against the inside of the cage. I stuck my fingers through the bars to touch its nose and rubbed its snout gently.

Thank you, it said.

I had a profound feeling of oneness with it; its cloudy eyes saw into my soul, and it was as if I was losing myself into it …

They've grabbed me, they're holding me, John said. *Run, Emma.*

'Run, Emma!' the Serpent said.

I turned, saw the King, and ran to stop him. He had his hands above his head and was crackling with pale blue light; he was in the process of generating a ball of black energy to throw at John, who stood below the dais held by the pair of demon Dukes who had been standing with him.

Even blind, John was more than a match for the two Dukes. He grabbed the left one's arm, swung it high and used it to slam its body onto the ground. He pulled the right demon down at the same time, flooring both of them in front of him, then blasted shen in a tight beam and destroyed them. He straightened, his hands still glowing with shen, and moved his head from side to side as he blindly tried to predict the path of the King's energy so that he could dodge it and attack the source.

The King's face went beatific, and with a whoosh as loud as a jet engine the pale blue energy changed to black. The King lowered his hands towards John and prepared to launch the black mass. If it hit John while he was this close to the Serpent, he would rejoin whether it killed him or not.

I made a giant leap to block the King's energy with my body. It had to hit me instead of John or all was lost.

'Mummy, what's happening?' a child said behind the dais, and everything stopped.

The King turned to the back of the dais, dropped the energy, and it disappeared. I landed on my side at his feet. I had made no attempt to land gracefully, fully expecting to be dead before I hit. I panted as I pulled myself back to my feet, clutching my bruised ribs from landing on my arm and still holding the claw in my pocket.

The child climbed the stairs at the back of the dais and stood next to the Serpent's cage. It was difficult to see its gender; it appeared about two years old, wearing a traditional Chinese jacket and pants. Then the shock hit me all the way down to my feet: it was profoundly similar to photos of Simone when she'd been that age. Its hair was a darker shade of brown than hers, but it was obviously half-Chinese and half-European as she was.

The King quickly changed back to Kitty Kwok form. 'You

shouldn't be here, Frankie,' she said. 'You were supposed to stay in your room. Where's your amah?'

'Who are you?' Frankie asked me.

'I'm Emma.'

The child shook its head, eyes wide. 'Mummy, stop hurting the big snake.' It saw John. 'You're the same.'

John reabsorbed the shen energy and turned his head from side to side, judging distance and direction from sound. 'Hello, little one.'

The King sagged slightly. 'Go back to your room, darling.' She crouched and put her arms out. 'Come and give me a kiss, then go back to your room, okay?'

'I want to stay with you, Mummy,' the child said, and its voice resonated through me. I'd heard that voice before ... in my dreams.

I backed to the cage, leaned against it and put my head in my hands, my throat filling. 'Holy shit, no. Don't do this to me, George.'

'Mind your language in front of my son,' the King said.

Frankie went to her and she hugged him and kissed him on the cheek. She smiled into his eyes with genuine affection and tousled his hair, making him giggle. 'It's your nap time and you're not allowed in here, you know that.'

'I know. Sorry, Mummy. Amah's had an ... accident. One of the big ones came in. I don't want to go back there.'

'I'll look after you.'

'That would be good.' He looked up at the King with adoration. 'Can I stay with you for a while? The big one was scary.'

'Yes, of course, darling.' The King spoke to me over his tousled downy head. 'Take your treaty and go. Go now, and I won't touch you.' She sat on the throne and lifted Frankie into her lap. 'Say goodbye to Emma, Frankie, she's going. I need to talk to the ladies standing at the front of the crowd here for a while.'

The Snake Mothers retreated from the dais, some of them hissing with fear.

Frankie turned to me and smiled, a sweet expression full of good nature. 'Goodbye, Emma.'

I could barely choke the words out. 'Goodbye, Frankie. I hope I see you again soon, because I'm your —'

'Shut up. That won't be happening,' the King said, talking over me. 'You have two days. Take your treaty and leave my dominion immediately.'

The words had the weight of an order. The Celestial's agreement to give the King dominion over his side of Hell still held and I was bound by it. I swiftly took the binder and carried it towards John. I hefted it under one arm and took his hand.

He gazed down at me, unseeing. *That child just saved your life.*

'I know,' I said. *Let's get the hell out of here.*

The hall disappeared around us.

* * *

I woke to find John dozing in one of the chairs next to the fire with the treaty binder open in his lap. Simone was sitting next to him and leaning on his shoulder as she read a book. She saw I was awake, closed the book and smiled. 'You okay?'

I sat up. 'I'm fine.' I saw the clock above the fireplace. 'I've been out for nearly two hours?'

'Edwin says it's exhaustion and to slow down.' She gestured with her head towards John. 'Him too.'

266

'I'm awake,' John said, moving upright and rubbing his eyes.

'Are you still blind?'

'No, they wiped the paint off after we left. I was … the Serpent was doing too much damage to itself hitting the walls of the cage.'

I sagged with relief.

'You were wrong, Daddy,' Simone said, digging him with her elbow. 'Emma's still here.'

He grunted. 'You've said that six times now.'

'I just like saying it,' she said with delight. 'Go back to sleep, Emma, I'll wake you for dinner.' She put her hand on his shoulder. 'You should nap as well, Daddy, you've been sleeping there for a while.'

'Okay,' I said, and settled back. I patted the bed next to me. 'Come on, John, nap time.'

'I have too much to do,' he said, squeezing the bridge of his nose. 'We have less than forty-eight hours.'

'Have a nap, Daddy,' she said, then went out, closing the door gently behind her.

I sat up. 'Thank you.'

'You're welcome,' the stone said. 'She didn't give me any trouble at all. I asked her to leave you and she just went. She knows something's up.'

'Have you shown him?'

'No, I waited until you were awake, and I knew you wouldn't want Simone to see.'

'Project it.'

A life-size projection of the child appeared between the bed and the fireplace. Little Frankie stood there, unmoving, his eyes wide.

John dropped his hand and stared at the image. The binder slid from his lap onto the floor and he ignored it. He glanced at me, then back at the child. 'This is not possible.'

'It could be a construct,' the stone said.

'It has to be,' John said.

'He's our child,' I said. 'They put him into a demon egg to take him to term.'

'Not possible,' John said, slumping in his chair. 'A human foetus would not survive that sort of treatment.'

'Look at yourself,' I said. 'Look at me. Now remember the origins of both of us.'

'This is not possible!' John said.

I gestured towards Frankie. 'He's been coming to me in dreams ever since I left the UK.'

John dropped his head into his hands. 'Me too.' He looked up at the projection. 'This is a disaster.'

'Only you would discover that we have a son and call it a disaster.'

'The King will turn him against you, Emma,' the stone said, its voice full of compassion. 'This child has a more powerful heritage than Simone, and look how powerful she is. When grown, he will have the capability to destroy everything.'

'You lost him six months ago. Look at him, he looks two or three and he's only just old enough to be *born*,' John said. 'Stone, given his advanced development already, how long before he is equivalent to fifteen years old?'

'Eighteen months,' the stone said. 'Although he may mature more slowly now that he's out of the egg.'

'Shit,' John said softly. 'I will not do this again.'

'No,' I said. 'Because if it becomes necessary, I will.'

John stared at me for a long moment. The image blinked out.

'You could not kill your own child, Emma. Trust me. I've done it.'

'If it came to this child or everything on the Celestial, I will run a sword through —'

I went silent. Just the mental image of doing that to a child, *my* child, stopped me dead. I dropped my head. He was right.

'Good,' he said. 'Because if you were to do that, you would be no better than one of them.'

'You've done it,' I said.

He spread his hands. 'Precisely.'

'They won't use the child in battle,' the stone said. 'The King loves him too much.'

'The stone has a point,' I said. 'Kitty's adopted him and loves him like her own. She won't put him in danger.'

'Oh, he's not there to be in danger,' John said. 'He's not there to be a weapon. He's not even there to be a hostage against our good behaviour.'

'Good,' I said.

'He's there to take the throne as the Jade Emperor.'

All the breath left me in a long gasp.

'I was wondering what the King had planned if the Heavens were to fall. He himself can't take the throne; his nature is incompatible. This child is the perfect puppet and his lineage is impeccable.'

'We can't let this happen,' I said.

'Emma,' John said, and his tone made me turn back to him. 'You need to accept now that we will never be parents to this child. He will never be ours. If the King wins, our son will be Jade Emperor and we will serve him as the puppet of a crucl master.'

'That's not an option —'

269

'Let me finish. If we win, this child will want to stay with the only mother he knows, and that is the King of the Demons. Hell is his home. There is a good chance the King will groom him to seize the position of Demon King if he is ever toppled.'

I pulled my knees to my chest and buried my face in them. 'I don't know which is a more horrifying outcome.'

'We could also destroy the Demon King — the only mother he's ever known — right in front of him and turn him against us forever.'

'That's the worst.'

'The best outcome is that we win this war, our son survives it, George keeps our child and loves him, and hopefully one day we will deal with a Demon King who is our own son and hardly knows us. That is the best possible future. Focus on that.'

I grinned into my knees. 'Calling him Francis was the final twist of the blade.'

'I know.' He came to me and put his arm around my shoulders. 'I'd say let it go, but I know how this is tearing your heart out, because it is tearing mine out as well.'

I grabbed him and held him for a long time. We sat in silence, grieving for a child we hadn't known we'd had and would never be able to love.

'War isn't about big brave soldiers and grand heroism and noble sacrifices,' I said into his shoulder. 'War is about hurting children and destroying families.'

'It always has been,' John said, holding me close. 'I only hope that one day there will be no more wars and I will no longer have a job.'

'We have to tell Simone.'

'I know,' he said, his voice low. 'Will you help me do it? I'll mess it up.'

'No, you won't, but I'll help you. Hey.' I wrapped my arms tighter around him.

'What?'

'She was right. I'm alive. Your prediction didn't come true.'

'Our son doing what he did was completely random and totally unexpected. He is like me: too powerful to be predicted by any of us. He really did save your life.'

'I hope I have a chance to thank him one day.'

'You need to rest so you can take the Elixir. Something like this is bound to happen again. Please stop plane-shifting.'

'I will.'

'No more, okay?'

'Okay. No more.'

'Really.'

'I mean it!' I said, pulling back to see his face. 'Now call Simone, we need to talk to her.'

'This will not be fun.'

'I know,' I moaned.

20

We showed Simone in the living room. She stared at the projection for a long time, her expression rigid with restraint.

'Don't tell anyone he exists,' John said. 'If they find out, there'll be constant petitions to have us removed from the war effort because our allegiance is compromised.'

She looked at us, from one to the other. 'Is it?'

'No,' we said in unison.

'Stop doing that. Did you talk to him?'

'We said hello. That was about it,' I said.

'Does he know who he is?'

'No.'

'You didn't tell him? Offer him an escape?'

'We never had a chance,' I said. 'I was shocked speechless, then the Demon King threw us out almost immediately. Your father was blind, so he didn't know who your brother was until we came back.'

'Can you talk to him now, Daddy?'

'No.'

'I see.' She straightened. 'And he's too powerful to be predicted?'

'Yes,' John said.

'Am I? Can you look into my future and see what I will do?'

John leaned back. 'There was a time when your future was bright and easily visible. As you have matured and grown into your power — no. You are as primal and chaotic as me. And him. You cannot be predicted.'

'Good,' she said. 'Is there any way at all we could get him and the Serpent out?'

'The long answer to your question is: going down there to the centre of their power and attempting a rescue would certainly fail and cost the lives of everybody involved as well as my freedom. The short answer is: no.'

'So we need to win this war, then we can pull your Serpent and my little brother out.'

'He may not want to be taken from the only home and mother he's ever known,' John said.

'Then we have to win this and then convince him that there's a better life for him here in Heaven.'

John and I both nodded a reply.

Simone rose and gestured angrily towards us. 'Now you're moving in synch as well. Stop it! Keep away from that damn Snake, Emma. And I changed my mind. Leave it in Hell!' She stormed out.

'You worry me, Emma,' he said mildly.

'Don't ask me for a separation, we'll be at war in two days.' I shrugged. 'And we're both so busy we hardly see each other anyway.'

'True.' He rose. 'You're right. I have too much to do and I can't sit around here with you, much as I would like to. You, on the other hand,' he gestured towards me, 'take the afternoon off, and that's an order. I will not risk you like this again. You are resting until you are well enough to take that damn Elixir whether you like it or not.'

'An order, eh?' I said.

He smiled slightly. 'A request?'

'Deal.'

I flopped back on the couch, unwilling to tell him that after the energy calming I was having trouble staying awake. But I was sure to have caged snake dreams later.

* * *

'Muu … ummy.'

'Frankie!' I ignored the fact that he still appeared as a foetus in a demon egg and slithered to speak to him. 'Stay here and talk to me.'

The hard bright eyes didn't blink and the gills opened and closed. 'Mummy?'

'I'm your Mummy. I'm your real mother.'

'But you're a snake.'

'Yes, I am. I'm a snake and a human and I love you with all my heart and I want to be with you.'

'But you left me. Why did you leave me?'

The egg turned blinding white, and suddenly he was his small male human form, standing alone in the huge dark space, wide-eyed and frightened. I wanted to approach but my snake form might scare him into wakefulness.

'They stole you from me, Frankie. Remember yesterday when the man and woman came into the King's throne room?'

'The King? Who?'

I tried to explain as quickly as I could before we lost contact. 'The woman you call Mummy.'

His face twisted.

'I'm your real mother,' I said. 'That woman you call Mummy, she stole you.'

He stared at me, unconvinced.

'God,' I said, and dropped my head. I put everything I had into changing to human form, and couldn't do it. 'Damn.' I raised my head. 'I'm the human woman who came to get the papers. I'm Emma. The man with me was your real father.'

He watched me silently.

'Frankie, if you ever get out of Hell, find us. Contact us. Call for me — I'm Emma. Or call your father, Xuan Wu, and he will hear you. We will care for you and love you, and you have a family in Heaven who will all look after you. We love you. We all love you.'

'You're my real mother?'

I lowered my voice. 'I really am.'

'It's scary here sometimes, when Mummy isn't around.' He turned and the room lit up. It was filled with Snake Mothers, advancing menacingly towards us. He shouted at them. 'You're not allowed to hurt me!'

'Your mother's not here to defend you,' one of the Mothers said.

'Yes, I am!' I shouted, and slithered to Frankie to protect him.

I woke before I made it. John wasn't in the bed next to me; I was alone. It was 1 am; he'd probably been held back in a late meeting. I checked my phone on the bedside table. There was a message from him.

Not happy with the disposition of the Hell forces, and liasing with the West on defensive barriers. May be a while. Don't wait up.

I rolled over and tried to go back to sleep; maybe Frankie would contact me again. It took me a long time.

* * *

I woke the next day to find John sitting in the armchair next to the fire in his Mountain uniform, reading a tablet computer on his lap. I checked the bedside clock: 10 am. I sat up.

'Don't rush. You're not needed for anything,' he said.

'We reject the treaty tomorrow and I've only equipped about a hundred of the senior students,' I said. 'What the hell are we going to do?'

'Only use the ones that are equipped, and only if we absolutely have to. Don't panic, Emma. The regular Disciples are fully equipped, and we have the Thirty-Six, the Elites and all the armies of the Four Winds on call. The students are just backup, and there's a good chance we won't need them.'

I bent my knees and rested my arms on them to run my hands over my tousled hair. 'You said yourself we're outgunned.'

'We don't use guns so it's irrelevant.'

'I still haven't received the full information about the military smuggling and the weapons that have gone missing on the Earthly,' I said. 'We need that intelligence.'

'We're ready for them.'

'We aren't!'

'Emma.' He leaned his elbow on his crossed knees and studied me. 'I'm the God of War. Trust me.'

276

I was silent for a moment. 'Okay. Point taken.'

'Good.' He raised the tablet. 'Thank you. This is excellent.'

'About time you finally sat down and read it. It's only details on the modern weapons that aren't classified anyway. I'm sure there's stuff out there that I couldn't find information on.'

'Don't worry. My nature is to be aware of all weapons; this just shows me who has what and how likely we are to face them. These small drone things are way more expensive and difficult to control than I expected. Dragons or flyers are much faster and more efficient.' He shrugged. 'A vast majority of weapons that work on humans won't damage demons anyway. Drop a nuclear weapon on a demon and it'll ignore the shockwave, shake off the heat, and walk through the fallout unharmed.'

'How do you know that?'

'The Tiger's done it. He thought a nuclear blast would be similar to pure yang, but it's much weaker — nearly ineffectual.'

I moaned softly. 'They could have nuclear weapons and our armies are humans.'

'Only on the Mountain. The armies of the Winds are mostly Shen. The Thirty-Six are mostly demons.' He put the tablet aside and came to sit on the bed next to me. 'Come and have breakfast. Today will be a busy day.'

'I'm surprised you're still here. Aren't people yelling at you to be all over the place?'

'Of course they are. And there are still many tasks that need to be done. But we face battle tomorrow and some things are more important.'

'Any word on our son? Has he tried to contact us?'

He shook his head.

'Okay.'

* * *

'Okay if I bring Bridget in to say hello?' Simone shouted from the entrance to my office.

'Sure. Hi, Bridget,' I said, rising and moving to the other side of the desk.

Bridget came in, accompanied by her two sons.

'Everything acceptable?' I asked her.

She shrugged. 'It's lovely. We'll miss being able to go anywhere we please ...'

Her younger son snorted with contempt.

' ... and the boys will just put up with it,' she finished.

'Let me show you around,' I said.

'Don't worry, I can handle this,' Simone said. 'You can go back to work.'

'What is BJ doing?'

'She's taken a shelf in the linen cupboard —'

'There isn't enough room in there for a mouse!' Bridget protested. 'She doesn't even have an air mattress. Where's the poor girl going to sleep?'

'She's a rock,' I said. 'She'll sleep on the shelf, she probably has a shoebox set up already. Don't worry about her.'

'She's a *rock*?' Phillip said.

'And she'll change to boy while you're staying there.' I spread my hands. 'Welcome to Wudang Mountain, where weird happens every day of the week.'

'How long will we be here, Emma?' Phillip asked me. 'I have a soccer match on Saturday.'

'We go into battle tomorrow, and when we win you can go home,' I said.

'A real — like war — battle?' his brother said with delight. 'With soldiers and guns and everything?' He looked from his mother to me. 'Is there any way we can watch?'

'Sure,' I said.

'Cool!' the boy said.

'I don't think so, Emma,' Bridget said.

'No, Bridget, it's fine. But if you want to watch, you have to come with me to the Mountain's mortuary first.'

That stopped him. 'The mortuary? Why?'

'To view some corpses.'

His excitement disappeared. 'I have to look at dead people?'

'Yes. A few of our soldiers are still there from the last battle. You have to view at least three bodies — one was torn into two pieces, one had half her face blown off, and another was burnt to death — before you can watch the battle tomorrow, because similar things will happen.'

'It's horrible,' Simone said softly.

The younger boy had gone completely white. 'Real bodies? Real people?' He hesitated. 'I never thought of it like that.'

'Good. Now you have.' I patted Bridget on the shoulder. 'Anything you need, you call me on my mobile. I'm here for you, okay?'

'Thanks, Emma,' Bridget said. 'Let's leave you to it. I don't envy you your job — what you just described are things I never want to see.'

'That's the whole reason I'm here,' I said.

She appeared confused for a moment.

279

'So that you never have to see them.' I went back around the desk. 'Come and have dinner with us in the Imperial Residence later.' I raised my hand. 'Never mind. You don't want to hear what we're saying on the eve of battle. Just enjoy the scenery and try not to be too bored.'

'Can I call David?'

'There's a phone in the house.'

'Simone?' I said after Bridget and the boys had gone out.

She turned back. 'Hmm?'

'My parents don't want to come up. Could you go and talk to them for me?'

She stared at me. 'Seriously?'

I shrugged. 'They think they'll be okay with Greg there.'

'They are completely insane.'

'Please, after you've settled Bridget's family, go and talk to them? Explain that this is serious and they're much safer here.'

She nodded. 'Okay.'

I sighed with relief. 'Thanks, Simone.'

'Hey, they're my Nanna and Pop, and my aunties and stuff. I want to see them safe too. They're my family as well.'

'You're absolutely right.'

'Uh ...' She hesitated. 'What if he'd *wanted* to see the corpses?'

'I know, I took a risk telling him that. Some people find death and dismemberment cool rather than scary.'

'So what would you have done?'

'Waited three years, then recruited him.'

* * *

John contacted me a couple of hours later. *Help, Emma!* He sounded desperate, and my head shot up. *I need your help ... Come to the training room in the Residence ... I don't know what to do ...*

I couldn't ask him what the problem was so I ran. I didn't normally stretch myself out to full speed, and the ground blurred beneath me as I raced to the Residence.

I arrived to find John and Simone wearing their Mountain uniforms and glaring at each other across the floor of the training room. He was holding Dark Heavens and she had her twin blades, Bo and Bei, loaded with her chakra energy and held menacingly in front of her.

I raised my hands. 'Whatever this is about, it can't be serious enough to need weapons.'

'You agreed,' Simone said.

'Please don't do this,' John said.

Simone didn't look away from him. 'Has he told you, Emma?'

'No?' I glanced from one to the other.

'Good.' She turned and saluted me with the blades crossed in front of her face. 'Defend yourself.'

'What?' I said, and jumped back as she swiped her right blade straight where my neck would have been. 'Simone —'

She attempted an upwards thrust through my abdomen and I dodged it.

'Summon your blade, Emma.'

'I won't fight you, Simone,' I said, backing up with my hands raised.

'Tell her, Dad,' Simone said, swinging at me again with the blades. I didn't move out of the way quickly enough and she stopped with the blade a centimetre from my waist. 'You agreed.'

John dismissed Dark Heavens and moved to the side. 'I can't tell you why, Emma, but you have to defeat her.'

'No Shen abilities,' I said. 'No Celestial Form.'

'Deal,' she said, crossed the blades in front of her face again and stepped back.

'Is she good enough to do this armed without killing me?' I said without looking away from her. I put my hand out and summoned the Murasame.

'I am thoroughly insulted,' Simone said.

'You'd better be good enough,' John growled.

Simone again tried to plunge her right-hand weapon into my abdomen and I blocked it. Her left came towards my head, so I pushed her right down and out of the way and stepped back to block her left. Her right came at me, again at waist height, and I twisted my blade around hers, pushed it down and smashed the blades into each other with a visible spark of her chakra energy.

'Good,' John said.

I didn't wait for her to recover; I spun with the movement and took a swing at her neck, but her crossed blades were already there to block me and she swung my sword down. She released one of her blades as mine was forced down and again attempted to take my head off. I dropped the Murasame beneath her push and somersaulted sideways to avoid her strike, feeling the blade whistle past me as I went underneath it. Close.

John must have been thinking the same thing. 'That was too close. Stop this now.'

As I righted myself I put my left hand out and the Murasame's scabbard flew into it.

'No!' Simone shouted.

She stepped forward and tried to put the point of Bo under my chin before I could ready myself to attack again. I used the Murasame's scabbard to block the blade coming for my throat while I used the sword in my right to block the other one coming towards my head.

Simone used brute force to push my blocks away and kicked me square in the abdomen, sending me sliding three metres across the floor. She was in front of me before I'd stopped moving and had a chance to recover. She held the tips of both viciously curved blades at my throat.

'I win,' she said with satisfaction.

She was at least three times stronger and faster than me and there was no way I could defeat her. I stepped back, turned the Murasame horizontally between us and formally slid it into its scabbard. 'I concede.'

She straightened, her expression full of triumph.

'Dammit, Emma,' John said with dismay.

I turned to him. 'I thought you'd be pleased. She's improved so much since you returned it's miraculous.'

'You. Will. Get. Yourself. Killed!' John shouted at Simone.

'You'll go back on our agreement?' she said, glaring at him. She pointed at me. 'I beat her. I can go tomorrow.'

'Oh, no way.' I dropped the sword and staggered as my knees buckled. 'No way. Simone, don't do this. Please, for us. You're *mortal*!'

'So are all the Disciples, the Elites, the Winds' armies ...' She looked from her father to me. 'I'm not special!'

'You're my daughter,' he said with anguish.

'Even more reason for me to go.' She gestured towards me. 'Five years of solid training with you and I just bested her. Easily. The Heavens need me.' She summoned yin and it spiralled around her. 'I could be the difference between victory and defeat.'

'You'll get yourself killed,' he said, his voice weak with misery. He put his hand over his eyes and went out.

Simone pulled the yin in, dismissed her swords and came to me. She put her hands on my arms. 'I have to do this, otherwise I wouldn't be able to live with myself. I have to help. All the Celestial, all the Earthly, all of it is at risk, and I would sacrifice myself without hesitation to protect it.' She gazed into my eyes. 'Didn't you just do the same thing a couple of days ago?'

'You're just a child,' I said.

'Like the Tiger said: he's had wives younger than me, and it's about time I grew up,' she said with grim humour. Then her expression softened. 'But you weren't thinking of going down and helping fight tomorrow, were you?'

'I have more sense,' I said, my voice thick.

'Good.' She raised her head and concentrated. 'He's coming back to give me as much training as he can before tomorrow.' She sighed. 'I hope he forgives me for this.'

'Just don't get yourself killed tomorrow, Simone. I don't know what I'd do.'

She embraced me. 'Don't worry, I'll be careful. Nothing will happen to me.' She pulled back to see me. 'I'll be fine.'

John came back in, his expression frozen into a grim mask. *Give her the Tiger's claw before she goes tomorrow.*

'I will,' I said.

You won't be able to explain what it's for.

'I know.'

'What? That's so rude!' Simone said.

'Contingency plans,' I said. 'I'll tell you later.' I picked the Murasame up from where it was floating ten centimetres above the floor. It quivered and felt heavy in my hand; it really hated it when I surrendered. 'If your father isn't sure you're good enough, please don't go.'

'He already agreed.' Her face softened. 'But I'll listen to his advice.'

'Start with the level three double-handed set,' John said. 'From the beginning.'

She moved into position in the middle of the room and brought her swords back out.

I headed back to my office, my heart heavy with dread.

21

Later that afternoon, I was checking the weapons in the forge with Moaner when the bells rang once and then stopped. I waited for them to pick up a code I knew, but nothing happened.

'Once?' I said to Moaner, and he shrugged.

Then it hit me so hard I staggered. I stared blindly at Moaner for a long moment, paralysed with shock.

'The Jade Emperor is *here*?' Moaner said, incredulous.

'What the hell?' I said, and ran to the great square in front of the Hall of the True Way.

'You're not dressed for him!' Moaner shouted behind me.

'He'll just have to put up with me,' I said as I arrived in the square and stopped next to John, who was standing in Celestial Form at the edge of the square to greet the Jade Emperor and his entourage. A crowd of students was gathering at the side of the square, jostling to see, with a few of the Academy dragons in the air above them.

Attention, John said, and the students settled, the taller ones moving back so the shorter ones could have a better view.

'Before you ask, I have no idea,' John said to me, and straightened.

The Jade Emperor appeared, floating slightly above the grey stone pavers in glowing Celestial Form, more than two metres tall. He wore his robes of Imperial gold, embroidered with six-toed dragons, and his flat square hat with beads hanging in front of his eyes. A pair of Celestial Palace fairies, in robes of pink and red, stood behind and to either side of him.

Er Lang and Venus flanked him, also in Celestial Form. Er Lang was in his human mid-thirties warrior form, wearing green-scaled armour and with his dog at his foot. Venus appeared as a Tang gentleman in robes of pale pink and violet with his long hair bound into a topknot and covered with a five-centimetre-wide filigree crown.

Everybody in the square, including John and me, fell to one knee on the pavers as the group approached, the Jade Emperor still floating slightly above the ground.

'Celestial Majesty,' John said, his head bowed. 'This humble Shen welcomes you and your —'

'No need, Ah Wu,' the Jade Emperor said. 'Up you come, this won't take long. War room, please.'

He settled onto the pavers and we stood to one side, heads still bowed, as he strode past us to the war room.

'We need a contingency plan if Hell should fall tomorrow,' the Jade Emperor said without any preamble as soon as we were sitting.

'Hell will fall?' I said with dismay.

'I keep forgetting you are young and mortal,' the Jade Emperor said with amusement. 'Ah Wu will explain later.'

287

He can't share his knowledge of the future because our actions will change in response, John said. *That could affect the outcome — and possibly not in our favour. We must trust him to guide us.*

'Or he will explain immediately,' the Jade Emperor said, still amused.

'Emma grasps concepts so quickly that there is no need for long explanations,' John said.

'True.' The Jade Emperor rapped his fingertips on the table. 'Contingency plans. I need to know that they exist and what they are. Lady Emma keeps telling everybody that defeat is not an option, when we all know that it is.'

I rose and pushed my chair back. 'It's all on my desk. I'll go and —'

Yi Hao came in and handed me my copy of the document.

'Never mind,' I said. I flipped it open. 'How much information do you need from me?'

'Do we have backups for every major Celestial?'

'All except you,' I said.

'The Number Ones are covered?'

'The Number Twos are up to date, except for the North where they're both ready to take over from each other,' I said.

'The Number Threes?'

'Each Wind is sharing as much information as possible, Majesty,' John said. 'We would need to lose a significant number of top-level people before our efficiency is compromised.'

'Good,' the Jade Emperor said. 'Have you stationed extra guards on the Courts?'

'Each Court has a full cohort of demons from the Tenth,' I said.

'Sufficient. I am giving you two Elites to assign to Pao in

addition to the cohort already present. Pao is to be guarded day and night.'

'Majesty.'

'Now tell me the contingency plan if Hell should fall.'

'We've erected barricades around Court Ten that should be impervious to all physical and elemental attacks,' John said. 'If they overrun the ends of the causeways, we will pull back to Court Ten and do our best to hold that. Even if the rest of Hell falls, as long as we hold Court Ten our people will be free to return to us, and we can use it as a base to retake our side.'

'Court One?'

John hesitated. 'There's a suicide squad in Court One, and they will fight until the end to hold it, but we will sacrifice Court One if needs be so we can retain Court Ten.'

'Majesty,' I said, my voice low, and everybody turned their attention to me.

'Miss Donahoe?'

'I've asked the Dark Lord this question and he does not know the answer. What if we place bombs in the Courts to destroy them if they should fall? How would the fate of our people be affected if the Courts don't exist?'

'Interesting concept,' the Jade Emperor said. 'Let me see.' He was silent for a moment. 'They would just land in the middle of the rubble.'

'The walls of the Court would not be around us?' John said.

'No.' The Emperor leaned back. 'I see your plan. There is a chance of escape and return if Court Ten has fallen but its walls are not around you.' He was silent for another long moment. 'A novel idea, but it would serve no practical purpose and make no difference in the end, apart from having to rebuild when all is over. Do not proceed in that direction.'

'Majesty,' John and I said together.

'Now. The treaty business tomorrow,' the Jade Emperor said.

'Majesty, may I once again —' John began.

'No,' the Jade Emperor said, interrupting him. 'We will not display any sign of weakness. They will only see our strength and confidence. We will not compromise our adherence to the protocols.'

'They didn't adhere to the protocols!' John protested. 'They attacked us in Hell when we collected the treaty.'

'And if they attack us in Heaven, I am counting on you to defend us,' the Jade Emperor said. 'I do not doubt your ability. Do you?'

John grunted with frustration. 'They have been doing things to themselves. The Western King —'

'Just be ready. They may try something. But we will not diminish the purity of Celestial Harmony by not adhering to the protocols! This is not negotiable. They will not terrorise us into any sign of weakness.'

'There's a vast difference between weakness and simple prudence —'

'The matter is settled. The negotiations will take place tomorrow in the Hall of Supreme Harmony.'

'At least evacuate the Celestial Palace,' John said, distraught.

'It has been. It will only be us and those required to maintain our presence.'

John rested his forehead in his hand, grim with defeat.

'Er Lang, Venus, dismissed,' the Jade Emperor said, and John's head shot up.

John and I shared a glance as the two men rose, went to the door, bowed to the Jade Emperor and went out.

I nodded towards the fairies.

'The Celestial Palace knows all that I know,' the Emperor said. 'Your secret is safe with it.'

'Majesty,' I said.

'I am pleased that the two of you have not concocted some ridiculously daring plan to rush in and extract your child,' he said. 'There is still hope that you both will attain some degree of wisdom before this is over.'

'It's the hardest thing we've ever done,' I said.

'I'm well aware of that. I have twenty-three children myself, Lady Emma, and eight of them are Elite guards. If Hell falls they will be at the mercy of the demon horde, and it is a certainty that they will not be adopted and loved by the King himself.'

'I understand and sympathise, Majesty,' I said. 'But this isn't about our child, is it? It's about me and his Serpent.'

'How many know?' the Emperor said.

'It's becoming obvious to everyone around us,' John said. He gestured slightly towards me. 'They hear me in her.'

The Jade Emperor leaned his elbow on the table and his chin in his hand.

We waited silently for him, then I realised why he hesitated.

'Oh hell, no,' I said. 'Not you too.'

He smiled slightly, still with his chin in his hand.

'This is absolutely none of your business,' John growled.

The Jade Emperor spread his hands, giving us the full benefit of his kindly old gentleman persona. 'I didn't say anything. I didn't order you to do anything.'

'All right,' I said, brisk and businesslike. 'If we were to do it — and I'm not saying I'm agreeing to you prostituting me here — how much would it affect the Celestial's chances of victory?'

'Not even a question, because if you don't want it, it won't happen,' John said, his voice still a low growl.

'I have not prostituted you, madam, because I have not told you to do anything,' the Emperor said with dignity. 'It would not affect the outcome of any aspect of the upcoming conflict with Hell in any way at all.'

'There's your answer then,' John said.

'But it would increase your chances of surviving this conflict from close to zero to about fifty-fifty,' the Emperor said to me.

'What?' John said, then gathered himself. 'I will Raise her!'

'Even so.'

'But if she's Raised,' John's expression darkened, 'how could she not survive? Give us more.'

'I don't need to.' The Emperor gestured towards me. 'She knows.'

'We'll merge before we can liberate your Serpent, and I'll be lost into you,' I said with resignation.

'There's still a fifty-fifty chance she'll be lost into me anyway?' John said, his voice hoarse with horror.

'No, because right now the likelihood of her being lost is a hundred per cent.'

'I would rather die than force my wife to submit to this,' John said.

'She is not your wife,' the Emperor said. 'And no force is necessary. All you need to do is reassure her that she will not be harmed and that the experience will not be unpleasant.

She is well on the way to saying yes anyway, Ah Wu, she just needs a little encouragement.'

John glanced at me and I smiled slightly. The Jade Emperor was right. I'd been unable to concentrate for most of the afternoon because I'd been debating whether I should ask John about it that evening, and the possibilities were driving me to distraction. All I needed when we were going into battle the next day.

The Emperor rose and we stood as well. 'My sincerest apologies for interfering in your private affairs in this way, but to be honest, Emma, I've grown quite fond of how you are completely unfazed by his grandiose displays of power and never hesitate to yank him off his altar when he becomes too arrogant.'

'I am never arrogant!' John protested.

'I'm more arrogant than he is,' I said. 'He's one of the most humble people on the Plane.'

The Jade Emperor went to the doorway, turned and slipped his hands into his sleeves. 'We need to hurry and have this Hell business out of the way so that you two can settle down together and we can all enjoy watching your antics. I am very much looking forward to that.' He bowed to us. 'I will leave you to it. Both of you are doing a fine job and the Celestial thanks you for your diligence.'

'Celestial Majesty,' we said in unison, and he and the fairies went out.

'Of all the interfering, intolerable, ridiculous old men —' John began.

'I try,' the Jade Emperor said outside the door. 'Venus, Er Lang, let's go.'

* * *

293

At 7 pm I went from my office back to the Imperial Residence to have dinner with the family. The dining room was deserted. I sat at the twelve-seater round table and Er Hao came in.

'They say they're on their way, ma'am. Do you want to wait for them or eat?' she said.

'I'll wait. Can I have some tea, please?'

She nodded and went out, then returned with a pot and three cups. I filled one and leaned back in my dining chair to wait for them.

Half an hour later, Simone stormed in. 'Sorry I'm late. I was with Leo and Ge Ge — they can't come but —'

She stopped, and I jerked upright. I'd fallen asleep against the back of the chair.

'Sorry, Emma,' she said more gently. 'I was just with Leo and Ge Ge at the Peak. We were teaching Buffy some martial arts.' Her eyes went bright with pleasure. 'She is so cute! I love her to bits. She's like a little sister. You should come down …' Her face fell as she realised I couldn't plane-shift and she changed the subject. 'Daddy's not here with you? You're all alone?'

'He'll be along when he's finished what he's doing,' I said.

She concentrated and nodded. 'He says to start without him, he'll be here as soon as he can.'

'Have you eaten?'

'No, I wanted to share this last —' She stopped herself again, then rallied. 'I wanted to be … with you. And Daddy. I asked Leo to come, but he's with Martin and Buffy, and that makes sense. Everybody should be with their family.'

'Did you talk to Nanna and Pop?' I said.

'Your family are stupid!' she snapped, then relented and sat next to me. 'Sorry. They wouldn't come. Something about the boys not wanting to come up here, so they all decided to stay together. They're stupid.'

'I only hope Greg's enough to guard them,' I said. 'Did you tell them to all stay in the same place with Greg while we give the treaty back tomorrow?'

'Yes, they —'

John interrupted her, stumbling into the dining room and falling into a seat on the other side of her. 'I'm here,' he said.

'Daddy, you look a million years old,' Simone said.

'I feel it,' John said, resting his face in his hand. 'What's that about Emma's family?'

'They're all together at Aunt Jennie and Greg's house, and Greg's guarding them,' Simone said. 'Greg will let me know if anything happens, and I'll go straight there.'

'Thanks, Simone. You tried, and that's what's important,' I said.

'Your family aren't coming up?' John said.

Simone harrumphed and crossed her arms. I didn't reply.

'Greg will be the first to fall if the worst happens, and if he's supposed to contact you —' John began.

'You are not helping,' Simone said.

'Sorry. I'll have some guards sent down for them.'

He concentrated and Er Hao brought in the plates, covered in aluminium foil to keep them warm. I poured tea for John and Simone as Er Hao lifted the foil off the dishes and put her hand over them to heat them.

'This feels like the third or fourth time that we've had dinner together on the eve of a battle, and every time the family shrinks a little more,' Simone said.

'That is the way of the world,' John said. 'People grow up and move away, people build families of their own, people —' He stopped.

She finished it for him. 'Die.'

'That is the way of the world.'

'Is it very hard, Daddy?'

He took my bowl and scooped steamed rice into it with the flat dimpled rice server. 'Sometimes.'

'I'll attain Immortality too. That way we'll always have each other,' she said.

He didn't reply.

'You said you couldn't see my future, but you can see Emma's?'

He nodded as he passed my bowl of rice to me, and reached for Simone's.

'She will be okay, won't she?'

He stopped with the bowl in his hand. 'There are many possible futures, depending upon our actions. As we act, the futures crystallise into the present.'

He filled the bowl with rice and handed it to her.

'What about Emma then?'

Neither of us replied.

'That bad?'

'We'll talk about it later,' I said.

'I don't want to talk about it later, I want to discuss it now,' Simone said.

'Actually I didn't mean you,' I said, and John's expression went grim.

'Would Emma merging with the Serpent count as her being Raised?' Simone said.

'No,' we said in unison.

'Don't lie to me, I can see it a mile off,' she said. She picked up some steamed gai lan from the dish in front of her and dropped it into her bowl. 'But if you merge, how can you two marry? You promised.'

I glanced up at John, full of hope, but his expression hadn't changed.

'Your promise will be gone with her?' she said.

John turned away from her and selected some mushrooms from one of the dishes.

'Just stay up here where it's safe, Emma, okay?' she said.

'Don't worry, I will.'

'Eat, Emma,' John said.

I looked at the smooth mound of rice John had put into my bowl, then at the vegetarian dishes spread before me. I'd dreamt of feasts like this when I'd been wandering cold and lost in the West, and now I couldn't face the food. I ladled some of the rich vegetarian broth with straw mushrooms and winter melon into my soup bowl instead, and choked it down.

'Kwan Yin hasn't even come to give us moral support,' Simone said.

'No Bodhisattva will ever assist any people at war,' John said.

'I know, that's exactly what Emma said.' Simone hesitated. 'That's *exactly* what Emma said. I love you two more than anything, and Emma, you're like a mother to me, but maybe you should separate for a little while? Emma, go and live in the West or the East or something when we win, and come back when Daddy's whole again? I don't want to lose you.'

'You heard me say I would talk to him later.'

'Oh.' She nodded. 'Okay.'

'So what's the plan for tomorrow?' I said.

'We'll return the treaty at the Celestial Palace at noon.'

'At the Celestial Palace?' Simone said, horrified.

'I tried to talk him out of it, but the Jade Emperor's being stubborn,' John said. 'He refuses to display any weakness in front of the Demon King. As soon as we reject the treaty, the Jade Emperor says they'll attack. The obvious first target is the Celestial side of Hell. They nearly took it last time, and if they can hold it every Immortal who dies will be in their hands.'

'How's the Serpent?' I said.

'I don't know, I'm not even looking,' John said, and lifted the bowl to his face to scoop some rice into his mouth.

'Good,' Simone said.

'What about that grill they put under the Serpent?' I said.

John shrugged. 'I've asked Ming to stand by during the meeting with ice packs to throw on me if they try to cook me, but it might be better ...' He didn't finish.

'Does that mean Leo will be on the Earthly with Buffy?' Simone said.

'Yes. One of them stays with her at all times. She's a target, as much as you were. There haven't been any tries for her yet, but it's just a matter of time.'

'Geez,' Simone said. 'I can see what you guys went through. How awful.'

'I'd like to give you some last-minute polishing on your swords tomorrow morning,' John said. 'After I've gone around and done a final check on all the defences. We'll talk to our elementals as well.'

'Okay,' Simone said. 'I like to think that this time tomorrow, we'll be here eating with everybody, and things will be back the way they should be. If we can get this all sorted, then I'll only have missed a couple of weeks at the university and I'll still be able to start.'

'I hope you're right,' I said.

'And then we can make plans to get your Serpent and my little brother out.'

'We will,' I said.

John put his chopsticks down. 'I've been summoned. Er Lang and Guan Yu want a last-minute review of the Gate defences.' He patted Simone on the back. 'Don't wait up for me, either of you. But Emma, I'll try to be back before you sleep so we can talk.'

'I will wait up for you anyway,' I said.

Simone hugged him from her chair and he clutched her with his eyes closed.

'I love you, Daddy,' she whispered.

'You are my life, little one,' he said. He rubbed her on the back and she released him. He rose, came to me and kissed the top of my head. 'Really. Don't wait up. I may be a while.'

'We still need to talk later, so wake me when you get home,' I said.

He put his hand on my shoulder. 'I will.'

He stalked out, his whole frame rigid with tension, and disappeared before he was completely through the door.

'Eat, Emma,' Simone said, waving her chopsticks over the food. 'You need to be strong.'

I ladled some more soup into my bowl.

22

He gently shook my shoulder, waking me. 'Emma.'

I put my arm over my eyes. The bedroom was dim and he was a dark shape sitting over me. I blinked with confusion. 'Has something happened?' I checked the bedside clock: it was after midnight.

'No. I just came in.'

I sat up. 'Wait for me, I'll be right back.'

When I came out of the bathroom, he was sitting on the bed in his black pyjama pants.

'We need to talk,' he said.

'Okay,' I said, and sat across from him.

He took my hands and spoke formally, as if he'd been practising this speech. 'Emma, you — and my daughter — are the most precious things in the world to me. I know what the Jade Emperor said, and I know that you're not sure. But your life is at stake, and this could be our last night together, so if you could —'

I didn't let him finish. I threw my arms around his neck and kissed him hard. He jolted with surprise, then slipped his arms around me and returned the kiss. We shared the feeling for a long time, his hands roaming my body. I wasn't even aware of the fact that we'd slid down to lie beside each other and our clothes had disappeared until he pulled back to see me.

'That's a yes,' I said, breathless.

His hair had come completely undone and he brushed it out of the way, then leaned up onto his elbow to see my face. He put his hand on my cheek and his eyes roamed my features, his expression intense.

'Your life is so precious,' he said. 'Anything that will give you a greater chance of survival …'

'I know. I said yes, John.'

He snapped out of it. 'Yes?'

I nodded.

He hesitated. 'Yes to what?'

I pushed him onto his back, climbed on top and nibbled along the edge of his jaw, making him breathe more quickly. I worked my way up the side of his face to whisper into his ear, a soft breath. 'I want your Turtle.'

His eyebrows creased and he moaned gently without moving.

I moved back down to the side of his throat, covered it with kisses, and drifted lower over his chest.

'Bring it out for me,' I said into his chest. 'I want it.'

'No, you don't,' he said, his voice warm and low. He ran his hand over my back. 'You're terrified. I can feel it. I changed my mind. Go back to sleep.'

'Terrified and excited. I want to make the leap.'

'You're scared, Emma, I can't do this to you.'

'I know I'm scared. But I want to do it anyway.' I shifted further down: he was thoroughly ready for this. I ran my tongue over him, enjoying his taut silken firmness and his breathless reaction. I looked up into his eyes. 'The fear just makes the excitement more intense. I want this so much …'

'I'm not sure.'

I moved back up to brush kisses over his face and covered his mouth with my own. He wrapped his arms around me and held me as if he would never let me go.

'You were just about to ask me to do it, to save my life.' I pulled back. 'It's what I want. Do it for me. I want the Turtle. Give me the Turtle.'

'I can't control it,' he said, his voice strained.

'Don't,' I said. 'This is what I want. Let it out. Your Turtle can have me.'

He made a rasping sound of defeat, rolled me onto my back and lay on top of me, his long hair a curtain around his head. He dropped to kiss me again, his whole body stretched against me. He pulled away to see me, looked me up and down, then moved his mouth down over my breasts and eagerly teased me.

I quivered beneath him and dug my fingers into his wonderful silken hair.

He smiled up at me, brushed his hair out of the way again, and moved further down to bury his face into me.

I squeaked and shuddered as his tongue pressed into me, and clamped my mouth shut to stop the loud sounds I wanted to make.

Make as much noise as you like, nobody will hear you, he said, and I let out a loud moan of pleasure.

'John, stop, stop,' I said urgently, and he raised his head, concerned. I gestured. 'Come up here and give me the Turtle.'

He looked down at me again, hesitating, then climbed back up.

'I'm ready,' I said.

'It shouldn't be something you have to be ready for. It should just happen.'

I smiled slightly and touched his cheek. 'Then let's make it happen.'

He closed his eyes and looked down for a moment, concentrating, then up into my face. 'Let me make sure I have control.' He took a few deep breaths as he lay with his hands on either side of me. 'Are you truly sure?'

I gazed up at his noble caring face and somehow managed to fall in love with him all over again. 'I truly am.'

'Tell me to stop any time and I will.'

I stroked his cheek. 'I won't need to.'

'I haven't done this before, I'm not sure …'

'Just tell me what you need.'

'This.' He put his hand under my shoulder and gently levered me over so I was on my belly, then pulled me up to my hands and knees. He brushed kisses over my back and spoke into my skin. 'Oh yes. This.' He shifted closer, moved into position and pushed his hips against me without entering. He filled his hands with chi and swept them up and down my back, and the energy flickered over my skin, cool and electric. I couldn't help myself; I gasped in response and pushed back against him.

'This is wonderful,' he said, moving with me, and I leaned back into him, wanting more. He bent so that his chest was against my back and ran his hands over me, trailing energy that flickered from warm to cool, sliding like water over my skin.

'Just say stop and I'll stop. I promise,' he said.

'I'm okay.' I dropped my voice. 'You're driving me crazy.'

'Good. Because the idea of doing this with you, like this … what's the word? Fantasy.' He took an audibly deep breath, then straightened and put one hand on my lower back. 'Okay.'

I went completely still, waiting for him.

'Can you drop down slightly?' He made a soft sound of appreciation. 'Nice. Spread your legs a little wider.' He made another low sound in his throat. 'Yes.' His voice grew husky. 'Oh, that's very good.'

He backed off slightly to glide his fingertip down over me, firm and teasing and touching exactly the right spots, making me quiver in response. He slid his finger inside me and touched me with energy and I collapsed forward to grasp the pillow, breathless and panting.

He ran his hands up to my shoulders and shifted back into position. 'I can't hold off much longer if I'm to keep control of it, having you like this is just too … damn … good. Are you absolutely sure?'

'I'm absolutely sure,' I said, panting against the pillow and desperate with need. 'If you don't do this soon …'

His voice was next to my ear. 'Just say stop and I will. Any time. I promise I will stop if it's too —'

I gripped the pillow, ready for his weight. 'Stop asking and do it.'

He was poised against me and I moved to let him in.

He jerked back. 'Don't.'

I froze.

'No, I mean … relax,' he said, running his hands over my back. He spread over me again and rested his cheek on my shoulder. His hair covered both of us as he spoke very softly, almost a breath, into my ear. 'Let me inside as Turtle.'

He panted a few times, his chest moving against me. 'Let me ... as Turtle. Let the real me inside?' He wrapped his arms around me. 'Will you?'

I raised myself slightly and freed one of my hands so I could take his hand and kiss it. 'I love you, Xuan Wu, and I will give you anything you ask of me. Your Turtle can have me. I am yours.'

A sharp hoarse sound of pleasure escaped him and he released my hand to hold my shoulders. I dropped back down to all fours, his weight shifted and there were flippers. I panicked at the sight of them and nearly told him to stop, but he pressed and then slid into me and hit every pleasure point with a vibrating delicious touch. He flooded through me, huge and cool and soft and hard, and my brain exploded. I was as big as the universe and the stars spread around me. I dropped lower to give him purchase, my vision sparkling with brilliant lights.

'Are you all right?' a voice whispered in my ear.

'John. John?'

'I'm here,' he said, and I relaxed. It was him.

Then my body responded and I moved with him as he slid cool and smooth across my back. The lights across my vision encompassed the world, and the energy surged into me until I thought I would pass out. Time stood still, the pleasure slowly building and his voice in my ear, saying words I didn't understand as I was lost in sensation.

It seemed like forever until we grew more urgent, losing ourselves into each other and abandoning control. The pleasure became a tiny point of intensity within me, fierce and ice-cold, driving me to seek reassurance that he was still there for me.

'John? John?'

'Emma!' he shouted, and the exhilarating cold surged into me and we tumbled over the edge together, moving fast and hard and leaving no more room for words. The energy resonated between us and my head filled with light, then our movements slowed as the light faded and I collapsed onto my stomach, unable to see, his weight reassuring above me.

His hands returned, his fingers dancing over my shoulders. I jerked and quivered, still experiencing feedback from what he'd done. I lay on my belly on the bed and his human weight was on top of me, his breath panting in my ear.

He flopped onto his back next to me, then turned his head to see my face, his expression full of concern. 'Talk to me. You seemed to enjoy it, and you never said stop, but if it was painful or too strange ...'

'I nearly said stop. Then it changed from freaky to ... wonderful.'

He relaxed back onto the pillow with a soft sound of relief.

'I can't move,' I said, still twitching with small spasms of pleasure. 'Give me a moment.'

He nodded. 'Neither can I.'

We both lay gasping for some time, then he took my right hand and raised it. 'Look.'

My arm was healed. The muscles that had wasted away after the demon essence was removed from my right forearm had returned. I turned my hand over, rapt; my skin was perfect and without a single freckle or blemish. I used his hand as a lever and he helped me to flop onto my back. I looked down at myself. I was glowing with good health and I looked twenty years younger; firmer and more muscular again. The rawness of my skin, a leftover from the burns I'd suffered, was gone and my many battle scars had disappeared. I was dying to see myself in a mirror but I could barely move.

I turned my head to see him. He looked about twenty-five. I'd never seen him so young.

I managed to wrap myself around him. 'How do you put up with doing it in human form after experiencing that?'

He ran his hand over my face, his dark eyes studying me. 'Pleasure is pleasure. Love is love.'

I raised myself on one elbow to see him. 'I'm surprised other Celestials don't seek out turtle Shen ...' I saw his face. 'Oh. They do.' I bent to kiss him. 'It was wonderful. It was worth taking the chance.'

He sighed with relief.

I smiled slightly and ran my hand over his chest. 'That was the most intense climax I've ever experienced.'

'Just one?' He winced. 'I'm losing my touch.'

'I was nervous. Next time I won't be.' I fell to lie next to him and stroked his skin. 'I very much won't be.' I raised my head slightly. 'How many times is usual?'

'Oh, eight, nine ... most lose count.'

'Whoa.'

He smiled and his eyes crinkled up.

'You can stop watching now, stone,' I said.

It didn't reply.

'Talk to me, stone. I know you were watching.'

'I was shut down. I never watch, you know I don't.'

'Stone, I know you were watching to make sure I'd be okay,' I said.

The stone hesitated, then said, 'Perhaps.'

'I asked it to,' John said. 'Emma, I —'

'Sorry, Emma,' the stone said, its voice small.

'To be honest, I'm glad you were keeping an eye on us,' I said, interrupting both of them. 'I wanted to ask you to supervise, but couldn't bring myself to say the words.'

John let his breath out with even more relief.

'Threesome,' I said.

'If it was a threesome, you'd be unable to move for very much longer,' the stone growled. Its voice grew sly. 'Turtle ...'

'Hmm?'

'It comes out of your *tail*?'

I turned to see John's face. His expression went completely blank.

'Seriously?' I said.

His face was still blank.

'Damn, I really must see that as soon as you're able,' I said with enthusiasm, and he relaxed. 'But why?'

John shrugged. 'The mechanics are complicated.' He smiled slightly. 'Just be very glad that the Turtle isn't the one in the cage with its tail cut off.'

'You have a point,' the stone said. 'Now if you'll excuse me, I'll be in my bunk.'

I sighed and flopped back to cuddle into John. 'God, I feel wonderful. Exhausted and satisfied and wonderful.'

'Satisfied?' he said, sounding disappointed. 'I wanted to do it again.'

'What, right now?'

His eyes wrinkled up.

'I think I need some time to recover.'

'Weak humans,' he said, and held me close.

'Insatiable turtles,' I said, then stiffened when I saw the bedside clock over his shoulder.

'What?' he said, concerned.

'It's 2 am.'

'Oh. You'd better get some sleep then.'

'We were at it for nearly two hours? It felt like ten minutes at the most.'

'Then I was doing it right,' he breathed.

* * *

We went to the Residence dining room for breakfast early the next morning — we didn't need much sleep. John was obviously still feeling as energised as I was from the evening's exercise, and both of us really did look twenty years younger. We sat at the table, John concentrated, and the demons brought us a huge tureen of mushroom congee and a selection of pickled vegetables to share.

Simone came in wearing a pair of jeans and a hoodie, and stopped when she saw us, her expression full of shock.

John waved for her to enter. 'Come on in. Plenty of food.'

She spun on her heel and went out again. John concentrated, then shook his head, talking to her. His face went grim.

'She's blocking me. I'm trying to tell her it's nothing ...' He sighed.

Meredith stormed into the dining room, grabbed me by the upper arm, ignoring my protests, and dragged me into the living room. She sat me down on one of the couches and sat across from me.

'Talk to me,' she said, studying me intensely. 'Are you all right? Do you need someone to talk to? How bad was it?' She turned away and wiped her hand over her face. 'We all knew this would happen eventually. I'm going to *kill* him.' She turned back to me. 'I should have spoken to you a long time ago, but he promised it wouldn't happen —'

I raised my hands. 'Meredith, stop.'

She watched me silently, and I felt more than her eyes on me. 'Oh, dear Lord,' she said softly.

I nodded, smiling. I showed her my right arm and she rose from the couch to take it, turning it over to study it.

'Damn. That's incredible.' She glanced up at me. 'You really agreed to this?'

I nodded again.

'You are *so strange*,' she hissed. 'You two are a completely matched set. Unbelievable.'

'Don't forget I'm a reptile myself, Meredith. Everybody keeps forgetting I'm a snake. I must take serpent form more often to remind you all.'

She sat back down on the couch, obviously relieved.

'Can I have my breakfast now?' I said. 'I'm starving.'

She sighed and shook her head. 'It's great to see both of you in such fine shape. Him, particularly.' She smiled slightly. 'Of course, the minute you walk out the door and everybody sees you ...'

'Good idea,' I said. 'I'll have him hide it so we look as terrible as ever.'

'Brilliant,' she said. 'The demons will never know what hit them. Do you think you'll be ...' She searched for the words. 'Repeating the treatment?'

'Oh, absolutely,' I said with enthusiasm.

'Good.' She rose. 'Go and have breakfast, and tell him to hide it. I'll let the Celestial Masters know not to quiz you about your new energy levels. You're so full of ching you're close on Immortal yourself.'

'He did promise to Raise me,' I said.

'I've never heard of this leading to Immortality, but from the looks of you it's a definite possibility,' she said. 'Ask him

310

about it; he'd know more than anyone. And now if you'll excuse me, ma'am,' she bowed slightly, 'I have to supervise the disposition of our defensive forces.'

She went out, and I returned to the dining room.

'Everything all right?' he said.

'Why didn't you come in and tell her it was okay?'

'You may have wanted to speak to her alone.'

I pulled my bowl closer; he'd already filled it with congee. 'I didn't.'

He tucked into his own as-yet untouched food. 'Excellent.'

Simone came in and stopped. John ladled some of the congee into a bowl and handed it to her.

'Don't say anything, I don't want to hear about it,' she said as she sat with her bowl. 'I. Do. Not. Want. To. Know.'

'We weren't going to,' I said.

'None of your business anyway,' John said.

'Pair of weirdos,' she said under her breath and stirred the congee with her spoon.

John and I shared an amused glance and ate our congee with gusto. We really were starving.

'So Emma can take the Elixir now?' Simone said after a while. 'She's strong enough?'

I lit up at that. I hadn't thought of it. I could take the Elixir and really be useful in the defence of the Heavens.

John studied his congee. 'This isn't true recovery. It'll fade after a week.'

'Okay,' Simone said. 'I hope we'll all be back here in a week and both of you look this good again.'

I glanced at her. 'Really?'

'Whatever it takes.' She shrugged and her voice thickened. 'All I want is to be able to share meals with my family. Is that too much to ask?'

'It's all we want as well,' I said, and John rubbed my back.

'Putting up with this is an unpleasant by-product of what we are,' he said. 'We are strong, and many people rely on our strength.'

'I know, and I'm ready to use my strength to help them,' Simone said.

'I'm proud of you.' John became more serious. 'When we reject the treaty at noon, the demons will immediately attack. Emma, please stay here on the Mountain where you're safe …'

'I plan to,' I said.

'Simone, don't risk yourself. Stay out of the main melee, be selective about who you choose to take on, and if things become too hard, don't hesitate to retreat.'

'Are you going to remind me to go to the bathroom before we leave as well?' she said, exasperated.

'Well, it's a good idea …' he said.

She raised her spoon. 'I'm nearly nineteen and I'm going into battle today. Cut it out.'

He looked from Simone to me. 'I don't want to lose either of you.'

'And we don't want to lose you,' I said. 'If they do something to disable you, we'll put you back in the cage, so be ready to take your smallest True Form.'

'And if you're in any danger at all, make sure you have that claw,' John said.

'No,' I said. 'I'm giving it to Simone straight after breakfast.'

'Dammit,' he said into his congee. 'I should have given you a piece of my shell last night.' He looked up. 'After what the Jade Emperor said, maybe you should keep it.'

'After what the Jade Emperor said, we know what my chances are, and the claw won't make any difference,' I said. 'I'm giving it to Simone.'

'What claw?' Simone said.

I put my hand out and the claw appeared in it. I passed it to her and she took it and turned it over in her hands.

'This is more than a good-luck charm,' I said. 'This is an item that could save your whole existence. Hold on to it. Keep it close. If you think you're going to …' I couldn't say the word. 'Make sure it's in contact with your skin.'

'What is it?' she said.

'The Tiger's claw.'

She looked at us, from one to the other. 'Why?'

'We can't say,' John said. 'Just make sure you have it in your hand.'

'I can do better than that,' she said, and shoved it down the front of her shirt into her bra.

John's eyes went wide with astonishment.

'Is that okay?' I said. 'The end's awfully sharp.'

'The sharp bit's sticking into the padding. I might go find some cotton wool to wrap around it as well. I have plenty.'

I didn't think it would be possible for John's eyes to go wider, but they did.

'Liu Cheng Rong is a wine nut — he should have a cork you can use,' I said.

She unfocused and snapped back. 'He says yes, he has one. Good idea, Emma.'

I finished my congee and checked the art deco mantel clock over the fireplace. 'We have five hours.'

John rose. 'I'll be in Hell for the next two hours, then I'm coming up here to supervise the disposition of the Mountain defences. After that I'll give you some last-minute tips, Simone. At noon, the King will return with the treaty. Emma, I'd like both you and Ming to watch my back in case they do something to me.'

'What about me?' Simone said.

'I will let you know when the situation is clearer.'

'Don't you dare leave me out of this,' she said. 'I have yin, and those black-armoured demons could be there.'

'I'm well aware of that,' he said. He put his arms around our shoulders and kissed our heads, one after the other. I raised my face and he kissed me with more passion, then stood straight. 'I'll be back about nine. Stay safe, both of you.'

'You stay safe too, Daddy,' Simone said. 'Be careful.'

He nodded to her without replying and went out.

She sat again. 'These are going to be the longest five hours in the history of the world.'

'I think you're right.'

'Uh ...' She pushed her nearly untouched bowl away. 'He was right about going to the bathroom. Suddenly my tummy's really wobbly. Can you stay here and wait for me? I'll be right back.'

'I'll be here,' I said, and she raced out to the downstairs powder room.

23

There was silence as we waited for the Demon King to enter. The Celestial Palace really was deserted; the only sound was the breeze through the clerestory windows high above us. John, in full Celestial Form with Seven Stars, stood next to the massive rosewood negotiation table in the centre of the hall. Imperial Elites in their red and gold armour stood along the walls of the hall, and Er Lang and Venus flanked the Emperor's throne on the dais. Martin and I waited at the side of the dais with ice packs and water in case the demons did something to John.

The Door Gods opened the double doors and a cohort of demon Dukes in human form, appearing as Chinese warriors wearing black enamel armour, entered the hall and formed an honour guard on either side of the carpet.

The silence thickened even further and both Demon Kings strode into the hall accompanied by a single Snake Mother, all of them in human form. The Eastern Demon King was short and slender, wearing scaled armour of red and gold, with his maroon hair long and in a traditional topknot. His fine fair features gave his face a classical beauty, marred by the cruelty in his red eyes. He watched with satisfaction as the Dukes positioned themselves around him.

The Western Demon King's human form was taller. He wore a double-breasted pinstriped suit and looked exactly like the dead Russian gangster on the tombstone: fair, with dark hair and eyes. He walked casually with his jacket undone and his hands in his pockets.

The two Kings stopped inside the door and looked around. The Eastern King nodded along the lines of Elites, obviously counting and weighing them up, and John stiffened. The Western King was more relaxed, looking around the hall with a small smile on his face. He saw me and his smile widened as he waved to me.

They moved to the table and stopped. The Celestials waited for the Kings to kneel, but they didn't. There was a long moment of silence as the two sides faced off. The Jade Emperor sat on his throne above them, glaring as he waited for them to show their respect. John dropped his head and his eyes burnt.

The Jade Emperor rose. 'Xuan Tian.'

'Majesty,' John said, his voice deep and resonant and as majestic as the rest of him.

'I delegate this negotiation to the Northern Heavens.'

John bowed slightly without looking away from the Demon Kings. 'Celestial Majesty.'

The Jade Emperor turned and walked down the steps at the back of the dais, with Venus and Er Lang following him.

John shrank in size to match the Demon Kings, took human form in his robes and armour, and made the table smaller to fit. He gestured stiffly with one hand, inviting the Demon Kings to sit at the table with him.

The Eastern King bowed slightly and held one hand out in reply.

The Western King took his jacket off and threw it on the table, then pulled a chair out, sat and leaned back with his hands behind his head. Both John and the Eastern King glared at him and he smiled and shrugged.

'Your *boy* dishonours you, Ah Mo,' John said.

'I know,' the Eastern Demon King said. He concentrated on the Western King. The Western King's smile didn't shift, and he shrugged again. The Eastern King gestured angrily towards him and his expression darkened. They had a silent argument, and the Western King sat straighter in his chair. Both their faces became fierce with rage. Eventually, the Western King threw himself to his feet, tipping his chair over. He grabbed his jacket, turned and stalked towards the door, gesturing angrily at the Dukes as he passed them. Two of them peeled off to escort him out of the hall.

Martin and I shared a look. John stood silent and dour, then bowed and gestured towards the table again. The Demon King bowed back and mirrored the move, and John pulled a chair out and sat.

The Demon King picked up the fallen chair and put it on the third side of the table between them. He smiled at me and gestured with his head. 'Come on, Brains, come and be a part of this. Without you involved, the Dark Lord's at a distinct disadvantage and I want these negotiations to be completely equitable.'

I hesitated. John nodded so slightly it was almost imperceptible, and I walked carefully to them. I stood behind John, to his left, and put my hand on his shoulder.

'Sit, Lady, sit,' the Demon King said, indicating the chair.

'I'll stay here with my Lord, if you don't mind,' I said, squeezing John's shoulder.

John nodded imperceptibly again.

The Demon King gestured up at the Snake Mother, who was standing behind him and mirroring my position. 'This is Lucinda; you might remember her. Brightest one I have, but doesn't want the job. She's acting Number One until enough people die and someone is still standing to take the position.' He glanced up at her, his eyes full of amusement, but she didn't move. 'She really should do it, but she'd prefer to stay female.'

'I think you mean alive,' I said, and Lucinda nodded to me, smiling slightly.

'Like I said, smart,' the King said. 'So do we have an agreement, Ah Wu? Will you let us play in the sun again? The little ones want to come out. They're jealous of the big ones being allowed to do stuff up top.'

John put his hand out and the binder appeared in it. He placed it on the table in front of him. 'The terms are not acceptable. The existing agreement is to stand.'

'You're rejecting it outright?' the King said, incredulous.

'I am. Go back to Hell.'

'I thought at least you'd negotiate something,' the King said. 'You know we'll try to take the Earthly by force if you deny us outright.'

'We will stop you.'

'Your nature betrays you,' the King said. 'You want to go to war.'

'I never want to go to war. But your terms are unacceptable.'

'Then let's negotiate something acceptable!' the King said, spreading his hands to emphasise the point. 'All we want is for more of us to have a longer time in the sunshine. That's all.'

'You want to torture humans.'

'They deserve it,' the King spat. 'They treat each other like shit. The men treat the women worse than animals. Everybody uses the children as slaves. They're repulsive. They deserve everything we want to give them.'

'They deserve a chance to become something greater.'

'Pah,' the King said with disgust. 'Only a tiny fraction of them ever learn true compassion. The rest spend all their time boosting their own self-importance by degrading their brothers and sisters. They're happy to wallow in their filth, polluting the air and fouling the water. Some parts of the Earthly make Hell look pleasant.'

'Then go back to Hell and let the humans manage their own domain,' John said.

'My children need to play in the sun,' the King said. 'Give us more time at Hungry Ghosts. Let us play with the really bad ones before they arrive in Hell. We won't harm the innocent.' He cocked his head to one side. 'It can't be that hard to negotiate something, can it? There has to be some middle ground, Ah Wu, let's not go to war over this. I could win, and if I do, you'll lose everything.'

'Ah Mo,' John said, exasperated, 'your children already break the terms of the agreement we brokered all that time ago, and we're flexible about it as long as they don't go overboard. We let the Princes have their business dealings — even when it's obvious they're hurting humans — as long as it isn't to excess. We let the Mothers wander around the Earthly for more than their allotted time to keep them occupied. You already have what you're asking for. All you need to do is go home and we'll be at peace again.'

'The little ones want more time,' the King said.

'There are tens of thousands of them,' John said. 'We can't give them more time. If I let them onto the Earthly many humans will suffer. When they grow large enough they can come up, and they know it. Leave them where they are. They're so small and mindless that it's not worth risking everything for them.'

'You have a point.' The King studied John for a while, then obviously made a decision. 'But when I took the throne, I promised them that I'd give them more time in the sun.'

'You gave your word?'

'Solemn oath, Ah Wu, in front of everybody. It's the only thing that's kept me alive.'

'You've broken your word before. You guaranteed our safety when you gave us this,' he raised the treaty, 'and you made a try for me anyway.'

'That was to you. This is to my own children. If I break this one, I'm dead and gone and you know it. They've been patient, but their patience is wearing thin, and now that I have your other half I have no choice. I must make a move.' He raised his hand and smiled. 'And don't even think about offering me asylum. I'd rather give my children a chance to be in the sunshine than be your slave.'

'Very well,' John said, and put the binder to one side on the table. 'But before we do this, let's talk about my family.' He raised his head slightly and the Elites saluted him, weapons in hand, and filed out. 'Dismiss your guard.'

The Demon King concentrated for a moment, his blood-red eyes intense, and the demon Dukes filed out of the hall as well. John waited a moment, then nodded confirmation that they'd actually gone. Both of them relaxed slightly.

'Sit, Emma, this includes you,' John said, gesturing towards the empty chair.

'What about Simone?' I said as I pulled the chair around to John's side of the table and sat next to him.

'I don't trust the King anywhere near her.'

The King smiled. 'Is Simone eighteen yet?' He saw John's expression and leaned back, grinning. 'No! No! Not like that. She'd make a brilliant Number One, you know? The training you've given her, her knowledge, skills and intelligence ... damn.' He shook his head. 'Exceptional. I'd love to have her as Number One and groom her for the job of King if I ever fall. Both of them together, her and lovely Frankie ...' His eyes were wide with admiration. 'They'd make a formidable team, particularly if they had Emma standing behind them to advise.'

'I think both Emma and Simone would die first.'

I nodded agreement.

The King shrugged. 'Worth a try.'

'I have an offer for you,' John said. 'I want to trade your life in the coming conflict for that of my family. It is inevitable that we will face each other before this is over, and if you can guarantee their safety I will ensure that you are spared.'

'We won't harm the boy. He's ...' The King hesitated, and dropped his voice. 'The light of my life, actually.' He nodded to me. 'He will be kept safe, Emma. But I don't have the time that he deserves, and the servants can't give him the stimulation an intelligent child like him needs. Why don't you come and be his nanny and care for him? All you have to do is say yes and you can spend all your time with him.'

I sat for a long time, intensely aware of John's fierce dark presence next to me. This was my son. This was my *baby*, and I could be with him every day ...

I leaned back and grinned. 'There you go, trying to get me into Hell again. What is this fixation on me? I'm small and human.'

'Exactly,' the King said. 'The only thing you have going for you,' he gestured towards John, 'is that he loves you and you're worth something as a hostage. But frankly, the two kids are worth way more. Look at him dropping the negotiation about the Celestial and talking about his family instead. He'd probably sacrifice you in a second if it meant saving Simone's life.'

'I'd sacrifice myself in a second if it meant Simone's life as well,' I said.

'There, you see? Some of the programming is even still there. It never ceases to amaze me that something as small and defenceless as you has managed to survive so long. I don't know how you made it through the night when we dumped you in the West. You should have died.'

'I'm a survivor,' I said with grim humour.

'That you are,' the King said, and turned back to John. 'So my life for the safety of your family? I have a better idea.' He leaned his elbow on the table and studied John. '*Your* life for the safety of your family.'

John glowered. 'Don't be ridiculous.'

'I don't mean kneel down right now and let me take your head,' the King said, exasperated. 'Use your brain, Ah Wu. Oh, I forgot, *I* have it.' He smiled slightly. 'There are no rules in war. Things will happen that are beyond our control. I'll try to protect Emma and Simone out of the respect I hold for you, but I can't guarantee anything.' He raised his hand. 'But if you come to me, change to True Form and go into that cage, I guarantee their safety. The boy too. They can come up to Heaven and live here as

322

a family under my protection when I win.'

John studied him for a long moment.

'Shut up, Emma, this is between him and me,' the King said without looking away from John. 'He's remained silent while you negotiated with me; do him the same courtesy.'

'Your word can't be trusted,' John said.

The King spread his hands. 'I'm going to a war I don't want because I promised them the sunshine, and I'm keeping my word to them.'

'You're going to a war you do want because you're holding a high hand and fishing for one more tile,' John said.

'You can't trust him, John. That's why I didn't take his offer,' I said softly.

'I told you to stay out of this,' the King said without looking away from John, his voice sharp.

'I know, Emma.' John rose and held the treaty out to the Demon King. 'If you had never broken your word, things may have been different. I will keep my word, though: as long as my wife and children are safe, I will not take your life in the coming conflict.' He nodded to the King. 'Contact me anytime if you wish to renegotiate a settlement. Anything is preferable to war.'

The King sighed without moving to take the treaty. 'Obviously we have to sort this out the hard way. Give the order, Lucinda. Start at five hundred volts.'

'Majesty,' Lucinda said.

John fell sideways and flopped onto the floor. His muscles seized so hard that he hit his head on the polished stone with a loud crack. Martin ran to us and crouched over John, obviously feeling helpless as John shook with spasms. I pushed Martin away, rolled John over onto his side and tried to put him into the recovery position as he fought me.

I attempted to check that he hadn't swallowed his tongue, but he moved too fast and hard and both of us had to step back as his limbs flailed. He kicked the table to the other side of the hall and it smashed into the wall.

'Stop,' the King said, and John went still, panting on the ground with his eyes open.

Martin put his arms under John's shoulders and assisted him to sit on his chair. John flopped, his eyes open but unseeing, and a dark stain spread over his pants: he'd lost control of his bladder during the seizure. I pulled my chair closer and sat next to him, slipping under his arm to keep him upright, but he was obviously unconscious with his eyes open.

The King stood. 'I didn't mean to embarrass him to that degree.' He bowed slightly. 'I apologise for this dishonour, Ah Wu.'

Martin positioned himself behind us and put his hands on either side of John's head. His hands glowed with shen energy for an instant and John snapped back to consciousness. He quickly dried himself and pushed me away to sit upright unaided, but was obviously still dazed.

'Have you finished torturing him?' I said. 'You're not achieving anything except to prove that you can't be trusted.'

'It had to be done. He has to be out of the way,' the King said. 'See you in Hell, guys. I tried to avoid this, and it's your choice to make it happen.'

He gestured towards Lucinda without looking at her, then rose and bowed to John and me. They turned and walked out of the hall together.

'There's another child?' Martin said.

'Wait,' John said, raising his hand. He relaxed. 'They're gone. They're not trying the Celestial; they're returning to

Hell.' He dropped his voice. 'I need medical attention. I can't see out of my left eye.'

Martin and I both assisted him to struggle to the Celestial Palace medical centre. His left leg dragged and he had difficulty with his balance. Halfway there he had another seizure. His movements were so violent that he writhed out of our grip and fell again. He scrabbled at the ground, his eyes wide, and made horrible garbled noises. After an eternal couple of minutes, the seizure stopped and John lay silent and unmoving on the ground with his eyes open, again unconscious, and with blood trickling out of his mouth.

'I can only do this two or three more times before it kills me,' Martin said, putting his hand, loaded with shen, on John's face.

John snapped back to consciousness, pulled himself onto his hands and knees, and looked around. He reached for me. I helped him to his feet, and he clutched me. Martin moved to his other side and we held him up. He wiped his hand over his mouth and winced at the blood there; he'd bitten his tongue.

John squeezed me and spoke, but what came out was meaningless gibberish. He tried to speak again, and again it was meaningless. His eyes widened and he switched to silent speech, but again the words were mangled beyond recognition in my head.

Martin levered John off him and turned to peer into his eyes. 'His left pupil is severely dilated, but the other one is okay. Brain damage? We need to find him medical attention right away, but if this is serious he may need an Earthly hospital.'

'John, do you understand me?' I said.

He didn't respond; he just leaned on me, panting.

'Shit,' I said softly. 'We need someone to take him to the Mountain. Can you?'

'I can try,' Martin said, and lifted John off me to take his full weight. 'What about you?'

'Can you take both of us?'

'No.'

'Just him then. We have to take him to the Grotto.'

'Why the Grotto?'

'We'll put him into the Celestial Jade cage. Take him to the Grotto and put him in —'

We landed outside the Grotto and I raised my head. 'Thank you!' I said loudly to the Jade Emperor. I dropped my voice. 'Ming. Go into the armoury where the Celestial weapons are kept — the Celestial Jade cage is there. Meet us back here with it.' John leaned more heavily on me. 'Hurry!'

I opened the Grotto door and carefully assisted John down the stairs, his feet dragging. I laid him on the cold stone next to the water and raised my head to speak to the fish.

'Everybody out. That's an order.'

Martin came down the stairs, the door closing behind him, and passed me the casket.

I put it on the floor and removed the lid. 'I hope he's conscious enough to change. Hold him, and when he changes put him inside. I'll close the lid.'

Martin held John's head up. John lay unmoving with his eyes open and his face slack.

'He seems too out of it, Emma.'

'Can you speak to him?'

Martin put one hand on the side of John's face and pulled it around to look into his eyes. He shook his head. 'He's too far gone.'

'We need him conscious and aware. The demons —'

Martin's head shot up, and I felt it as well. The Jade Emperor had called battle stations. The demons had attacked Hell.

John made some garbled noises, pushed Martin away and struggled to climb to his hands and knees. He bent his head for a moment, panting, then lurched to his feet and staggered, nearly falling. With visible effort he regained his balance and took Celestial Form with Seven Stars on his back. He bent, took my hands, raised them to his face and kissed them; then stood straight and turned to hold his hand out to Martin.

Martin hesitated for a moment before he grimly clasped it and both of them disappeared.

'Goodbye,' I said.

I stood silently for a couple of minutes, then shook myself out of it. I needed to find Simone and make sure she was okay, and that she knew what had happened to her father. I put the cage into its casket and climbed back up the stairs, each of them seeming ten metres high.

The minute I was out of the Grotto the stone spoke to me. 'Simone's gone to fight, Emma. Go put that cage away and I'll keep you updated.'

'Can Zara go with him and relay for us?' I said as I carried the casket towards the armoury. All around me, Disciples hurried to their positions.

'She won't. She doesn't want to bring him bad luck.'

'How about you then?'

'I vowed to stay with you.'

'Find someone, please. I need to know what's happening.'

'I'm looking. There aren't many of us left, and we have to use mundane technology to communicate from Hell —'

'— because it's underground. I know.'

Lucy Chen was distributing weapons at the entrance to the armoury, and nodded to me as I passed her. I went through the empty shelves to the end of the room and walked through the wall. The Murasame was the only Celestial weapon remaining in the high-security section. I closed my eyes to walk through the gold bars, and placed the casket at the far corner of the room against the stone wall.

I passed the box containing the Elixir of Immortality as I headed out, and stopped for a moment. I made a snap decision and put my hand on the featureless black surface. The box shimmered into nothingness, revealing the black and silver jug. I picked up the jug, held it down by my side so Lucy wouldn't see it, and went back out again.

They were all gone when I exited the armoury, so I carefully carried the jug back to the Imperial Residence. Smally was standing in the entrance hall, her eyes wide and frightened.

'There's no demon master, ma'am, we don't know what to do,' she said.

'Return to barracks,' I said. 'Tell all the other demons to return to quarters immediately.'

She nodded, concentrated to share the information, then hesitated. 'Can I stay with you?'

'No. Go back to the demon quarters, and lock them up when you're all in there.'

'Ma'am,' she said, and went towards the rear of the house.

I followed her into the kitchen and watched the demons head out to their quarters. I found a sports bottle in the kitchen cupboard, carefully poured the Elixir into it, and sealed it tight before the powerful scent of it made me pass out.

'You're wasting your time. There's nobody to take you to Hell,' the stone said.

'There are two very easy ways I can get there,' I said.

'Two?'

'I can change to serpent and teleport myself as well.'

'As well as what?' the stone said, confused.

'As well as the obvious way of getting to Hell.'

I went into the living room and sat on the couch, rigid with dread and holding the sports bottle.

'You do that to yourself and I will never forgive you. Nobody else will either,' the stone said, its voice sharp. 'And the Elixir won't go with you, so don't even think about it.'

'I promised Simone I wouldn't, don't worry.' I raised my head. 'How's John? Is he still alive?'

'Surprisingly, yes. I think the Jade Emperor's helping him. Martin is also giving him a hand. It appears that they're using him as a weapon — pointing him at things and having him destroy them.'

'Who's winning?'

'Too early to say.'

'Okay.' I pulled my legs up to sit cross-legged on the couch with the bottle in my lap, and tried to relax as I waited for them. 'Keep me updated on Simone. I wish you would leave me and go to her.'

'I promised.'

I leaned back on the couch. 'I understand.'

Its voice softened. 'Emma …'

'I know,' I said.

'You know?'

'He's not coming back. Whether we win or lose, he won't be coming back.'

The stone was silent for a while, then said, 'Okay. I'm here for you.'

My throat thickened. 'Thank you. Just keep me updated on Simone.'

'At the moment, she and her horse are doing magnificently.'

'Let me know if the situation changes.' I raised the sports bottle in front of my face. 'And let me know the *second* there's any chance she'll need this.'

'Of course.'

I sat in silence, waiting for word from them.

24

Zhenwu

Of all the brain injuries to have, damage to the language centres was absolutely the worst. John couldn't give orders and Martin couldn't provide information; instead, they communicated through raw emotion and with non-verbal direction, passing images between them. They stood side by side in front of the barricades that blocked the entrance to Court Ten, the last line of defence. Martin fought next to him, indicating demons for John to attack, but John wasn't able to direct the army and had no idea how the battle was progressing. On top of that, he was close to death, half-blind and had no idea whether Simone was safe or not.

John sent Martin a picture of Simone's face. Martin sent him a reassuring emotion and John silently thanked him; Simone was okay. He sent a blast of shen energy to destroy the Mothers around him, then turned to Martin and sent him a query.

331

Martin responded with despair, giving John an overview of the situation. The demons had overrun the Celestial island and were marching on Court Ten. Courts Two to Nine had already fallen, and Court One was ... As Martin sent the image it changed. The demons were in One. The Celestial forces had pulled back to Court Ten, but they'd been devastated by the forces of Hell — both types of demon, East and West — and the Celestial army was a fraction of its initial numbers. Only a hundred or so of the biggest Celestials — the Winds themselves, and the Generals — were falling back to form a ring around Court Ten, with the horde savagely trying to break through the lines.

They needed reinforcements. The Twelfth was guarding the Earthly and some of them could be pulled down quickly to bolster the defence. He sent the number twelve — a cross with two horizontal strokes beneath it — to Martin.

Martin sent back bewilderment.

John sent the Western twelve and a soldier.

Martin nodded understanding and hesitated, passing the order on. Maybe they could do this after all. Martin moved into position next to John and raised the Silver Serpent. If they couldn't break this final attack, they would retreat behind the barricades and shore up Court Ten for siege.

Martin sent him an image of Pao behind them, standing in front of his court with a sword in his hand and a resolute expression. John sensed Pao's desperation: the judge was frantic with concern that the Court would fall and every Shen sent to it would be imprisoned by the forces of Hell. Pao was probably prepared to stay with his Court to the end; he had a level of stubbornness that made Emma look pliant.

Martin indicated five black Western demons approaching. John hefted his sword and prepared to fight them. He didn't have much left, but by the Heavens he would take out as many as he could before he fell. Martin attacked two and John attacked three, but their blows glanced off.

Oh shit.

Martin made his sword sing and it slowed them, but the black demons didn't stop.

Martin sent futility: a suggestion that they fall back.

John sent determination and summoned yin. It floated around him in a cloud of destruction and he pushed his left hand out towards the demons and released it into them. They shredded in its cold cloud, and he fell to one knee with the effort of calling it back to him. Martin patted his shoulder as John clambered back to his feet. John nodded; they could do this together.

Martin broadcast shock and sent John an image. There were more than two hundred of these black demons approaching; they had overrun the Celestial lines and were descending on them. Behind them came a cockroach the size of a bus, its shell the same shiny black material as the demons. The insect would be able to dismantle the barricades around Court Ten with ridiculous ease.

John lifted Seven Stars and prepared to fight them to the end. It wouldn't be long and he would rejoin, and even if he was to suffer at the hands of the demons it would be a tremendous relief to be whole once more.

Simone rode in on a sweat-lathered Freddo behind the demons and generated a cloud of yin that destroyed them. Martin raised his hands and sent yin into the vanguard of the armoured demon's forces. Their yin clouds were a fraction of what John could generate. If John could add his full capability without destroying everything, they could still win.

He gathered himself, leapt high above the demon force and prepared for a final release that would destroy most of what remained.

The Serpent was shocked with electricity again and he lost control. He reached the apex of his leap and fell, helpless. The pain was excruciating and his muscles heaved in spasms until he hit the ground hard and lost consciousness.

* * *

Emma

I heard voices behind me and turned. Martin and Simone had appeared in the Residence's courtyard, Simone mounted on Freddo and Martin next to the horse's head. They were blackened with demon essence. John was thrown across Freddo's back behind Simone.

Simone dismounted, then she and Martin lowered John onto the grass and knelt next to him. I rushed out to see them.

'Are you okay?' I said.

Simone rubbed her hand over her forehead and smeared demon essence over her face. She looked at her hand and grimaced, then dropped it. 'We lost.'

'Hell has fallen,' Martin said, raising John's eyelids to check his eyes. 'They shocked him just before the final push and knocked him out as they charged the Court Ten barricades. Our lines were overrun and Court Ten is theirs.' He looked up at me. 'Most of our forces are dead or their prisoners.'

'It's awful,' Simone said and broke down, shaking with silent sobs. Martin reached around and pulled her into a hug and she clutched him.

I fell to sit on the grass, stunned. I took John's hand. He was unconscious and Martin obviously didn't have enough left to bring him around. At least he hadn't rejoined, but he looked close to death and if that happened the demons would have him. He was so far gone that he would probably take off and rejoin the minute he woke up.

'You're safe here,' I said. 'The Disciples are here to defend. We'll be fine.'

'They have Michael!' Simone cried, distraught. 'Oh my *god*, poor Clarissa.'

'Do they have any of the really senior people?' I asked Martin.

'They took down the Dragon, but obviously they don't have another cage because he came back almost immediately. They don't have any of the Winds or the Generals, but there isn't much left of the army and many of our senior officers are prisoners. The Jade Emperor ordered us to evacuate when Father went down and the cockroach attacked the barricades, so the last of us made it out. Anyone left in Court Ten is theirs.'

'A cockroach?'

'I think I'm going to be sick,' Simone said. She pulled herself free from Martin and ran to the powder room.

'Ten metres long and covered in that armour you were talking about,' Martin said. He looked down at John. 'We need to get him to the infirmary.' His eyes unfocused. 'Never mind, it's full of casualties. Edwin can examine him later. Let's clean him up and put him to bed.'

'Your patience is impressive, Freddo,' I said without looking away from John. 'Return to the stables. You've earned your rest.'

Martin glanced back at Freddo, who had been standing quietly the entire time. 'Go and clean up and tell the mafoos you've earned an extra feed. Well done, my friend.'

'I wish I could stay and help Simone,' Freddo said. 'It's a pain being such a large animal sometimes.'

'You saved her life more than once,' Martin said. 'You were courageous in battle and defended her fiercely. You are a huge asset as you are.'

'Thank you, my Prince,' Freddo said, and disappeared.

* * *

Edwin released John's wrist after checking his pulse. 'Hard to say. It could just be exhaustion, or it could be a coma from the brain damage. I'd love to do a scan but no stones are available.'

'Where's Gold?' I said.

'Coordinating from the Celestial Palace,' the stone said. 'He'll be busy for a few hours; he's acting as an information relay.'

'You?' I said.

'I can't do it,' the stone said with regret. 'I'm too ...' It hesitated, then its voice dropped. 'Old and weak.'

'I know the feeling,' Edwin said. He checked his watch. 'It's 6 pm. If he hasn't come around by tomorrow morning, I'll put him on a drip and we'll ask Gold to stab him in the brain again.'

'Can you just leave him like this? If we bring him around he'll rejoin,' I said.

'If we leave him in a coma, I'll have to catheterise him, put him on a drip, insert a feeding tube ...' Edwin looked him up and down. 'Believe me, having him awake is a much better option.'

'I understand,' I said. 'How are the Disciples in the infirmary?'

He smiled without humour. 'There are only ten, and they're not badly injured. I'm hearing similar reports from the other medical centres. The ones we have are the ones that were on the back lines, or reinforcements that weren't called up. The ones that fought the demons ... all died.'

'I see. Thank you, Edwin. Go find something to eat, and rest. I don't know how long we have before the demons make their next move.'

'Ma'am,' he said, saluted me and went out.

'I need to go check on Leo and Buffy,' Martin said. 'Will you be okay?'

I nodded. 'Just one thing before you go.' I patted the quilt and he sat next to me on the bed. 'If I change to serpent, I can feel his Serpent's call, know where it is and go straight to it. Would you be able to follow me?'

He was silent for a long time, his refined features intent. Eventually he shook his head. 'I don't know.'

'I think it's worth a try.'

'But we have you already, and you sound exactly like him.'

'I'm small, human, mortal and inexperienced. We need him now, more than anything.'

Don't even think about it, Simone said.

'Stop listening.'

She came into the room wearing a bunny robe over fleecy pyjamas and slippers, her long hair wet from the shower. 'No. Don't even think about it. You'll end up in that cage as well.'

'We don't know if the cage works on people other than the Winds.'

'And we never will, because you won't try.' She sighed, exasperated. 'He'll absorb you, Emma.'

'We'll have to open the cage before he can absorb me. If the cage is open, he'll be free. It would be worth it.'

'Not to me.' She bent and took my hand. 'If it comes to that, I'll go myself.'

'Promise me you won't do this without consulting me first,' Martin said. 'If you do it, I will come along and take out the trap that is probably there waiting for whoever attempts this.'

'Deal,' I said, and both Martin and Simone relaxed slightly.

'By your leave, ma'am, I really do need to check my husband and daughter,' Martin said. 'Leo says they're okay, but I can't be sure until I hold them in my arms.'

'You really like saying that, don't you — husband and daughter?' Simone said.

He smiled at her. 'It's the best feeling in the world. They're my light within this darkness.'

'Go, Martin, and give them a hug for me,' I said. 'Come back soon. I think we have a lot of planning to do.'

'Emma's right,' Simone said. 'It's only a matter of time before the demons take the next step, and we need to be ready for them.'

All our heads shot up. The Jade Emperor had summoned us to the Celestial Palace for a debrief.

'So much for that,' Martin said.

'Can you take me?' I said.

'I am a Number One. Of course I can,' Martin said. He sighed and stood, and looked at the palms of his hands. 'Can I use your bathroom first? I'm still filthy.'

I gestured towards the bathroom. 'Go right ahead.'

Simone hesitated in front of me. 'Me too?'

'The Celestial knows what he's doing. Put some pants on,' I said.

338

She concentrated and changed her pyjamas to a Mountain uniform. She pointed at the floor next to my feet. 'Why are you carrying that One Direction bottle everywhere?'

I looked down at the sports bottle: she was right. 'It has the Elixir of Immortality in it.'

'In a *One Direction* bottle?'

I shrugged. 'It was the first one I grabbed out of the cupboard.'

'But why —'

'Smally's a huge fan.'

'Oh. I keep forgetting how young some of them are.'

'They may be young but they're not children.' I picked up the bottle. 'I should probably put the Elixir back in the armoury before we go.'

'And throw that bottle away.'

'No way. It would break Smally's heart.'

* * *

The Emperor met us all in a large audience room. It was the first time I'd ever seen every single senior Celestial in the same room together and their Celestial Forms were huge and intimidating. Everybody looked tired and bedraggled from the battle; even the Shen were too exhausted to clean themselves up for the audience. The Emperor sat on his throne on the dais and everybody else gathered, standing, around him.

'Marshall Ma. Status of the Thirty-Six,' the Jade Emperor said after the obeisances had been made.

'Of our original twenty-five battalions that went into this battle, only three have enough soldiers to still be called a battalion,' Ma said. 'The others were almost completely wiped out. We have just over fifteen hundred soldiers remaining.'

'Winds?' the Emperor said.

The three Winds stepped forward.

'I have less than a hundred birds left,' the Phoenix said. 'The demons took pot shots at them with sniper rifles.'

'Fifty dragons,' Qing Long said.

'A hundred and fifty Horsemen,' the Tiger said. 'Half of those were stationed at the palace guarding the Western border as you ordered. The other half were active in the Hell engagement.'

'Northern Heavens?'

Martin stepped forward. 'Twenty-three reptile Shen and a handful of humans. That is all.'

'Elites, Er Lang?'

'Three left, Majesty,' Er Lang said, his voice rough with emotion.

'Three?'

'Majesty.'

'Lady Emma, status of the Mountain?'

I stepped forward. 'The hundred junior Disciples who were not called into battle remain on the Mountain. Five of our Celestial Masters and twenty-seven Shen Disciples obeyed your order to evacuate Hell and have returned.' My voice broke when I saw the faces of my dead students in front of me, then I pulled myself together. We still had a long way to go. 'The rest are lost.'

The Jade Emperor raised his voice to be heard by all. 'Before you ask, the Demon King electrocuted the Dark Lord and he is in a coma. If he is roused he will probably rejoin with his Serpent. Either way, he is lost as well.'

I lowered my head and wiped my eyes.

'We do not have the means to take Hell back from those armoured demons,' the Emperor said, and it wasn't a question.

'I suggest a stealth mission to release our people held in Hell,' Martin said. 'There must be at least three hundred Immortals held by the demons now that Court Ten has fallen.'

'Good idea,' Er Lang said.

'You would fail,' the Jade Emperor said with finality.

Martin opened his mouth to argue and closed it again.

'Give me permission to get the Serpent out,' I said.

'No.'

'You were quite happy for me to go down to certain death two days ago,' I said.

'That was just your life. This is your whole Immortal existence,' the Emperor said. 'If things become extremely dire I may consider permitting you to make an attempt for the Serpent, but this sort of sacrifice goes against everything that the Celestial stands for.'

'The Celestial stands for nothing if it has fallen,' Guan Yu said.

The Jade Emperor rose and stood in front of his throne. 'Before anyone says anything, do not blame Lady Emma for this. Anyone who does will be reprimanded. This has been coming for a long time, and this is the most intelligent and devious Demon King we have ever faced.'

'Of course he is, he was originally a human woman,' Er Lang said. 'It's not surprising that many human men are so terrified of their females that they oppress them.'

'And oppression breeds hatred. It is a vicious cycle,' the Jade Emperor said. He paced the dais with his hands behind his back. 'Regardless of his background, this was inevitable from this King. Our own honourable nature has been a large factor in this result, and we will not compromise our principles and lower ourselves to their level.'

'Even if the Celestial falls?' Guan Yu said quietly.

We were all silent at that.

The Jade Emperor stopped in front of the throne. 'Venus is down there right now. He's offering them what they asked for in the first place: the Earthly in return for our half of Hell and safety on the Celestial.'

'They won't agree,' Guan Yu said.

The Emperor paced again. 'I know. I'm keeping them busy so they don't immediately go and celebrate on the Earthly. I don't expect them to agree to something that they already have in their hands.'

'Once they've regathered, they can take the Earthly by force,' Guan Yu said.

'They do not plan to take the Earthly by force. They will take it by stealth, infiltration and economic incursion, the same way they did it in the West with no Celestials to impede them. The humans will never know that they have been subjugated by demons. All they will know is that the few and wealthy control them absolutely, through their government, legal system and economy.' He continued to walk up and down in front of his throne. 'Once the demons' hold on the Earthly is secure — and they are well on the way already — they will make a try for the Celestial. And their plans for the conquest of Heaven are not nearly as bloodless.'

'How long do we have?' Er Lang said.

'We have about three weeks. Their losses in this latest battle were as large as ours. They only have those armoured demons remaining, and they will need a large force to take and hold Heaven. They will attack us constantly for the next two weeks to soften us up while they hatch a new army. Then they will make a big final push at the end of spring, aimed at conquering the entire Celestial.' He ran his hand down his beard and suddenly appeared very old. 'Bai Hu, order a small team of your best Horsemen — and women — to capture one of those black demons to experiment on. Qing Long, have your people find a way to use our blood as a weapon. All the Winds are to start donating blood immediately. My blood is to be taken as well.'

The Tiger and Qing Long silently saluted the Emperor.

'Take our blood too,' Ma said.

'You are too human,' the Jade Emperor said. 'Only the blood of the five elemental creatures will work.'

Wait, what? Simone said. *The Jade Emperor's an animal too?*

Tell her about his animal nature and that nobody's really sure what he is, I said to the stone.

Nobody to relay; tell her when you're home, the stone said. *We stones have long speculated that the Wind of our element is a qilin, but many say he is a dragon.*

'Go and rest, all of you,' the Emperor said. 'They are as battered as we are and they will not attack again for a few days. Take this time to be with your families and arrange for the safety of those closest to you. Things will be worse before they are better.'

He walked down the stairs at the back of the dais and disappeared without another word.

25

I sat at John's bedside watching him. It was very late and I should have been sleeping, but I didn't know how long I had left with him.

Simone spoke silently to me. *Marcus is here.*

'Come on in, Marcus.'

The minute he entered and I saw his face, I knew.

He pulled a chair close to the bed and studied John. 'I wanted to tell you after we'd won. I'm sorry I have to tell you after we lost. How is he?'

'I'm hoping that I can keep him here when he wakes up, but we'll probably lose him when he does. He'll go straight to his Serpent and be gone.'

Marcus wiped his hand over his eyes. 'Monica passed away earlier today. There'll be a memorial service in Hong Kong ...'

That pushed me over the edge. All my students and friends, the love of my life, my son, and now this wonderful woman who was a part of the family ... I couldn't face it any more. I ran into the bathroom and closed the door, then sat on the lid of the toilet and let go.

The stone changed to human form, picked me up, sat on the toilet lid, pulled me into its lap and held me close as I wept.

'It's been nearly half an hour, Emma, you should stop,' the stone said eventually, still holding me.

'I can't,' I said. 'I'm trying and I can't!'

'Oh, that's bad,' the stone said.

The door opened and Meredith came in. Simone hovered, concerned, behind her. Meredith knelt in front of us and put her hands on my face.

'Emma,' she said gently, 'the best thing for you right now is to sleep. I'll knock you out and we'll put you into the spare bed.'

'I can't be asleep,' I said, still choking. 'I need to be here if he wakes up.'

'I am awake,' John said behind Meredith, and I leapt off the stone's lap, ran to him and threw my arms around him.

He picked me up and held me, buried his face in my hair, and carried me out to the bedroom.

'It's okay,' he said softly. 'You need to rest. I'm not going anywhere. Come and I'll put you to bed and you can sleep it off. Anybody would crack under this sort of pressure.'

'Stay with me,' I said, clutching him.

'I will,' he said into my hair. 'Dismissed.'

The stone returned to my ring, and Meredith ushered Simone out of the bedroom and closed the door quietly behind her.

John laid me on the bed and brushed his hand over my face. 'I'll be here. Just as you are always here for me.'

'I love you,' I said, then his cool hand was on my forehead and I didn't remember anything else.

* * *

When I woke, it was dark and he was sleeping beside me, his hand protectively on my back. I sat up, slightly dizzy and with a throbbing dehydration headache. My throat still hurt from crying too much.

He woke, sat up beside me and put his hands on either side of my face. 'Stay still.'

I remained completely motionless and fell into a light trance. He rested lightly on the surface of my consciousness, barely touching it, like an insect suspended on the surface tension of water. The force was there, we were still trying to merge, but he held back and controlled it with skill that I could only aspire to.

He released me and nodded. 'I don't know what Meredith did to you, but it worked.' He shook his head. 'Human minds are beyond me sometimes. You seem completely fine.'

'Good, I can go back to work.' I dropped my voice. 'Don't tell anyone I lost it.'

'I won't.'

It all came surging back to me. 'Dear Lord, Hell's fallen. We need to regroup and take it back.'

'We are. It will take time to reorganise our resources. I also need to spend some time in the cage as soon as I can. I'm still blind in one eye and my balance is ruined.'

'Let's go now,' I said, throwing the covers off.

'No need,' he said, putting his hand on my arm to stop me. 'We can do it tomorrow. The demon army is busy occupying Hell and sorting out their prisoners. If you rest and have plenty of,' he smiled slightly, 'extremely excellent intimacy with the very best of me, in two weeks we should both be close to a hundred per cent and I'll be strong enough to lead a surprise attack before they're ready for us.'

'Really?'

He nodded.

I was filled with new enthusiasm. We could do this. We could take Hell back and sort this out once and for all.

'Sounds like a plan.' I lay back down and pulled the soft silk quilt up. 'Let's get some sleep; we've both had a hell of a day.'

He lay beside me, and we clutched each other silently as both of us took a long time to go to sleep.

I woke late the next morning alone, and to a Mountain that was eerily silent. I couldn't hear a single shout or clash of weapons.

Full of foreboding, I pulled my uniform on and headed downstairs. Smally met me at the dining room.

'What's happening?' I said. 'Where's the Dark Lord?'

'In his office, preparing to speak to the students,' she said. 'They're all gathered in the mess waiting for him.' She gestured towards the dining table. 'We have breakfast for you, ma'am.'

'I'm not really hungry,' I said, distracted by the silence.

'Tea?'

'Maybe later.' I headed out the front door of the Residence, then turned back. 'Where's Simone?'

'Still asleep, ma'am.'

'Leave her be. Don't wake her up.'

'That's what the Dark Lord said about you, ma'am.'

'I see.'

I headed through the silent Mountain — the only sound was the warm spring breeze through the pines and the soft patter of gentle rain — towards the administrative area. As I neared the far side of the compound I heard subdued conversation from the mess.

Zara wasn't at her desk and I went into John's office. He was studying his computer intently and she was in her stone form on the desk next to him.

'Good, you're up,' he said. 'Come and look over these figures for me.'

'The numbers are correct,' Zara said, indignant.

I went to him, put my arm around his shoulders and we shared a kiss. We both turned to the sheet and I saw that he was working out how many evacuees we would have if every student brought their immediate family up to the Mountain.

'We could do it at a squeeze,' I said. 'Four hundred will stretch our resources, but it's doable.'

'They'll want to bring more than their immediate families though,' he said, scrolling through the sheet. 'Grandparents. Their siblings' families. Aunts and uncles — the number could easily be double.' He sighed and stretched. 'Time to go talk to them, I suppose.'

'Big rousing speech?' I said. 'Boost their spirits, reassure and inspire them to new levels of enthusiasm?'

'No. Grim truth,' he said. 'Bring them down to earth and let them know exactly how bad things are so they can make an intelligent informed decision about whether they stay or go.'

'This is why I love you,' I said.

He rose and nodded to Zara. 'I'd appreciate your help as well, Zara.' He took a deep breath and ran one hand down his face. 'All right, let's do this.'

* * *

The students were sitting around the tables with the remains of their breakfasts in front of them; the demons were clearing plates. All of them became absolutely silent when they saw us enter.

John stopped at the front of the room. 'Leave the dishes,' he said, and the demon staff went back to the kitchen. 'No, I want you to hear this as well. All staff to attend me.'

The demons crept out of the kitchen, some still holding towels.

John turned to the students and raised his voice. 'Listen to what I have to say, then there'll be time for questions when I'm done talking.' He linked his hands behind his back and paced in front of them, his soft voice boosted by telepathy to be easily heard by all. 'It seems only yesterday I did this for the first time when the Academy was based in Hong Kong. And now I'm doing it again.' He stopped, sighed and lifted his head. 'Hell has fallen. The Celestial armies are close to wiped out. We hope to regroup and retake Hell, but right now there is nothing to stop the horde of Hell from marching on the Earthly Plane and subjugating it. You are all that the Mountain has left. Except for a very small group of Shen, every other Disciple …' He hesitated, and when he spoke his voice was rough with misery. 'Every other Disciple is dead.'

A few of the students broke down, crying into their table napkins, and others comforted them.

John continued to pace in front of them. 'The demons' next objective will be conquest of the Earthly. If you are down there, you will be a target; but I want to give you a choice. You can stay here where you will be safe, and help us defend the Mountain if the horde try to invade Heaven. I can also offer sanctuary to your immediate families. No one else. Parents and siblings, that is all. No in-laws, no nieces or nephews, uncles, aunts, cousins or grandparents. Your immediate families only.'

One of the students waved his hand, obviously wanting to ask a question.

'I said when I'm done, Bernie,' John said with amused exasperation. 'I swear you are the most impatient Disciple on the Mountain. Let me finish.'

Bernie dropped his hand.

'The other option is that you return home to your families on the Earthly.' A few hands shot up. 'The answer to your question is: no. We are not expecting open warfare on the Earthly Plane. The demons have not planned to take the Earthly by force; they will take it by economic infiltration. Your families should be reasonably safe if you do not draw attention to yourselves, and you can use your skills to defend them against the oncoming invasion if things become much worse.'

The hands all dropped.

'Good,' John said. 'I will give you the rest of the day to make the decision: go down and protect your wider families, or bring your immediate families up here. Immediate families only. *There will be no exceptions.* Now ask your questions.'

'I have two children with my ex-wife,' one of the Disciples called out.

'Isabelle and Dominic can come, Rene,' John said. 'Alison, your ex, can't.'

'My parents died when I was young and my grandmother raised me —'

'I know that, Beatrice,' John said. 'If I make an exception for you, everyone else will want the same lenience. If you are that concerned about her, go down to the Earthly and be with her.' He looked around at them. 'Any further questions?'

Nobody put their hand up. A few of them put their arms around each other's shoulders or held hands in silent solidarity.

Emma, can you arrange this? It will be complicated.

I nodded.

Thank you.

'Very well. Lady Emma will manage this. I remind you again, Disciples: no exceptions. Immediate family only. Speak to her when you have made your decision. Dismissed.'

'Salute your Master!' I shouted.

As one, the students rose from their chairs, fell to one knee and saluted John. He nodded to them and went out.

I shouted again. 'Come and see me in my office when you've decided. And I remind you again: no exceptions, and I will hold fast to that rule.' I dropped my voice. 'Let's go and wait for the deluge, Zara. I think a lot of students are going to be very upset.'

Zara squeaked with dismay.

* * *

It was after lunch before I'd worked through the queue of students and processed their requests. Many of them were still thinking about their options and hadn't made up their minds.

'No more right now,' Yi Hao said from the office door. 'Take a break, ma'am, you work too hard.'

'She shouldn't be working at all, it's Saturday,' my mother said loudly outside my office. 'Oh, hello, Yi Hao. It's about time Emma gave you a name, you know.'

'You don't understand, Mrs Donahoe,' Yi Hao said. 'It's a tremendous honour to be the Dark Lady's Number One.'

'Mum!' I yelled. I ran to her and embraced her in a huge hug.

All the family were there, crowding into Yi Hao's office and overflowing into the courtyard outside: Mum, Dad, both my sisters, their husbands and their children. Tears filled my eyes as I hugged everybody, laughing with delight.

'Thank you,' I said when we'd settled. 'Thank you for coming up.' I hugged my father again. 'You have no idea how glad I am to see you here.'

'Greg talked us into it,' my father said, still holding me. He pulled back to see me and his mouth flopped open. 'Good Lord, Emma, what have you been doing to yourself?'

I stopped, confused.

'You look at least ten years younger,' my mother said, and lit up. 'You're Immortal? You did it without telling us?'

'No, no, it's some energy treatment that John's been giving me.'

'Well, make him share!' my father said.

'I'm afraid it's Emma only,' John said behind them, and again we were lost in the chaos of hugs and excitement.

We moved into the Residence's living room where we could all talk.

'I convinced the family to move up here,' Greg said after we'd settled onto the couches. 'It's too dangerous down there now — people are being replaced.'

'Thank you, I appreciate it,' I said. 'But everybody except Mum and Dad have to go back down, we don't have space.'

'Yes, we do,' John said. 'You can have the Imperial Residence in the Northern Heavens, and the Crown Prince's residence as well. We spend most of our time here anyway.'

'We can't break the rules we just applied to our own Disciples, John.'

'That's why they're going to the Northern Heavens, and not the Mountain,' John said.

'That's a convenient loophole and morally wrong —'

'Your family are three times the targets that any Disciples are, Emma. The King wants their genetic material to make more hybrids,' John said. 'If they stayed on the Earthly it would only be a matter of time before he discovered their location and took the boys again.'

Jen blanched and held her toddler tighter, and Greg put his hand on her shoulder to reassure her. The older boys looked nauseous.

'All right. That makes sense,' I said.

'Crown Prince's residence? What happened to Martin?' my mother said. 'He is all right, isn't he? I heard so many were taken hostage ...'

'He's fine. He and Leo have set up house in the Peak apartment with a little girl they adopted together,' I said.

'Oh, I'm so happy for them,' my mother said with genuine delight. 'They'll make wonderful fathers.'

'Wouldn't they all be safer up here?' Amanda's husband, Allan, said.

'A child can't travel here without its mother to protect it from the transition,' Greg said. He nodded towards John. 'That's what started this whole mess in the first place — Simone's mother dying.'

'This whole mess has been coming for a while,' John said. 'And you're right about them being good fathers — I've never seen a little girl quite so cherished.'

'More than Simone?' I said.

'About the same,' John said. 'But Simone has all your family to spoil her as well.'

'That's a grandparent's prerogative,' my father said.

John stopped for a moment, then said with wonder, 'I suppose it is. My son has a child, and that makes me a grandfather.' He shook his head. 'This is a first.'

'Feel old?' my mother said with a smile.

'It does tend to creep up on you,' John said, returning the smile.

'Don't be ridiculous, Vincent's your great-great-grandson,' I said with scorn.

'Vincent?' my mother said.

'We found him a couple of years ago,' I said. 'He didn't know who he was, only that he changed into a huge snake. He was thrilled to bits to discover that he had a home and a family.' I gasped as I realised. 'Oh dear Lord, he was an Imperial Elite Guard and only three Elites are left. He's probably dead.'

John nodded silently, his face grim.

I rested my forehead on my hand. 'People keep popping up … not there. So many dead.'

'Are you okay?' my mother said. She came and knelt in front of me. 'Emma?'

John moved behind me and put his hands on my shoulders.

I sat straighter and smiled for them. 'No. I'm fine. We have too much to do. We'll win Hell back and everything will return to normal.'

My mother shot John a glance. He obviously said something telepathically to her that they both tried to cover. I didn't bother calling them on it.

'Let's take you over to the Northern Heavens and settle you in,' John said. 'I'm sure Emma will want to talk your ears off, and Thirty-Eight will be delighted to have a large family to look after.'

I looked up at John. 'You're supposed to be resting.'

'I know,' he said. 'First thing tomorrow morning, I'll go down and take a nap.'

'Are you all right, John?' my mother said, concerned. 'I saw you limping. Are you okay?'

'I will be,' John said. He released my shoulders. 'Let's go.'

* * *

Martin and Yue Gui had breakfast with us the next morning, to discuss strategy before John went into the cage.

'Before I go down, Emma,' John said, 'I need to give you something. Come upstairs.' He nodded to Yue and Martin. 'We won't be long.'

'Don't be two hours,' Martin said with mischief, and Yue slapped him on the arm. He winced and rubbed it. 'You're a turtle too,' he said with indignation, and she slapped him again. He raised his hands. 'All right, all right.'

John shook his head and led me up the stairs to our bedroom.

He went to the end of the bed and opened the camphorwood chest carved with a scene of pagodas on pine-covered mountains that looked very much like the peaks of Wudangshan. He rummaged through the silk quilts and pulled out a small ebony box. He guided me to sit on the bed and opened the box; it contained a pair of black jade earrings in the shape of ancient coins: round with a square hole in the middle. Each hole was filled with a black diamond on a post.

He passed them to me and I turned them over in my hands. 'How many of these do you have?' I said, incredulous.

'I think altogether I have about fifteen pairs,' he said. 'The Demon King has a great many of them, for obvious reasons, and when he gambles he tends to use them as currency.' He shrugged. 'They become extremely valuable after a hundred years or so up here, and I give them as funeral gifts for people whose relatives have died.'

'I'm sure they appreciate them.'

'They do, but unfortunately it reinforces my image as a creature aligned with darkness and death.'

'Black jade — I'll be sure to wear them at the wedding, just to cause trouble.'

'That would be a scandal all over the Celestial,' he said. 'I love it. Make sure you do.'

He closed the chest and rose.

'Wait, this is why you brought me up here?' I said, glancing down at the earrings.

'Yes. Wear them, please.'

My breath left me in a long rush. 'You think I'll be lost again?'

'I don't know. I want to be sure.'

I looked up at him. His face was rigid with restraint and his eyes were glittering.

'John ... what's the matter?'

'Nothing. Just please wear them.'

'I don't think you've ever lied to me before, Xuan Wu, and I hate to think you'll start now. Tell me why you're giving me these now instead of when you come out of the cage ...' My voice trailed off. 'Oh geez.'

'I have no sense of time while I am in there; my sentience is gone. If I am not back within two weeks, Ming and Ma will lead the armies and we will try to retake Hell anyway.'

'Two *weeks*?'

'I have ordered them to release me from the cage if the battle is close and my True Form could be the difference between victory and defeat. The Turtle may attack the demons before it rejoins.'

I choked on the words. 'Don't go into the cage then. Don't risk it — we need you too much.'

He dropped his voice. 'If I don't go into that cage soon, I will be lost anyway. I cannot resist the Serpent's call for much longer — its suffering is too much for me to bear.'

'It's that bad?' I looked up into his pain-filled eyes. 'Never mind. I can see.'

'Emma.' He took my hands in his. 'This is just a precaution. Wear the earrings, and it's quite possible I'll be back out for dinner and looking for some,' he smiled slightly, 'extremely invigorating intimacy with the Lady love of my life.'

'Okay.' I wiped my eyes with the palm of my hand and took a deep shuddering breath. I removed the black pearl earrings he'd given me for my last birthday from my ears and put the coins in. 'I wish you hadn't told me this; it will be in the back of my mind all day with my family.'

'Don't worry about me. Yue will watch me, and I will have her try to wake me at dinnertime if I haven't come back.' He put his hand on the side of my face. 'But please, ease my concern and wear the earrings all the time until this is resolved.'

'Okay.'

'And if I'm not back before you go down for the funeral the day after tomorrow …' He slipped his arm around my back and pulled me into an embrace. 'I know better than to ask you not to go; I know how much Monica meant to you. I would go myself if I could, she was part of the family. But please, be very careful down there. Always be with Martin or Simone. As long as the King has our son, he needs you.'

357

I buried my face in his shoulder. 'I know. Don't worry, I'll be careful.'

He pulled back to study my face and moved a stray lock of hair out of the way. 'I still worry about you.'

'Don't,' I said. 'Rest in the cage.'

He kissed me for a long time.

'I said *don't* be two hours!' Martin called from downstairs, then howled with outraged pain. 'Jie Jie, that was unnecessary!'

We rose together, and I put the pearl earrings onto the bedside table as we went out.

26

After dinner with my family, Simone took me back to the Mountain and I went down to the Grotto. John was in the cage on the bench next to the water, but Yue was nowhere to be seen.

'Yue?' I said. I knelt in front of the cage. 'John, are you okay?'

The Turtle didn't reply.

Yue surged out of the water in turtle form and changed to human. She waved her hands in front of her as she approached us. 'Sorry. The water is invigorating. Don't worry, I've been watching him.'

'The fish have been complaining nonstop about being constantly evicted.' I nodded down at the cage. 'Any change?'

She shook her head.

'Go get some dinner. I'll take over,' I said.

'No need.'

I put my hand on her arm. 'I want to.'

Yue sighed. 'All right.'

* * *

Late that night I blearily raised my head from the inflatable mattress as I heard tiny bells above me. It was Yue Gui, the silver ornaments in her hair tinkling as she came down the steps.

She sat on the end of the mattress and folded her legs under her silver robe. 'Enough's enough, Emma. Stop arguing with me. Go upstairs and go to bed. You'll catch your death of cold down here in the damp.'

'Cold and damp don't make you sick,' I said, my voice thick with sleep as I pulled myself up to sit.

'If your immune system is compromised and you let your core temperature drop, they certainly can,' she said. 'And I haven't seen an immune system quite as compromised as what I'm looking at right now. You're so chilled your lips are blue, and you're probably anaemic as well. I'll take over. Go upstairs and have a soak in a hot bath and go to bed.'

I opened my mouth to argue, then realised that a hot bath sounded really, really good. My fingers and toes were freezing and my nose was so cold it hurt.

'What time is it?'

'It's 1 am.'

I collapsed forwards over my knees. He'd been in there for fourteen hours and hadn't come back to us.

Yue pulled herself gracefully to her feet and held her hand out to me. 'Come on. Either he'll return, or he won't. What happens will happen regardless of whether you're here or not.'

'But he might come back for me,' I said.

'Tomorrow morning we will all gather here and bring him back together. Until then, go and rest and warm up.'

'All who?'

'All of his family who love him.'

She helped me to stand, and I went to the cage and crouched to see him. The outside of the cage was covered in a light layer of frost that formed a delicate tracery of crystals over the surface of the jade. He was asleep inside it, his beak forming a sad smile that was only an illusion of awareness.

'Come back to me, Xuan Wu,' I whispered, but the Turtle didn't move.

'Go. I have him,' Yue said. 'Tomorrow we'll all come down here and wake him.'

I hugged her, and she embraced me back, resting her cheek on top of my head. She was as tall as her father.

She released me. 'Go rest.'

I saluted her Western-style. 'Yes, ma'am. See you in the morning.'

'I'll be here.'

It felt wonderful to be warm and clean after the bath, and I snuggled under the silk quilt, already missing John's comforting presence beside me.

* * *

The next morning, Martin and Yue joined Simone and me in the Grotto. We moved the cage onto the floor and sat cross-legged around it.

'So what are we supposed to do?' Simone said.

Yue shrugged. 'Make it up as we go along, I suppose. Just speak to him, Simone, ask him to come back.'

'Daddy.' Simone gathered herself and sat straighter. 'We all need you. I need you. Come back to us, please.' Her voice broke and she bent to wipe her hand over her eyes.

'Father,' Martin said. 'The Heavens are on the edge. Hell has fallen, and the Earthly will shortly follow. We need your strength, your knowledge ... we need *you*. Return to us.'

'Ba Ba,' Yue Gui said, and her voice gained a childlike edge I'd never heard before. 'Even though you knew what I was, you let me come out with you. I want to stay with you. Come back to me.'

'John,' I said, keeping my voice tight and determined not to lose it, 'I love you with all my heart, and I am lost without you. Your children need you. Come back so we can have a huge overblown wedding that we will both detest.' I reached and touched the cage, then drew back at the cold. 'Come back to us, Xuan Wu.'

We waited silently for him to respond.

'Daddy?' Simone said.

The Turtle didn't move.

'Try again, Emma,' Yue said.

'John,' I said. 'Please come back to me ...'

After an hour and a half of begging, cajoling and reminding him of good times together, it became extremely obvious that he wouldn't reply, and we gave up. We shared a morose breakfast in the Residence and then went our separate ways. We had to inform the Celestial that the Dark Lord was probably gone for good, and to prepare for the assault on Hell that had a good chance of failing without him.

I hadn't even been there to give him a final hug when he'd gone into the cage. I'd been in the North with my family and I'd never even said goodbye.

I tried to go back to work. I met Lucy Chen and Moaner at the forge, and we sat on stools around a black ceramic outdoor table with a pile of requisition sheets and a few sample swords on the table in front of us.

Lucy Chen held up one of the sample swords and eyed it appraisingly. 'How long to make fifty of these?'

'Twenty days,' Moaner said.

'How many can you make in ten days?'

Moaner pulled a requisition closer and scribbled on it with a ballpoint. 'Twenty if we work day and night.'

Lucy put the sword down, carefully minding its edge, and sighed. 'Better than nothing. Armour?'

'Twenty swords will take all of our time. Swords or armour — choose,' Moaner said.

'Contact the Celestial,' I said. 'The Elites wore modern Kevlar body armour. See if they have any surplus.'

'Good idea,' Lucy said, writing on the paper in front of her.

My mobile phone rang and I checked the caller: Bridget Hawkes, David's wife. I answered it. Bridget sounded scared and breathless, and I sat straighter.

She whispered into the phone. 'Help, Emma, get us out. It's not him.'

My mind worked furiously. 'Is it a copy of him?'

'Yes!' She gasped with relief. 'You know! Help us.' Her voice was tight with desperation. 'Help us!'

'Where are you?'

'In the bathroom at home. The house in Shek O. I'm hiding from him, I'm pretending that I don't know ... but it's not him, Emma.'

'Can you and the boys get away to be picked up?'

She sounded terrified. 'I don't know!'

'Listen carefully,' I said. 'I'm going to hang up —'

'Don't hang up!'

'And someone will call you back immediately. When they do, keep a normal conversation your side, and they will give you directions on where to go to be picked up —'

There was a splintering crash and she shrieked.

'Oh dear Lord,' I said as I heard the phone hit the bathroom floor. They struggled silently for a moment, then she collapsed into terrified sobs.

David's copy picked up the phone. 'Why hello there, Emma,' he said, his voice sly. 'Were you arranging to rescue her?'

It wasn't worth pretending that I didn't know. 'What do you want in exchange for her?'

'Nothing. I need her to keep my cover. They didn't have the resources to make a copy of her too, so I have to use the real one.' He grunted and she made a soft noise of pain. 'Now, *honey*, you'll do what I tell you when I tell you, and the boys won't be hurt.' He returned to the phone. 'None of them will be hurt provided you stay well away and don't blow my cover. I need them unharmed for this to work, so keep it quiet and stay out.' He hung up.

I bent over the table. 'They've already started to replace powerful people in this region.'

'We knew it would happen,' Lucy Chen said.

'I know,' I said. 'But it's happening to my friends.'

Moaner hesitated, then shifted the papers in his hands. 'If you can find us one or two extra demons we can make you more weapons, and maybe try for some armour as well.'

'I'll see what I can do,' Lucy said. 'What about spears? Can you make spearheads?'

I didn't hear his answer because Yi Hao contacted me telepathically. *The Emperor of the West is in your office looking at your files. I tried to stop him, ma'am, please come quickly.*

I jumped to my feet. 'The goddamn Tiger's in my office going through my stuff. I'll be right back.'

Lucy and Moaner nodded, distracted, both of them looking at the personnel lists and forge schedule.

The Tiger was sitting behind my desk, going through my emails. Kenny was in one of the visitors' chairs watching him with a panicked expression.

'That was quick, I didn't even have time to play with your Facebook,' the Tiger said. He moved around the desk, leaned on the wall and grinned. 'Don't worry, Emma, I didn't hurt anything.'

I sat behind my desk and checked my computer. He'd been in the middle of updating my Facebook status with something coarse and unfunny. I deleted it and turned to Kenny, who still appeared stricken.

'Are the orphans okay?'

'The kids are fine. This one,' the Tiger nodded towards Kenny, 'asked me to bring him back.'

'Is something wrong?' I asked Kenny.

He rose, fell to one knee and saluted me. 'It's good to see you still strong after losing so many of your students.'

I studied him carefully. He wasn't being sarcastic, he really meant it.

'They died doing what they loved and fighting for what they believed in,' I said. 'It would be a disservice to them to sit around here moping when I have a chance to finish what they started. We are determined to win this, in their honour.'

365

'I am too,' Kenny said. 'Every Disciple counts, Lady Emma. I want to return and assist in the defence of the Mountain. I know I said I wasn't a soldier, but this is more important. Will you take me back?'

I sat silently considering him for a long time. He'd been equipped before heading down to the orphan camp and was fully armed. He'd be an extra sword when we were short so many.

'Please?' he said.

'Are the kids sufficiently guarded without him?' I asked the Tiger.

'Sufficient,' the Tiger said. 'But this one's full of survivor guilt. He followed his heart in not fighting; he made the choice that was right for him. I'd think twice about letting him rejoin.'

'I don't care what it's called. Guilt or no guilt, I want to protect the Mountain,' Kenny said.

'You'll die,' the Tiger said.

'All my friends are dead already,' Kenny said, still on one knee.

'The children need you,' the Tiger said.

'The Mountain needs me more.'

'You won't make any difference,' the Tiger said. 'The Mountain army is so short-handed that if the demons make a try for you, it'll be over in five minutes.'

'Will it?' Kenny asked me. 'Will it make no difference? Tell me the truth.'

I hesitated again.

Kenny rose. 'I will make a difference! Who do I report to?'

I ran one hand through my hair, which had already started to come out of its tie with all my running around. 'Report to Lok in Leo's office.'

Kenny's expression went strange for a moment.

'I saw that,' the Tiger growled. 'Share.'

'Suddenly,' Kenny said with wonder, 'it was like a big bell, right in the middle of me, rang to say, "This is the right thing to do."'

'Go and report to the dog,' the Tiger said, his voice soft with compassion. 'Fight with honour, Dark Disciple.'

'Celestial Highness.' He saluted the Tiger. 'Ma'am.' He went out.

The Tiger flopped to sit in one of the visitors' chairs. 'Do you really think he'll make a difference?'

'If it comes down to it, it's possible,' I said. 'I was just contacted by the wife of one of my Earthly liaisons, a good friend. They replaced her husband with a demon copy after Hell fell. She's terrified.'

'They killed her husband and she's living with a demon?'

'Yes. She called me, but the demon discovered her. He said that provided she behaves, she and the kids won't be hurt.'

'So stay away.'

'I am.'

He studied me. 'And look at you. Happy as a turtle in mud. Thoroughly in your element.'

I stopped for a moment and realised he was right. I wanted this to end, but I hadn't felt so calm and focused on a task in what seemed like forever.

I shrugged. 'I think Meredith did something to me. And I'm an adrenaline junkie anyway.'

'No. You're being just like him. Totally in his element and revelling in the chaos. When he comes out of the cage, move away from him for a while.'

'He's not coming out of the cage, Tiger. He's been in there more than a day and there's no sign of sentience. He's gone.'

I smiled slightly. 'The demons have one half of the Xuan Wu in a jade cage, and we have the other. The symmetry is delightful.'

'There you go again: totally inappropriate reactions. Whatever.' He levered himself out of his seat. 'Come with me to Ah Wu's office, there's something we need to do.'

'What?' I said, walking around the desk to join him.

'You'll see. Oh, we caught one,' the Tiger said as we headed for John's office. 'We took one of those armoured demons down. And you wouldn't believe it — those useless fucking laser weapons we developed destroyed it.'

'That's excellent news,' I said. 'How many lasers can you make before we assault Hell?'

'Not enough. Best we can probably do is five or six, and a senior child of mine has to run it — it chews up massive amounts of energy. Liaise with my Number Four, he's in charge of the project. And my Number Two as well. He'll be doing a great deal of management in the near future until we take Hell back and pull my One and Three out.'

'Did the blood weapons work?'

'They work, but they won't last long at full blast.' He raised his head as we approached John's office. 'Excellent, they're here.'

The Dragon and Phoenix were waiting outside John's office. The Winds stopped and held a silent conversation. They all shared a nod and the Dragon spoke to me.

'We are planning an attempt to bring Ah Wu back, Emma, and you can come along provided you vow not to interfere. This is an extremely dangerous procedure, and any wrong move could result in disaster.'

'Don't do it then,' I said.

'We can't win without him,' the Phoenix said. 'Having

you nearby will encourage him to return. Do we have your word? Give us your word and you can be present.'

'And if I don't give my word?'

'We'll leave you out here and try it without you,' the Tiger said.

'You could be the difference between him returning and this procedure failing and costing us a great deal,' the Phoenix said. 'Please, Emma.'

'I vow not to interfere.'

'You must vow to neither assist nor impede us. Vow to watch without acting.'

'You have my word. What the hell are you planning?'

'All right, let's get it over with,' the Tiger said.

* * *

We proceeded to the Grotto and found Yue sitting on the bench next to John.

'You cannot help us,' the Phoenix said to Yue. 'Return to your duties, Princess, and wish us success.'

Yue rose and bowed to them. 'Your courage will inspire songs and poems for many millennia.'

'Fuck that, I can't stand poetry,' the Tiger said.

Yue smiled, shared a small embrace with the Tiger, kissed him on the cheek, and headed up the stairs.

The Tiger studied her speculatively as she went up. 'Maybe I will finally have a chance to see what this turtle fuss is all about. If I do, this whole thing will be thoroughly worth it.'

'Not on your life, Devil Tiger,' she said softly and went out.

He chuckled, and the three Winds went to the bench where John's cage was sitting.

The Tiger crouched to study the cage. 'May I again remind you, Lady Emma, you have vowed not to interfere. No matter what happens, do not touch any of us.'

'I promise.' I dropped my voice. 'What are the chances of bringing him back?'

'Absolutely no fucking idea,' the Tiger said, and stood. 'Okay, I'm ready. Who does what?'

They shared a silent moment of telepathic communication, and nodded. The Phoenix summoned a curved red sword with a gold-plated guard and a handle wrapped in red leather, and stood next to the cage. The Dragon positioned himself on the other side, and the Tiger stood directly in front of the cage.

'We do not perform human sacrifices!' I said urgently.

'I'm not human,' the Tiger said. He glared at me. 'You gave us your word, Emma.'

'Stay out of this,' the Dragon said. 'On the count of three.'

All three of them nodded in unison, then the Dragon flipped the cage open and the Tiger plunged his hand in and placed it on top of the Turtle. His hand glowed with shen so brilliantly white that it was dazzling, the rays of light shifting as they radiated from the cage.

'He's taking it,' the Tiger said through gritted teeth. 'On my word.'

'He'll absorb you completely,' I said. 'Don't do this, Bai Hu.'

'Quiet,' the Dragon said, concentrating.

'I'm slipping into True From, bring it down,' the Tiger said, then raised his head and yowled with pain. 'Down!'

The Dragon quickly lowered the cage onto the floor and the Tiger took True Form, still with his paw on the Turtle's back.

'Not yet,' the Tiger said. He panted. 'Holy shit, he's cold. Not yet!'

'You don't have much left,' the Phoenix said, distraught. 'Don't risk it. Give the word!'

'Not yet!' the Tiger yelled. His True Form became smaller and more slender and grew transparent. 'More. I need to give him more!'

'Do it, Ah Que,' the Dragon said.

'No!' the Tiger yelled. 'I'm not there yet!'

'Do it!' the Dragon roared. 'Before he takes it all. Do it!'

The Phoenix swung the sword and lopped the Tiger's head off. The body fell sideways and the head rolled a couple of metres until it came to rest next to the lake.

The Dragon leaned on the back of the bench and sagged. 'So close. So close.' He shook his head. 'We nearly lost him, stupid damn cat.'

'Ah Wu?' the Phoenix said, touching the Turtle's back.

'It didn't work,' the Dragon said, putting the lid back and slipping the latches in place. 'The Tiger is in the demons' hands for nothing.'

27

The next day, as Simone and I exited the Celestial gateway in Wan Chai, I turned to speak to the Nine Dragon Wall. The dragons moved to the centre of the wall as its two sides slid together.

I saluted around at the dragons. 'Honoured Shen, thank you for your diligence in guarding the entrance to the Heavens.'

The dragons poked their heads out of the wall and bowed in response.

The central gold one replied, 'We serve the Celestial and it is our privilege to guard the gateway in this time of uncertainty.'

I dropped my hands. 'Are you guys okay?'

One of the purple dragons came closer. 'It's exhausting, Emma. They try us all the time. Zhi,' she nodded to one of the blue dragons, 'is concerned about her children. She hardly sees them.'

'I'll talk to the Dragon King about finding you relief.'

'Don't worry about it,' one of the gold dragons said in his warm male voice. 'We already did. He can't spare anyone. So many dragons are being held hostage in Hell; we're the lucky ones.'

The other dragons nodded agreement.

'How often are they trying you?' I said.

The dragons shared a look, their heads waving in front of the wall, then turned back to me. 'We've already had about ten small demons thrown at us today.'

'But it's only 11 am!' I said.

'And we're due for another attack, so perhaps you should head to where you're going,' one of the white dragons said. 'You shouldn't be down here anyway — it's too dangerous.'

'I have to attend the funeral of a family member,' I said.

'Leo's here, Emma,' Simone said behind me.

'I'll bring you guys some cakes when I come back,' I said, and the dragons grinned in response. 'Stay strong, and remember that the Celestial treasures you.'

'Of course it does, we are treasures,' the gold dragon said, and they returned to their spots on the wall and merged into it, becoming inanimate. The wall shrank and the marble balustrade emerged from the ground in front as it returned to its normal appearance.

'I've never seen those dragons so cooperative,' Simone said as she waved to Leo in the driver's seat of the family car.

'It's remarkable how being at war makes people forget their petty differences and pull together,' I said.

* * *

After the priest had given a carefully worded but generic memorial service for Monica, her husband, sisters and brothers went up to the front of the chapel to speak. More than a hundred of Monica's Hong Kong-based friends had come to the service; people who were unable to attend the complicated funeral in the Philippines.

'Monica came over to my employers' apartment on Stubbs Road one Chinese New Year,' her sister Erica said. 'She took me to the flower markets and we bought sweet-scented flowers that filled up the apartment and made the whole place so happy ...' She choked on the words. 'So many family were there over that holiday break. And then I went home to the Philippines, and she kept in touch, and came to visit us on holidays. She helped Rosa and Paul to go to university,' she locked eyes with her children where they sat, 'and Rosa will be a doctor. She will be a doctor because of Monica's help. I think, I think ...' She had trouble getting the rest of the words out and wiped her face with a tissue, then blew her nose. 'Monica always thought of her family. All the time. It was all she thought about ...'

She broke down and returned to her seat, where her son and daughter patted her on the shoulder. They turned to me and gestured for me to get up and speak.

'Can you say something, ma'am?' one of Monica's relatives said from the row in front of me. 'Marcus would like that. He says you're very important.'

'I'm not that important,' I said, protesting, but Simone and Leo pushed me to my feet and I wasn't aware of walking up to the pulpit until I saw everybody's faces shining in front of me. Fortunately I still had my packet of tissues in my hand and I pulled one out to clutch it as I spoke.

'I remember once, we all went to Australia. Simone was very tiny, probably only about four or five. Monica came with us to help look after Mr Chen, who was recovering from a serious injury.'

They went very still as they listened to me. Simone's eyes were unfocused as she remembered.

'I offered to take Mr Chen to dinner at a restaurant there, so that Monica wouldn't have to cook and could have some time off,' I said. 'We were at a tourist resort; I thought she would enjoy the break. She refused. She refused very loudly! She said she would much prefer to look after the family.'

Some of her relatives nodded at my words.

'Looking after the family wasn't work, and she didn't want a holiday from it because she enjoyed it so much. She really did love caring for everybody around her. Giving to you, to all of you, of her time, her energy — it wasn't something you were taking from her, because she loved doing it so much. The joy that filled her face and her voice every time she talked about how much she was helping you was wonderful to see, and she never regretted not having children of her own, because she had all of you.'

They were nodding more now, and I breathed a small sigh of relief that I wasn't being as tongue-tied and brainless as I felt I was.

'Thank you for inviting us here today. Monica was a huge part of our family, just as much as she was a part of yours, and we are all richer for having known her.'

I left it at that, and returned to sit between Leo and Simone. I hadn't broken down; in fact, I felt remarkably calm. Meredith had done something to me and I silently thanked her.

* * *

375

After the service, Leo drove us up to the Peak to have dinner with Martin and Buffy. He stopped the car at the gates when he saw a tall strongly built black woman in her mid-sixties standing outside the building entrance and arguing with the security guards.

'Oh shit,' he said softly.

He backed the car down the drive, but the woman saw us and ran towards the car. 'Leo! Leo! Where are you going? It's me!'

Leo banged his forehead on the steering wheel. 'Oh *shit*.'

'Who is it?' Simone said. 'She looks like ... oh shit.'

'Yep,' Leo said. 'That's my sister.'

He took the car back up the drive and the guards opened the gates for us. His sister stormed along next to the car, yelling at him to stop and explain himself.

He parked the car in its space, got out and put his arms out to her. 'Elise.'

That silenced her. She threw herself into his arms and started to sob. 'We thought you were dead!'

'I'm not dead,' he said, holding her close. 'Things happen. Come on up and meet the family.'

She turned to see Simone and me, her eyes glittering with tears. 'Is this your family?' She moved closer to me. 'Is this your wife?' She turned to Simone. 'Daughter?'

'No, but we're like family,' I said. 'Are you explaining?'

'I am,' Leo said. He guided Elise to the lifts, past the grinning security guards who were enjoying the show. 'Elise, I have a partner upstairs, and a daughter.'

She lit up. 'We knew you'd come to your senses eventually. This is wonderful. Is she Chinese? I hope there'll be a wedding soon. If you have a child you should get married and be a proper family.'

He rubbed the back of his neck. 'The partner's a he.'

She sagged with disappointment and followed us into the lift.

* * *

Leo sat on the couch with Buffy in his lap and Martin leaned on the couch behind them.

'I saw someone that looked like you on Discovery Channel, so I came to see,' Elise said from the other couch. 'It was a show called *The Monk With A Thousand Children*, about this wonderful Chinese man who cares for the poor orphans. There was a shot of a playground in the background — I was sure it was you. Max didn't believe me, but I checked the foundation, and it's funded by the estate of John Chen Wu, so I checked again and that was your boss all the way back then, so I came anyway.' She spread her hands. 'And here you are. Alive. I can't believe it.'

'I'm happy here, I have a family,' Leo said. He pulled Buffy, who obviously didn't understand what was happening, closer to him. Martin reached over the couch to put his hand on Leo's shoulder, and Leo covered it with his own. 'I know you all disapprove, so I kept quiet. It's good to see you, Elise, but please don't judge me. I'm happy. Can't you just let it be?'

She glared at Martin. 'Who are you anyway? Did you lead Leo into this?'

'I am John Chen Wu's son.' Martin gestured towards Simone. 'This is my little sister, Simone. We inherited our father's fortune and we're running the orphanages together.'

Simone nodded, obviously desperately wanting Elise to understand. 'Leo and Martin have looked after me since I was a tiny girl. Leo's like a second father to me, and Martin's the best brother I could ever ask for.'

'Thank you,' Martin said softly.

'And you?' Elise asked me.

'I'm their stepmother. We're one big happy dysfunctional family, all caring for each other.'

'That's what family is,' Leo said. He dropped his hand from Martin's and put it around Buffy's waist. 'And this is our newest member. She's one of the orphans that the documentary was about.'

'You should not be caring for a little girl,' Elise said. 'That is so wrong!'

Martin was confused. 'Why not?'

'Leave my Daddies alone,' Buffy said. 'They look after me.'

'Look, Leo.' Elise took a deep breath in and out. 'I'm not Mom. I know you're like you are, and I won't try to change you. But you can't be in a relationship like this and have a child involved. It's just not fair on her. How will she grow up normal if she has no mother?'

'She didn't have a mother anyway. What's important is that she's loved and has a family,' Leo said, sounding tired. 'We're all happy, don't worry about us. And if you were to return home and tell everybody that I'm dead it would be the greatest favour you ever did for me.'

'Don't be ridiculous,' she said. 'You can't just ship me off like that. I'm staying here for a few days to talk to this child. This little girl needs a proper family with a mother and father, not this perv—' She stopped and spread her hands. 'It's not natural! I can offer her a safe family back in Chicago. She'd be much better off there with us.'

Buffy's eyes widened and she grabbed Leo's arm.

'You can't take Buffy away from the only family she's known,' Simone said, distraught. She rose and moved to stand next to Martin. 'My brother would give his life for either of us in a second. He's probably the most caring father a little girl could ask for.'

'We'll see about that,' Elise said. 'I want to talk to the little girl by herself, before you have a chance to coach her.'

'Go right ahead,' Leo said. 'And when she tells you she's being loved and cared for as if she was our own child, you can go straight home.'

'I want to stay a few days and make sure.'

'Very well.' Leo rose and slid Buffy off his lap. 'Come into Buffy's bedroom and ask her anything. But if you traumatise this child and make any suggestions that will prey on her mind in later life, heaven help you, Elise.'

'I would never dream of it.'

The intercom buzzer went off next to the front door, and Martin went to answer it as Leo and Elise took Buffy to her room.

'Wei?' Martin said.

'Delivery from the supermarket's here,' the security guard said on the other end.

Martin unfocused, obviously asking Leo if he'd ordered from the supermarket, then turned to Simone. 'Did you order anything to be delivered here?'

'No, of course not.'

'Me neither,' I said. 'Damn, they're bold.'

'Send him up,' Martin said into the intercom. He summoned the Silver Serpent and waited at the door.

The doorbell rang and he opened it. A delivery guy stood on the other side of the metal gate, holding a large cardboard box full of groceries and grinning. He saw the

Silver Serpent in Martin's hand and his eyes widened with confusion.

'Simone,' Martin said without moving.

Simone summoned one of her short curved blades and stood next to Martin. 'Damn, I have no idea.'

The language charm kicked in. 'I'll just leave this stuff here for you,' the delivery guy said, obviously alarmed by the weapons as he placed the box on the floor. 'It's all paid for ... uh ... yeah. Bye.' He spun and ran to the stairs.

Simone opened the gate and poked her head out. 'We didn't order anything!'

'Just keep it,' he yelled, his voice echoing in the stairwell.

Simone checked the box. 'The order's for one of the flats downstairs, they sent it to the wrong address.' She knelt next to the box. 'I'll take it down for them.'

'Don't touch it!' I said as she reached for it. 'Have a look inside, it could be a bomb.'

Her eyes unfocused and she shook her head. 'No, nothing but groceries.'

'Yin it anyway. It could be something we haven't encountered before.'

'Ge Ge?' Simone said.

'Emma's right, it could be a trap.' Martin held his hand out to Simone. 'Let's yin it together — we'll have more control.'

They concentrated and yinned the box without putting a dent in the floor. They came back inside and Martin closed the gate and front door. He went to the couch and sat on it.

'Give me a moment,' he said. 'I need to let the Generals know that they may be targeting us and trying to send us to Court Ten.'

'But was that a human or a demon?' I asked Simone.

'To be honest, Emma,' she said, flipping her hair over her shoulder, 'I have no idea.'

'Holy shit — *Elise*,' I said, and we ran to Buffy's bedroom.

Martin threw the door open and the three of us charged in. Leo raced into the room from the bathroom at the same time. Elise was sitting with Buffy on the bed, sharing a picture book.

She looked up at us, confused. 'What?'

Leo gestured towards us. 'Ming, come and have a look and make sure. I see her as human.' He gently led Buffy to the doorway.

Martin crouched in front of Elise and put his hands on either side of her face. Her face went slack.

'Human all the way through, I sense no demon here at all.' Elise's eyes went wide and she squeaked with pain. 'This is most definitely human. Do you want me to adjust her attitude while I'm in here? It would make our lives considerably easier.'

'No,' Leo said. 'Leave her be. Don't mess with her head. She's my goddamn sister.'

'Don't fix her head now. Do it later, and only once so you minimise the damage,' I said. 'When you take her to the airport, fill her mind with the fact that she didn't find Leo and send her home. Leave him dead.' I turned to Leo. 'Sorry, Leo, just a suggestion.'

'Actually, that works,' Leo said softly. He looked down at Buffy and patted her back. 'You okay, sweetheart?'

'Yeah, we're doing our superhero thing,' Buffy said. 'I know.'

'I'll release her and go invisible, she won't even know I did this,' Martin said. 'Buffy, come and sit with Aunty Elise and everybody else — out.'

'Okay, Ba Ba,' Buffy said, and climbed on the bed next to Elise. She pulled the book around so that it was in the same position, and shooed Leo away. 'It's okay, Daddy, I'll make sure she doesn't know anything happened.'

Leo kissed the top of her head and went out through the connecting doors. Simone and I went back to the living room and sat on the couches.

'Are we going overboard with the paranoia?' Simone said, leaning one elbow on the arm of the couch.

'I'd rather be paranoid and alive,' I said.

She nodded once sharply. 'Yeah.' She bounced to sit straighter on the couch. 'I should have kept one of the packets of ramen in the grocery box. I'm *hungry*.'

'I'm hungry too!' Buffy shouted as Elise brought her into the living room, holding her hand.

'Do you have a ticket home already? Do we need to buy you one?' I asked Elise.

'You'll just buy me an airfare to the US?'

'My dad was really rich,' Simone said. She shrugged. 'We can if you want us to.'

'I have a ticket to return in three days,' Elise said. 'I don't need your money.'

'You are welcome to stay here with us, you're family,' Martin said. 'We have a spare room for you.'

'I think I will,' Elise said. 'I want to make sure she's okay.'

Leo concentrated on Martin. Martin shook his head. Leo gestured, irate, and Martin turned his back on him to speak to Elise again.

'We still haven't found a domestic helper and there isn't a scrap of food in the house, so how about we go down to SoHo and find something to eat?' He nodded to me. 'After dinner we'll drop you in Wan Chai.'

'SoHo?' Elise said, confused.

'South of Hollywood Road,' Simone said. 'It's a district of Mid-Levels. There's some nice foreign restaurants there.'

'Foreign?' Elise said.

'Pizza!' Buffy shouted, waving both little hands with glee.

Simone smiled slightly. 'Anything that's not Chinese is foreign.'

'I think this whole place is foreign,' Elise said under her breath.

28

'This deep-dish pizza is all wrong,' Elise said, staring at the large rectangular baking dish holding the five-centimetre-thick crust covered with lashings of ground beef, tomato and cheese. 'It's supposed to have the sauce on the top.'

'It's Hong Kong style,' Simone said, pulling one of the square chunks out of the dish. 'It's closer to the way they serve it in some parts of Italy where it was invented.'

'Deep-dish pizza was invented in Chicago,' Elise said.

'Uh, okay,' Simone said.

'Can I have some too, please, Aunty Simone?' Buffy said, her eyes wide with anticipation.

'This is yours,' Simone said, passing the plate to her. 'The vegetarian ones are for everybody else.'

'Yum,' Buffy said, and tucked into the fluffy bread crust.

'What do you say?' Leo said sternly.

'Thank you, Aunty Simone,' Buffy said in a sing-song voice through the pizza.

Simone used her knife to cut another square section off. 'Would you like some?' she asked Elise.

'I suppose I can try it,' Elise said. 'It doesn't have anything ... strange in it, does it?'

'You are embarrassing me more and more every minute, Elise,' Leo said, his voice a low rumble.

'You have embarrassed me all my life,' she snapped back, then stopped. 'Sorry.' She nodded thanks to Simone as she put a piece onto a plate and handed it to her. 'Now tell me what you're doing with yourself. I knew you were alive, I had a feeling.' She patted his shoulder. 'Last I heard you were a bodyguard for that opera singer, then I heard she died, then they told us you were dead too! What happened?'

'That opera singer was Simone's mother,' Leo said.

'It's okay, Leo,' Simone said gently.

'Oh, I'm sorry,' Elise said. 'I didn't mean it that way. I'm just confused. What happened?'

'I wanted to be left alone,' Leo said into his untouched pizza.

'We're your *family*,' she said, then gazed out the window. 'How can he ride around like that?'

I looked out as well. A gas delivery man was riding a sturdily built heavy Chinese bicycle along the narrow street with two full gas bottles in the basket in front of him.

'That's a common sight in the narrower streets that aren't easy for trucks,' I said. I dropped my voice; he'd stopped outside the restaurant and obviously seen us. 'Heads up.'

The delivery man pulled a piece of paper out of his pocket, checked it, then climbed back onto his bicycle and rode clumsily away.

'We really are paranoid,' Simone said. 'Buy some groceries and find a helper, Ge Ge. This is ridiculous.'

'We'll go shopping tomorrow,' Martin said. 'We're just having trouble finding the right domestic help.'

'I can give you one of my ... staff,' I said.

'Your staff?' Elise said. 'How many staff do you have?'

I thought frantically for a moment, trying to place the demons in a situation where they'd fit on the Earthly. I'd been spending far too much time on the Celestial.

Martin came to my rescue. 'One of Chenco's subsidiaries is an employment agency. Emma helps us manage the company. It's a huge enterprise.'

'Oh, I understand.' She looked from Martin to me. 'How big is this company anyway?'

'Big enough,' Leo said. 'Your pizza's getting cold.'

Elise cut a piece of the thick pizza off with her knife and took a bite. Her eyebrows shot up and she nodded enthusiastically, making pleasurable sounds in her throat.

'That's why we came here,' Simone said. She nodded towards Buffy, who had nearly finished her square of pizza. 'She likes it more than anything.'

* * *

We walked back along the narrow street; its surface was shining from the rain that had just passed over and slick with oil. Steam rose from the warm asphalt, and the coloured signboards above the street and along the Mid-Levels escalator route reflected in the water. The streets ran parallel to the hillside and the lanes between them that carried the escalators were steep and slippery.

'This time it's definitely the real thing,' Simone said, looking around.

'Yes,' Martin said. 'Hurry.'

Leo took Buffy from Elise and hoisted her onto his hip to carry her.

'We need to hurry, it will rain like anything in a minute,' Simone said. She raised her phone. 'Thunderstorm warning.'

'A little rain won't hurt us,' Elise said.

'Hong Kong doesn't do little rain,' Simone said, and stopped.

Four Mothers in human form stood in front of us. Elise backed up and turned to run, and another appeared behind her. She trembled with fear. Mothers could drive humans wild with terror just by looking at them and Elise was close.

'Elise, take Buffy and stay calm,' Leo said. He handed the little girl to Elise, who clutched her. 'Look after her for us, okay?'

Elise nodded over Buffy's head, braver now she had the child to protect.

I stepped forward with Martin at my right. 'Whatever you want, you aren't getting it. The King's guaranteed my and Simone's safety through this, and if you're acting outside his orders, you are in serious trouble and your best bet would be to go home right now.'

'I guaranteed your safety during the coming conflict,' the King said from behind them, his voice mild. They parted and he stepped between them. 'And the best way to ensure it is to have you in custody.'

He raised one hand and pointed at Leo. A shot rang out and Leo fell.

'Leo!' Simone shouted and knelt next to him. 'Leo?'

Martin grabbed me and covered as much of me with his body as he could.

'Not me!' I shouted. 'Protect Elise and Buffy. He needs me alive.'

Martin moved in front of them and I summoned the Murasame.

'I know what my sword will do to you,' I said.

'I told her to aim for his knees,' the King said, still mild. 'But at this distance her aim isn't very good.'

'He's hit in the head,' Simone said, and summoned a pad to stop the bleeding. 'Leo. Leo?' She rose and turned to the King, summoning yin around her hands. 'You will *pay* for this.'

The King raised his hands. 'Before you do anything rash, Princess, remember there's a sniper above us with her gun trained on the black woman.'

Simone disappeared.

'Oh, bad idea,' the King said, and pointed at Elise.

Another shot rang out and the bullet hit the ground next to Elise's feet. She shrieked and jumped.

'Her aim really is very poor,' the King said with interest. 'I told her to shoot above the black woman's head.'

Simone reappeared. 'Why can't I find it?'

'Because she's one of my special creations,' the King said. 'Stay here, Simone, or the black woman will have both her legs shot off. Or as close as my terrible sniper can manage.'

Elise made soft gibbering sounds of terror, still clutching Buffy.

The King sighed with feeling. 'Calm down, I'm not here to kill you. Do what I ask and nobody will be hurt. Nobody *else* that is.'

'What do you want?' I said.

'You know what I want, Emma. Give it to me, or I'll pick your family off one by one. The Immortals will come to play with me in Hell. The mortals ...' He smiled kindly at Elise and Buffy. 'Well.'

388

I dropped my head and dismissed the Murasame.

'Good girl,' the King said.

I looked into Simone's eyes. Her own were full of desperation. I wished I could speak telepathically to her.

I have a relay, the stone said.

Tell her I'll go with him, change to snake, and run to the Serpent. If she can find me, she can meet me there.

'That really is extremely bad manners, and if you don't stop right now someone will find a bullet in them,' the King said.

Deal, Simone said.

I raised my hands. 'Don't hurt them. I'll come with you.'

He smiled with satisfaction, took my upper arms, kissed me quickly, and the world around us disappeared.

* * *

We arrived inside what appeared to be a small single-storey villa, with timber interior walls and large windows that overlooked a pleasant garden. The living room had a mix of modern leather furniture and extremely ancient Chinese rosewood. I was in Hell again, trapped again, and a roaring filled my ears as everything faded to white.

When I came around, I sat up. A really big demon in male human form was sitting on a couch across from me and there was nobody else around. I changed to my smallest snake form, slid off the couch onto the floor and hid under the couch.

'The villa is snake-proof, Emma,' the demon said, perfectly calm. 'The King has ordered me to take you to see Prince Francis, so please change back and we'll go.'

I hesitated, thinking about my son. Then I searched for the Serpent. I sent out my awareness, searching for it, and

389

couldn't find it. I poked my head out from under the couch and the demon didn't move, watching me with amusement from where he sat. I emerged from under the couch and scouted around the room, looking for the Serpent and not finding it anywhere.

'Don't you want to see your son, Emma?' His expression became concerned. 'You are sentient like that, aren't you?'

I ignored him and concentrated on the room where they were holding the Serpent. I focused my internal eye on the shape of the cage and willed myself to be next to it. The room shimmered around me, then it was like hitting a wall — the shock vibrated through me and sent me hurtling backwards. I landed upside down on the floor of the villa with a massive headache.

'Did you just try to teleport? I didn't know you could do that,' the demon said with wonder. 'Emma, the villa's *sealed*. All of Hell is sealed. You can't go anywhere, except with me to see your son. Don't you want to see your only child? We haven't told him you're coming; it will be a wonderful surprise for him.'

I changed back to human form, pulled myself to my feet, then flopped to sit on the couch and put my throbbing head in my hands.

'Emma,' the demon said kindly, and I looked up. He was holding a box of painkillers towards me, and I took them. He gestured over his shoulder. 'The water in the kitchen is perfectly good to drink.' He smiled slightly. 'I know what that feels like — sometimes we forget and hit the wall ourselves. The seals have only been there a few days. Dad secured all of Hell when he won.'

I staggered to my feet, went to the villa's compact kitchen, found a drinking glass and filled it, then gulped down the painkillers. I filled the glass a few more times and drank it down; the pizza had been very salty. I leaned on the bench as I remembered the pizza, the family ... that had been less than an hour ago. At least they were safe ...

'Are my family safe?' I said.

'Ah! She does speak,' the demon said. 'Yes, we left them after we took you. The King only wanted you. He needs you if his plan is to succeed, and he knew you wouldn't cooperate if they were hurt.'

'Leo was shot in the head.'

'Her aim was terrible, and she apologises. She was supposed to hit him in the leg. He's not dead, he's in hospital in a coma, so he won't be coming down here for us to play with.' His tone changed to regret. 'Such a shame.' He brightened. 'But if you behave, I'm sure we can arrange for him to be spared if he does make it down here.'

I studied him and the shock of recognition went through me. He'd aged himself about ten years and now looked mid-forties, but it was my friend April's husband. April, who had borne a child she'd been made to forget, and who had ended up in pieces in a dumpster in Kowloon City.

'Andy Ho,' I said.

He nodded acknowledgement.

'Were you the father of that Simone copy April gave birth to all that time ago?'

'Yes. I have a similar heritage to you — I'm quarter European. So was April, by the way. We are all descended from the Island of Holy Serpents, and the King was hoping to breed from the three of us. He was extremely cross when we lost you; he had us set up to be a grand little threesome. You and April were to be my two wives, and I was on the way to creating a lovely little nest of my own with a few really

391

exceptional Mothers as well. When we lost you, the King blamed me for not treating you well enough and punished me severely. He killed my entire harem and April as well — her job was done anyway, the copy was created. I survived, but it's taken me a long time to redeem myself.'

'The reason I left had nothing to do with the way you treated me, Andy, and everything to do with the fact that you and Kitty totally creeped me out.'

He shrugged.

'How many did you have to kill to reach Number One?' I said.

'Three hundred-odd.'

'No, since the last Number One died.'

He smiled.

'Damn. You took a serious piece out of the horde.'

'Not really. Three hundred out of three hundred thousand ...' He shrugged.

'But they were the biggest.'

'Plenty more to replace them. There are always more small demons wanting advancement than there are places for them.' He rubbed his hands together and rose. 'Now, how about we go see your little boy, eh? He's a lovely kid. Shame I'm not the father, but you can't have everything, I suppose.'

He guided me out of the villa and through a garden of lawn and carefully tended flower beds to another identical villa. Both villas stood behind a large double-storey courtyard house with an upward-sweeping roof, red walls and black pillars.

'Is that the King's own palace?' I said.

'That it is. These villas are the residences for the human wives; he doesn't have any at the moment.' He glanced sideways at me. 'He's always hoped that you might be living in one eventually. He'll be thrilled to bits to see you in there.'

'I'll kill myself before I let him do anything to me,' I said.

'You can't kill yourself; you promised Simone you wouldn't.'

'How do you know this?'

'We have control over the Celestial side of Hell, Emma, and *we* decide who goes to the Pits. Nobody in there can remain silent forever.'

'Damn.'

He stopped in front of the door into the other villa. 'The villas are very comfortable. I lived in one of them for many years myself. But before we go in, there's a few ground rules I have to go over.'

'I'm sure there are.'

'If you tell him you're his mother, we'll break his other arm.'

'His *other* ... What? You *broke his arm*?'

'Dad and Uncle Francis are tag-teaming the brainwashing. Dad's the good, loving and indulgent parent. Francis is the cruel one.'

'And what did he do to deserve having his arm broken?'

'We're *brainwashing* him, Emma, he didn't do anything. But he's frantically trying to work out where he failed so it doesn't happen again. Remember: don't tell him you're his mother. Don't tell him anything about topside. No stories of the family. You can be with him as much as you like and teach him the ways of the world, but don't make any attempt to turn him from us or he will suffer, and suffer horribly, for it.'

'I see.'

'Dad and Francis will be back in a couple of hours and they'll be very happy to discuss his future, and your role

393

in it. Until then, I'm sure you want to spend time with your child.'

He opened the door and we went in. My son was sitting on the floor in the middle of the living room with a demon in older female human form, a nanny. Frankie looked six months older already, and had black rings under his eyes, which were red from crying. He was surrounded by toy cars, his left arm in a bright pink cast from his hand to above his elbow.

I ran to him, then slowed when I saw his panicked expression. I approached him more slowly with my hands in view.

'Do you remember me?' I said gently.

He shook his head.

I knelt to speak to him. 'My name's Emma.' I glanced back at Number One, then returned to Frankie. 'I'm here to teach you things.'

He flinched, put his arm in front of his face and started to sniffle. He was too terrified to run away from me and waited for the blow to come.

'No, not bad things, nice things,' I said. 'I'm here to teach you interesting stuff, and I'll never hurt you.'

He dropped his arm to see me, and my heart twisted. He resembled me; and he had some of John's features as well — his strong jaw, softened by youth, and his dark eyes. His hair was a fine dark brown, the same colour as mine, and his skin was as fair as my own. He really was our child.

I didn't try to hug him; that would come later. Maybe one day he would even call me Mummy.

'Number One,' I said loudly, 'I need Lego. Lots of Lego, a few basic sets, and a computer with internet access. I don't care how much your father complains — limit outgoing,

I don't care. This child needs to see more nature than this garden, and I'll need to research which books I want to order for him. A television and DVD player — I'll give you a list of DVDs later. I want a complete list of everything you're feeding him; he looks like he's not getting enough vitamins. He needs sunshine, dammit, he's whiter than me! The King will need to arrange something. Drawing materials, a *lot* of paper, crayons, paints, Play-Doh.'

I turned to see Number One leaning on the wall next to the front door and smiling with satisfaction. 'Are you writing this down?' I said.

'I don't need to, Emma. And you can call me Andy, if you like. I'd really prefer it.'

'I'll think of more things later, *Number One*.' I swept my hand over the rug covered in miniature cars. 'Is this all he has?'

'The King buys him toys but he's usually too young to play with them, ma'am,' the house demon said. She dropped her voice. 'And they're taken away as well.'

I checked Frankie. He was sitting on the rug, petrified with fear, his face blank and withdrawn.

'Move me in here with him,' I said.

'Ask Dad about that,' Number One said. He sat on the couch. 'He'll be here soon. Why don't you get to know the child before he comes?'

'What time is it?'

'Only nine, still early.'

'He should be getting ready for bed.'

'He can go to bed after his mother and father have been in to say goodnight,' Number One said.

I made a soft sound of frustration in my throat, sat on the carpet across from Frankie and picked up one of the cars.

29

Two hours later, Frankie and I had made an imaginary town on the carpet using pencils and paper that Number One had scrounged for us. We drew roadways on the paper, and drove the cars through life and family situations. Frankie's life experiences were close to nonexistent, but he was a fast learner.

The Demon King arrived in Kitty Kwok form, accompanied by the Western Demon King, Francis. Both of them plastered smiles on their faces as they came in through the door.

'Ah, Emma, so good you're here,' the Western King said. 'Little Frankie's been a bad boy and I had to hurt him. I hope it won't happen again.'

'It won't happen again, Father,' Frankie said.

'I can take over caring for him,' I said.

'No, you can't, Emma dear, you don't have the same set of goals as we do,' the Eastern King said. She sat on the carpet

396

next to Frankie and pulled him into her lap. 'Has your arm stopped hurting, sweetheart? We can give you more Panadol if you like.'

'It's not too bad, Mummy,' Frankie said, and put his head on her chest. 'I missed you.'

She put her arms around him and held him close. 'I missed you too.' She smiled over his head at me. 'That's not a good look to be showing the boy, Emma. Your face is venomous enough to kill at ten paces.'

I tried to change to blank. 'Can you blame me?'

'He would not be alive if not for me, and you'll never have another one.' She stood, still holding Frankie in her arms. 'Bedtime now, my darling.'

Frankie threw his arms around her neck and kissed her cheek. 'I love you, Mummy.'

Her face filled with genuine affection. 'I love you too, sweetheart. Go with Three Fifty and I'll come in later and say goodnight.' She lowered him. 'Say goodnight to your father.'

He bowed formally to Francis. 'Good night, Father. I'm sorry I messed up and I'll try to do better.'

'I hope you do, Frankie,' Francis said, full of regret. 'I hate disciplining you. You need to try harder.'

'I will.' Frankie turned to me and his face went blank. He looked from me to Francis, obviously close to panic — he'd forgotten my name.

'I'm Emma,' I said. 'Goodnight, Frankie.'

He sagged with relief and bowed to me. 'Goodnight, Miss Emma.' He took the nanny's hand and she led him to the bedroom.

Kitty watched him go out, full of indulgent affection. When the door closed behind them, she became more brisk, sat on the couch, and changed to male form. 'Okay, Emma, if you don't want to stay and help out with him, say the word and we'll put you in a nice warm cell.'

'I'll stay with him,' I said. 'I've already given Number One a list of things I need.'

'We'll provide everything you ask for, and you can spend your time teaching him. Agreed?'

'Agreed,' I said.

'This is too easy,' Francis growled.

'I know what it's like to be a mother. She'll give anything and do anything for her child,' the Demon King said.

I dropped my head. He was right.

'I want something from you in return for giving you time with the child,' the King said.

'Why am I not surprised?' I said without looking up.

'I want you to give him the Murasame and teach him how to use it. It was once his father's, it became mine, it's now yours. I think it's entirely fitting that the blade becomes his.'

'He's too young to learn to use it,' I said.

'His coordination is —'

'Nothing to do with his coordination,' I said. 'Everything to do with his size. He's too small to wield the blade. He'll need to grow at least another thirty centimetres, and probably more, before the tip isn't digging into the ground every time he swings it down.'

'Oh,' the King said. 'You have a point. Very well, give him the blade now and we'll put it on a rack until he's big enough. And when he is big enough you teach him. Understood?'

'The blade won't destroy John, George. You're wasting your time giving it to him.'

'It won't destroy John, but it may take out the Jade Emperor.'

That stopped me. He saw my face and grinned.

'I'll need a small bokken to train him first,' I said. 'He needs to be able to master the basic moves, otherwise the Murasame won't obey him and may hurt him.'

'We can't have that. I'll arrange it,' the King said. He rose, and Francis stood as well. 'Let's go to the other villa — your villa — and lock you in for the night. If you behave, I may give you free run between your house and his.' He gestured towards the door and I went out with them. 'Tomorrow morning you start teaching him everything he needs to know to live on the Celestial.'

* * *

Back in my own villa, I sat cross-legged on the bed and closed my eyes, ostensibly meditating before sleep.

You there? I asked the stone.

Yes. I'm linked to the wireless network here, but it's heavily encrypted and I'll have to use brute force to open a connection. It can be done, but it will take a while.

I sighed. I wasn't in any hurry to leave Frankie, but I knew what I had to do.

Good. I was worried that you'd changed your mind when you were playing with him. Number One was right: he really is a lovely kid. Don't forget that you'll be able to come back for him once we're free.

I hope so. Any progress on finding the Serpent?

I need to make this wireless connection work so I can find it. When you go to spend time with Frankie tomorrow, 'forget' me back here. I'll have a look around and see if I can't find some copper wire or fibre optic or something. That is much easier to break into.

399

Hopefully they'll have a computer and internet for me tomorrow as well.

If that's the case I'll be able to break in immediately. Is the plan still the same?

Yes. Somehow break out of here, go by foot — or whatever — in snake form to find the Serpent and let it out. Come back and free Frankie, then the Xuan Wu Serpent teleports Frankie and me home to Heaven. Take the Serpent to the Grotto, and cry like a child when John is finally whole again. Retake Hell and soundly thrash George and Francis. Get married and have a real family with two lovely kids and probably cry again. Happy ever after and shit.

Definitely sounds like a plan. Get some sleep and I'll continue to try to break into this network and find out where the Turtle's better half is.

I slipped between the covers and nearly lost it at sleeping alone again. I missed John so much it hurt.

Put me to your forehead, the stone said.

Thank you. I didn't remember anything else.

* * *

The next morning I went straight from my villa to Frankie's, eager to spend time with him. He was eating congee at the table next to the kitchen, the demon nanny supervising.

'Good morning,' I said, cheerful to be doing something so ordinary with him. I nodded to the demon. 'Any extra?'

'Ma'am,' the demon said, and went into the kitchen to serve me a bowl. She handed it to me over the kitchen counter.

'Thank you,' I said, and she stared at me with shock.

I sat next to Frankie and my heart twisted — I'd done this so many times with Simone when she was small. His dark eyes — John's eyes — shone at me over his bowl.

'So what were you planning to do today?' I asked him.

'Normally I just watch TV and stuff. It's pretty boring until Mummy comes,' Frankie said. He brightened and sat straighter. 'Can we do the thing with the cars again?'

'If Number One brings the things I asked him for, we can do much more than that,' I said. 'I gave him a list of really fun things we can play with together.'

His eyes were wide with wonder over his congee.

'Have you ever had dreams?' I said casually, watching the demon nanny busy in the kitchen from the corner of my eye.

'Sometimes. Sometimes they're scary,' he said, still eating with gusto.

'Snake Mothers?'

'What are they?'

'Never mind. Do you dream of snakes?'

The demon nanny went very still.

'Sometimes,' Frankie said.

'Talking ones?'

Frankie didn't reply, he just took another spoonful of congee.

'Talking snakes tell the truth in dreams,' I said, and took a spoonful myself. 'They'll always tell you the truth.'

'No ...' he said, unsure.

'Always. And if you listen to the snake's voice —'

'I think that's enough of that,' the King said from the doorway. He was in Kitty form. 'Nice try, Emma. He told you he dreams of snakes?'

'Mummy!' Frankie leapt out of his chair and ran to her.

She bent to speak to him. 'Don't run too fast after eating, you'll be sick.' She tousled his hair. 'And how's my best little boy?'

He threw his arms around her neck and hugged her. She smiled over his shoulder at me, then gently eased him off and kissed him on the cheek. 'Finish your breakfast, then we have to do something.'

He froze. 'Do something?'

'Yes. Up you go.' The King lifted him, little legs dangling, and sat him at the table again. She sat next to him. 'Eat up, and then Emma will give you a present.'

Frankie looked from the King to me, eyes wide. 'Really? Is it the stuff you said about, Emma?'

'The stuff I was talking about, yes,' I said.

'No,' the King said. 'Emma's going to give you a sword. A really cool one.'

I was silent at that.

'Or. Else,' the King said with quiet menace, tapping her fingers on the bright pink plaster cast.

I pushed the congee away, suddenly not hungry.

The Demon King chatted with Frankie as he ate his breakfast, and wouldn't let me speak: she either interrupted me or talked over me when I tried. When Frankie was done, the Western King Francis entered, with two Dukes in human form attending as guards.

'Living room, there's more room there,' the King said, and we all filed in.

Francis and one of the Dukes stood behind me; the King, Frankie and the other Duke stood in front. They weren't taking any chances.

'Try anything and you know what will happen,' the King said. 'Give him the sword.'

Frankie stood silent and uncomprehending. I hesitated, then held my hand out.

'It won't come,' I said. 'It doesn't like Hell.'

'Don't be ridiculous,' the King said. 'It *loves* Hell. Little finger first? Or two fingers? Take your pick.'

The Murasame appeared in my hand and I wavered. If I tried for the King now, my son would see me kill the only mother he knew.

'Just do as you're told, Emma,' the King said, reading my mind. 'Then you can spend the rest of the day playing with him. You said it yourself: he's too small to use it, and you know nobody else will be able to. It will sit on the rack untouched. Give it to him. It's only a blade and you have plenty.'

I said goodbye to the sword and asked it to care for my child. It sat in my hand like a callous bird of prey, silently waiting to attack anything that moved. It didn't give a damn who owned it as long as they brought it gifts of chaos.

I knelt and held the blade horizontally in front of Frankie. His expression was a mixture of awe and fear.

'It's pretty cool, isn't it?' I said. 'It's a magic blade, and it's yours because you're a Prince.' My heart broke; as the son of Xuan Tian Shang Di he really was a Celestial Prince. He should have been taking his place in the ranks of Heaven and learning the magic of the Celestials. I pulled myself together and continued. 'You're too small to use it right now, but I'll teach you how and in time you'll be big enough to wield it.'

Frankie shook his head emphatically.

'Take it, little love, it is yours,' the King said.

'Take the damn blade. I have better things to do,' Francis snapped behind me.

Frankie jumped as if stung, and approached me.

'Wait a second. I need to tell the sword that it belongs to you,' I said. 'Nobody but you will be able to touch it.' I glanced at the King. 'Do you have a rack to put it on?'

'They're bringing a lovely ebony stand from my house right now — the Murasame's old home,' the King said. 'Go ahead.' Her voice sharpened. 'Now.'

'Put your hand over mine,' I said.

Frankie put his hand where I directed, then ripped it away again. 'It bit me!'

'Emma,' the King growled.

'It doesn't want to go to him; it says he's too small,' I said. 'Give me a moment.'

I tried to reason with the sword but it was like arguing with a piece of furniture. Eventually I fiercely ordered it to accept my child, and showed it who Frankie's parents were. That worked. The sword saluted me, and the blaze of pain from holding it was so intense I had to drop it.

'Pick it up, it's yours,' the King said to Frankie.

Frankie approached me carefully, bent and picked up the sword. He had no trouble lifting it — it wasn't particularly heavy, it weighed less than a kilo — and his face went slack with wonder as the sword settled into his ownership.

'The sword's name is the Murasame, the Destroyer,' I said. 'Wield it with courage and honour, my son.'

Francis struck me on the side of the head from behind so hard that I hit the floor with a smack.

* * *

'And this is a natural dog,' I said later that day. 'My drawings are terrible, but if we get a computer I'll be able to show you videos of dogs being cute.'

404

'What do they do?'

I grinned conspiratorially. 'If you throw a ball or a stick, they'll bring it back. They love that game.'

'And they really can't talk?'

'They really can't talk. They're not that clever. They just love you and play with you and cuddle you and,' I bent closer, 'lick your face!'

'Ew!' he said, recoiling with theatrical distaste. He came closer again. 'Can I have one?'

'I'll talk to your ...' I bit the words out, 'mother and father.'

Number One came into the villa without knocking. 'Emma.'

I stood to speak to him. 'Is that a laptop?'

'Yes, it is.' He pulled it out of its bag and put it on the desk, then leaned on it with one hand. 'We've severely limited what you can do with it, and we'll be watching you every second.' He opened it and plugged it in. 'Apart from that,' he said, checking the screen as it booted up, 'do whatever you like. If you want to order something, let me know.' He turned and smiled at Frankie. 'Are you having fun with Miss Emma?'

Frankie crept slightly behind me, his eyes wide. 'I like Emma.'

'Good. Emma, with me.' He gestured for me to follow him out of the villa, and stopped in the garden. 'You can have the computer but you have to hand over the stone.' He gestured towards my left hand. 'Which is probably a good idea, considering what it's up to. Hand it over.'

'I forgot to put it on this morning, it's in my villa,' I said.

'Seriously?' he said, laughter in his voice. 'That's the best you can come up with?'

I led him into my villa and made a show of looking for it. 'It's gone.'

'If it's gone then Frankie will have two of his fingers broken,' Number One said.

'So sorry, I was asleep,' the stone said, and floated out of the bedroom. 'You forgot me again this morning, Emma.'

'Oh for fuck's sake, give me a break and stop with the playacting,' Number One said, exasperated. He pulled a small stone casket from his pocket. 'In here.'

'Let me say goodbye,' the stone said.

'No. Into the box.'

The stone changed to human form, gave me a hug and slotted a map straight into my head like an ice blade. It held me in the embrace as I sagged, almost falling from the shock of the data insertion.

'If you do not enter this box immediately the child will suffer,' Number One said, becoming irate. 'Now!'

The stone folded up and flew into the casket. 'Good—'

Number One snapped the lid shut. 'All right, back you go. We'll go through the logs and find out what it gave you. We saw everything it did.'

* * *

'And these are ponies,' I said, bringing up a video and trying to ignore the map nagging at the back of my head. I would look at it later. 'The White Tiger of the West has plenty of them, and gives them to his children to ride.'

'They're furry! They're so cute!' Frankie said, watching the video. 'But they don't have wings. Can they fly?'

'No, they can't fly.' I remembered. 'You've ridden flyers before with your mother, haven't you?'

406

Frankie nodded. 'I saw ...' His brown brows creased. 'I don't know what I saw.'

'You saw a battle. A fight. Between the forces of the Celestial and the forces of Hell.'

'Is that what that was?' he said with wonder. 'Why were they fighting?'

'Forbidden topic, ma'am,' Three Fifty said from the other side of the room where she'd been quietly listening.

'That's the fourth one today!' I said, exasperated. 'I can't teach the child anything!'

Three Fifty shot to her feet. 'Your parents are here, Prince Francis.'

Frankie's face went blank then composed into an expressionless mask. So young to be hiding his fear already. We both rose and turned to face the door.

The King in his Kitty form, accompanied by Francis and Number One, came in.

'Frankie,' Kitty said, warm with pleasure, and crouched and opened her arms for him.

Frankie ran to her and smiled up into her face. 'I missed you, Mummy.'

She kissed the top of his head. 'I missed you too, darling.' She dropped her voice. 'Quickly, call your father before he becomes angry.'

Frankie extricated himself from the King's grip — the King deliberately holding him to slow him — and turned to bow to the Western King. 'Good day, Father. It is good to see you.'

'Why don't I get a hug?' Francis said, irate.

Frankie eased himself carefully towards Francis and held his arms out for the embrace. Francis knelt and gave Frankie a cursory hug, then quickly pushed him away to glare at him.

'That was only half a hug. You love your mother more than you love me,' Francis said in a menacing tone.

'No, Father, I truly love you,' Frankie said desperately. He hugged Francis again, and Francis didn't return it. 'I do love you, Father.'

'Emma, with me,' Number One said, and opened the door.

I started to speak and the King stopped me. 'Nothing you can say or do will make any difference whatsoever to the child, except that you'll be put somewhere else. Be quiet and go while we spend time with our son.'

I nearly growled with frustration as I went with Number One and he escorted me out of the villa.

Inside my villa, Number One went to the kitchen and made himself a cup of coffee.

'Want one?' he said.

'Please. Milk and sugar.'

'This is a proper coffee machine, Emma, haven't you looked? How about a latte?'

'Thank you.'

He busied himself in the kitchen while I sat on the couch, straining to hear what was happening in Frankie's villa, hoping that I wouldn't hear the poor child scream.

Number One handed me a mug. He took a five-centimetre-wide brown stone out of his pocket and put it on the table between us, then sat across from me.

'Don't say anything. I only have a minute or so. I want a pact that if Dad loses, you'll give me Hell to rule as Demon King. I'll swear a blood oath to stay on our side for perpetuity and never try for the Heavens or the Earthly again. Back to what it was.' I opened my mouth and he raised his hand to stop me. 'No, don't speak. I want a backup plan in the unlikely case that Dad loses, and this is it. As a show of good faith: they've moved the Serpent; it's now about two kilometres southeast of where it will appear on the stone's map. That's all I have time for. Say yes if you're willing to give me your word, and we'll leave it there.'

He picked the stone up and put it in his pocket. 'I know you wanted to order things for the child with the computer. I'll provide you with one of Dad's credit cards later so you can order online. I'll need to give you the Earthly address for delivery, though, and I forgot to bring it. Is that okay?'

I sat for a long time, weighing his offer. The information about the Serpent was probably a trap for me if I escaped. If he was doing this on behalf of the King, the agreement only came into force if the King was gone and we'd won anyway, so no loss on our part.

'Yes,' I said.

He visibly relaxed. 'Good to hear.' He waved at my mug. 'Finish your coffee, then I'll take you back when they're done and give you the credit card details.'

I nodded and sipped the coffee. It was excellent.

30

'Emma,' a woman said into my ear. I jerked awake and jumped out of the bed in a long defensive stance.

It was Simone. I ran to her and crushed her to me, holding her tight. I whispered fiercely into her shoulder, 'You're here! You're here.'

'I'm here.'

I pulled back to see her. 'Dear Lord, you're not trapped here too, are you?'

'No, I came to get you out.'

'Frankie's in the house next to me. We can take him with us.'

'Is he?' She lit up. 'Really? That's wonderful. Do you know where Daddy is? Have you looked?'

'Wait … which Daddy?'

'The Serpent. The Turtle's still stuck at home in the cage.'

'Phew. Okay. I have a rough idea where the Serpent is …'
There was the sound of running feet and I pushed Simone

away. 'They're watching me, they saw you. Let's grab Frankie and run.'

She took my hand, dropped her head and concentrated, then collapsed.

'Simone. Simone!' I held both hands on her face, unwilling to slap her into awareness. 'Simone, they're coming, wake up!'

She took a huge deep breath and her eyes snapped open. 'That was like hitting a wall.'

'Seals. Everywhere. No teleporting out, we have to walk.' I raised my head to listen: they were outside the house. I summoned the Murasame and it didn't come. 'Dammit!' I helped her to her feet. 'We have to fight our way out. Can you call me a weapon? Will Dark Heavens come to you?'

'Just call your sword, it should come.'

'I gave it to Frankie.' The demons threw open the door, and hesitated when they saw how big Simone was. 'Weapons. Now!'

She held Dark Heavens out to me without looking away from the demons in the doorway, then summoned her own blades and filled them with her energy centres. Her voice went ice-cold. 'I am here to take my family out of here, and any of you that are in my way will be destroyed.' Her voice filled with even more menace, and yin wrapped around the blade of her left sword. 'Get. Out. Of. My. Way.'

The demons ran into the room and attacked.

I parried the first blow coming at my head, swiped it down, and tried to make it through the demon's guard but it was too fast. It closed and went for my head again, and I had to take a step back as I parried. As it followed me, it moved closer to Simone. Without looking away from the three demons she was facing, she threw energy into it and made it explode.

I generated a ball of energy on Dark Heavens and threw it at the next demon, and gaped as five of them disintegrated in the blast. The energy returned from the sword and hit me in a wave of power. It flooded through me, filling me with dark vicious cruelty, and I sent the energy straight back out to destroy five more. I shouted with delight at the havoc, and shot three balls into the remaining demons, destroying them all. I lowered the sword, panting with a combination of exhilaration and disappointment that the demons were all gone.

Simone turned to me and her face filled with concern. 'Emma, can you hear me?'

I raised the sword in a guard position and grinned at her, pleased that I had something else to fight.

'Emma, it's me, Simone. We need to find Frankie and pull him out,' she said.

Simone. Frankie. All my breath left me and I sagged, lowering the blade. I stared at it. 'What the hell?'

'Your eyes went black,' she said. 'That was one of the scariest things I have ever seen.'

I held Dark Heavens out horizontally and asked the blade to bring its scabbard to me. It obliged, and I put it away and dismissed it.

'I didn't know Dark Heavens could do that,' I said.

'Neither did I. I always thought it was just an ordinary demon-killer, with a bit of extra oomph from energy. Leo never said anything about it being particularly special.'

'Let's find Frankie before the next bunch of demons arrives. It looks like George and Francis aren't nearby to direct them.'

We went out of the villa together and ran across the grass to Frankie's villa.

I stopped at the door. 'Be aware that Frankie's been heavily brainwashed by the demons, and he thinks George is his mother. Take it slowly.'

'We may not have time to take it slowly.'

The door of Frankie's villa wasn't locked and we went inside. I led Simone to the analogue of my bedroom, and Frankie was there, small and vulnerable, curled up in the middle of the queen-size bed.

I shook his shoulder. 'Frankie. Frankie?'

He gasped and scurried away from me. Simone turned on the bedside light and he jumped out of bed and ran to cower in the corner when he saw her.

'Frankie, this is your sister Simone, from a different Mummy and the same Daddy. She's here to take us somewhere wonderful.'

He looked from Simone to me, eyes wide with fear.

I crouched to reassure him without touching him. 'Trust me, Frankie, I'm your real Mummy. I've been seeing you in dreams for a while now. I'm the snake in your dreams.'

His face was blank with shock.

Simone knelt next to me. 'We have a wonderful home in Heaven for you, Frankie. I really am your sister, and Emma is your real mother. Come with us, and we'll take you out.'

'I don't want to go out,' he said. 'I want to stay here with Mummy.'

'But Emma's your Mummy,' Simone said, still gently forceful.

He screwed up his face. 'You're lying. You're not my Mummy. My Mummy comes every day and hugs me.'

'I'm your real mother. That woman stole you,' I said.

'That's what the snake said.'

'That's because I was the snake.'

413

He put his hands over his face and screamed. He took a deep breath and screamed again. 'Mummy, come!' he screamed. 'Mummy, there's people here! I'm not a bad boy. Come and take them away.' His voice rose in pitch. 'She's a *snake*!'

Simone put her hand on his arm and he screamed higher and louder.

'Frankie! She won't change to snake, she's not scary!' she shouted through the screams. 'You're safe! You don't need to do this!' Her head shot up. 'There's a bunch of *really* big demons coming. Duke level.' She looked from Frankie to me, desperate. 'They're too big and he won't stop screaming.'

I rose and she did as well. Frankie had collapsed into sobs, bent double on the floor and calling for his mother.

'Come with us,' Simone said to him.

'Go away and leave me alone,' Frankie said. 'Go. Away! You'll get me into trouble!'

'I could just grab him ...' Simone bent to pick him up and he fought her off, kicking desperately and screaming again.

'You have to come with us,' I said. 'I love you. I'm your mother, and I will look after you.'

'Go away!' he screamed, his voice hoarse. 'You're a bad snake and Daddy will hurt me if he finds you here!'

'Come back for him after we find the Serpent,' Simone said. 'Let him think about it.' She raised her chin again. 'Emma, we need to go now.'

'I'll stay here with him. You go,' I said. 'I'll talk to him and we can take him out when you come back.'

'Okay, that works. Tell me where the Serpent is.'

I grabbed her hand and put it on my forehead. I concentrated on the map the stone had given me.

'I can't do that, Emma, I've never learned. Just tell me. Quickly!'

'I can't, it's too complicated.' The Dukes appeared in the doorway: ten of them, all bull-heads. 'Dammit!'

'There'd better be a back door.'

'The window isn't barred.'

I shot one last despairing look at my terrified child, threw a chair through the window and jumped out. We ran across the lawn as the Dukes charged through the house, accompanied by Frankie's screams. I'd been planning my escape all evening, and there was one exit from the King's garden. It led straight through a tunnel into the Nest of the most senior Mothers.

I led Simone to the tunnel with the Dukes crashing through the villa behind us. They went silent as they followed us across the grass towards the tunnel, but couldn't close on us. Both Simone and I were ridiculously fast when we ran flat out. We put a good distance between us and them, and I stopped at the end of the fifty-metre tunnel.

'Take your snake form, the weird one,' I said. 'Carry me in your hands. If any of the Mothers ask, you're one of the King's breeding experiments and I'm your dinner.'

I changed to snake and Simone took her serpent form: a big black snake with tiny arms and human hands covered in scales. She attempted to pick me up but her hands were too weak.

'Mouth,' I said, and lay flat on the ground.

She lowered her head, carefully picked me up in her mouth, and slithered through the gates and into the deepest Nest of the biggest Mothers.

I couldn't see much hanging upside down from her mouth. The cavern echoed with the dry rustling of the Mothers sleeping in their nest hollows. A few were talking softly nearby, but most appeared to be in the demon equivalent of sleep.

The Dukes stormed into the Nest, and Simone slithered into a group of sleeping Mothers, then turned. The Dukes didn't recognise her snake form and ran through the Nest and out the other side.

Can you give me an idea of direction? she said.

I jabbed my nose in what I hoped — upside down — was the right way.

I was expecting you to point right through the middle of them. That's actually not too far away ... Oh no.

'Hello, my lovely, are you here to play? Oh look, you brought us a toy,' one of the Mothers said.

Simone tried to speak around me in her mouth, then gave up and went silent.

'Really?' the Mother said. 'That would explain why you're so fucking ugly.'

Simone must have replied silently because the Mother raised herself on her coils and hissed. I flinched. All we needed was Simone picking a fight and waking them all up.

The Mother stayed still for a moment; Simone was talking to her.

'Did you break out or did he let you out?'

There was a pause as Simone answered.

'I know,' the Mother said with misery. 'We never see him either. He's always off with that Francis prick. I haven't served him in *months*.'

Simone replied and some of the Mothers laughed.

'We could tell the King about you and win extra toys,' the first Mother said, her voice sly.

They were all silent for a moment.

'I want one too!' the second Mother said.

'I don't believe you,' the first Mother said. 'No way you have two.'

They were silent as Simone spoke to them.

'Really? That makes sense,' the second Mother said. 'It must have been pretty boring in the lab — nothing to do and no toys. How long were you in there? How old are you anyway?'

There was a long silence, and both Mothers moved back to allow us through.

'I know where the lab is,' the first Mother said. 'If you don't pay up and give me the account codes by the end of today, I'll find you and eat you *and* your dinner.'

'What's going on? And what the fuck is this ugly thing?' another Mother said.

Simone tightened her grip on me and I hissed.

Sorry. Some more woke up. We're attracting attention.

'Oooh, food. I love snake,' another said.

'Nope, she's under my protection,' one of the first Mothers said. 'Hands off.'

'But I'm *hungry*,' another growled. 'Fight you for her? Winner eats both?'

'I can take you, Four. I'm bigger than you,' the first Mother said with menace.

Bigger than Four? Simone nearly dropped me, and I had to control my urge to wriggle out of her grip. Neither of us had realised exactly how huge these Mothers were. A group of them would be a challenge even for John.

'For your position as well, then. I can take you, and this thing looks tasty.'

'Nah, we're letting her go. She's one of the King's pet projects from the labs. She's looking for the Little Grandfather.'

'Oh,' all the other Mothers said in unison.

'I still want your position,' the other Mother said.

'You'd never take me down in a million years.'

Simone began to back away slowly as attention focused on the standoff between the two Mothers. From my limited vision it appeared that a circle was forming around them.

'We'll see about that!' the first Mother said, and attacked with a hiss that was echoed by the rapt spectators.

Simone slithered away as quickly as she could, her grip on me so tight I could feel her small individual teeth digging into my scales.

There were two demon guards flanking the door on the other side. Simone tried to move past them as casually as she could.

'Where are you going?' one of them growled.

Simone answered silently.

'The King never told us that.'

Simone raised herself on her coils and hissed. The higher vantage point gave me a better view of them. They were big humanoids, but the two of us could take them down if necessary. Whether we could do it without bringing the entire Nest of Mothers down on us was another matter.

'He was in the Pits last time I looked,' one of the guards said. 'You *have* to go down there, it's *wonderful*. Every single Celestial we've taken is in there. Nonstop fun. They even have the White Tiger on level nine! If you see him, take some photos for me. He killed half my nest mates a couple of hundred years ago.'

Simone nodded and the movement made me dizzy.

'If you find Da Shih Yeh, say hello for me,' the other guard said. 'I owe him my life.'

Simone nodded again, hefted me in her mouth and slithered to the end of the tunnel. The doors opened for us and we were in another tunnel. Simone followed as it wound for three hundred metres, then stopped.

Fork in the road, three-way.

I pointed with my nose.

Gotcha.

After fifteen stress-filled minutes, the tunnel opened out and the echoes changed. We were in a cavern that smelled even more rank than the Mothers' Nest: a combination of sweat, fear and damp.

Wow, this cavern is huge, Simone said. *It's like a demon office — they even have desks! It looks like Immigration back in Hong Kong, except stuck in some sort of time warp. They're all sitting behind their desks, completely frozen. Must be parked for the night.*

Immigration? This really was Hell.

I think this is the staging area for the Pits, Simone said. *Let me find a quiet spot in one of these tunnels and put you down so we can talk.*

It was another long ten minutes of wandering through corridors and avoiding patrols until we reached a quiet alcove and she put me down.

She dropped her head to speak to me. 'Can you see the Serpent?'

I concentrated, looking for it. 'No.'

She raised her head and looked around. 'I can't see it either. There's a gateway to the surface on the other side of this cavern, Emma. I could take you out right now ... No, don't bother saying anything. I need you to find the Serpent. We'll lose the war without it. Just make sure you're not nearby when I release it. You said you had a map?'

'The stone gave it to me, but King found out about it. They took the stone away and moved the Serpent. What did you offer the Mothers?'

'Level ninety World of Warcraft characters with max gear and epic mounts.'

'They play WoW?'

'They have their own server. They chased everybody else off it.'

'And they believed you had the characters?'

'Of course they did. I told them the ID and they knew me. On the server, that is. We have a couple of people who watch them play and listen to their conversations. Very informative.'

'Was watching them your idea?'

'No, Justin's. Where to now, Emma? Word must have gone out — they'll be looking for us everywhere.'

'They don't know what you look like, so we have that advantage. The King really has been experimenting, so hold on tight to that story as long as it works.' I figured out where we were, traced a route to where the Serpent was held and sagged. 'Damn.'

'You okay?'

'We went too far. We have to go back through the Pits to reach the spot where they had the Serpent.'

'But you said they'd moved it.'

'I may be able to find it if they haven't moved it too far.'

'That makes sense. So let's go to the Pits.' She bent to pick me up in her mouth.

'Wait,' I said, and she hesitated above me. 'The Celestial prisoners are in the Pits, Simone. You have to stay strong.'

She was silent for a long moment. 'Humans have been going through there for centuries. It's about time the Celestials were reminded of what it's like. The Pits need to be closed; and when we win this war that'll be the first thing I'll take up with both Daddy and the Jade Emperor. Seeing

420

what happens in there will only give me extra ammunition to close it down.' She picked me up in her mouth. *Let's go. Point the way.*

She slowed at the end of the tunnel between the staging area and level nine, the Pit where the very worst criminals were punished. It was completely silent; there wasn't a single sound, not even the air moving around us.

Is this it? Simone said.

'Put me down,' I said, and she gently lowered me. 'Yes. This is it. You probably don't need to carry me any more, they'll be ... busy.'

'Okay. What if they stop us? How about we say you're my child?'

'Demons eat their children, Simone.'

'Oh yeah. Wife?'

'They don't form loving relationships.'

'Slave.'

'That works.' I hesitated. 'Stay quiet from here on. There will be demon guards.'

She nodded and we entered the Pit cavern. The air was freezing cold and dank with the odours of fear and death. The cavern was so large that the far side wasn't visible, and had a low dark ceiling and a rough stone floor. Floor-to-ceiling stone columns with metre-long jutting blades — the Trees of Swords — were scattered through the area with limbless corpses impaled on them.

I couldn't speak silently to Simone, so I just nodded in the direction we had to go: around the edge of the cavern to level eight on the other side. She hesitated, staring at the Trees of Swords, and I gestured with my head again. We had to do this.

She lowered her head and turned it away, obviously wishing she could close her eyes. Many of the corpses had slid down the blades and all that was holding them there was their skulls or collarbones. Their skin was pale; they'd bled out when their limbs were cut off. Their eyes were white and sightless: they'd been blinded as well as dismembered. I recognised some of my most senior colleagues from the Mountain and it took all my courage to go past their unmoving bodies without saying a word. There was still no sound. Obviously the demons had left their victims on the trees overnight, frozen in death.

One of the corpses moved, and Simone squeaked and slithered away. The corpse lifted its blinded face. Simone made a quiet sound of pain. 'Michael.'

'Simone?'

The corpse on the other side of the tree from Michael growled softly and raised its head. 'What's she doing here?'

'Tiger,' I gasped.

'Simone, whatever you're doing here, if you can run, run,' Michael said.

'You pair of stupid fucking bitches! What the hell?' the Tiger growled under his breath.

'I have to get you down,' Simone said, and changed to human form. She stood in front of Michael's body, obviously working out how to lift him off the blade.

'We have to leave them,' I said. 'They can't do anything until they regrow limbs in the morning. We must find the Serpent!'

'Let me see,' the Tiger said, and concentrated for a moment. 'About two hundred metres to my left. Go!'

'I have to bring you down!' Simone said, desperate.

'If you pull us off we'll just fly straight back on again,' Michael said. 'It doesn't work like that. This torture is designed for Celestials as much as humans. Simone ...' He moved his head from side to side. 'Simone?'

422

'I'm here.'

'If we lose, I'll be stuck here for a very long time. Promise me something?'

'Anything,' she said.

'Stop this stupidness and run,' the Tiger said.

'Shut up, Dad,' Michael said. 'Promise you won't wait for me. Go and find someone else. One day it will happen for us, you know it will. But it isn't the right time yet. You're too young, and I'm too stupid.'

'Oh, Michael,' she said, smiling through the tears. 'I know that.'

'I know something too,' the Tiger said, and made a sound of pain at the movement of speaking. 'I know that you two morons need to run, and run fast, because two hundred metres to my left there's a fucking enormous Serpent that will win this for all of us. It's our only chance of freedom. And two hundred metres to my right, there's a good number of demon guards who can hear echoes of talking through the caverns and are waking up to check on us. So stop with the romance novel bullshit and *run*!'

'He's right, Simone. Change back and let's get the hell out of here,' I said. 'Tiger, Michael, stay strong.'

'Don't tell Clarissa you saw me!' Michael said.

'Of course not.'

The Tiger growled again. 'Will. You. Shut. The. *Fuck*. Up. And —'

'We are.'

Simone changed and we raced out of the cavern together.

31

A large arched passage led to level eight. The Pit was the same size as level nine, but there were no bladed columns; instead, the entire interior was a lake of red liquid that looked like blood. A guillotine, looking similar to one used to cut paper but two metres long, stood next to the lake. This type of guillotine had been the preferred execution method for many years: simple and effective. A severed head floated to the top of the lake. Its eyes appeared to blink for a moment, then it submerged again.

As we approached the lake, a tunnel opened from the right of the passage. There was another staging area to the side, probably for the victims of eight and nine, and it was almost exactly where the Tiger had said the Serpent was. I realised with a jolt that it was where Number One had said the Serpent would be as well. Maybe he wasn't leading us into a trap.

Simone was watching the pool's contents with fascinated horror. I tapped her on the back of the neck with my snout and she visibly jumped. She turned to see me and I gestured with my head. She nodded and followed me down the tunnel, hopefully towards the Serpent.

The tunnel was about a hundred metres long and winding, narrow and claustrophobic. When we reached the staging area, we hesitated at the entrance: double doors blocked the way.

'This could be it,' Simone said. 'I sense a big snake on the other side but it's kind of blurry. Stone shields?'

'Possibly. Watch my back while I open the door.'

She moved back and I grasped the ring on the door and pulled it.

I was flattened by a snake demon, and five more slithered over the top of me to get to Simone. A turtle hybrid stomped on me, making me hiss with pain, then opened its beak and grabbed my throat. It crushed my windpipe and I sent my breathing tube out, but it was ineffectual. The sharp edges of its mouth were cutting through my scales. It was about to take my head off.

The turtle slammed me into the floor, then did it again. It released me and I slithered away, then turned to see that Simone had the turtle hybrid's neck in both hands and was banging its head on the floor. She released it, stepped back and yinned it. The cold from the yin caused frost to form on my scales and I backed up further.

Simone turned her glowing white eyes onto the room where the snake and turtle hybrids had been, then rose to full majestic Celestial Form with her hair streaming around her, summoned her blades and strode into it.

I followed, and watched with awe as she loaded the blades with her chakras and sliced through the snake and turtle demons with fierce battle frenzy, her face frozen in a cruel mask. When all the demons were gone, she spun, raised her swords and ran towards me.

'It's me!' I said.

She stopped and lowered her blades, and her eyes went back to normal. Her hair fell around her into a tangled mess. She dismissed her blades and ran her hands through her hair. 'I wish it wouldn't do that. I must have it cut short when we're back home.' She turned away again. 'It's not here, Emma.'

I sent my senses out and found the Serpent fifty metres away on the other side of the hybrid room.

'I have it!' I said, trying to keep my voice low.

I flicked my tongue to taste the air around me, and headed through the room that had contained the hybrids to another tunnel going in the right direction. The delicate fragrance of fresh air wafted from the tunnel before us: the scent of a Celestial. Simone's scent was more floral; the clean alpine coolness was definitely the Serpent. I flicked my tongue again and Simone followed me as I traced it.

The tunnel opened into a plain grey cavern, two hundred metres across, with blindingly bright lights set up around the edges and all facing the Serpent in its cage. No wonder John hadn't been sleeping well. Two thick black cables led from an electrical box with buttons and dials to the metal grill under the Serpent: the electrocution device.

Five cockroaches squatted on their six legs under the lights; each four metres long, shiny and black. I recoiled when I saw that where the mouth parts should have been, each cockroach had a female human face of disturbing ethereal beauty, calm in sleep.

Stay here, Simone said, and silently crept around between the back end of one insect and the front of another. *God, they have faces! Did you see that?*

426

The cockroach facing her woke before she made it between them, and raised itself on its four hind legs. It attempted to stab her with its two sharp forelegs and she jumped back. She summoned her weapons and moved into a defensive stance.

I slithered past her as fast as I could to reach the cage.

'No, Emma!' she shouted. 'Stay back!' Her yelling woke the rest of cockroaches and they rose on their legs and fluttered their wing cases. 'Shit!'

One of the insects moved between me and the Serpent's cage. Weapons for these. I changed to human form, summoned Dark Heavens and launched chi into it in an attempt to stun the insect for a quick kill. The energy blast hit the cockroach's black shell and did nothing. It rose on its hind legs to impale me, and I somersaulted backwards, hitting another insect behind me. I rolled sideways, wishing I had the all-around view that my serpent eyes gave me. I checked the positions of the demons. Simone was facing three of them, dodging their forelegs and hitting them with her blades without effect.

'Clear!' she shouted.

I threw Dark Heavens up in front of my face to block the leg attempting to impale me, and felt more than heard the other insects behind me readying to strike. I somersaulted sideways again and leapt onto the cockroach's back. I tried to jam Dark Heavens between its wing cases, but the blade did nothing. I made an experimental slice where the head met the abdomen and understood with a chill — these demons were armoured. We couldn't hurt them.

'Clear, Emma, clear!' Simone shouted again.

Oh. I had to be clear of the area so she could yin them. I jumped off the cockroach's back and ran to the other side of the cavern, the insects following me at similar speed. As I ran them around the edge of the cavern towards her, they gained on me — they were faster than I was. I somersaulted sideways again, then backwards, hoping that I was clear enough for her to get a good yin shot at them.

Three were already gone.

Simone dropped her head slightly and focused the yin around her as one of the cockroaches prepared to impale her. She was too slow. The timing was too close. She wouldn't make it, she was overconfident, she couldn't do it …

Its foreleg went through her as she smothered them all in a cloud of yin.

The demons disintegrated. She collapsed and returned to human form: a small pale shape on hands and knees in the centre of her cloud of darkness.

I went as close to the yin as I could. 'Simone, call it in!'

She made a low sound of effort, which became louder and more intense until it was a shout of anguish. The yin disappeared and she fell to lie on her side on the floor.

The cockroach had split her from the middle of the abdomen down, an ugly wide slash. I put my hand over it, then ripped my shirt off and pushed it into the wound. Blood was pouring out of her. Too much damage. She had less than five minutes.

She concentrated, and the blood flow seemed to reduce for a moment, then pumped out of her again.

'Get … Daddy,' she gasped.

She was right: the Serpent could heal anything.

I jumped to my feet, raced to the cage and opened the door. The Serpent lay unconscious, flat and unmoving on the electric grill. I shoved it. 'John. Wake up!'

It didn't respond.

'John!' I shouted. 'Xuan Wu! Your daughter is dying ...'
I choked on the words. 'And she needs you. For heaven's
sake, wake *up*!'

It didn't respond.

I looked around for the controls for the electric shock;
perhaps I could torture it awake. I found what looked like the
right switch, set it to two hundred and fifty, and turned it on.
The Serpent writhed until I released the switch, then went still.

I climbed into the cage to check on it. It was breathing,
but only just. It was as close to death as she was ...

'Emma,' Simone gasped behind me.

I ran to her, knelt and held her hand. I pushed the blood-
soaked pad harder into her wound.

I looked up and shouted, 'George, Francis, anyone, if you
can hear me, I'll give you anything in exchange for her life!'
My voice went hoarse. 'Anything.'

She was deathly pale and her lips were blue. My throat
thickened. 'Summon the Elixir!'

'I love you, Emma. Please go on with Daddy and look
after him,' she said.

'No!' I shouted, my voice even more hoarse. A sob
escaped me. 'Summon the Elixir!'

'No. For you,' she said.

'If he loses both of us, he'll turn. One of us has to survive.
Do it!'

She grimaced and the Elixir, still in its sports bottle,
appeared in my hand. I popped the top, gasping with grief
and relief as I squeezed the liquid into her mouth. She
swallowed, choking on the fluid. She coughed and pushed
the bottle away, and I let her regain her breath then forced it
on her again. She sucked weakly on the bottle, then her eyes
rolled into her head and she fell limp and unconscious.

Half the Elixir remained. I wiped the infuriating tears out of my eyes, pulled the shirt pad away, then pushed the end of the bottle into the wound and squeezed. Squirting it straight into her had to be the same as her drinking it.

I wiped my eyes furiously as the Elixir bubbled out of her, looking exactly like mercury — reflective and shiny. The aroma mixed with her blood and became almost unbearably pure.

She was very still. I hadn't seen her stop breathing. She was still breathing, wasn't she? I checked her pulse and couldn't find it. I frantically moved my hand over her neck, looking for her pulse, and still couldn't find it. I put my hands over her chest to perform CPR and leaned into her. Blood gushed out of the wound from the pressure, adding to the pool around her. I was just killing her faster.

I bent over her too-still body and held her hand. Her eyes were half-open and her expression was blank. Her hands were growing cold. She wasn't breathing.

I fell over my knees and closed my eyes.

The light became very bright against my eyelids. The demons must have found me and turned the spotlights brighter. I raised my head and opened my eyes, blurred with tears.

The lights hadn't been turned up; it was Simone. She was glowing with a golden purity that shone from her, and a radiant heat that forced me onto my feet and back.

She floated upright, her expression beatific. She smiled at me, nodded, and then exploded into a brilliant golden light that shifted and faded into a million luminous particles before it disappeared.

I collapsed on the floor and wept with relief. She was in Court Ten. I had to hope that the Demon King would keep his word and protect her. I curled up over my knees. Both of my children were held by the King.

My children. I had to get them out.

I rose and staggered, then wiped my eyes, took a deep breath and steadied myself.

I was wearing only blood-soaked jeans and a bra; my shirt was saturated with Simone's blood so I left it. The air was cold on my wet skin as I dragged myself to the door of the cage. I didn't have long before they would come running and lock the Serpent up again. I had to get the damn thing out of that cage and it was five metres long and nearly a metre around.

I grabbed it as best I could at a narrow part near its tail and hauled at it with both hands. I managed to make it out the door with its tail, but the rest of it wouldn't budge. It was too heavy. Even with my strength I couldn't move the whole thing.

Nothing for it: I had to free it the old-fashioned way.

I summoned Dark Heavens and clambered around the Serpent's coils to its head. I pulled the head back, revealing its throat, and prepared to make the most effective throat cut — the point of the blade horizontally into the side and then the whole blade ripping out the front. I shifted into position, hampered by the size of the Serpent and the smallness of the cage, and made the thrust. The sword disappeared.

I resummoned it and it returned to my hand. I tried to ram it through the Serpent's eye into its brain, and it disappeared again. The blade would not destroy its master, however dire the need. Dammit.

'Energy it is,' I said, and grunted as I let its head fall. I sighed and put my hand on its head. 'I don't even have the stone here to record a message for you or anything. I have

431

no other choice, John, we need you so we can win this. Everything we both love is at stake. With our children held here in Hell, we have to do this.' I dropped my voice. 'I guess Kitty wins after all. She programmed me to want to be one with you, and she's finally getting her wish. If you can hear me at all, I'd appreciate an effort to keep my individuality intact.'

The Serpent didn't move or reply. It was probably in a similar brain-damaged coma to John's Turtle form. I wondered if the Serpent had a human form distinct from the Turtle, or whether they would be one human form when they rejoined. The Serpent had a female-sounding voice — perhaps the two human bodies that John had hinted at were one of each sex. It was so weird that I wouldn't put it past him, but nobody had ever mentioned it.

'I guess I'll find out soon,' I said. 'I'm sorry it had to end this way. We knew what the chances were —'

I heard a sound and raised my head. Footsteps, echoing down the tunnel. I didn't have any more time. I put both hands on its head behind its eyes and fed it chi.

It worked; the chi flowed through it and lit up its intelligence, making it glow with awakening. I tried to stop the flow but I'd lost control of it.

'John, you're draining me,' I hissed. 'Ease up.'

'Huh?' the Serpent said.

My hands sank into its back. I attempted to pull them away, but the vacuum holding them in place was too strong. I sat on the floor of the cage, put my feet on the Serpent's side and tried to lever my hands out, all the time becoming weaker as the energy was sucked out of me. I kicked at it, yanking at my hands, but they were drawn into the Serpent's back. I was up to my elbows. I pulled away with all my strength, with no result. My strength gave out and my face was slammed into the Serpent's side by the force of the suction. I panted, eyes wide, as my face was dragged into it. I wouldn't be able to breathe ...

The energy drained from me, going into the Serpent, and I couldn't hold myself away any more. I was drawn in and surrounded by suffocating darkness. It was dark. It was *dark* ...

Not good enough; this was not happening. Totally unacceptable. I threw my will at it: *You are not absorbing me, Xuan Wu. I am in charge here and you will do what I say. You will stop pulling me into you and you will let. Me. Go!*

I popped out next to the cage and panted with relief. Mentally ordering it to stop taking me must have worked. I wasn't absorbed; in fact, I'd gained a tremendous amount of energy from the short time we'd been merged.

I turned to check it, and it was gone from the cage. Not surprising after I'd released it. I searched for it, sending out my consciousness, and horrified realisation blossomed: the Serpent was within me.

It was like huge stone blocks sliding into place. Many of the things I'd said and done in the past — and the future — resonated from this moment; ripples through time from when I combined with the Xuan Wu. It was an immense black sun; dense, cold, silent, profoundly intelligent — and intensely aware of what we had just done. Our serpent natures orbited each other, separate but equal. It sat barricaded in the back of my brain, quiescent in its exhaustion. It hadn't absorbed me; I had absorbed it.

More like possessed, it said.

I'm possessing you?

433

I'm very drained, Emma. You must move fast. As I recover I will grow, and I will not be able to stay so small. Your mind will not hold me. I will expand and encompass you.

You'll take me over?

You must hurry. Take us to the Turtle. Open its cage, let it out. If the Turtle is in front of me, I will ignore you and go to it.

How do I —

Emma, even talking to you is making me grow. I must shut down and stay small otherwise you are lost. Take me to the Turtle!

* * *

I couldn't teleport out. I had to wind my way back through the Pits to the staging area to reach the gateway to the surface. I heard voices and footsteps coming. There was only one way out of there — the way the demon guards were coming in.

I had an inspiration and went to the door of the cage. I broke off the tiny rod of jade that would slide into the hole to hold the door in place, silent in wonderment that such a small brittle thing could hold something as big as John. Rather like me holding the Serpent.

I went into the cage, pulled the door shut — fortunately it stayed shut, even without the latch — and changed to my biggest serpent form, lying on the floor of the cage.

'Wah!' one of the demons said. 'What the fuck?'

'There's blood everywhere!' another one said. 'Looks like a serious fight and they all lost.' It dropped its voice. 'Damn, what a waste of good blood.'

434

'Shit!' one of them said, and ran to the cage. 'No, it's still here, and still asleep.' It gasped with relief. 'Whew. Dad would tear our scales off if it was gone.'

'We'd better head back and report. Dad will be furious at losing five of those cockroach things.'

'They did their job though,' the other said as they turned away to leave. 'So much blood — they must have torn the human to pieces. No body parts, though, why ... Oh.'

'What?'

'No body — it must have been a Celestial! I wonder which one it was. When Dad is back from the West he'll have another one to play with.'

'Damn, and we missed seeing it being torn to bits,' the other one said, and they laughed together.

After they'd left, I checked around for surveillance equipment and didn't find any. Their monitoring was probably much less mundane than simple electronics. I pushed at the cage door and nearly cried with relief when it opened. I changed to human form and closed the cage behind me.

The Serpent studied the cage with loathing. So much suffering — the bottom of the cage was stained with excrement and blood and scattered with loose scales and my skin.

I grinned with grim malice, leaned my hand into the side of the cage and shifted my feet into position. I took a deep breath in and out, centred my chi, pulled my hand back and tapped the cage with my index and second fingers. It disintegrated into glittering dust that slowly fell with a soft sound of powdery spatters.

I turned and silently followed the demons. I had a very good idea where I needed to go; I just needed to make it there with a minimum of fuss.

I summoned my sword and Seven Stars appeared in my hand.

Shit. I hadn't thought about it too hard and John's sword had come to me ... to us. Wonderful.

I dismissed it and called Dark Heavens, and the unadorned blade sang with delight as it appeared. I held it by the scabbard in my left hand, ready to draw. Using it was probably as bad an idea as using the big one; both of them were attuned to the Serpent within me.

The Serpent lay inside me, quiet and unmoving, watching me with its serpent eyes.

The Serpent lay quiescent, observing without acting, small and invisible, watching and silent

I reached the end of the tunnel and the room where all the snake and turtle hybrids had been.

The Serpent wailed with grief at the loss of so many of its children, used to make these unnatural abominations

And made myself invisible.

No, Emma, using my abilities will blur the edges between us. Dammit, don't do things like that!

Like I had a choice.

The two demons were in the room, reporting to that damn eye thing that the King used as a security camera. The new eye demon was different colours from the old one: purple and orange with much fewer eyes in it. Obviously he had started a new collection.

I slipped invisibly past them and down the tunnel towards levels eight and nine.

The Serpent suffered many years of torture here, ordered by the Celestial as fitting punishment for its crimes before it turned —

Shut *up*, John, I need to concentrate here.

436

The Serpent settled into the back of my mind and I sighed with relief. I needed to hurry; I wouldn't be able to keep it contained there forever.

It was nearly dawn and the demons would be moving again, bringing the corpses down from the Trees of Swords so they could regrow their arms and legs and be dismembered again. I hurried past the trees, not looking at my friends, colleagues, my brother the Tiger ...

'Ah Wu?' he growled softly.

'I will return for you,' I said.

'Thank the Heavens,' he breathed. 'Hurry up and rejoin and get us the fuck out.'

'I will.'

'Go,' he whispered.

I pelted down the tunnel on the other side and came out in the staging area: Immigration. The demons were awake and some of them were Mothers. Dammit.

'Invisible Celestial over near the door!' one of the Mothers shouted. 'Someone stop it.'

A small group of Mothers in True Form surrounded the end of the tunnel. I tried to push through them, and one felt me passing and grabbed my arm. She jerked me back and slammed me against the wall of the cavern, hitting my head hard and stunning me so that I dropped the invisibility.

'Holy shit, it's the Xuan Wu!' someone shrieked.

The Mother released my arm and backed away.

Don't you dare take my Dark Lord form. You'll make things a hundred times worse, the Serpent said.

I concentrated on my Emma form and grew physically shorter. I grinned with menace, drew Dark Heavens, loaded it with energy and threw the energy at the Mothers. They weren't completely destroyed, but the blast was enough to

437

knock them back and in the confusion I ran between the desks to the other side of the cavern.

They followed me. One of them tackled me and I fell heavily. I couldn't roll and recover with her locked around my lower legs, so I kicked at her. She held me firm.

'Shackles or something — quickly!' she shouted.

No way. I changed to serpent, slid my tail out of her grasp, and slithered to the gateway on the other side of the cavern. I dodged a few blows, and ducked as a blast of dark energy flew over my head.

I reached the gateway, changed to human form, and ran through it to the surface.

I charged out into the middle of a busy sidewalk in a city in China. There were more bicycles than cars, wending their way along the path marked out for them at the side of the road. A pagoda stood on the crest of a hill not too far away, and the shock of many memories rattled through me: Jingshan Park, directly north of the Forbidden City. Okay: Beijing, and not far from the Imperial Palace.

The Ming was the best time. I had a charming, comfortable house next to the palace and enjoyed wise discourse with the highest levels of the Empire's scholars. The Earthly Emperor suspected who his military advisor truly was and treated me with awed respect. We shared tea, and wine, and the Emperor even offered me his own concubines — and was more certain of my identity when I politely refused them. We wandered the carefully tended gardens together, discussing the needs of the Empire and whether there would be enough rain for the coming harvests —

The gateway was obvious. I didn't need the Serpent's *old-man recollections, and I wish they would stop*

Sorry.

438

I'd seen the Gates of Heaven on the Celestial Plane and knew exactly where I needed to be.

The Earthly analogue is not Tiananmen; it's Wumen, the Meridian Gate. The third and final barrier before the palace itself.

People around me stopped and stared at the half-naked European woman covered in blood. Five big demons stormed out of the gateway behind me and looked around. They shouted when they saw me.

I ran into the crowd of pedestrians, then took the Turtle's usual small, middle-aged Chinese female form, dressed in black slacks and a silk jacket. I shoved my hands in the pockets of my jacket, put my head down and gaped in exactly the same way as everybody around me. Humans never saw Shen transformations; as far as they were concerned, the European woman had just disappeared as if she'd never been there. All of them had the confused look of people who didn't believe their own eyes; a look I'd seen many times before.

The demons pushed through the pedestrians, even shoving me out of the way in the urgency of their search. Good luck finding me in *this* mob, particularly when they were looking for a topless, brown-haired foreigner among the black-haired locals. As a dumpy, plain-faced, middle-aged woman I couldn't be more invisible if I tried.

I made my way towards the Imperial Palace, and saw barricades and signs at an entrance to the subway. It was early morning and there was a queue outside the entrance as limited numbers of people were permitted to enter the overloaded system. To hell with that; it would probably be quicker to walk the kilometre or so to Tiananmen, the first gate, even through the choking pollution that would be sure to weaken me. The walk sign lit up on the crosswalk and I

439

dashed across between the cars that, as usual, failed to stop for pedestrians.

The demons faded behind me and I filled with fierce exhilaration. I was free and *soon I would rejoin and then nothing would stop me from exacting justice upon the demons that had dared to harm my family, my subjects, my children ...*

'I'm Emma, I'm Emma,' I mumbled over and over, thinking of my past and my family, concentrating on who I was. Emma. I'm not the Serpent. I'm not Xuan Wu.

Regrets

Just shut UP and let me get you there. Not far now, and I'll be back in Heaven with my family ... My children. By the Heavens, my children!

Gold!

My Lord?

Simone's in Court Ten. She was Raised. Find out how she is. I don't care how you do it, just do it. Is the Turtle still in the Grotto?

Yes. Simone was Raised? Is that you, Emma? How are you talking like this? What happened?

I have the Serpent with me. I'll be at the Gates of Heaven in about ten minutes. I need a ride from there to the Mountain, as fast as possible. Be ready to open the Grotto for me.

My Lord.

My Lord?

'Shit,' I said under my breath, and charged towards the Gate of Heavenly Peace.

32

Modern Beijing had a ten-lane highway between Tiananmen and the square, with pedestrian underpasses to negotiate the ridiculously huge road. I stopped and looked around; it had been a while. I sneered with contempt at the ugly Stalinist-style halls that blighted the square, then turned towards graceful Tiananmen itself.

The cries of the dying students echoed in my ears. That was a bad time.

Mao's portrait still hung on the gate, and I wondered again how long it would be before it was removed.

It was surprising that it had lasted so long. 'Don't make my image perfect, show my flaws,' he said, so they made his image perfect except for a mole on his chin. Hypocrites.

I ducked into the underpass, unremarked by anyone around me. A dumpy, middle-aged woman was invisible; but a dumpy, middle-aged woman whose face was fierce with determination was terrifying.

Mao started the way most Earthly leaders start: full of fire to improve the world and make it a better place for everybody. He grew corrupt, the way most Earthly leaders do: seduced by the ease of power and privilege. Blinded by power, he led his people — my people — to mass starvation.

John, you need to close down you're engulfing me …

The Serpent pulled back, horrified at its creeping growth.

I came out on the other side, under Tiananmen.

'*But you can use the middle gate as well, can't you?*' the Emperor said.

'*Not this one,*' I replied. '*There is another, though, and I do not use the middle there either. It is not my place, either here or there.*'

'*Where is your place?*'

'*By your side, assisting you, Majesty.*'

'*And I am glad for your counsel.*'

'*Majesty.*'

John! I can't keep you down if these flashbacks don't stop.

I have no control over them. It's been a long time …

I went through Tiananmen; it wasn't nearly as majestic up close, purely because it was so huge. The paved court on the other side led to the next gate. The trees were a nice touch. During the Imperial times, these courts had been completely bare of any greenery except for the occasional display of potted flowers.

Duanmen was next: the main gate. Not long now. People didn't notice me as I lowered my head and charged through the gate towards the Wumen, the Meridian Gate, and the entrance to the Imperial Palace Museum.

I smiled. What would the Ming Emperor have said if I'd told him that one day the Forbidden City would be a public museum that even the lowest peasant could walk through? I could imagine the look on his face.

The gate was red and imposing, an inverted U-shape with its arms reaching towards me on either side above the fifty-metre-wide moat that surrounded the Palace. The red walls were brighter than they'd been in centuries. The damn Qing had let the place go; even the library hadn't been used ...

'Counsellor, the library can't have a black roof, what are you thinking? The fung shui is most inharmonious. All the Imperial buildings must have roofs of gold!'

'The library is the most susceptible to fire damage. Its contents are a thousand years of our history, Majesty. Making the roof black will align it with the power of the Xuan Wu, the force of water, to protect the scrolls ...'

'So the Xuan Wu knows which building to protect first in case of fire ...' The Emperor stared at me, mouth open, for a long moment. Then he said, 'I think I may have a black roof put on my own quarters as well.'

'No need for that, Majesty,' I said equably. 'Just ensure that the lantern I gave you is alight outside your pavilion when you are in residence.'

'And are you privy to the secrets of the Shen, as other Taoist Masters have claimed when they kneeled before me?'

I bowed acknowledgement. 'Black roof, Majesty, I advise it most vehemently.'

He waved me away. 'Arrange it.'

I wandered up to the red wall on the left. I was even more invisible here; everybody was heading to the main gate and the entrance to the palace museum, and there were far fewer plain-clothes secret police wandering around than in the square.

Wumen had always been my favourite gate. Tiananmen was squat and massive, Duanmen was simple and smaller,

443

but Wumen, straddling the moat with its five central arches and five elegant turrets, was harmonious and lovely with its red walls and gold roofs. Archers on top of this gate could surround any would-be invader on three sides from a perfect elevation and make the entrance to the palace nigh on impregnable.

I put my hand on the red wall and concentrated.

'Majesty, we have been having this argument for a year now, and I will resign if you do not approve my proposal. You must release me to prepare your defences.'

'Stop arguing with me; this will work. I'm doing it. I don't care what you say. I've decided. The Edicts have been signed and the orders have been sent: the army is to be disbanded. The money I save from not having a standing army will be distributed to the people and everybody will share the benefit. Even the lowest peasant will be wealthy.'

'You cannot disband the army, Majesty, not while the Manchurians are massing north of the wall. Have you been drinking the tonics that quack gave you again? Mercury will drive you mad and kill you.'

'It's already done!' The Emperor turned and faced me, his eyes dark from the poison and glazed with obsession. *'You are Immortal yet you refuse to share your secrets. The Sage says that I will gain Immortality from these medicines. I will be as you are!'*

'I am not Immortal, Majesty.'

'I know you are. I know who you are. You've been helping my family for years — my father knew you when he was young! You and the other three Winds will protect the Empire against the threat of the Manchu.'

'I am not an Immortal, there are no Winds — Majesty, this is madness. Allow me to return to the army and prepare

your defence. The Manchu are strong and you will need everything you have to stop them — the wall may not be enough.'

'No. I order you to do this. The army is to be disbanded, the wealth shared with the people, and the Shen of Heaven will protect the realm. It is done.'

I slipped my hands into my sleeves and bowed. 'If you continue this track I will retire, Majesty, and return to my estate in Hubei.'

'You cannot. I decree it! You must stay with your Shen armies and protect the realm!'

'Farewell, Majesty.'

'No! Where are you going? You have to stay and advise me! I order you to defend my realm! You helped my father ... Where are you going? Come back! No, Counsellor, I need you! Where ... Guards! Stop him!'

But I was gone. I cursed my stupidity. I had greedily basked in their awe as they suspected my true identity, and they had relied on me far too much. Never again would I so directly meddle in the affairs of the Earthly.

The Ming Dynasty would fall and it was partly my own stupid fault. The echoes of my mistakes would follow me through history.

The wall of Wumen blurred and I was beneath the Gates of Heaven. Guan Yu must have sensed me because he appeared in front of the gate, holding his halberd, and charged down the hill to me.

He stopped. 'Ah Wu?' He grinned broadly. 'Ah Wu!'

I took my normal human form and his face filled with confusion. 'Lady Emma?'

The Turtle felt my presence in the Heavens.

The Turtle called.

The ground shook.

'Holy shit, what the hell was that?' Guan Yu said, looking around.

I couldn't resist its mighty, demanding call …

'Get the hell out of my way!' I shouted, and shot straight into the air.

The Serpent flew over the serene hills of Heaven, towards its Mountain, its other half, its Turtle …

The Turtle called again and I screamed with anguish. So close, so close … I took Serpent form and raced through the air. I couldn't stop myself, I called back …

The Serpent called. The Turtle answered. The skies of Heaven rippled with their roars …

I reached my Mountain, shining black and beautiful. It had been so long … But few Disciples remained. Strategies filled my head for using them to defend the fortress. It could be done, provided the force thrown at it was not too large …

The Turtle roared again, making the Mountain shake. The Serpent screamed in reply and dropped to land in the Great Court, cracking the tiles beneath its coils …

Meredith raced out of the training area and tried to keep up with me as I slithered as fast as I could to the Grotto.

'Clear the area around the Grotto for three hundred metres,' I said. 'Order the fish out now! If anyone's in there, get them out.'

The Turtle called, a deep roar of anguish, and the Mountain shuddered. Glass shattered and Disciples were knocked off their feet around us.

I screamed in return and Meredith fell to her knees and covered her ears.

Liu appeared next to us, knelt and put his arm around her, and they spoke silently together.

'Clear the area!' I shouted. 'Lock the Disciples down to barracks! I can't hold back much longer. Get everybody out!'

Liu dragged Meredith to her feet and they ran. I put my head down and breathed, trying to hold back the urge to race to the Turtle. My Disciples jumped to their feet and scurried around me as the bells rang in lockdown. I hadn't heard my bells in so long, it broke my heart ...

I couldn't resist any more and rushed to the blank stone wall that was the entrance to the Grotto. I slammed inside and flew down the stairs. Yue was on her knees next to the cage, clutching the bench, her face pale with terror.

'Get out!' I roared, and she ran up the stairs.

The Turtle screamed and the Mountain shook again. The temperature dropped to near freezing. I approached the cage.

'All of you out!' I bellowed. 'Out. Now!'

The water in the Grotto surged around me. The fish thrashed in the maelstrom and disappeared. The Turtle in its cage was swept off the ledge and down into the freezing black depths. The Serpent swam to follow it, took the cage in its mouth, dived to the bottom and smashed it into the floor of the cave.

The Turtle was free. Its cries rocked the Mountain and cracked the stones around them. It ran to the ocean and the Serpent followed it, roaring with frustration.

The vast black Turtle pushed through the water, every stroke of its flippers a wave of force. It moved through the thick ebon seas, searching. It cried out. There was nearly an answer. It cried ...

There was movement. The Serpent approached. It slashed through the deep like a gaping dark wound. The Turtle stopped to regard it.

447

The two great giants appraised each other. They were an even match.

The Serpent rushed forward. The Turtle pounded through the water to meet it. They clashed in a mighty thrashing that was felt to the ends of the oceans …

The Serpent seized the Turtle and wrapped its coils around it in a death grip. The two enormous heads rose up, mouths open in defiance. They roared at each other silently within the waters. The Serpent's grip tightened, squeezing the life from the Turtle's shell …

They merged. They were one. They were complete. They were Xuan Wu …

* * *

John woke beside himself. Both of him were lying in his bed in the Imperial Residence on the Mountain, side by side. He hadn't had two bodies in a very long time; a probable side effect of being apart for so long.

He stared at the ceiling and looked inside the Serpent. 'Emma?'

I hope I give you a massive dose of indigestion, asshole.

Both of him sat up and rubbed their faces, then stared at each other with shock. His human forms were all wrong. Male Chinese Turtle, female European Serpent … what?

'John, what the hell happened to you? Where am I? What am I?' I said.

'I rejoined. I think you were caught up in it.'

No, I'm right here…

So am I, love.

'Uh … two voices? John …?'

448

He took my hand and led me from the bed to the bathroom, and stood us in front of the mirror.

'No, that's wrong: the Turtle is female and the Serpent is male,' I said. 'Why am I female?' I dropped my head. 'No, that's wrong: the Turtle is male and I'm Emma, I'm female, I'm separate ...' I ran my hands through my wild black hair. 'What the hell happened to me? ... Oh.' I turned to John; he was silent, watching me as I worked it out. 'I see. But I don't feel any different. I just feel like me ... No. The Serpent's here too.'

'I am staying as small and quiet as I can so that you will remain intact.'

'But I can't stay like this forever, Emma ...' I said. 'Oh. Can I be extracted?'

'We can ask the Jade Emperor. He's done it before, he can probably teach me ... us.'

'We have to pull me out quickly so I'm not completely consumed by you.'

'I know. Are you up to travelling?'

'Of course, I feel wonderful. The Serpent is immensely powerful and I'm somehow one with it. But John ...' I took a deep breath. 'Why the hell does it feel completely wrong to be female?' Understanding hit me. 'Oh dear Lord, that's what caused everything in the first place. We are yang and yin, always in motion, one into the other ...'

'... and we cycled. You didn't need to go off and sulk just because you turned female, Serpent.'

'It was all right for you — you turned male! I'm feeling the panic of being female, inferior ...' I shook my head, horrified at the Serpent's attitude inside me. 'John, you really do have some serious subconscious issues with gender, which

449

is freaking hilarious for someone who's both sexes at the same time. No wonder the Dark Lord is always male.'

'The Turtle had no issue at all with the gender change,' he said, indignant. 'I thought someone had forcibly split us after it happened. It never occurred to me that you would panic and run away. If you'd just shared your confusion, Serpent, we could have fixed this together.'

'You changed to male — you had it easy! Changing to female was too awful to think about,' the Serpent said with misery.

'I need to spend some serious time female and get myself over this,' he said.

'John Chen Wu, don't you dare!'

'Emma?'

I hesitated. 'I'm not sure who I am right now.'

Ah Wu, the Jade Emperor said. *Stay as you are. Both of you come here right now.*

We stayed as two bodies and teleported to the Celestial Palace, not enjoying the disconnected sensation. We wanted more than anything to rejoin, Turtle and Serpent as one again, but the Emperor knew what he was doing.

'Majesty,' we said, kneeling in front of the Jade Emperor. 'Help me. Help us …'

'I can see the problem, Ah Wu. Take True Form.'

We hesitated. True Form could force Emma even more deeply inside the Serpent.

The Emperor sighed with exasperation. 'I know what I'm doing, Ah Wu. Take True Form and let me look at you.'

We dropped our heads and changed into the combined Turtle and Serpent. We enjoyed a blissful moment of completeness before feeling the jarring pain of Emma's essence within us.

'Serpent, off. Come here and let me examine you,' the Jade Emperor said.

The Serpent separated from the Turtle and slithered to the Jade Emperor. I lowered my head before him.

The Jade Emperor put his hands on either side of the Serpent's head. 'Let me see what we have here.'

Both Serpent and Turtle felt the Emperor's regard; it was like liquid gold running through the combined essence.

'Equal spirits, sharing the same awareness,' the Emperor said. 'Three became two, became one.' He opened his eyes and tweaked a small smile at the Turtle. 'All this because the Serpent became female and couldn't cope with it? Ah Wu, I would expect much better from you and I am deeply disappointed.'

'So am I, Majesty,' the Turtle said.

'Let me see. Turtle: separate for many years, so reasonably independent. Serpent ...' The liquid gold feeling intensified around me. 'Two serpents orbiting each other, so finely matched in intelligence and spirit, with the smaller stubbornly refusing to be eclipsed by the larger. You have a will of iron, Miss Donahoe.'

'Please help us, Majesty. Emma's independence is worth more than my life,' the Turtle said.

'It is a shame that this is the outcome. I had high hopes that a different future path would be taken.' The Emperor sighed with feeling. 'All the portents indicated that you would be safe at the funeral, Emma. Leo's sister is not of my realm and I could not predict her arrival. She disrupted everything.'

'What's done is done,' I said. 'Can I be extracted?'

'Yes,' the Jade Emperor said, and the Turtle nearly collapsed with relief.

451

'What will it involve?' I said. 'This can't be a simple process.'

'You are still the brains,' the Jade Emperor said with amusement. 'I will need to release your spirit and send you through the Courts. You will land in Court One. If you can hold yourself together and remember who you are, he can bring you out from there.'

'And if she forgets who she is?' the Turtle said.

'Then she is gone for a thousand incarnations, just as you were when you Fell.'

The Turtle lowered its head with grief.

I consoled it. 'Don't worry, John. We've done this before. We can do it again.'

'No, you haven't, Emma. That was me.'

I hesitated. 'Was it? I remember doing it ... I'm sure it was me. Which part is me?'

'We need to do this right now, Majesty!'

'We cannot,' the Emperor said. 'We cannot send Emma through the Courts until we have taken Hell back and you can enter the Courts and Raise her. If you don't, she will be lost completely.'

'But if we wait, the Serpent will devour her.'

'I know. If we are to release Emma, we must resolve this quickly and reclaim Hell.'

'I don't want to live without you,' the Turtle said.

'Even if the Serpent completely devours me, I will still be a part of you, my love,' I said. 'I always will be.'

'Not good enough,' the Turtle said. It lowered its voice with grief. 'Emma waited so long for me. I cannot do this to her.'

'I'm right here,' I said.

'I know. But for how much longer?'

'The Celestial comes first, John. Now you're whole, we can go home, round everybody up and retake Hell.'

'How do we tell them that I've absorbed you?'

I was silent at that. My family would be devastated.

'Don't tell anyone,' the Jade Emperor said. 'Serpent, take Emma's form. Be Emma. Tell them the male human form is the combined creature.'

'Can you do that?' the Turtle said.

'Only one way to find out,' I said, and took Emma's form. It was surprisingly easy, probably because Emma was still halfway independent.

'Oh, love,' the Turtle said. 'You're still there.'

'I know,' I said. 'I can feel it too.' I looked up at the Jade Emperor. 'How long do I have?'

'It depends how hard you fight it. If the Serpent remains still and quiet and allows Emma to be the main personality, she may last weeks. If you spend all your time in True Form as the combined creature, then Emma will be gone in a matter of days.'

'Damn,' the Turtle and Serpent said in unison. Finally free and complete, and unable to take a combined True Form.

'Let's go home and brainstorm,' I said. 'Now that you have me and my intelligence back, the strategy should flow much more easily.' I knelt and saluted the Jade Emperor. 'Majesty.'

'Take care, Emma, you sound like him.'

'I've sounded completely like him for months now. I don't think anyone will notice.'

'Dismissed,' the Emperor said.

Turtle and Serpent teleported back to their Mountain.

33

Gold, we said.

My Lord?

Did you find Simone?

I'm sorry, my Lord. Short of going down there myself, there is no way I can communicate. I've called her but received no reply. Her phone has disconnected; it appears to be dead. His voice dropped with misery. *Profoundest apologies, my Lord, I have failed you. Would you like me to go down there myself to try to contact her?*

No, never mind. I'll try. Return to the Mountain; we have important plans to make.

On my way, my Lord. Is ... His voice trailed off.

What?

Is Lady Emma with you? Is she all right? If Simone is in Court Ten ... His voice in our heads grew desperate. *Oh, Lord, is she all right?*

Emma is with me. She is unharmed.

I heard you rejoin. That was ... extreme.

For me as well. Come to the Mountain, Gold, we have a Hell to retake.

My Lord.

* * *

The Disciples were picking over the wreckage on the Mountain; mostly broken glass, but a couple of landslides had destroyed smaller buildings as well. We landed on the Great Court and winced at the damage done to the black slate tiles by the Serpent's coils. The replacement tiles wouldn't have the same degree of weathering and would be an obvious patch, marring the perfection of the court.

Meredith charged up to us. 'Is everything okay?'

'Emma will pass the orders on,' John said. 'I want a strategy meeting with the leaders of the armies immediately. We must retake Hell as quickly as we can. I'm heading down to the Grotto and I'll be out in time to chair the meeting.'

'You're not going back into the cage, are you?' Meredith said, concerned.

'The cage is in a million pieces on the bottom of the Grotto,' I said. 'He's never going into that awful thing ever again.'

'I have to make some calls and I don't want to be interrupted,' John said. He gestured towards me. 'Emma is taking over.'

He disappeared into the Grotto.

'Come with me to my office, we need to arrange this,' I said. 'He will be about twenty minutes.'

'Emma, are you okay? You look ...'

I waited for her to finish, but she just stared at me. 'Yes?'

'I don't know. Are you two sure you're all right? That was intense.'

'I'm fine.' I headed towards my office. 'Contact the Phoenix and Dragon for me; they need to be involved. The Tiger's Numbers Two and Four. Summon Jade; Gold is already on the way. Both my Number Ones. Er Lang, Guan Yu, Ma, you and Liu.'

Meredith stopped walking and I stopped with her. She was staring at me again.

'What?'

She pointed behind me. 'Your office is that way.'

I looked. We were outside John's office.

I thought quickly. 'I need some papers from his office, and I need to talk to Zara.'

'No, you said *both your Number Ones*, Emma. Or should I say Lord Xuan? You're the Serpent, aren't you? Not Emma at all.' She turned away from me. 'How could you do that to her, John? We loved her.' She wiped her hand over her eyes. 'She was like a *daughter* to me. What you did to her is worse than death, and you're *lying* about it.' She turned back and fell to one knee. 'Lord Xuan, I resign my commission —'

I cut her off. 'There's no need for that, Meredith, I'm still here. It's me. I'm Emma.' She didn't move. 'Meredith.' I took her arm and pulled her to her feet. 'Really. Emma and the Serpent are equal and sharing right now. My personality is still intact. I can be extracted; ask the Jade Emperor if you don't believe me. I'm not gone.'

She studied me, and I felt more than her eyes on me, then she sagged with relief. 'I see. We must hurry and extract you.'

'We will, but we need to take Hell back first. Don't tell anyone what's happened. They'll react the same way you

456

just did. In the meantime, help me out; let me know if I slip up.'

'I will. So what's it like being Emma and Xuan Wu Serpent at the same time?'

I was silent as I tried to describe what it was like, and shook my head as words failed me. 'Let's just call it multiple personality disorder, except the personalities aren't taking turns, they're all here at once.'

'That must be very uncomfortable.'

'It's extremely distracting. The Turtle is on its way to the bottom of the Grotto to try to contact Simone, and I'm there with it. Now let's bring these people together and prepare to retake Hell. All of my closest friends and both my children are down there, and we need to get them out.'

'*Both* your children?'

'Damn. I'll explain on the way.'

'My Lord.'

'No. Treat me as Emma.'

'Ma'am?'

'Better. Let's go.'

John drifted to the bottom of the Grotto and squatted in Turtle form among the shards of the shattered cage. *Simone. Simone. It's me, your father. It's Daddy. Simone, speak to me.* He put more into it. *Simone, it's Daddy. Talk to me, sweetheart.*

Her voice was small, like a child's coming from far away. *Daddy!*

Are you … Are they hurting you?

No! I'm in one of the villas on the Celestial island, one of the holding cells for Court Ten. I'm being cared for, but I can't leave the villa. All of Hell is sealed and nobody can teleport out.

I understand. Stay open to my call; you can be my eyes in Hell while we prepare our attack. We will attempt to retake the Celestial side soon.

You need to retake the demonic side! Everybody's in the Pits!

I know that. I rejoined: I am the Serpent as well now. I saw them.

'Emma, you said that out loud. Take care,' Meredith said.

'Shit,' I said under my breath, and clamped my mouth shut.

Oh, Daddy, you rejoined — that's wonderful. Is Emma okay? She was there when I ... when it happened. I haven't seen her here in Hell, she is all right, isn't she? I was so worried ...

Emma's fine. Please stay open for my calls and watch everything that happens around you.

I'll spy for you.

Thank you. I'll be in touch to let you know how you can help.

Love you, Daddy.

Love you too, sweetheart. Oh, and congratulations.

Why? Oh. Raised and stuff. I don't feel any different.

I think you were already there.

Why do you sound like Emma? You didn't merge with her or anything did you?

Emma is fine.

He turned his attention to his other child. *Frankie. Frankie?*

No reply. Blankness.

Frankie, this is your real father. Your real mother is here as well. We love you, Frankie, and we have a beautiful home for you in Heaven. We are your real parents who will never

458

hurt you. Just say the word and I will free you from the cruelty of those awful people.

A minuscule shift, a breath, then a barrier was raised.

Time for the meeting. He headed out of the Grotto and up to the War Room.

* * *

'Opinions,' John said. 'Here's the plan. We send a small force — all Immortals — against Hell and lose. We are routed. We run back to the Gates of Heaven and hope to the Heavens that they follow us, believing that our last defences are gone and Heaven is theirs. We lead them to the Gates where our main force is waiting for them — and at the same time we send a small group to take back the Celestial side of Hell while it is vacant. Secure the Celestial side of Hell, free our Immortals held there and head to the Gates with them to attack the demons from the rear, engage them from both sides and defeat them. The question is: will they fall for it?'

'What happens if we lose and they open the Gates?' the Tiger's Number Two said. 'They will overrun Heaven.'

'Their next target will be the West, if they stick to their plans,' John said. 'They'll take down the four Bastions, then the Mountain, then the Celestial Palace itself.'

The Tiger's Number Two grunted agreement.

'The West is evacuated, isn't it? Jade?' John said.

'People have been moving back, convinced that Heaven is safe,' Jade said.

'Move them out again.' John's voice went hoarse with emotion and I shared his anguish. 'If they take the West, Number Two, yang it to bedrock with all of them in it.'

459

'With all due respect, if you order that, my father will rip your scales off, my Lord,' the Tiger's Number Two said.

'Good.'

They were all silent, considering.

After a couple of minutes, John drew their attention back. 'I'm still waiting for opinions on whether they'll fall for it and run to take Heaven after routing us. Are they that lacking in self-control? My gut says yes, but it's been wrong before. Many times.'

'Put the right Shen in front of them and they won't be able to help themselves,' the Phoenix said. 'If they see you running scared, Ah Wu, they will chase you to the ends of the Earth.'

'Good idea. Use their intense loathing of you to draw them out,' the Dragon said.

'I wanted to be at the front of the main force waiting for them at the Gates, but that is definitely a better option,' John said. He dropped his voice. 'Simone is in Court Ten.'

He waited for someone to point out that we were risking the Heavens for selfish reasons, purely so we could pull our own daughter out. Nobody did.

'Congratulations,' Ma said, and everyone nodded agreement.

'So the plan?' John said.

'It's a good plan,' Er Lang said. 'The risk is worth it.'

'Very well,' John said, still feeling as if he was throwing the rest of Heaven under a bus to save his daughter. Under a bus? John glanced at me with concern; it was an expression he'd never heard before. It was from me. We brushed it off and he continued. 'I want volunteers for the feint attack on Hell. If the plan fails, these people will be stuck in the Pits, so volunteers only. About two hundred if we can round them up. They must be Immortal: it's effectively a suicide mission.

460

Let me know by this time tomorrow who has agreed to it. We have a total of just less than two thousand troops left. I will give you the assignments for the rest of them as soon as we have these deployed. Anything else?'

Everybody shook their heads.

'Dismissed. Crown Prince Ming Gui, remain.'

They filed out, discussing the plan. The general atmosphere was positive; they liked it.

You always seemed so confident, I said. *You doubt your ability to that degree?*

Without the Serpent's intelligence, frequently.

You have me back now.

I don't want you back if it means losing Emma.

We will free me. Do not doubt.

Ming moved closer and sat. 'My Lord?'

'Leo was shot. Did he survive?' John said.

Martin ran one hand down his face. 'Leo is brain dead. The doctors wanted to turn off the life support, but neither Elise nor I would let them. Elise because she doesn't believe he's dead; me because I don't want to send him to Hell. As his partner but not his husband, I have no rights. Elise is the next of kin and has power of attorney over him and custody of Buffy. If we could marry as we wished, my rights would be clear. As it is now, I have no control at all over the fate of my husband or my child.' He dropped his head. 'Elise took both Leo and Buffy to the United States to care for them there.' His voice became a low moan of pain. 'The first family I ever had, the first real happiness, and it's gone forever. Our family is destroyed. Buffy's cries as Elise took her away will echo in my ears for the rest of my life.'

'When we retake Hell, you can release Leo's spirit and send it to Court Ten,' I said.

'Then Leo will be dead and Elise will retain custody of Buffy,' he said.

'No,' I said. 'Release him, then take his place. Have a miraculous recovery in Leo's form and bring Buffy home.'

'That's brilliant,' he said with awe. 'Intelligence worthy of Father's —' He looked from me to John. 'Oh.'

'Don't tell anyone. For now, I'm Emma and he is the combined Xuan Wu,' I said.

'And who are you really?' he said.

'Close enough to Emma for it not to matter,' I said.

I felt his ice-cold gaze and the Serpent within me leapt to meet him. Parent and child regarded each other with cool affection and quiet delight to be together again.

'I see,' he said. 'You will need to be quick if Emma is to be removed, Father.'

'I know,' I said. 'As soon as we have taken Hell, we will release me.'

'Is that all?'

'If I lead the feint, I would like you to lead the main force guarding the Gates,' John said.

'I am honoured by your confidence. I will serve to the best of my ability.'

'Dismissed.'

He saluted John. 'Mother.' He saluted me. 'Father.' He smiled slightly, rose and went out.

John and I shared an astonished look; Martin was right.

* * *

We went out of the war room to find a large number of students standing in the courtyard of the administrative section. There were so many that they overflowed onto the breezeway and out towards the barracks; there were even about fifty of them sitting on the roofs of the administrative buildings. It was all of them.

We stopped and stared at them, and as one those on the ground dropped to one knee to salute us, then stood again.

One of the phoenixes moved to the front of the group. 'Welcome back, Lord Xuan.'

'Thank you, Lai.'

'We heard you rejoin, my Lord. Are you really the combined creature again?'

Oh dear, I see where this is going, I said. *We can't change in front of everybody without them seeing me merge into it.*

Think quickly, my serpents, John said.

'Yes. I have rejoined,' he said out loud.

The students erupted in cheers, to John's bemusement and my delight.

'Please show us, my Lord,' Lai said.

'We want to see!' one of the students shouted from the back.

'Real Xuan Wu!' someone yelled from the rooftop.

I quickly presented John with a solution and both of us willed it to work. He raised one hand, and the noise abated.

He linked his hands behind his back. 'We were just in a meeting with the leaders of the Celestial alliance. We will strike Hell within the next few days and attempt to both reclaim it and drive the demon horde off the Earthly and back to where they belong.'

'We can do it!' someone yelled from the rooftop, and whooped with enthusiasm.

'You are extremely loud, Sakamoto, and if you don't shut up you will be doing more push-ups,' John said.

'Worth it,' Sakamoto said more softly, and a few students laughed.

'I will not take True Form until the Courts of Hell are ours,' John said.

The students went silent with dismay.

'Your Immortal colleagues are held in Hell. I will not show you my True Form until they are free, and all my Disciples have returned to the Mountain.' He raised his voice to be heard by all, and the air went still around us. 'When Celestial Hell is restored and the Immortal Disciples have returned, I will go to the centre of the Great Court, in front of the Palace of Yuzhengong, and I will take my largest and darkest True Form for all my Disciples to see. This I swear.'

The students erupted in cheers. Two of them fell off the roof of John's office and we had to run to catch them. This caused even more mayhem, and we led them back to the mess with the delighted students capering around us with glee.

* * *

Ma was waiting outside my office when I arrived. I waved him in, and he closed the door, then sat across the desk from me and put his clasped hands on its surface. He studied me with more than his eyes, then leaned back, his expression full of restraint.

'Let me tell you what I see. I see Emma, somehow merged with the female Serpent, which is separate from its male Turtle. What the hell happened?'

'Emma was caught up in the rejoining, and we will extract me when we have retaken Hell.'

'Emma can be extracted?'

'Yes. I'll have to be sent to Court One, but it can be done.'

'So you're the female part now, Serpent?' Ma said. 'Has the Xuan Wu separated into two creatures again?'

He spoke with quiet hope. 'When Emma's extracted and reunited with her Turtle — is there a chance for us, Ah Wu?'

John dropped everything and teleported straight into my office, his eyes wide with alarm that rocked through me as well. The memories flooded back. Me as the female Turtle before we'd joined — me with Ma ...

'Holy fucking shit.' I looked up at John and he stared down at me, horrified. I jabbed my finger at Ma as I yelled at John, 'How could you do that to this wonderful man? He's a Celestial Worthy of the highest calibre and you just *ditched* him when you joined with me. That is so wrong!'

John sighed, ran his hand over his eyes, and sat next to Ma. He took Ma's hand and clasped it. 'Look at the memories, Emma. It was mutual.'

'I loved the female Turtle,' Ma said with infinite longing. 'The joined Dark Lord ... is male. I see him as a friend. A brother.' He spoke more softly. 'Never as a partner.' He spoke to John. 'When you were female with me ... it was the best thing in the world. A dream come true.'

'But we haven't been female for nigh on four thousand years, and you still stay with us,' I said.

You've taken female form with me, I said to John. *How could you do this to him?*

The Turtle was female. After I combined, the Serpent part of me refused to be female, even for him.

And that was me. I leaned on the desk and put my head in my hands. 'We are such a bastard.'

'No,' Ma said, and he squeezed the Turtle's hand. 'You are the Dark Lord. You are male and perfectly aligned, and so am I. I would not change to female for you, so here we are.'

Neither of us would be female, so as he says: here we are.

I looked up at Ma. 'You were right. The Serpent has changed to female and the Turtle is male. We cycled.'

His face filled with understanding. 'You are the essence of both yang and yin. Of course you cycled, it was inevitable.' He hesitated, then leaned forward over the desk. 'So where does this leave us?'

'With Emma right in front of us,' John said with heavy meaning.

'As well as the Serpent Xuan Wu.' I sighed with feeling. 'I love you dearly, Ma.'

His face crumpled; my words had nearly broken him.

You let him suffer for centuries, then went to the Earthly and did exactly the same thing to Leo!

I did nothing to them. They did it to themselves.

'Ma.' I rose, went around my desk and crouched in front of him to hold his hand. 'Hua Guang, look at me.'

He raised his head to look into my eyes, his own full of longing.

'When I'm extracted, I hope I will retain the Dark Lord's memories and feelings. Because I love you so much ...' I checked John's reaction; he wasn't jealous because he felt the same way. His love for me wasn't diminished by his ancient bond with Ma; and neither was my love for him. I hoped that wouldn't change. 'When I'm extracted, I'll talk to the Dark Lord. What we've done to you is so wrong, and now that we've cycled,' I glanced at John, 'and learned so much about ourselves, I'm sure we will find a place for you in our hearts.'

'I know I have a place there already, Emma. There is no need for you to be unfaithful to each other,' Ma said. 'I know the Xuan Wu's number is one. I respect your relationship, and I am so happy that the Dark Lord finally found someone who is his equal in intelligence and,' he tweaked a small smile, 'bad-tempered brain-dead stubbornness.'

'That's us,' John said.

I moved to kiss Ma, and his face filled with intense longing before his expression cleared and he put his hand out to stop me.

'No,' he said. 'It's time. You're right.'

Time for him to move on; something we'd been telling him for years.

I nodded and moved back behind my desk. 'I'm glad you have our backs tomorrow, Marshal.'

Yi Hao spoke outside my office. 'She's with someone. Do you want to come back?'

'Come on in, Jade,' I shouted at the door.

Jade threw open the door and strode in, her green robes floating around her and her face a mask of fury. 'That asshole in the East has once again refused my requisitions,' she said. 'I need you to sign them, Emma. The Dragon's refusing to accept my authority just so he can see more of me.' She realised who I was with and saluted around. 'Sorry to interrupt, my Lords.'

'It's all right, we were done anyway,' John said, and rose. He gestured towards Ma. 'Give Jade a hand, will you?'

Setting me up again, Ah Wu? Ma said with amusement.

The Dragon's been chasing her for nearly fifteen years and she's turned down all his proposals, I said. *Feel free to tug his chrome-plated tail.*

Oh, with a great deal of pleasure, Ma said, and grinned broadly, his eyes sparkling. 'Princess Jade, I believe I have the authority you seek as the Dark Lord's second-in-command. May I escort you to the Eastern Palace so we can take this ugly blue beast down together?'

Setting me up again, Emma? Jade said, and I just smiled.

She held her elbow out for him to take. 'I thank you for your assistance, General Ma, and your authority will be more than sufficient.'

He took her arm and they disappeared together.

John and I shared a look. He felt my amused wonder; I felt his pained guilt. We shook our heads at each other and returned to work.

34

I woke the next morning in a warm haze, having dreamt of swimming through the beautiful clear waters of a coral reef, both of me dodging between the brightly coloured corals, the water sweet in our mouths. I opened my eyes to find myself wrapped around John, warm and comfortable. The pale pre-dawn light and the sound of songbirds echoed through the closed shutters.

I tried to move away from him to go to the bathroom and couldn't. I pulled my hand: it was stuck to him. I was wrapped around him and couldn't get free.

Wild panic seared through me, waking him as well. My arm had disappeared into him, and my breasts had merged into his chest. I struggled to free myself and only succeeded in hurting myself where we joined.

'Emma. Stop,' he said, his voice calm. He deliberately forced waves of relaxation through both of us, and I stopped to breathe, panting with terror. 'If you struggle you'll lose yourself even more. Relax.' His cool consciousness settled over me and I calmed. 'Good.'

'I need to get free from you!' I said, wondering if this was a nightmare where my worst fear — of him absorbing me completely — had been realised.

No nightmare, he said. *Real enough. Relax and we will disentangle you.*

His composure settled me; he could separate us. As I forced myself to relax and stop fighting him, I felt his relief — and under that, his own terror at absorbing me.

'We need to concentrate on Emma's separate consciousness,' he said. 'What are the names of your parents?'

'Brendan. Barbara.' Images of their faces — they'd only been in my office, what? Less than a week ago. My entire family.

'Pull gently. Concentrate on your family. Do you remember the flat you shared with Louise?'

'It was so tiny. We didn't even have room for a four-seater table ...' My hand came free and I gasped with relief. 'My bed went from one end of the room to the other, and I didn't have space for a proper wardrobe ...'

He pushed me away and my body was free. My other hand popped out of him with a sudden release of pressure.

I scrambled back, away from him. 'Shit, that was awful!'

'Tell me about it,' he said, rubbing his chest where I'd been released. 'You have to sleep separately until we fix this.'

'And no sex!' I stopped. 'Wait. Is it still sex? Or is it masturbation now?'

'I have no idea. Is it?'

'Good Lord, Xuan Wu, are you so weird that sometimes you confuse even *yourself*?'

'Frequently,' he said.

I grabbed my dressing gown and summoned Smally to make up the spare bed for me. 'I'll sleep in the spare room.'

He rolled onto his belly and thumped his head on his hard ceramic pillow. 'I cannot tell you how much I hate myself right now. This is unspeakably awful.'

'Since I'm you as well right now, I can only agree.' I threw the robe around me and stomped out to find Smally ready for me with the bed linen. 'In here, Smally.'

* * *

Something moved in front of my face and I snapped back. I was sitting at my desk and Yi Hao had waved her hand in front of my eyes.

'Sorry,' I said, shaking my head.

'You were just sitting there, blank,' Yi Hao said with concern. 'Are you all right, ma'am?'

I'd slipped into a link with John, assisting him with the disposition of the forces for the coming attack on Hell, and hadn't realised how close we had become.

'I'm okay, Yi Hao. The Dark Lord was talking to me.'

'When did you change your hair? I liked the brown better.'

I pulled a strand to my face to see it: black and tangled again. Dammit.

I thought quickly. 'It was an experiment to cover the grey — I thought I'd go the same colour as everybody else around here. It's a bit strong, isn't it? I'll dye it back to brown …' I smiled. 'Or do you think I should go blonde?'

'I liked your hair colour before. I never saw any grey,' she said with stolid loyalty.

We both heard a noise outside and turned. The Grandmother bustled in, in her usual human form of an elderly Indigenous Australian woman in flowing robes of red and gold. She leaned on my desk with one hip and crossed her arms, opened her mouth to say something, then stopped. Her eyes widened.

I raised both my hands. 'Please don't say anything. Yi Hao, leave us and close the door.'

The Grandmother disappeared, and appeared in front of John. She went around his desk to tower over him with her hands on her hips.

'Dammit!' I said, and ran to his office.

She was poking him in the chest as she spoke. 'That was a *human*, and I liked her. How could you do that?'

'I'm still here!' I said, entering his office and closing the door behind me. 'We're retaking Hell and then we'll extract me. Ask the Jade Emperor if you don't believe me. He says it can be done.'

Her eyes unfocused for a moment as she spoke to the Jade Emperor, then she snapped back. 'Asshole.' She rounded on John again and he cringed. 'You too! Asshole. How could you do this? What the hell ... which side are you on anyway?'

'The Celestial,' he said. 'Always the Celestial. We are moving tomorrow to take Hell back and free our own — and yours as well. There must be dozens of your children held by the demons, and when we retake Hell they will be freed.'

'I know, the diamond in your anteroom told me,' she said, relaxing and sitting across the desk from him. She waved for me to join her and I sat as well. 'I have something for you.'

'We would appreciate your help, my Lady,' John said with reverence. 'This situation has gone on long enough and we must put them in their place.'

'Good,' she said. She turned to me. 'And your stone is gone too?'

I nodded and wiped my eyes. 'I really miss it. I hope it's okay.'

'All right,' the Grandmother said. 'I didn't want to be involved in this; this is organic business and I wanted no part of it. But many of my children are being held by these brutes and you can free them for me.' She gracefully pulled herself to her feet and opened the door. 'Here you go. Out here.'

We accompanied her to the courtyard. For a moment I thought the students had camped out in the courtyard again, looking for John's True Form. Then I realised — these people were stones. At least two hundred of them in human form stood around the courtyard and out onto the breezeway, much as the students had the day before.

Gold was standing at the front. 'Take us as the feint,' he said.

'How many of you are trained?' John said.

'Except for about twenty of us, none,' Gold said.

'I can't lead untrained soldiers into Hell!' John said, exasperated, and turned to the Grandmother to send them home.

'No, wait,' I said. 'They don't need to be trained if we're planning to lose.'

'Exactly,' Gold said. 'Just throw us at them and let us fail.'

John opened his mouth and closed it again. They were right.

'Send the word out among your own as well,' the Grandmother said. 'I'm sure there are people in Heaven who would volunteer. Save the real soldiers for the real fight.'

'If we lose ...' John said.

She poked him in the chest in time with her words. 'Then. Don't.'

Gold snickered.

John fell to one knee and saluted her, then rose, turned to the massed stones and saluted them. 'You profoundly honour me with your offer. You could be the difference between victory and defeat.'

The Grandmother nodded. 'Good. And *you*.' She waved her finger in my face. 'Fix this up and then come visit me, okay? I have something for you in the Red Centre.'

I knelt and saluted her, then rose again. 'My Lady.'

She pointed at us, from one to the other, and her voice went very stern. 'Sort this out as soon as Hell is returned to us. This isn't the way we do things here.'

'You have my word, Lady,' John said.

'Good.' She exploded into a cloud of red and gold particles that descended through the air and disappeared.

John raised his voice to be heard by the stones. 'Come with us to the mess hall and I'll provide you with the strategy for the coming assault.' He lowered his voice. 'Can you handle the rest, Gold? Accommodation for them until we head out tomorrow?'

'My Lord,' Gold said. He looked from John to me. 'What was all that about?'

'Didn't she share the information with you?' I said.

'No?'

'She says this hair colour looks terrible and I should dye it back to brown.'

'I agree with her,' Gold said, then grinned with mischief. 'Did you go emo or something? Or have you turned into a metalhead like the Dark Lord?'

We both glowered at him. 'Mess hall, Gold.'

The next day, the Celestial forces gathered at the Gates of Heaven to prepare for the assault. Two thousand troops and the remaining Generals and Immortals stood grim and determined, armed and ready to defend the Gates with Martin at their head. Phoenixes and human archers were perched on top of the Gates, and dragons floated in formation above us, ready to rake the attackers. Three hundred of the toughest demon foot soldiers were separated off, led by Marshal Ma and ready to secure Celestial Hell when John drew the demons out of Hell and to the Gates of Heaven.

John gathered his stone force, and I stood with him as the final orders were relayed. The stones were as determined as the soldiers, all in their battle forms: human shapes of rock. Even untrained, stones could be tremendously destructive when they used brute force.

The Tiger's people arrived and we went to speak to them. They carried five of the laser weapons and four blood weapons. The laser weapons were long tubular devices with a simple barrel and looked more like a laboratory experiment than a weapon; some of the wiring was even held together with duct tape. Number Four was carrying one with a cable running from the grip to a band circling his wrist.

'How robust is that? It looks very flimsy,' I said.

'We didn't have time to make them robust. One good knock and they're ruined. We'll have to be careful.' Number Four nodded towards the Horsemen who were holding the other weapons. 'Those laser weapons need Dad and the other high-level sons — and daughter — to run them. I hope they're capable of using them after being in the Pits. The blood weapons can be used by anyone, and we have a few trained to take them if the people using them fall.'

'How long do the batteries on the lasers last?' John said.

Silly Turtle, there aren't any batteries there at all. Can't you see that?

... We have to hurry and extract Emma, I need your brains!

Damn straight you do.

'No batteries,' Number Four said. 'We power them as we go. So ... as long as we're able to stay conscious, they'll work.'

'I see,' John said. He summoned Ma, who appeared next to them. 'When you take Hell, have Pao release the high-level cats first and tell them to go to the top of the Gates.' He turned to the Tiger's Number Four. 'Wait on top of the Gates and pass the weapons to them when they arrive.'

Number Four and Ma nodded understanding and returned to their groups.

John went back to stand in front of the stones. He was imposing in his Celestial battle form with Seven Stars on his back.

I watched Number Four and his cohort move to the top of the Gates, then stopped in wonderment. *The Jade Emperor is on top of the Gate with Er Lang and Guan Yu,* I said.

What? John saw them. *Stupid old man. He should be in his palace where he's safe.*

I want to see how this turns out, the Emperor said. *If they attempt to breach the Gates I can help hold them back.*

Do not risk yourself, Majesty, John said. *You are the Heavens personified. If they take you, this is all for nothing.*

Fate be on your side and the One guide your hand, Xuan Wu, the Emperor said.

We had the disturbing joint understanding that the Emperor thought we had a good chance of failure.

All ready? John said.

The other leaders sent their affirmations.

John raised his voice to speak to the stones. 'On my mark, we will all travel to the roof of Yanluo Wang's building. Fight hard and fight as if all of Heaven is at stake, but listen for my call to run.' He dropped his voice. 'Your courage will be spoken of for centuries.'

The Celestial honours your noble contribution, the Jade Emperor said. *Fight well, and when we win you will not be long in Hell.*

'On my mark ... go,' John shouted, and he and the stones disappeared.

Lady Emma to me, the Emperor said.

I ran to the gate and straight up the red wall to the top where the Jade Emperor and his two guards stood.

The Emperor put his hand on my shoulder. 'Share.'

'What?' Guan Yu said.

'The demons have removed Hell from my dominion and my supervision, and she will be my eyes.'

'How can you see through her?' Guan Yu said, even more confused.

'If we win, it will be inconsequential. If we lose, it will be even more inconsequential. Share, Emma,' the Emperor said.

I linked with John, and the Emperor shared my vision through John's eyes.

* * *

John and the stones landed on the roof of Yanluo Wang's office building. The ten Courts of Hell spread around them, each one at the end of the causeway that led to its respective Pit.

Simone, we're in Hell. We're coming to free you.

I'll help as soon as I have this door open!

Ride the wind to Court One, John said to the stones, and made himself invisible.

He flew to Court One, studying the demon garrison below him. The stones floated in a cloud with him. The demons had set up camp in the centre of the island, with standard demon soldiers supplemented by small numbers of black-armoured guards stationed at the Courts.

'The demon numbers don't add up,' I said to the Jade Emperor. 'There aren't many there.' Both John and I turned our heads, studying the layout below us. 'Where are they all?'

We landed at Court One and John took out the twenty demon guards with shen energy, then yinned the two armoured ones.

The stones took their battle forms, and some scouted the area, looking for more demons, while John opened the Court and destroyed the demons inside. There was no judge in Court One. Yanluo Wang himself was the administrator of this Court, and new arrivals were sent straight to Court Two for their first judgement.

'Minimal resistance,' I said. 'What the hell?' Both our heads shot up as we understood. 'They were waiting for us to assault Hell, Majesty, and they're coming to the Gates!'

The horde appeared at the Gates: front lines of thousands of low-level mindless thralls, with a similar number of larger ones behind them, and a hundred of the black-armoured demons bringing up the rear. There were far more than we'd anticipated. The demons hadn't had

478

time to hatch a new army in just three days; these demons must have been in reserve. Thousands of them.

'These are Western demons and they shouldn't be able enter the Eastern Heavens!' the Jade Emperor said with frustration. 'That maniac is making appalling hybrids.' He turned to me, his eyes unseeing. 'Tell the Turtle to continue clearing out Hell.'

'I am, Majesty,' I said, and changed to silent speech. *Ma, don't bother with Hell; there's nobody there. Take the rear of the demon force here at the Gates, and hold the armoured ones until the cats arrive.*

My Lord ... my Lady.

The Heavenly defenders were pinned against the Gates. They threw themselves against the demon attack.

Marshal Ma's small force appeared behind the demons, and the rear guard of armoured demons turned and sliced into them.

Martin flew overhead to yin the armoured demons, but they were so huge he could only take out one at a time.

'Go to Court Ten first, Ah Wu! Release Pao, then secure the rest,' the Emperor said.

'On my way there already, Majesty,' I said.

John and the stones flew as quickly as they could to Court Ten, next to Court One on the island wheel. A couple of black-armoured demons guarded the entrance, and John yinned them.

'Pull that yin back, Emma,' the Emperor said.

'Whoops, sorry,' I said, and absorbed the yin into me.

'Good to know you can use it too; we may need it,' he said under his breath.

'You know that's an extremely bad idea.'

'Sometimes bad ideas are the only ones we have.'

Martin ordered those holding the blood weapons to attack the armoured demons, and directed the rest of the Heavenly army to strike the normal demon warriors. Guan Yu leapt off the wall into the middle of them, swinging his halberd with a rage so furious his skin glowed red.

'We're overmatched, and they probably have reinforcements,' I said.

'So release Pao now!' the Emperor said. 'We need our Immortals from the Pits and those lasers working!'

John strode into Court Ten, yinning a couple more armoured demons as he charged through.

Pao was in his chair on the dais, bedraggled and weary. 'Ah Wu! Thank the Heavens. You have no idea how glad I am to see you.'

'The demon garrison at the centre of the island has been alerted and the guards are coming, my Lord,' Gold said, his voice urgent.

'Shut the doors,' John said. 'Can you barricade the Court?'

'We'll stonewall,' Gold said.

They'd chained Pao to his chair and John freed him. Pao jumped to his feet, threw his arms around John's neck and let go into his shoulder with high-pitched wheezing gasps. 'It was a nightmare. They made me sentence everybody. They're all in the worst Pits —'

'You need to release them,' John said gently, easing Pao off him. 'We need them. The Gates are under attack and the demons from the garrison in the middle of the island are on their way here. Pao?' He bent his head to gaze into Pao's eyes; Pao was beside himself with grief and relief. 'Pao. Pao!'

Pao visibly pulled himself together, hesitated for a moment, then swept the chains aside and sat back in his chair. He pulled the book of sentencing closer and inked his brush.

'Free the big cats first, this is most important,' John said. 'The Tiger and his biggest sons and daughter.'

'With a great deal of pleasure,' Pao growled, sweeping the brush over the sentencing entries with wide strokes.

Loud thumps echoed through the walls. 'Gold. Is it holding?' John said.

We have it, my Lord. They can't get in. It seems all the biggest armoured demons are at the Gates; these are just small unarmoured ones. His voice changed to dismay. *They've thrown everything they have at the Gates.*

The Tiger appeared in the middle of Court Ten and collapsed. Michael fell to lie unconscious next to him, and John ran down the stairs to them.

Simone has appeared on the other side of our wall and is taking down the demons, Gold said. *She is quite magnificent.*

The Tiger's Number Three landed next to Michael and collapsed as well. John went to the Tiger first and put his hands on either side of his face.

'About time I had the chance to pay you back for Guangzhou,' he said, feeding the Tiger shen.

The Tiger woke, saw John and grabbed his arm. 'Ah Wu. Ah Wu. Ah Wu!' He pulled himself up, put his hands on either side of John's face and kissed him hard, then pulled back to stare at him as if he could disappear any moment. 'Holy fuck, am I glad to see you.'

Simone appeared next to them and lowered her weapons. 'Goodness, that felt strange.' She raised her voice. 'Close it up again, Gold!'

Already.

My attention returned to the Heavenly Gates as the Jade Emperor spoke. 'We need those cats up here now!'

A blood-weapon wielder emptied his reservoir onto an armoured demon and it screamed and dissolved where the blood hit it. The reservoir was empty and the soldier tried to back off, but was torn to pieces by the armoured demons following.

Our forces were dwindling and more demons appeared on other side of the Gates, sandwiching Ma and his small elite force and tearing them to pieces.

Martin had stopped calling yin — probably too exhausted to control it — and had moved so that his back was to the wood of the Gates, the Silver Serpent singing as he swung it with focused ferocity. The Heavenly soldiers fell around him, their screams filling the air and their blood soaking the grass.

'We need reinforcements, Ah Wu,' the Emperor said. 'If we don't have the cats up here soon, the Gates will fall.'

'We're waking the cats now,' I said.

'Simone, are you able to give Number Three some shen energy? We need these cats up and fighting,' John said as he put his hands on Michael's face and brought him around. 'Tiger, head straight to the top of the Gates of Heaven. Go to your Number Four — he has a laser weapon for you. Hurry! They're at the Gates and we don't have many left.'

The armoured demons at the Gates ran over the top of the blood-weapon wielders, safe now that their reservoirs were exhausted. Martin fell, and there was nothing between the demons and the Gates. The remaining Heavenly army were surrounded by the demons, fighting with desperation.

'You should retreat, Majesty. They're ready to breach the Gates,' I said.

The Emperor concentrated and raised his arms and a wall of rock appeared behind the wood of the Gates, reinforcing them so they would be impossible to open. 'Not until this falls as well.'

There are no demons left here, they're all at the Gates, Gold said.

More demon reinforcements appeared down the hill from the Gates: hundreds of armoured demons, human-shaped and four metres tall.

The Tiger landed next to us on top of the Gates, grabbed one of the laser weapons from the Horseman holding it and connected it to his wrist. He shared a word and a nod with Number Four, then he roared and jumped into the air, shooting the armoured demons from above. He focused the laser to a tight beam on an armoured demon until he'd bored a hole through its shell, bringing it down in clouds of filthy-smelling smoke.

Number Three woke on the floor in Court Ten and Simone spoke urgently into her face. 'You're needed up at the Gates to use one of the laser weapons, Katie. Are you up to it?'

'Fuck yeah,' Number Three said, and disappeared.

'Simone!' John shouted. 'Secure this area. Revive the Celestials as they're returned and station them around the Courts. Hold as much of the Celestial island as you can; we need One and Ten as an absolute minimum. Then send everybody else up to the Gates to help defend. Minimal numbers down here. Got that?'

'I understand. Go!'

'Gold, bring your war-trained stones with us and leave the rest here as barricades,' John said. 'Simone, Martin just fell and he'll arrive here soon. Keep him here to help. Okay?'

'I have it. I'll send Martin to you to help defend the Gates.'

'Let me know if you need him then. Gold, with me.'

'My Lord.'

The demons had destroyed the wood of the Gates and were scrabbling at the Jade Emperor's stone barrier. The Heavenly force continued to whittle at the rear of the demons, but the armoured ones far outnumbered the laser carriers. The demons struck a heavy blow on the stone barrier and the Jade Emperor bent double, his face weak with pain.

Er Lang and I rushed to assist him and held him up.

'You should go, Majesty,' I said.

'No, I can hold this indefinitely. They can't get in,' the Emperor said.

'You'll need to rest eventually, Majesty,' Er Lang said.

The Eastern Demon King appeared on the blood-soaked ground next to the Gates and crossed his arms over his chest. He watched with satisfaction as the demons threw themselves at the Jade Emperor's wall, destroying themselves in their frenzied assault. The stones cracked and the Jade Emperor staggered, his face ashen.

John appeared in the middle of the demons and swung Seven Stars, destroying them around him. The tall armoured demons strode through the middle of the demon force, crushing their fellows underfoot, until they reached John. John guided the stones to battle them. The demons couldn't injure the stones, but the stones couldn't hurt the demons either. Instead, they kept them occupied while the Tiger and his three children picked them off slowly with the laser weapons.

John jumped into the air and floated next to the Tiger, helping him destroy the demons with concentrated shafts of yin; but controlling it soon became too much and he landed again to strike at the non-armoured demons with Seven Stars.

I hurriedly closed the link between us as he was overrun by them and decapitated, landing in Court Ten with the rest of the downed Immortals. Pao scribbled furiously in his book, trying to keep pace with the bodies piling up in front of him.

John went outside the Court and found Simone; she and Marshal Ma were working together to direct the stones to hold Hell.

'We've destroyed the bridges the demons built over the ends of the causeways, and the stones are enlarging the holes so they can't come back,' Simone said. 'You said the Tiger has laser weapons that will destroy the armoured demons?'

'They do,' John said. 'But we're close to losing the Gates. We must hold this island.'

'If we can station the laser weapons around the Courts, we should be able to hold the island without difficulty,' Ma said. 'Your daughter has done a most meritorious job in securing the island.'

'Thank you,' Simone said.

'Pao just released me,' John said, and headed up to the Gates, joining us on top.

The Celestial army was defeated. The remaining soldiers joined us on top of the Gates and the demons stopped attacking the stone barrier. The demon army pulled three metres back from the Jade Emperor's barrier and there was complete silence as they stared at the stone wall.

The Demon King smiled up at us from his position next to the Gates and five glowing fluorescent slime demons appeared. They flew onto the stone and stuck to it, and the Jade Emperor screamed. His eyes went wide with horror as his robes and the skin of his hands dissolved as if they were bathed in acid. The fabric of the robe disintegrated to reveal his naked body, thin and pale. It was a distressing blow to his dignity for us to see him so exposed. The skin of his abdomen dissolved in front of our horrified eyes.

'Is Hell secure?' he shouted.

Simone?

Yes?

Is Hell secure?

Yes.

'It is, Majesty.'

I can't hold this much longer, the Emperor said in broadcast mode. *When it falls, follow them to the West and let them take it.* He quivered with agony as the slimes dissolved the wall and him with it.

'No! You can't have my Western Palace!' the Tiger roared. 'It took me two thousand fucking years to build that beauty! You are *not* having it!'

He jumped off the top of the wall and ran his laser weapon over the slime demons. The beam burnt them, producing acidic, foul-smelling smoke, then the burn holes closed over and the demons continued to eat at the wall.

'Tiger, come back, you're wasting your time,' the Emperor said. 'Be ready. You'll be needed in Hell soon.'

'Fuck, I don't believe this,' the Tiger said as he returned to us. 'They cannot fucking win.'

The slime demons shrank; melting the wall was a destructive process for them. The Jade Emperor collapsed, leaning heavily into me and moaning with pain. The slime demons shrank to nothing, their work complete, and the Emperor panted with relief.

The rest of the demon army hit the stone wall and the Gates shook. The wall crumbled and a hole appeared through its middle, mirrored in the Jade Emperor's abdomen.

The demons hit the wall again, and the hole grew to thirty centimetres across.

There was a breathless hush of anticipation from both sides as the demons drew back to hit the wall again.

'Let it go,' I said into the silence.

Laser-equipped warriors to Hell and hold it against the armoured demons, the Jade Emperor said. *Heavenly forces*, his voice changed to deep regret, *retreat. Fall back to the Celestial Palace.*

The demons rushed the stone wall, and as they struck the Jade Emperor dismissed it. The demons roared with victory and charged through the Gates into Heaven. The Demon King summoned a flyer, mounted it and led the demons west.

'No!' the Tiger yelled, and ran to follow them.

Tiger, to Hell. Now, the Jade Emperor said. *Number One son of the Tiger, Michael, are you there?*

Majesty, Michael said.

Go with Ah Wu to the West and observe. When they are settled there, his voice changed, *yang it to the ground with all of them in it. Extra commendation if you can take the King with them.*

Majesty, Michael said, and he and John headed west.

'Emma, the Serpent is to liaise with Ming Gui as to the disposition of laser-equipped cats in Hell. We must hold Hell at all costs.' The Emperor collapsed into Er Lang, his skin and robes returning as he healed. 'As soon as Hell is absolutely secure, both of you come to the palace. You're almost completely merged with him and if we wait much longer I will not be able to extract you. Er Lang, help me to the palace.'

'Majesty,' Er Lang said, gruff with grief.

35

John and Michael followed the demons to the Western Palace and positioned themselves in the desert not far from the walls. They watched as the demon army, with the King at its head, marched triumphantly through the gates of the palace. A few of them stopped to urinate on the walls before they entered, but the King angrily prevented them, destroying any that broke ranks.

'They can't see us?' Michael said.

'I have it,' John said. 'They don't know we're here.'

'There are still some demon servants there,' Michael said. 'There are about seventy demons in our main hall.'

'Order them to leave immediately.'

My Lord, Franklin said.

Leave now, Franklin, John said.

My Lord. We know the demons are coming. We will talk to them, welcome them and keep them in a limited location so they can be yanged without destroying the entire palace.

You are worth more than that ugly pile of rock, John said.

What he said, the Tiger said. *All of you, out. They're just stones and I can rebuild.*

You want to destroy all of them, Highness, and this will ensure it, Franklin said.

Dammit, you are the last of your kind and so close to Ascension it doesn't matter. You are not to do this, I forbid it! John said.

We waited a long moment before Franklin replied, *No.*

Franklin, dude, the Tiger said. *If you can disobey him, you're in the middle of Ascending. Get the fuck out of there because if you're yanged before you do it —*

The King is here, my Lords. The other servants have obeyed you and left the palace, but I'm holding him for you. They are in the main hall; we prepared a feast for them.

All the wives and children are out, right? Michael said.

They are. It is just me here.

Did you at least get the fucking horses out? the Tiger said.

Uh … that's the feast, Franklin said.

The Tiger howled with rage and pain in John's head.

I'm ready. Do it, Franklin said.

Are you seeing gold yet, Franklin? John said.

No, Gold's not here. Oh! Oh. I see what you mean. Wow. Gold. Everything's gold. His voice became urgent. *The King is gathering a large force to move to the next Bastion. You need to do this now!*

'Do it, Michael,' John said.

'But Franklin —'

'Do it, that's an order. And don't just take out the main hall; yang the entire thing to bedrock. Everything.' He lowered his voice. 'That is a direct order.'

'Please witness my execution of this order under extreme duress, Celestial Highness.'

'Acknowledged,' John said. 'Now *do it*!'

Michael stood, dropped his head and stared at the Western Palace. He raised his hands and the sky glowed.

Memories flooded John as he watched the sky ignite above the red stones: the good times he'd spent there with his brother the Tiger. Helping the Tiger design the ingenious system of cooling fountains; arguing over the finest steeds to stock his stables. Feasts and merriment, shared with their families. All to be destroyed.

I am so sorry, brother.

Fuck this. When I rebuild, you're paying for it.

Of course.

John hoped that Franklin had made it out before the twenty-metre-wide circle of blindingly white light appeared directly above the centre of the palace. It expanded to fifty metres and the waves of heat coming from it made the stones of the palace appear to ripple. Michael made a soft sound of effort and a shaft of hot white light exploded from the sky into the earth with a deafening roar that made the ground shake.

'Nice control,' John said softly.

A ring of light shot from the pillar, then two more. They expanded so fast they were almost invisible, rushing outwards past Michael and John into the distance and fusing the sand and every stone around them into glass.

The deafening shockwave hit a moment later, full of dust and debris, and the ground shook again.

The circle in the sky contracted. The pillar of light crashed into the earth with another tremendous impact felt through the ground, and spread in a dome of light, kilometres across, that expanded then shrank to a white-hot dot in the centre of a circle of destruction.

The dot disappeared, the stones fell from the air and there was silence; the only sound the pinging of the fused stones cooling around them. No mushroom cloud in the aftermath; the destruction was complete. A smooth polished circle three kilometres across remained where the Western Palace had been.

Michael fell to his hands and knees with grief. John held him, then sent his senses out, searching for demons, and found none.

'Majesty?' he said. 'I can't sense any. Did we destroy them all?'

I cannot sense any, the Jade Emperor said.

John sagged with relief. The cost had been appalling, but they'd won.

'Did Franklin Ascend?' he said.

There was a long silence, then the Jade Emperor said, *No*.

John punched the ground and the glass surface shattered over the dust beneath.

He silently helped Michael to his feet and escorted him to the safety of the Celestial Palace. There, he would meet with Emma — and kill her.

* * *

'I think we're good to go here,' I said as we did one last pass over the demon camp in Hell. 'They're all gone —'

A fake stone elemental surged out of the ground and grabbed me, one arm around my waist and another over my mouth.

Simone summoned yin around her hands and stood frozen.

491

I tried to free myself and failed; Emma wasn't strong enough. The Serpent could break the demon's hold, but I knew what that would do to Emma — to me. I stayed still and waited, ready to strike against it.

'I have her, Majesty,' the demon said in a very cultured English accent. 'Yes. Emma. Yes. No. Majesty.'

The Celestial island blurred around me and I landed on the dais in the Demon King's throne room. The room was completely empty; no demons or guards were present, just the two Kings reclining on the throne together, kissing with passion.

Shit. They weren't destroyed.

'Majesty,' the demon holding me said, its voice rumbling through me.

The Kings jerked up, then separated and rose, fixing their clothing.

'Well done,' the Eastern King said, and the demon nodded its head over mine. The King sauntered to stand in front of me and put his hands behind his back. 'This is what we're going to do.'

John charged out of the Celestial Palace and straight to the Celestial island in Hell. Simone was still standing, stricken, in front of the hole that had held the demon. It was a clever ambush: none of his family could sense the stone elementals.

He checked Emma's location — the King's throne room. He tried to teleport directly there and couldn't. That side of Hell was still outside Celestial jurisdiction and sworn Celestial Retainers like himself were barred from entry. Perhaps Simone …

The King slapped me across the face and I landed back in my own head.

'What?' I said.

'That worked. Who were you talking to? When did *you* learn telepathy?'

'You need me, right?'

'Of course I do.'

'If you don't release me right now, I'm gone anyway. Look at me. Take a good hard look, George.'

He put his hand on my face and held my chin and his cruel essence lanced into my brain like a hot knife. I tried to stay silent and failed, whimpering as he tore my head open and roughly examined me. The Serpent surged inside me, threw him out and slammed my head shut so that he couldn't re-enter.

He fell back, stricken. 'There it is again, that same snake thing inside your head. You're the *Serpent*? You were the Serpent all along? No — I had the Serpent. What the fuck was that then?'

'I've merged with the Serpent,' I said. 'It's consuming me. I must go to the Jade Emperor so he can extract me.'

'Is she still Frankie's mother?' Francis said. 'We need his mother more than we need the stupid Serpent.'

'She's both at the same time.'

'She's way too small to stay separate. It will eat her.'

'Let me look. Hold her tight,' the King said to the armoured demon.

It gripped me, and he took my face again and examined me more carefully. The Serpent sat coiled at the back of my head and glowered at him.

John walked along the street in Beijing. There were the pagodas of Jingshan Park, there was the entrance to the subway … the bicycles flowed everywhere. Where had the gateway been? He sent his senses out and found it. He pushed through the crowd and couldn't enter the gateway; it was blocked to him.

The Demon King slapped me again, bringing me back.

'Let the Turtle in,' I said. 'Let him take me to the Jade Emperor and extract me. If I'm not extracted soon I'll be gone. You will lose any chance of taking my son to Heaven for the next fifteen years.'

Come and destroy them, Turtle. Merge with me in True Form and take them both down. We can do it.

If we take True Form, Emma will be gone. I know how little of you remains, love.

Worth it.

No!

I jerked my head back. 'Don't hit me, I was talking to him. Let him in.'

The King looked me in the eyes, studying me. 'How joined are you? If I talk to you, will he hear me?'

'Yes,' I said with both voices.

He grinned with malice. 'Let's do a deal.'

Shit.

Just agree to everything they offer. Then come and take merged True Form and destroy them, I said.

No!

'I'll let you have her, Turtle, but if I ever want to take the child to Heaven, she has to escort him for me.'

We hesitated.

'That'll only happen when I win, Ah Wu. And you'll be gone anyway. Your Lady and child will be safe in Heaven.' The King moved closer to see into my eyes. 'Not such a sacrifice, eh? Give me your word and you can take her.'

'Guarantee Simone's safety as well,' I said.

'Done. Turtle?'

You vowed to protect the Celestial, Xuan Wu, and you can end this now. Agree to everything they offer, then combine with the Serpent and destroy them when you are here.

The Turtle was silent for a long time, considering. He could renounce his Celestial alignment, throw it all away, and come to collect me and keep me safe …

And you can't extract me yourself. Stop pretending you could betray the Celestial and come destroy both Kings with one strike. I love you, John. Come and take these monsters down and free the world from their cruelty.

No!

Once they are gone, the King's Number One will become King. He has agreed to stay on his side of Hell and renounce all claim to the Earthly. Make sure he keeps his word with a blood oath, and both the Earthly and Heaven will be safe.

He was silent for a long time, then: *You were the best thing that ever happened to me, Emma.*

Thank you, Xuan Wu. Free our son when they are gone and tell him that I loved him.

I will.

'You have my word as the Xuan Wu,' I said. 'Release Emma into my care, and when you need her to escort the child into Heaven, she will do it.'

'Good,' the King said. 'Meet her in Tin Hau station in Hong Kong.'

'No, let me in to collect her. We need to hurry!'

'Don't be ridiculous. Let you in here? No. Tin Hau. I'll let her out from the gateway there.'

John was full of relief as he teleported from Beijing to Hong Kong. He no longer had the option of merging and taking down the Kings. Emma would be safe, and now she could be extracted.

He arrived at Tin Hau station with the evening rush hour — so normal and mundane. These humans had no idea of the conflict that had occurred above them.

Emma stood blank and unseeing on the concourse before the turnstiles, in front of the unmarked metal door that was the gateway to Hell. People swirled around her, paying her no attention. He took her hand and she didn't respond. He checked inside her and it was like looking into a mirror: his own consciousness looked back.

'Emma? Can you hear me?'

She didn't respond.

He sought her inside himself and heard an echo, a glimmer ...

We may still be able to extract her, the Jade Emperor said. *Bring her now.*

* * *

John followed the Jade Emperor's guidance to his own quarters in the Celestial Palace. Simone was there waiting for them.

'You need to do this now, Ah Wu. Emma is almost completely you,' the Jade Emperor said.

The Jade Emperor was right. Emma stood stiff and unseeing when John released her hand. He waved his hand in front of her face ...

And I snapped back into my own head.

'Now, Ah Wu.'

'I can't just kill her!' John looked into my eyes, desperate. 'You must survive this.' He nodded over my head to the Jade Emperor. 'Give her a scale or a claw or something. Anything!'

496

'She's already back inside your head, Ah Wu,' the Emperor said, and John pulled back to see ... Emma was blank again.

'Emma? Return into your own head, Emma. What are your parents' names? Brendan. Barbara ... No — you speak, Emma. Return to yourself. I'm trying —'

'She's gone,' the Emperor said.

'Hurry!' Simone said. 'We can't lose her.'

'You already have.'

John held his hand out to the Jade Emperor. 'Scale. Come on, old man, help us out.'

The Jade Emperor hesitated.

'We won't tell anyone. Scale. Please!'

The Jade Emperor passed John a gleaming silver scale and John pressed it into Emma's hand.

The scale was like a brilliant point of freezing white light in my hand and the shock of the cold pushed me back into my own head.

'Now do it. You must send her to Court One immediately,' the Jade Emperor said.

'What's the easiest and fastest way?' I said. 'Just take my head?'

'I can't watch that!' Simone said, distraught.

'No,' John said. 'Decapitation is quick and painless, but kneeling and waiting for the blow to fall is very unpleasant. Trust me, it's awful.' He turned to the Jade Emperor. 'Majesty, can you?'

'No! You do it, John,' I said. 'You're the only one I trust. Please. Hurry.'

He turned back to me. 'I can't!'

'Get your damn sword and cut off my head!' I said. 'I'm slipping away, I can feel it.'

He put his hand out and Dark Heavens appeared in it. I closed my eyes and waited for the blow.

'I can't,' he said, desperate.

I opened my eyes. He was standing slumped with defeat. 'I can't do this to you.'

'John …' we said in unison.

'Do it, Daddy!' Simone said.

'Ah Wu, you are losing her. Do this now or she is gone.'

He stood, balanced on the indecision that I felt as well. I could lose my identity in Court One and be gone. He couldn't do it.

'Oh, for fuck's sake, Dad!' Simone shouted.

She summoned her blades, took two huge strides and ran one of them straight through me. She ripped it upwards, scraping it along the bones of my spine and tearing my ribs away with a remarkable feeling of separation, then hit my breastbone with enough force to lift me off my feet. The blood filled my lungs and everything broke inside me.

She held me impaled on her blade and looked me in the eye. 'I love you, Emma.'

'No!' John shouted as Simone pulled the blade out. He caught me as I fell.

'It's time,' the Jade Emperor said. 'Move back.'

John gently lowered me to the ground. I tried to see him but he had narrowed to a tiny tunnel of light, his burning dark eyes the only thing I could see. I searched for Simone with my narrowed vision and saw her standing with her blood-stained sword, tears running down her cheeks.

'It's all right, Simone,' I said. 'You always were the brave one. Find a way to get your little brother out. He deserves better.'

'I will, Mum.' She smiled when she saw my face and

shook her head through the tears. 'You were my dad for a while. Close enough.'

I looked up at John again, and coughed up a vast amount of blood. He wiped my face with his sleeve, already soaked and blackened with it.

'I love you. I love you both ...' I said, the words bubbling out of me.

I am so sorry, my love, he said.

Do not be. Even if this is the end for me, I would not have lived my life any other way. I am happy to end it here. And if it is not the end, I will serve the Celestial by your side with complete contentment.

My life slipped away and I tried to remember who I was. It was important that I remember. I stopped breathing and it wasn't significant. My hand was weak and I couldn't hold the important thing in it ... I couldn't remember why the thing was important and it fell out of my hand. The cold filled me from my centre out and everything faded.

The Jade Emperor reached into me with heat and gold and ripped me out of my body, leaving the Serpent alone and bereft.

The warm golden force threw me and I shattered.

I exploded into a million joyful shards of golden light and drifted down.

* * *

I landed in Court Ten and staggered. I was wearing the white of a convict and Judge Pao sat at his desk on the dais above me, his arrogant composure obviously restored after we'd regained Hell. He glared at me from under his dark brows.

'Kneel before your judge,' one of the guards said.

I crossed my arms over my chest. 'No.'

Pao sighed with exasperation and tossed his brush onto the desk in front of him. 'The Jade Emperor promised me you'd land in Court One!'

I grinned without mirth. 'Too bad, here I am. And you can't Raise me, Pao, the Dark Lord has to do it.' I raised my chin. 'First time ever?'

'I would not Raise you, Miss Donahoe, you are not ready. You are too wilful. You need more incarnations of suffering so that arrogant streak is beaten from you.'

'If I was a man you'd call it strength, not arrogance.'

'Nonsense. You are disobedient, overconfident and conceited, madam, and you should not be Raised.' He picked up his brush again and spoke with grim satisfaction. 'Emma Donahoe, I find you Unworthy. Return to Court One and prepare —'

'I don't think even you have the power to override one of the Dark Lord's vows,' I said, interrupting him. I sent my senses out and found him: he was charging from Court One already. 'Oh good, here's my ride.'

John stormed into the Court in his Celestial Dark Lord form — the first time he'd taken it since his Serpent was free of me. He was taller, leaner, darker and much, much fiercer. I smiled. I liked this new Dark Lord a *lot*.

'Are you okay?' he said. 'I couldn't do it, and you were —'

'Don't worry about it, John, I understand. I'm here now and that's all that's important.'

'The Jade Emperor said you'd land in Court One!' he said.

'Of course he did.' I gestured with my chin towards Pao on his dais. 'You know how Pao would react if he knew I was coming here.'

'He'd try to send you to Court One anyway,' John said.

I turned back to Pao and looked him in the eye. 'Yep, he just did.'

Pao didn't reply as he sat glaring at both of us.

'You said the Jade Emperor would never lie,' I said to John.

'Oh, he'll lie to your face when it suits him. It's Kwan Yin who never deals in untruths.' John stood next to me, facing Pao. 'You'd better not get in my way,' he growled.

John was too tall. Not good enough. I reached into my dark serpent nature and grew as well. My hair darkened and twined around my head. Echoes of being joined with the Xuan Wu still resonated inside me and probably would for the rest of my ... Immortal existence. I had a small moment of satisfaction when my white convict clothes changed to my black robes and armour, as scuffed and worn as they always were. I concentrated and they changed to clean and new, shining black and silver in the light of the Judge's courtroom.

Pao's eyes widened and his mouth clamped into a grim line.

Impressive, John said.

Thank you.

I shot him some images of *exactly* what I wanted to do with him while we were both in these forms and he fought to control his smile. He sent back images of what *both* of him wanted to do with me and I had similar trouble holding back my own smile.

'I have one regret, Xuan Wu,' I said without turning away from Pao.

John glanced down at me, concerned.

'I never had a chance to take you down, one on one, while I was the Serpent.'

John turned back to Pao. 'I share your regret, Emma. But I think with some training you will be a definite challenge for me.'

'Oh, come on, John. You know damn well nobody will ever defeat you in a fair fight. You're the best.'

He slumped almost imperceptibly. 'I know.'

I turned to him and gazed into his eyes and saw everything he felt in them. He was full of joy to be here with me, and I wanted to break down and weep at the strength of the love we shared. Our souls were joined in more intimate ways than any human would know; reptiles together.

'Together,' I whispered.

'Joined,' he said, and held his hand out.

I took his hand and he fell to one knee before me. The guards made quiet sounds of wonder.

'Celestial Worthy Lady Emma Donahoe, Dark Lady. Will you marry me and share my home, my dominion and my Mountain as Empress of the North?'

'I am greatly honoured by your proposal, Supreme Emperor of the Dark Northern Heavens, and I respectfully accept. It would give me no greater joy.'

The court guards broke into spontaneous applause. John smiled up into my eyes and stood. We embraced and shared a long kiss, and the guards cheered and whistled.

'Damn reptiles,' Pao said under his breath, and added more loudly, 'This is most inappropriate in my courtroom!'

John pulled back to gaze into my eyes again. *This will feel extremely strange*, he said. *Don't fight it, go with it.*

'But you don't have the Elixir. Won't I have to wait here for it to be ready?'

'No,' John said. 'I am equal in precedence and authority to Pao. Ready?'

I nodded.

Here goes; I've only done this once before. He put his hands on either side of my face. 'I am First Heavenly General Zhenwu, Demon-conquering Celestial Worthy, Celestial Minister of Jade Emptiness, Master of the Glorious Teachings of Primeval Chaos and the Nine Heavens. Arise, Emma Donahoe, you are judged Worthy. Take your place among the Celestial and rejoice.'

'Your wording is incorrect,' Pao said.

'Too bad,' John said.

My feet weren't touching the floor. I was floating with John's hands on either side of my face. The gold that had been sitting quiescent within me since the Jade Emperor had sent me to the Court flamed into a huge ball of wild energy that I couldn't hold. It surged out of control and I exploded.

The last thing I heard was John's voice, speaking softly. 'You've promised to marry me, and I hold you to that. Come back to me soon, love; please don't leave me.'

I shifted sideways and out of everything. I floated outside all of creation, separate from it. I could enter the Second Platform if I wished; I could join the peace and harmony and be forever free of the suffering of striving and never achieving, free of space and time itself ...

No. Not my time yet. Still things to do; so many things to do! And my Dark Lord needed me. I'd promised him.

I landed sitting on a mountain top, profoundly still and silent. The sky was the pale blue of extreme altitude, and snow-covered peaks filled the landscape all around me. I had no idea where I was, but I could see for a very long way; the sea seemed to shimmer on the horizon.

I sent out my new senses, rapt in their sensitivity and depth — and they would only improve with time and training. I searched for my children, and found more than two. There were two now, mine and John's, but in the future there would be more. Many more. I would free Frankie, but not just yet. Simone was full of joy that both of us had Ascended. And John. John ...

The Xuan Wu was on its Mountain, our Mountain. He was standing in human form in front of the Palace of Yuzhengong with all of his Disciples, human and Shen, gathered on the Great Court around him.

Liu shouted at them and they grudgingly moved back and into ranks with the shortest at the front, giving John room to change to True Form.

John moved to the centre of the paved square. He turned completely black with a loud snap that made the students jump. He became an intensely dark cold hole in reality, his form shifting and changing from human to something wild and otherworldly, existing outside of our normal dimensions and impossible to focus on. A black cloud seeped up from the ground around the hole and a whirling tornado two metres across, full of ice and black water, appeared above him. The mist and ice swirled into him, making him grow and change and appear even more grotesque and strange, then everything stopped moving. The ice, mist and water all remained completely frozen in their swirling forms, unmoving around him. There was complete silence.

Then with a sound loud enough to break nearby windows, the whole thing exploded outward and was sucked back in again and John's True Form stood on the pavers, five metres long, black and horrifying, the Serpent wrapped around the Turtle's shell.

The Turtle's head was a cross between a lion's and a dragon's, but much uglier. A black frill surrounded it, and its shell had bumps and ridges. Its massive feet had huge, cruel claws.

The Serpent's head faced the Turtle's tail; the top of its head was also frilled and covered with a collection of spikes and spines that bristled out around it.

The Turtle looked backwards on its long neck and the Serpent turned its head to face it. The two reptiles glared at each other, mouths open in defiance, then the Serpent slithered around the Turtle so that its head hovered above the Turtle's, swaying on its coils still wrapped around the Turtle's shell.

Both heads were facing the students, and opened their mouths together.

'I have returned,' the Xuan Wu said in a voice of ice and cold and death.

The students stood silent and awestruck at the side of the square, then slowly, one at a time, they fell to one knee and saluted their Master.

The Xuan Wu looked up into my eyes and smiled their reptile smiles at me, and I knew where I needed to be. I pulled myself to my feet and took a deep breath of the cold fresh air, then travelled back to our Mountain.

36

'Didn't anyone notice when Martin changed from a big black guy to a big Chinese one on the plane?' Simone said.

'Humans don't notice Shen changes,' John said. 'Their usual reaction is to think they saw wrong the first time.'

'They're that gullible?' she said, incredulous.

'More than that,' I said.

'I consider myself human and I am mortally offended,' Leo said.

'Then tell Martin to stay in your form and walk out as your twin brother,' John said, and grinned. 'Lion.'

'Too late, they're here.' Leo shifted, impatient. 'They're waiting for their luggage to come out.'

Leo went very quiet and still as we waited outside the arrivals hall. After half an hour of near complete silence, obviously following them telepathically, he straightened and his face filled with joy. He grinned broadly and Martin came through the glass doors, pushing a trolley with Buffy sitting on top of the suitcases.

We moved back from the railing as Martin wended his way through the crowd and between the rails, then they were in each other's arms, making soft sounds of delight. They pulled back, smiling hugely, then hugged each other again. When they separated, Leo grabbed Buffy under her arms and hoisted her, making her shriek. A few other waiting people around us laughed at her ecstatic reaction. Leo put her on his hip and embraced Martin again, this time one-handed. Martin pulled back and they gazed into each other's eyes.

'Come on, Ba Ba, give Daddy a big kiss. I know you want to,' Buffy said.

'The people around us wouldn't like that,' Martin said. She opened her mouth and he raised his hands. 'Not because we're both men, but because kissing in a public place like this makes people uncomfortable. It's bad manners.'

She huffed with exasperation. 'Then make yourselves invisible. Honestly, Ba Ba, you really are very hopeless.'

'Later,' Leo said.

'Now. We can wait,' John said.

They blurred into invisibility for a long time, then Buffy's little voice said, 'You're squishing me!'

'Sorry, sweetheart,' Leo said, and they reappeared.

Martin nodded to John. 'Father.' He smiled slightly at me. *Don't you dare*, I said.

'Lady Emma. Ah Ma.'

'Oh, that's worse,' Simone said.

'Mei Mei.'

'Ge Ge.'

'Enough,' I said. 'Skip all the family calling stuff, let's take you home.'

507

'Home,' Martin said softly.

I took the trolley and pushed it for them as they walked with their arms around each other, with Leo holding Buffy. John levered me away so he could push the trolley and nodded to Buffy with a small smile.

'Yeah, let me back on,' Buffy said, and Leo placed her on top of the bags.

'You be careful there,' Martin said sternly.

'I will, don't worry, Ba Ba. Yeh Yeh's looking after me.'

Yeh Yeh? I said, amused.

And you're Poh Poh, old lady.

I huffed and John ignored me.

'Did you find a new domestic helper, Daddy?' Buffy said.

'Emma gave us one. Her name's Er Hao and you'll really like her.'

'Can she make udon?' Buffy said, her little face unsure.

'She makes the *best* udon.'

'Yay!'

'And the demons are truly defeated?' Martin said. 'No reappearance?'

'The Kings aren't destroyed, but their entire armies are gone, armoured demons and everything,' John said. 'We're meeting with them in the next couple of days to forge a new treaty that hopefully will bring things back to the way they were.'

'Have they ceded the Earthly?'

'Not yet,' John said grimly. 'There's no outright warfare here, but they do have a great deal of influence. The copies are still in place and must be removed. This will be a major part of the new treaty; we hope to win the Earthly back without bloodshed.'

'I hope we can regain control,' Martin said.

'We will,' John said. 'Now, who will go in the car? There isn't room for everybody.'

'Not me,' I said. 'Flying's way too much fun.'

'You have enough skill already?' Martin said.

'With help,' I said, and smiled at John.

'I'll come with you. Daddy and Emma can take themselves,' Simone said. 'I want to catch up with my niece.'

'Okay!' Buffy said, and climbed into her child restraint. 'I can tell you all about America!'

'Did you like it?' Simone said as she buckled her up.

She pursed her lips. 'Kind of. Auntie Elise was all right once I got used to her. Uncle Max was okay. The cousins were weird. Their food was strange and they had no udon.' She shook her head. 'I'm just glad to be home with my daddies, but we promised Auntie Elise we'd go visit her sometime soon.'

Leo glared at Martin, who ignored him.

After they'd driven out of the car park, John and I took the lift to the roof.

John took my hand and I shook it free. 'Let me try myself.'

He shrugged and moved back.

'Are we hidden?'

'Of course.'

'Okay. Here goes.'

I touched my centres; already doubled since I'd been Raised. I needed to do more energy work to build their size. I raised them and felt the thrill as my feet lifted off the concrete of the roof.

'Very good,' he said. 'Before you go further, let them go again.'

I dropped back onto the roof.

'Excellent. Up you go.'

I lifted my energy centres and the experience was exhilarating. John paced me, floating beside me, as I rose. I stopped about a hundred metres up, level with the top of the airport hotel.

'Nice,' he said.

The airplanes were parked on the tarmac all around me; dozens of them, moving through the busy terminal. An A380 took off as I watched, majestically lumbering into the air, appearing too big to fly.

The next bit was hard. I shifted my centres from 'up' to 'forward' and lost it. I fell through the air and tried to centre them again as the roof of the car park rushed to meet me.

John took my hand and helped me to hover. 'Nearly had you back in front of Pao,' he said.

'Oh hell, no.' I had a sudden worrying thought. 'He was really pissed at us — he can't send me back to Court One and sentence me to Fall, can he?'

'No. You're one of us now. He doesn't have the authority to sentence you to Fall. Best he can do is hold you at his leisure.'

'Or send me to the Pits,' I said.

'Only with a damn good reason. The Jade Emperor would censure him hard if he did it out of malice.'

'Everything he does is out of malice,' I said.

John didn't reply, agreeing with me. He squeezed my hand. 'Do you want to try again?'

'They have a good head start on us. Can you guide me to the Peak?'

'Sure.'

He shifted hands so he had a better grip and waited for me to move again. I concentrated, and this time managed to move up and towards the Peak.

'Well done,' he said.

'More practice. I need more practice!'

'You will have it. We have all the time in the world.'

We passed over Lantau Island, the Tsing Ma Bridge bright with reflection and expansive below us. The immense container terminals were next: hectares of stacked containers with the cranes busy moving them, thousands of them.

'Oh,' I said. 'Speaking of Pao, I wanted to ask you.'

'Yes?'

'You said you'd done it once before. Who was the other one you Raised? Was it Martin?'

'No.' He dropped his voice. 'It was Peony. The Serpent Concubine.'

'What, so Peony's still around? I know you executed her —'

'No. I executed her and then she was sentenced to Fall by the Jade Emperor himself. She is gone.'

'That is so wrong. She was ill, John, not a criminal. With modern mental health treatment her paranoia could probably have been brought under control ...'

'We know that now. Back then, all we could do was release her from her broken body and brain and send her to the Earthly in the hope that she would Ascend again with an incarnation less damaged.'

'Did she?'

'Once someone has Fallen — or passed through Court One — they are gone and we cannot know where they are.'

'So nobody can find someone and Raise them before they're ready for it. I understand. What about me?'

'Oh, you were ready.'

'Despite what Pao said?'

He harrumphed a short laugh. 'Pao says that to every woman who passes through his Court. He's been reprimanded for it in the past.'

'Next time I see that man I am going to punch him in the nose.'

'Join the queue.'

We passed over the harbour, bright with busy waterborne traffic. The daylight was fading and the brilliant artificial lights were coming up on both sides; a stunning display of colour.

'Do you miss it?' he said when he saw me watching.

'I do sometimes. It's good to have family in the Peak again. But when I'm down here, all I can think about is returning to our lovely Mountain.'

'You make me so happy sometimes, Emma.'

I squeezed his hand. 'Good.'

He guided me up the side of the Peak; the steep ascent was difficult for a novice like myself. We plunged into the low-lying clouds and he kept us dry as we made our way up to One Black Road. We arrived outside the living room windows on the top floor, and he teleported us into the apartment.

Everybody was already in the living room with the bags, and Er Hao had crouched to speak to Buffy. 'Welcome, little Princess. I am Er Hao and I'll be very happy to help look after you.'

'My name's Buffy, I'm not a princess,' Buffy said. She smiled. 'Except when me and Daddy wear our princess dresses together.'

Martin grinned and Leo looked mortified.

Next time let me know and I'll put on some tulle as well, I said. *I hope you have a spare set of wings and a wand for me; everybody should have the chance to be really pretty now and then.*

Tell that to Martin, he'd die first, Leo said. *I'm sure you can borrow Simone's.*

512

'No, you're a princess, my Lady,' Er Hao said.

Buffy put her hands on her hips, ready to tell Er Hao otherwise, and Simone cut in. 'Actually, Buffy, your Ba Ba is a prince, your Daddy is a lord, and your Yeh Yeh is an emperor. You really are a princess, just like me.'

Buffy turned the frown on John and looked him up and down. I choked back the laugh; I could see her point. He was barefoot, wearing his plain black cotton Mountain uniform pants with a faded black T-shirt thrown over the top, and his hair, as usual, was all over the place.

He spread his hands and glared at me. 'What?'

I sent him a mental image of himself and he subsided. 'I like this T-shirt. It's comfortable. And these pants have no holes in them!'

'For a change!' I shot back.

'Unlike you!'

I looked down and frowned at the slash in the left knee of my jeans. 'I don't know how that happened.'

'I think we'll leave the princess business, Er Hao,' Simone said, ignoring us. 'It's more trouble than it's worth, and I know I wanted to be a normal kid more than anything.'

She crouched as well and put one arm around Buffy's waist. 'Did you buy anything cool in America?'

'Yeah, Aunty Elise bought me a bunch of new clothes. She was having fun so I let her.' Buffy screwed up her face. 'What is it with grown-ups and buying everything pink? I don't want another pink thing for*ever*.'

'I know what you're talking about,' Simone said. 'Let's take your bag to your room and you can show me.'

Her head shot up and the rest of us did it as well. A big phoenix was heading straight for us, falling out of the sky.

John disappeared and reappeared on the roof of the apartment building, and everybody else joined him. I didn't have teleportation down yet and had to run.

'Er Hao,' I said, 'mind Buffy. Take her to her room. Something's going on.'

'Demons, ma'am?'

'Not as far as I can tell, but keep in touch and let me know if anything happens.'

I ran up the stairwell and banged on the rooftop door; it was kept locked. The chain rattled on the other side and Simone opened the door for me. John, Leo and Martin were all standing on the roof, looking into the sky, and I felt it as well. I looked up and saw it: a fireball, heading straight for us.

'Is that Zhu Que?' I said.

'No, it's a smaller phoenix, maybe one of her children,' John said.

'It's my friend Ting, but he's not talking to me,' Simone said. 'Something's really wrong.'

'Ming, with me. Leo, stay.'

John took off into the air with Martin next to him, and didn't get very far before the flaming phoenix in True Form plummeted, limp, into his arms. He ignored its fire, landed on the roof and gently laid it on the concrete. Its eyes were closed and its red feathers were all aflame with waves of heat coming off it that forced me back.

'Ting!' Simone shouted, kneeling next to its head. 'Ting?'

The phoenix didn't respond, and she cradled its head in her lap.

John crouched next to its head and put his hand on it. He lit up with shen energy and the phoenix quivered all over, its feathers shaking. It spread its wings and attempted to rise, then collapsed prone again.

It opened its eyes and spoke with a male voice. 'Simone?'

'It's me, Ting,' she said.

'Simone. I found you. Is that your father?'

'Yes.'

'Good. I found him.' The phoenix gasped with pain. 'My Lord Xuan Wu, they came. Stones, artificial stones, so many stones … They killed all the babies and smashed all the eggs. We ran and we flew, but they killed so many of us.' He quivered again, his pinions fluttering, and the flames danced around him. 'Mother sent us to the four corners of the Heavens to find you. The demons have taken our palace under the volcano. The South has fallen.'

The turtle and serpent had merged.
They were complete.
They were Xuan Wu.

Characters

(*Ordered by first name*)

Andy Ho: Husband of Emma's friend April; later turned out to be a demon.

Audrey Au: Wudang Wushu Master.

Archivist, The: Immortal responsible for the management of the Heavenly Archives, a collection of all the world's literature and the Celestial Records. Usually takes the form of a twelve-year-old boy.

Bai Hu: the White Tiger, God of the West. His element is Metal.

Barbara Donahoe: Emma's mother; in hiding with the rest of the family in Perth.

Black Jade (BJ): stone Shen, child of Gold, created when he was damaged in battle.

Blue Dragon: Qing Long, God of the East. His element is Wood. Father to Jade's three dragon children.

Brendan Donahoe: Emma's father; in hiding with the rest of the family in Perth.

Bridget Hawkes: wife of David Hawkes; executive in a large Hong Kong company.

Chang: human, ex-Shaolin monk. Worked as an assassin/bodyguard for a demon prince until he refound the Way and returned to the monastic life.

Clarissa Huang: human. Was engaged to Michael MacLaren until she was captured and tortured by demons, giving her lingering physical and psychological after-effects.

Da Shih Yeh: the Little Grandfather; ancient mystical demon that wanders the Halls of Hell comforting those who are in most need. Rumoured to be a demonic incarnation of Kwan Yin.

David Hawkes: human executive director of one of Hong Kong's large family-owned companies; husband to Bridget.

Demon King (East): calls himself George. Has several male and female human forms, one of which is Kitty Kwok. His True Form is similar to a Snake Mother (human front end, snake back end) but red instead of black.

Demon King (West): calls himself Francis. Has teamed up with the Eastern Demon King and they are building an army together.

Edwin: Wudang Mountain's staff doctor.

Elise Alexander: Leo's sister from Chicago.

Emma Donahoe: human Australian woman who can change into a snake; engaged to Xuan Wu.

Er Hao: tame demon, major domo of the Imperial Residence on Celestial Wudang.

Er Lang: Second Heavenly General, the Jade Emperor's left hand and John's assistant in defence of the Heavenly realm. Has a third eye in the centre of his forehead and is most often seen in the company of his Celestial Dog.

Franklin: last vampire in existence. A hybrid of Eastern and Western demons, which makes him very fragile even though he is powerful.

Francis: *see* Demon King (West)

Frankie: John and Emma's son; aborted when he was three months old and brought to term in a demon egg by the King of the Demons, who adopted him.

Freddo: Freddo Frog, Simone's half-demon horse.

George: *see* Demon King (East)

Gold: stone Shen, child of the Jade Building Block. Works as the Academy's legal adviser. Husband to Amy, stone parent to BJ, and human father to Richard and Jade Leong.

Grandmother of All the Rocks: Uluru, the massive stone in the centre of Australia. Spiritual mother of all the stone Shen in the world.

Greg White: human Immortal husband to Emma's sister Jennifer. Used to be the White Tiger's Number One son; resigned to marry Jennifer and now lives in Perth with the rest of Emma's family.

Guan Yu: Also called 'Guan Gong', Marshal of the True Spirit and Guardian of the Gates of Heaven; one of the Thirty-Six.

Jade Emperor: supreme ruler of Taoist Heaven, God of the Centre and the element of Earth.

Jade Girl: Daughter of the King of the Dragons; John's earthly accountant, now Wudang PR Director.

Jennifer: Emma's sister, mother to Colin and Andrew with her first husband, Leonard. Divorced, and remarried the White Tiger's previous Number One son, Greg. Living in hiding with the rest of Emma's family in Perth.

John Chen: Xuan Wu, the Dark Emperor of the Northern Heavens; God of the North and Martial Arts. His True Form is a snake and turtle combined together. His element is Water.

Justin: A son of the Dragon of the East who specialises in IT. Dated Simone for about two weeks.

Kitty Kwok: Emma's previous employer, who ran kindergartens in Hong Kong; revealed to be the Eastern Demon King in female human form.

Kwan Yin: a Buddha, one who has attained enlightenment and has returned to Earth to help others. Goddess of Mercy and Compassion.

Leo Alexander: African-American bodyguard to Simone when she was a child; now a Taoist Immortal. Engaged to Prince Martin Ming Gui, son of Xuan Wu.

Lily: human Immortal; one of the administrators of the Northern Heavens.

Liu, Cheng Rong: the Academy's Immortal Shaolin Master; married to Master Meredith Liu.

LK Pak: Wudang Demon Master.

Lok: A dragon who was cursed into the shape of a dog and was Wudang residential manager while the Academy was in Hong Kong.

Louise: Emma's good friend for many years; married the White Tiger and became wife number ninety-seven. Lives in the Tiger's Western Palace.

Ma Hua Guang: Vanguard of the Thirty-Six; one of the Thirty-Six (now Thirty-Five) Heavenly Generals and John's right hand.

Marcus: Son of the White Tiger, married Monica while she was in the Western Palace.

Margaret Anathain: physician, and headwoman of the serpent people in the Welsh town of Holyhead.

Martin Ming Gui: turtle Shen, son of Xuan Wu, elder brother to Simone, younger brother to Yue Gui; Prince of the Northern Heavens and John's Number One son. Engaged to Leo Alexander.

Master (Miss) Lucy Chen: Wudang Weapons Master.

Meredith Liu: the Academy's Energy Master; a European Immortal; married to Liu Shao Rong, the Academy's Shaolin Master.

Michael MacLaren: Number One son of the White Tiger; son of Rhonda MacLaren.

Michelle LeBlanc: Xuan Wu's first human wife, Simone's mother. Killed by demons when Simone was two years old.

Moaner: Head Demon of Wudang Forge.

Monica: Filipina domestic helper for John and Michelle when they set up house; married the Tiger's son Marcus.

Number One: an honorary title given to the most senior son (or daughter). Most rulers have a Number One to assist them in running their realms, and a Number One has precedence second only to their father/mother.

Pao Qing Tian: Celestial Judge of the Tenth Level of Hell. Responsible for releasing Immortals back to the world when they're killed; also makes the decision on who is Worthy to be Raised to Immortal.

Paul Davies: human housekeeper of John's UK house in Kensington; husband to the butler, Peta Davies.

Peony: the Serpent Concubine. John's concubine during the Qing Dynasty; became mentally ill, murdered her servants, and was executed.

Qing Long: the Blue Dragon, God of the East. His element is Wood.

Red Phoenix: Zhu Que, Goddess of the South. Her element is Fire.

Rhonda MacLaren: the only one of the White Tiger's wives with the strength of will to leave him. Was destroyed by drinking the Elixir of Immortality.

Ronnie Wong: half-demon son of the Demon King; in hiding from his father's assassination attempts on him. Works as a Fung Shui Master; expert on demon seals. Married to stone Shen, Silica.

Silica: stone Shen living on the Earthly to avoid repercussions from a previous romantic entanglement; Ronnie Wong's wife.

Simone: Simone Chen, Princess of the Dark Northern Heavens; daughter of Xuan Wu and his human wife, Michelle LeBlanc.

Stone: the Jade Building Block of the World; the stone that sits in Emma's engagement ring. One of the stones created by Nu Wa to hold up the Heavens when the Pillars were damaged by an angry god, but was never used for this purpose. The ring Emma wears was created for the Yellow Empress.

Venus: God of the planet Venus; emissary for the Jade Emperor.

White Tiger: Bai Hu, God of the Western Heavens. His element is Metal. Michael MacLaren's father, and husband to more than a hundred wives.

Xuan Wu: Dark Emperor of the Northern Heavens, God of the North and Martial Arts. His True Form is a snake combined with a turtle. His element is Water. English name: John Chen Wu.

Yang Piao: Marshal Yang Piao the Earth Spirit, one of the Thirty-Six.

Yanluo Wang: God of the Underworld and the Dead. Administrative manager of the Celestial side of Hell.

Yellow Empress: wife of the Yellow Emperor, a fabled ruler from ancient times who taught humanity the basics of civilisation.

Yi Hao: tame demon, Emma's secretary on Celestial Wudang.

Yue Gui: turtle Shen; Xuan Wu's older daughter, older sister to Simone and Martin Ming Gui, mother to Sang Shen. Manages the Northern Heavens' administrative side.

Zara: a diamond stone Shen that works as John's secretary. Used to be the stone that was in both Rhonda's and Clarissa's engagement rings.

Zhu Que: the Red Phoenix, Goddess of the South. Her element is Fire.